HEIDI HEILIG

FOR A MUSE OF FIRE

Greenwillow Books, *an Imprint of* HarperCollins*Publishers*

Content notes: Mental illness (bipolar), blood use in magic, gun violence, war, colonialism, racism, descriptions of dead bodies, mention of reproductive coercion, mentions of torture, mention of suicide

For a Muse of Fire
Copyright © 2018 by Heidi Heilig
Map illustrations copyright © 2018 Maxime Plasse
Music for "La Lumière," "We Meet by the Light of the Moon," "The Dream," and "Untitled" copyright © 2018 by Mike Pettry; lyrics copyright © 2018 by Heidi Heilig. Reprinted with permission of the authors.

www.epicreads.com

The text of this book is set in Minion Pro. Book design by Sylvie Le Floc'h

Library of Congress Cataloging-in-Publication Data
Names: Heilig, Heidi, author.
Title: For a muse of fire / by Heidi Heilig.
Description: First edition. | New York, NY : Greenwillow Books, an imprint of HarperCollins Publishers, [2018] | Summary: "Jetta, a teen who possesses secret, forbidden powers, must gain access to a hidden spring and negotiate a world roiling with intrigue and the beginnings of war"—Provided by publisher.
Identifiers: LCCN 2018008135 | ISBN 9780062380814 (hardback)
Subjects: | CYAC: Fantasy. | Magic—Fiction. | Theater—Fiction. | Manic-depressive illness—Fiction. | Mental illness—Fiction.
Classification: LCC PZ7.1.H4446 For 2018 | DDC [Fic]—dc23 LC record available at https://lccn.loc.gov/2018008135

18 19 20 21 22 PC/LSCH 10 9 8 7 6 5 4 3 2 1
First Edition

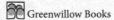 Greenwillow Books

To the mad ones

CAST OF CHARACTERS

The Ros Nai

Jetta Chantray. *A shadow player.*

Samrin Chantray. *Her father, a singer from a long line of shadow players.*

Meliss Chantray. *Her mother, a flautist and drummer.*

Akra Chantray. *Her brother, once a shadow player, who left to join the armée during the famine known as The Hungry Years.*

The Denizens of Le Perl

Leo Rath. *The mixed-race proprietor of Le Perl, a show hall in Luda.*

Cheeky Toi. *A dancer at Le Perl.*

Eve Ning. *A dancer at Le Perl.*

Tia LaLarge. *A singer at Le Perl.*

Mei Rath. *Leo's mother, a chanteuse and the owner of Le Perl before she died.*

The Aquitans

General Julian Legarde. *The leader of the Aquitan armée in Chakrana and half brother to Le Roi Fou, emperor of Aquitan.*

Capitaine Xavier Legarde. *His son, trying to fill his father's shoes.*

Theodora Legarde. *The general's daughter, called La Fleur d'Aquitan, considered the most beautiful woman in Chakrana and engaged to Raik Alendra, the Boy King.*

Eduard Dumond. *The armée questioneur. A torturer.*

Lieutenant Armand Pique. *A veteran of the long occupation of Chakrana.*

Antoine "Le Fou." *The emperor of Aquitan, obsessed with shadow plays.*

At the Capital

Siris Kendi. *The proprietor of Le Livre, an inn in Nokhor Khat.*

Raik Alendra. *The Boy King and last of his line, whose older brothers were slaughtered during La Victoire.*

PROLOGUE

Some people say that all the world's a stage.   1
But here, a shaky scaffold in the paddies
Can hold a universe inside an hour.

For on this humble platform of bamboo
A shadow player paints an epic tale.   5
She works behind the silk, and at her back
The flames throw embers at the velvet sky.
Sweat beads her brow, but triumph lights her eyes
As darkness dances for the fiery muse.

Across the pale swath of silken scrim   10
Her shadows cast a story like a spell:
Great dragons battle tooth and nail with wolves,
A humble peasant takes a prince's throne,
The gods themselves, of life, and death, and knowledge
Walk among the mortals that they serve.   15

Beyond the veil of silk there is the crowd
And in her world, they can forget their own:
The way the foreign merchants seem to prosper,
Their fortunes tantalizing, out of reach.
The rebels stalking all sides in the jungle.   20
The armée men, too quick to draw their guns.

Better to escape inside a story.
For most, it is the only way they can.

So for an hour the audience is rapt.
A hundred people laugh and cry as one.   25
Applause comes like the gust of monsoon rain
That falls upon the thirsty, eager earth.

They cheer for her—the master of the shadows—
A girl who'd leave this broken land behind
Like ash and eggshells from a phoenix, rising,   30
Or the tattered body of a soul set free.

ACT 1

TONIGHT!
TONIGHT! TONIGHT!

THE ROS NAI

WILL PRESENT

THE SHEPHERD AND THE TIGER

COME SEE THE GREATEST PUPPET TROUPE IN ALL OF CHAKRANA!

AMAZING! ASTOUNDING!

"SHADOWS WITHOUT STICK OR STRING."

CHAPTER ONE

The most thrilling moments in life are when everything comes together.

The delicious chords when harmony joins melody. The way a scrap of leather, a shaft of light, and a clever player can make a shadow come alive. Or the roar of an audience after a show—when they become a creature with many heads and one heart.

Sefondre, the Aquitans call it—to coalesce. I love that word. Madame Audrinne once used it to describe our performance as she toasted us in the parlor of her plantation. I've remembered it ever since.

Will it happen tonight at La Fête des Ombres? The signs are promising. The weather is holding clear—just right for the outdoor stages. Papa's voice is rich and steady as it floats through our roulotte's carved scrollwork; he is singing a story song as he drives. Beside him on the bench, Maman keeps perfect time on the thom. Inside, I direct the little shadow play that flickers on the silken scrim that makes up one side of our roulotte. A thick stack of flyers lies next to me, ready to tout tonight's show. And I'm wearing my best costume—a scarlet wrap with ruffled edges, a red silk shawl draped artfully over the rippled scar on my shoulder, and a striped corset in a nod to Aquitan fashion. My dark hair is swept into a twist, the stray ends patted down with a touch of oil, my eyes smudged with bone black and my lips with lucky red. A compelling picture for the Aquitans in the audience: local color, foreign polish.

Everything is nearly perfect. All except for the ghost of a kitten that won't stop pouncing on my fantouches.

I don't know where she came from, or where her body is. The little arvana must have crept into our roulotte when we stopped for a quick meal on the edge of town—tempted by our food, no doubt. Then again, does it matter why or where? There is no shortage of spirits in Chakrana. The more pressing question is, how can I get her to leave?

Being easily distracted is one of the tamest parts of my malheur, and I can't afford any distractions tonight. Not at La Fête des Ombres.

"Shoo," I whisper for the third time, fluttering the stack of flyers at her, but she only scampers behind one of my pillows. Spirits usually aren't so persistent—unless they smell an offering. But I have put away the rice and the incense too—nor am I about to offer her any blood.

At least she isn't interfering with the play itself. Her little paws, formed of flickering orange flame, pass right through the silk and leather of my fantouches, my shadow puppets. The souls I've tucked inside them ignore her better than I do. They dance in the air, between the scrim and the palm-oil lantern, going through their choreography with minimal direction from me.

They know the play by rote. It's the one we perform every time our roulotte crosses into a village—a traditional folktale about long-lost lovers meeting under the moonlight. A little taste of our skill, a way to drum up an audience as we travel through town. The two lovers are played by jointed leather dolls no larger than my hand and ensouled with the spirits of hummingbirds; the moon is a disk of gold silk stretched over a circle of green bamboo, buoyed up by the spirit of a carpenter bee. But I can't take my eyes off the kitten's ghost as she bounds back and forth across the floor of the roulotte.

Thankfully, I'm the only one who can see her; she casts neither light nor shadow to the small audience we've already gathered. I catch glimpses of them through the scrollwork: a rambunctious pack of Chakran children, barefoot on the road, a pair of older men walking slowly side by side. A modest group, but there is delight on their faces as they watch the graceful dance of light and dark: the lovers meet and part and meet again, moving in time to the music, and all without stick or string. Just as it says on the flyers. That is what sets us apart from all the other troupes in Chakrana, why some people say the Ros Nai is the best shadow troupe in the country—maybe even the empire.

I grimace as the kitten starts to climb the scrim: the praise might not be so effusive if the audience knew how I controlled my fantouches. Souls and spirits are the realms of monks and their magic, and all the old ways are forbidden ever since La Victoire, when the armée pulled Le Trépas from his bloody altar and imprisoned him in his own dark temple. If they knew what I was doing, I could be thrown in the cell beside him. Though it chafes, Maman's refrain is the most important line I've ever learned: never show, never tell.

We keep our secrets close. There is a latch on both sides of the door to the roulotte, and when we perform on stage, my parents guard the wings. Despite the danger, I can't afford to stop. When my brother joined the armée, my parents and I had to find a way to keep performing without him—especially after his letters suddenly ceased, along with the money he was sending home each quarter. No one would pay to watch a show with only one puppeteer—not if we were using the traditional methods.

But even if we could, I don't want to go back to the way things were. There is a thrill in fame. Besides, who would look at me and guess what I could do? I am no tattooed monk, no nécromancien, no power-hungry monster who thinks herself a god. I am just a shadow player. Le Trépas and I are nothing alike.

The three-strike rhythm of Maman's thom brings me back to the play—this is the part where the lovers lose each other.

"Cross left," I whisper to one fantouche—or rather, to the soul inside her—and she obeys. She must—I'm the one who gave her life. But the kitten follows, clawing at the trailing silk of her dress. "Go away! Not you," I add quickly to the soul of the bee; slowly, the moon drifts back to the center of the scrim.

This has gone on long enough. I can't let the kitten's antics throw me off. I have to concentrate—not only on this little shadow play, but on tonight's performance: *The Shepherd and the Tiger*, on the main stage at La Fête des Ombres. The most important performance of my life, though I'm trying desperately to pretend it's just another show. There are whole minutes where I have myself convinced. I am a very good actor.

But it comes back—it creeps in, just like my malheur: the knowledge that our performance has to be magnificent. We need sefondre tonight. We must do well—no, better than well. We must be the best.

For just like our sugar and sapphires, shadow plays are prized in the empire. Usually, the rare troupe that can tour must gather quite a sum to make the passage across the Hundred Days Sea. But this year, in honor of the Boy King's eighteenth birthday, he will be taking a grand tour to Aquitan, and General Legarde will be choosing the best shadow player to send with him. There, in a land of light and luxury, Legarde's half brother—Le Roi Fou, the Mad Emperor—is enamored of fantouches d'ombres. They say he pays a lead player their weight in gold for a single performance, and that once he smashed his throne for kindling when his favorite troupe ran low on fuel for light.

They also say he bathes in a magic spring, and the water is the only thing that keeps his illness at bay. While gold is tempting, we have that here in Chakrana. What we do not have is a cure for my own malheur—that thing only an emperor might dare name madness. Of all the things that stand in my way, the ghost of a kitten cannot be what stops me.

So I draw out the pin that holds my shawl over my shoulder and prick the pad of my thumb. Blood wells like vermilion ink, and all around me, stacked on their shelves and bound in their burlap bags, my fantouches rustle. Even the lovers shudder—the moon trembles—though they do not stray from their positions by the scrim. They have had their taste of my blood—it's what binds them to their new skins, what makes them obey. But that doesn't mean they don't hunger for more.

The kitten spirit hungers too. At last she turns from her pursuit of the golden moon.

Lowering my hand gently to the stack of flyers, I draw the symbol of life on the top page—a line and a dot, like the sun on the horizon. A path to a new body for a hungry soul. Already others are drifting in through the scrollwork, glowing like embers, drawn by the scarlet liquor of my blood: vana, the littlest spirits—flies or mosquitoes, once. But the kitten is faster. She pounces, and with a flash of light, her arvana disappears into the page.

At last. Later, after the show, I'll burn the paper to set her free. Then she can fade after three days and find rebirth like any normal soul. For now, I can fold her up and tuck her under a pillow. But the page slips from my fingers.

Usually souls take a moment to adjust to new bodies, but the kitten is not wasting time. The flyer leaps into the air as though caught by a breeze, bounding once more at my fantouches. And this time, in her new, unwieldy paper skin, she blots out half of the show. Frantic, I grab for her, my own shadow falling over the lovers—an arm, impossibly long—before I can snatch the flyer out of the light of the little oil lantern. Then a knock on the front panel of the wagon makes me jump.

"Jetta?" Maman's voice. Only now do I realize my parents have played the last notes. The show is over. Quickly

I crush the flyer in my fist, snuffing the lantern as Maman slides the panel open. She peers into the gloom, but with my fist tightly shut, there is nothing for her to see—not now. Still, her eyes are suspicious. Does she know? "We're almost there."

"Yes, Maman," I say, but she doesn't close the panel. The paper tickles my palm. "Do you need something?"

She scrutinizes my dress, my face, my hair. Then she casts her eyes to the pile of puppets on the floor beside me, the fantouches set aside for tonight's performance. They are still bound tight in burlap and silk—the shepherd, the tiger, the herd of sheep. I breathe easier now; those spirits, she knows about. "I need the performance to go well," she says at last. As if I didn't know.

"It will, Maman," is all I say.

She looks about to say more, but then Papa's voice floats in, gently chiding. "Meliss, stop distracting her."

Maman bits her lip, but she nods, the lines around her eyes deepening as she gives me one last look. "It's almost time for the flyers. Get ready."

At last she shuts the panel, but inside I curse. Where had the hour gone? I push the crumpled flyer under a pillow to deal with later. Then I gather the lovers and the moon, tucking them into their little burlap sacks. Had they even performed the ending? Quickly I press my eye against the scrollwork and curse again, this time aloud. No wonder Maman was worried. We have lost what little audience we'd gathered.

No matter. They aren't the ones we need. At least that's what I tell myself, though any performer knows that the bigger the audience, the better the show.

Pushing the thought from my head, I pull the lever that closes the wooden shutters over the scrim. At least now there is nothing left to distract me. Taking one last look in the mirror, I pin my scarf back over my scarred shoulder as I run through tonight's play in my head. I can't afford to get it wrong. It is another old tale—the swineherd and the tiger—but I've rewritten it just for the festival. New words flowing over familiar notes.

In my version, the swineherd has become a shepherd to honor General Legarde—the Shepherd of Chakrana, they call him since La Victoire, though we do not have sheep in our country. I hope my sheep fantouches look convincing. Still, the leader of the rebellion is the Tiger, so the story hasn't changed much. But a slip of the tongue would humiliate us—lucky it is Papa who sings the story songs. He never slips. I'm told they mock swineherds in Aquitan, calling them simpletons. I don't know why. Pigs are very clever. Back in Lak Na—our home during the rainy season, when the fields were green and the roads too rutted to travel—not a week went by but some brassy old sow escaped her pen to wallow in the cool mud of the paddies and gorge on black crabs.

The memory brings a smile to my lips—my brother and I, splashing and shouting through the pale green rice to chase pigs away from our own dinner. But my humor fades quickly. Akra is gone. And I'll never see Lak Na again either—at least, not if tonight goes well.

"Jetta!" A knock on the front panel, and Papa's voice. "It's time!"

Turning from the mirror, I gather up the flyers. We don't usually use them—so few Chakrans can read, at least in the villages. But this is Luda. This is La Fête.

This is the most important show of my life.

I pin my lips into my best smile and open the back door of the roulotte. The ruddy light of sunset floods in, warm on my skin. We have passed right through town. Fallow fields unroll before me on either side of the road. Half the year, they hold rice; I can still see the earthen walls that regulate the river water. But now it looks as though someone planted bullets in the dusty earth, and up sprang an encampment d'armée.

Waxed canvas tents march across the field in neat rows, bounded by a picket lined with horses—those great foreign beasts, all muscle and fire. Soldiers walk briskly to and fro, most of them Chakran, except for the officers. A pang hits me—the last time I saw my brother, he was wearing a uniform like these men do. I blink away the emotion, raising my eyes to try to drain away the threatening tears. Then I see it, in the center of the encampment: the red wolf flag flying over the general's tent. Legarde is here.

My heart quickens, and I search for a glimpse of him. I've seen him before—on the posters that commemorate La Victoire, of course, but also years ago, here in Luda, from very far away. He was surrounded by a cadre of soldiers, watching the show on the main stage. That was before we were good enough to perform there. This year, we have top billing.

This year, Legarde will see us.

The stages are just past the encampment, between the armée and the river. It's time for me to collect our audience. Making sure my shawl is still in place, I step out onto the little platform at the back of the roulotte, pulling my shoulders back and tilting my face to the light. Then I cock my knee so it slips from the ruffles of my sarong; might as well do all I can to catch the soldiers' eyes.

"Messieurs!" My voice is pitched to carry; it floats over the camp. Soldiers look up at the sound. They stare; I smile. And there it is—that intoxicating thrill of having an audience in the palm of your hand. "Tonight, on the main stage, come and see the greatest troupe in Chakrana, the Ros Nai!"

I toss a fistful of flyers like confetti. For a moment, they flutter, buoyed by the warm breeze. Then an explosion rips the air in two.

ACT 1,
SCENE 2

In the town of Luda, a dingy theater called Le Perl slouches in a back alley near the docks. To judge by the carved marquee and the cracked gas lamps, it must have been beautiful, once. Now there are puddles in the alley and holes in the roof, and a crooked sign reading GIRLS GIRLS GIRLS *over the peeling door.*

Inside, it's hot as hell, with twice the temptation. On a scarred stage lined with stained curtains, a local girl with black eyes and a blond wig croons a sultry song to the light, lazy notes of a piano. Her voice is smoke and brass, and the footlights fall to pieces on the sequins of her hem. Slowly she removes a single glove. In the wings, the other girls whisper as they wait for their turns on the floor.

EVE: It's so humid.
CHEEKY: Then pull your knees together.

Their laughter is sweet and rough.

EVE: The way my thighs rub? I'd kindle a fire.

CHEEKY: Can you do it on cue?

In the audience, men wait just as eagerly. They are crammed around rickety tables, soldiers with soldiers, civilians with their own kind, and each side avoiding the other's eyes. With the rebellion gaining strength, they might be enemies outside these walls, but Le Perl is a place for forgetting such things.

The drink helps with that. So behind the battered wooden counter stands a boy in his element, making sure the liquor flows despite the rationing. His first name is always Leo, though his last name changes depending on who he's talking to; the Aquitans prefer his father's, the locals know his mother's. And in his face, a bit of each side. But he sells anyone drinks and tickets, both at outrageous prices, though the winks and jokes are free.

Between mixing rounds, he checks his watch—a gesture that looks almost absent, but for the fact that he checks it again just a few minutes later. When a knock comes at the theater door, LEO goes to open it. EDUARD DUMOND stands outside in his uniform, a rifle slung over his back. He is the armée questioneur—the kind less at home with words than with implements. LEO ushers him in like they're old friends—

but LEO has grown up around people who had to pretend for a living.

LEO: Eduard! Sava? Come in, quickly, quickly!

As the soldier enters, LEO glances over his shoulder toward the street—a quick and practiced look—then shuts the door firmly.

How long has it been? A year? Too long, anyway. Ah, wait!

LEO holds up one hand.

You remember the rule? No guns past the bar.

EDUARD jerks his chin at the pistol tucked into LEO's belt.

EDUARD: You have a gun.
LEO: And here I am, at the bar. *(A small pause.)* This isn't a new rule, Eduard.
EDUARD: But this is a new rifle.
LEO *(laughing)*: I won't scratch it!
EDUARD: I mean a new type. It's called a repeater. Seven

shots before reloading. A new invention. Very expensive.

LEO: Courtesy of the armée scientist, eh?

EDUARD stiffens.

EDUARD: The armée has no official scientist.

LEO (*laughing again*): Perhaps they grow the guns in the fields, then, next to the sugar. Either way, I'm guessing if you lose yours at a burlesque, the general will shoot you with his.

EDUARD: You know how he is.

LEO: I do. Oh, I do.

LEO's grin has an edge to it now. He nods to the stage.

Then again, you know the girls. If they see I've let a rifle past the bar, they'll disarm the both of us. And they'll take our guns too.

EDUARD: All right, all right.

Making a face, EDUARD hands over the new rifle. LEO puts it behind the bar with the others—almost a dozen, now. La Perl is more popular with the soldiers than the shadow plays.

Then LEO claps his hands and gestures to the greasy bottles on the back shelf.

LEO: Bien, now to more serious matters! Do you still drink l'ouragan? I'll mix you one so strong you'll hardly remember you had a gun in the first place.

With a flourish, LEO mixes the drink, heavy on the rhum, pouring the glass full to brimming. As EDUARD makes his careful way toward an empty table, LEO checks his watch one last time. Then he ducks behind the bar and pulls open a dirty trapdoor. He has just tucked the last rifle into the crawl space when the explosion rattles the grimy glass of the chandelier.

Quickly, he slams the trapdoor shut and sweeps his hand across the bottles on the back of the bar. As the glass shatters on the floor, he draws his gun and smashes the butt of the weapon across the bridge of his own nose. Wincing and swearing, he leaps over the counter and runs down the hall, shouting back over his shoulder to the murmuring audience.

LEO: They're getting away!

Received at 2016h
Capitaine Durand at Morai
To: General Legarde at Luda

SABOTAGE AT SUGAR MILL STOP BOILERS
DESTROYED STOP PLANTATIONS BURNED

Received at 2019h
Capitaine Roche at Kah Le
To: General Legarde at Luda

CONTACT LOST WITH GARRISON STOP REBEL
ACTIVITY SUSPECTED

Received at 2024h
Lieutenant Gerard at Sekat
To: General Legarde at Luda

MUNITIONS STOCKPILE RAIDED STOP
REMAINDER SET ABLAZE

Received at 2037h
Capitaine Moreau at Dar Som
To: General Legarde at Luda

ROUTINE PATROL EXECUTED BY REBEL
FORCE STOP TOWN IN TURMOIL

CHAPTER
TWO

As the blast ripples through the air, the wagon lurches forward, throwing me into the road.

My shoulder crunches as I hit the dirt, and my breath is knocked free like a tooth. Gasping, I push myself up on one elbow, my hair tumbling loose from the comb. Dust coats my teeth, stings my eyes—our roulotte vanishes into the cloud kicked up by the wheels.

"Papa!" Can he hear me? All around, there are screams, cries, the pounding of feet. Servants and cane cutters push past their employers, all of them running in the same direction. Those who can't run are screaming too—not in panic, but in pain. Dazed, I pull myself up to keep from being trampled. The shifting smoke near the stages hides the worst of it, but in the dark clouds I can see the bright souls of dead men.

Had we arrived a few minutes earlier, we might have been among them.

I am bleeding from half a dozen scrapes—I must be. The little vana drift closer, hopeful. I ignore them. A fire is raging along the riverbank: the stages blown apart in blazing smoke. How? Any shadow player knows the fear of flame—indeed for me, it is not a fear but a memory . . . the choking smoke, the searing heat, the acrid smell of burning hair. . . .

The scar on my shoulder is burning, but it's only where I connected with the road. I swallow the sourness of it all. But in the theater, fire creeps in by stealth, not force: a draft taking a curtain, the gas leaking from a lamp. In the theater, there are no explosions.

This wasn't someone's mistake.

Rebels. It must be. We've all heard the stories. Sabotage. Assassination. Guerrilla attacks. As quick and deadly as their leader's namesake: Legarde's enemy, the Tiger.

The soldiers guessed before I did; as the audience and

performers flee to the town, the armée runs toward the scene, pulling their rifles over their shoulders.

The roulotte is heading that way too. Water buffalo have terrible eyesight; Lani must have panicked at the sound of the explosion and simply started running. Hitching up my torn silk skirts, I race after her alongside the soldiers, bare feet pounding the road.

Sharp stones prick my heels; my shoulder is starting to ache, the skin scraped raw. As I run, vana gather in my wake. Arvana too—bigger souls like rats and birds, crawling up out of the earth, dipping down out of the sky. Their fiery orange glow swirls in the air around me. The soul of a dog follows at my heels. Beautiful. Distracting. Gritting my teeth, I put on more speed, but I can't outrun the spirits. Nor can I close the distance between myself and the wagon. Lani is charging ahead through the smoke and the crowd. Can my parents stop her? Do they even know I've fallen? "Papa!" I call, but my cry is lost in the sudden crack of gunfire.

Flashes ahead, in the smoke. Beside me, a soldier stumbles, his pale face going paler still as he drops to his knees, clutching the spreading red stain on his uniform. Biting off a scream, I careen off the road and into the fields: I do not want to be a target, and I do not want to watch the man die—to watch his soul spring free. But another soldier races by, shouting orders. "Fan out!" he calls to the other men. "Take the full field! You and you, follow me! Use the wagon as cover!"

My ragged breath hitches as I recognize him—General Legarde.

He speeds toward the fire, toward the roulotte, and his men follow his lead. For an irrational moment, I am giddy. Legarde is a hero. He will keep us safe. And ahead, Lani has finally veered from the conflagration, scared by the sound of gunfire or the scent of the thickening smoke. But as the wagon bounces off the road and down into the dry paddies, it lands with a crunch and the rear wheels splay sideways.

The back stair of the wagon hits the dirt. A broken axle. Lani stumbles, lowing, as the roulotte plows to a stop. Papa is flung forward over the bar; Maman pulls him back onto the seat. I turn course, stumbling down the embankment into the field, dodging furniture and instruments and half-eaten picnics, abandoned by the audience as it fled. But the soldiers are heading the same way, trying to put the wagon between themselves and the rebels.

Gun smoke and dust mix with the drifting ash of the fire. The soldiers aim a volley into the haze, and the rebels shoot back. Ahead, another soldier drops to the dust, leaving his akela standing over his body in shock—a column of golden light, the soul of a man. But Legarde doesn't spare a glance for the soldier's body and cannot see his soul. He only leads the living toward the stricken roulotte.

As we approach, Lani tries to run too, straining against her harness, but the wagon drags in the dusty fields. My parents are trapped in the crossfire. I'm close enough to hear Maman screaming; she covers Papa with her body as he tries to cover her with his.

Gritting my teeth, I drag my hand across my bloody shoulder. She'll forgive me, won't she? She has to, if I save her life.

I don't slow as I reach the roulotte, spirits still swirling behind me. With one hand, I grasp the doorframe and scramble through it—with the other, I leave a scarlet mark on the back step. At my heels, the soul of the old dog leaps. As I pull the door shut behind me, there is a flash of light in the dark of the wagon—lightning only I can see.

"Up," I whisper, and the floor seesaws; souls are so strong, and dogs are always eager to please. "Not so much!" Then outside, another round of rifle fire. Lani leaps forward again and the wagon follows, buoyed by the spirit inside.

We roll through the rutted field, but the wagon no longer bounces and swings; the ride is smooth. Are the wheels even touching the ground? The dust and smoke give us cover, at least, and in the confusion, who would notice a wagon's wheels? I peer through the scrollwork to see if we're being watched. Then I scream as a figure bursts out of the haze and leaps onto the wagon.

I scramble away from the wall, pressing myself into the silk scrim as the roulotte sways with new weight—not once, not twice, but three times. Dirty fingers worm through the scrollwork as the men find handholds. Frightened eyes peer in.

"Help me," one says—his voice is high with youth and panic. I can hear his ragged panting, smell the sour sweat of fear on his sooty country clothes.

Behind us, the call comes—Legarde barking orders. "They're on the wagon!"

My eyes go wide in the dark; my heart is pounding like Maman's drum. Are these the Tiger's men clinging to the side of the roulotte? They sound like boys. Then again, my brother was my age last I saw him, when he left to fight rebels like these. And their age didn't stop them from bombing the stages. Should I pry their fingers loose? Before I can decide, a bullet crunches through the wagon, whistling past my ear. I flatten myself on the floor as one of the rebels falls screaming into the field.

Then the wagon tilts upward as Lani heaves herself up an embankment. I slide back against the door, and it swings open wide on the hinges. There are the soldiers, surrounding the fallen rebel, rifles at the ready. But Legarde is still chasing us—this is not how I wanted to be seen. "Arret!" he shouts.

I raise one bloody hand. "Don't shoot!"

"Stop the wagon, now!"

"We're trying!" But as the roulotte rights itself, another shot sounds, much closer; one of the rebels returning fire. I slam the door shut and latch it as Legarde takes aim.

We're back on the road. The sound of hoofbeats on stone means we've reached the docks. Two rebels still ride on the wagon, one keening in fear, the other clambering up toward the roof—to hide or to shoot? I scramble to the front panel, sliding it open. Fresh air swirls through the smoky haze in the roulotte as we careen past the seedy bars and dance halls on the edge of town. "Papa! We need to stop!"

"She won't!" he calls back, but Maman is staring at me.

"We *were* stopped, Jetta!" Her eyes are fiery as damnation.

She grasps my bloody hand. "What did you do?"

My mouth falls open, but no answer comes. Then, straight ahead, a man bursts out of an alley and stops in the middle of the street. His nose is bloodied, and a group of soldiers is right behind him. At first I think they're chasing him—is he another rebel? No, he's dressed too finely, in Aquitan style, though he doesn't look foreign—not quite. "They fled to the fields!" he shouts to the soldiers, pointing directly toward us. Then his eyes widen when he sees Lani barreling down on him.

"Out of the way!" I scream. Papa hauls on the reins, but Lani has the bit in her teeth. One of the soldiers pulls a pistol out of the strange man's belt, aiming at her—or at us? "No!"

The strange man swears, grabbing for the gun, forcing it upward and firing at the sky. Lani snorts, startled, and skids to a stop just inches from his outstretched hand.

The rebels leap from the wagon, but where can they go? This new group of soldiers is standing before them in the street, and Legarde is charging over the embankment behind us. "Stop them!" he calls, and the soldiers obey, surrounding the two rebels before they can reload their weapons.

The stranger ignores them, reaching up to Maman, blood still running down his face. "Come with me."

I half expect her to protest, but Maman scrambles down—though she doesn't take the hand he offers. Papa follows as I crawl through the opening on the front panel and onto the seat, scraping my raw shoulder on the frame. The stranger holds out his hand again, impatient; now that I'm closer, I realize what is so strange about him. The word surfaces in my mind before I can banish it: moitié, the Aquitans say, mixed, and always with a sneer. I can't meet his eyes lest he see the thought on my face, but he's watching Legarde approaching, not me. I put my hand in his—my legs are shaking, unsteady—and he pulls me away from the scrum.

"Wait, Leo!" One of the nearby soldiers steps in front of us—the one who'd aimed the gun. He's still holding on to it, the barrel pointed somewhere between the ground and Papa. As he stumbles closer, I can smell the alcohol on his breath. "The general might have questions."

"I'm sure he will, Eduard, but does he want my answers?" The stranger—Leo—leans in toward the soldier like a conspirator. "Maybe *you* stopped the wagon. Maybe *you* caught the rebels. Who knows? *Maybe* that will cancel out the part where they stole your new rifles."

Without waiting for an answer, Leo steps around the

soldier and hustles us down the side alley, past the sign: GIRLS GIRLS GIRLS. For a moment, I hesitate, but then I see Legarde, striding up to the wagon, dragging the stricken rebel by the collar.

"Don't look back," Leo says, pulling me along behind him. "This isn't going to be pretty."

Sent at 2104h
General Legarde at Luda
To: Dar Som, Sekat, Kah Le, Morai

LUDA SECURE STOP DO NOT PURSUE

CHAPTER THREE

I should have listened to Leo.

But isn't it human nature to watch?

Or if not human nature, it is my nature. And though Leo hustles me inside the building, the door hangs loose on the hinges, so I turn and press my eye to the crack.

The soldiers line the rebels up, kneeling in the alley. Three in a row—one already wounded: small and skinny, and filthy with soot and soil. Country boys. Chakran boys. Like my brother was once—like he always will be, now.

No. Nothing like my brother. These boys are the reason my brother is gone.

So why do I shudder as Legarde raises his gun? The Shepherd, they call him, but his banner is a wolf. And don't shepherds slaughter as they tend?

I can't hear his question, only the soft murmur of his voice, but I see the defiant look the wounded boy gives him. Does he know what happens next? My hand goes to my mouth as Legarde pulls the trigger, and my muffled scream is lost in the crack of his gun. The body falls—the soul flees, bright gold. Wet blood pools on the street. Then a different wetness spreads beneath the rebel on the left as Legarde adjusts his aim and asks again.

"Come away." The whisper makes me jump—Leo is standing just behind me in the hall. He's cleaned the blood off his nose, but something about his face still puts me on edge. Or maybe it's everything else. Either way, this time I listen.

Numbly, I let him lead me through a dim corridor lined with doors and lit only by drifting spirits. Leo cannot see them—can he? But he walks with such certainty in the dark. I am more trepidatious. The air here is close and cloying, tacky with perfume and smoke and sweat. The boards creak and sag underfoot; the souls of dead vermin skitter across the floor. My mind goes back to the sign outside. "What is this place?"

"My theater," he replies.

"*Your* theater?"

His back stiffens; he turns to study my eyes. "What about that surprises you?"

"Your age," I tell him truthfully. "You don't look much older than me."

"Ah." His shoulders fall, but so does his face. "It was an inheritance."

The explanation is simple, the meaning profound. Losing Akra was hard enough—I cannot imagine losing both my parents. I suck air through my teeth, ready to offer some inane politesse. But then I hear another shot outside, and a boy starts screaming.

The sound cuts through me, through the shell-shocked shroud that had fallen when the stages exploded. Only as it melts away do I realize it was ever there. To my surprise, a sob escapes my lips, and another, and I can't stop them. They crawl up my throat and force their way into the air, they take me by the shoulders and shake me with a shocking violence. I reach out to steady myself, tears hot on my face, and suddenly his arms are around me. For a moment, I grasp at the comfort he offers—this stranger. "It's all right," he lies. "It's all right."

I push him away, horrified. "It's not!"

His hands are up, his expression cautious, his back against the patched plaster of the wall. "Fair enough." Another scream rattles the air between us. "Though it could be much worse," he adds through his teeth.

I swallow bile, wiping my face with the back of my hand. Then I take a deep, tremulous breath. "Is my family safe here?"

"I won't hurt you."

"But what about them?" I gesture wildly toward the flimsy door. "Will they come for us next?"

"You tell me!"

"What do you mean?"

"You were running," he says with a look. "What did you do?"

"There was an explosion!" I shudder again at the memory. "We were on the way to La Fête when the stages blew apart. Lani panicked. She wouldn't stop until . . ." I half turn then, looking back down the hall. "She's still out there."

"She'll be fine," Leo says. "Though the soldiers may search your wagon, considering you drove in with rebels aboard."

My heart stutters then—what would the armée find, if

they really looked? They'd have to crawl to see the broken axle. But might they unbind my many fantouches, suffused with the souls of the dead? Or reach beneath Maman's pillow to find the little enamel box and all the money we've saved? But the rebel boy is still screaming, and I can't go back out there, I can't.

"I'll go out and guard your things," Leo says quietly. "As soon as . . . as soon as *that's* over."

I don't have to ask what he means. I wet my lips; my mouth is so dry. "Won't they . . . might they hurt you too?"

"Me?" Leo barks a laugh. "Non. Not if they know what's good for them. Half the armée is in love with my girls," he adds then, and his look makes me take a step back. "And half are afraid of them."

"I see." Carefully, I school my expression, though the implication of ownership makes me queasy. Or is that only the sounds from outside? "Thank you. And thank you for . . . for stopping the wagon. That was brave."

"What can I say?" A wry smile flickers across Leo's face, and he pitches his voice to carry. "I'm good with animals."

"*I heard that!*" Another voice floats through the gloom, soft and feminine. Out of the shadows, a Chakran girl appears, wearing little more than rouge and rhinestones.

"Oh! Cheeky." Leo smothers his smile as he turns to her. "Didn't hear you coming."

"Never will, with an attitude like that." The girl arches a perfect eyebrow. Then her face freezes as she turns to me, taking in my torn shawl, my bloody shoulder. "You don't look so good."

I blink at her—the dark, tousled pin curls, the wide eyes winged with bone black, the soft expanse of bare golden skin. I'm not naive—I saw the sign out front. I know that shadow plays aren't the only sorts of shows there are. And Maman has told me the truth of it—that work is work, no matter what you have to work with. Still, knowing is different than seeing, and the girl comes as a bit of a shock. Or is it only the wide gulf between death and beauty that has my head spinning? And how can they joke at a time like this?

But she reaches out to me, her hand hovering a few inches away from my skin. "May I?" At my nod, she slips her arm through mine, and her touch is warm and gentle. "Come with me. We'll get you cleaned up."

"Where are my parents?" I ask as she leads me onward.

"Samrin and Meliss? Just down the hall. Leo!" She calls his name over her shoulder. "Wash some more glasses, will you? She'll need a drink too. Welcome to La Perl," she adds with a grand gesture and a mocking smile as she sweeps aside a curtain.

I blink in the sudden light. "La Perl?"

"Well, doesn't it look like a dive to you?"

We've entered a wide room, lit by dozens of candles on at least as many café tables, each surrounded by chairs that don't match. There's a narrow stage at one end, with gas footlights— there are even red curtains and a real piano, though the velvet is balding and the piano has been painted several times, like an aging star. On the far side is a bar near the main entryway, though the rhum is stored in old kerosene jars, and half the bottles have been smashed across the floor in what looks like an altercation. Whatever audience there was must have left in a hurry—some of the furniture is knocked over, and there are half-full glasses scattered about. But Maman and Papa are there, as promised, and I pull free of Cheeky's grasp when I see them.

"Jetta." Papa stands, reaching out; I run to him, falling against his chest. He wraps his arms around me, but I hiss when he touches my shoulder—new wounds, old scars. "What happened to you?"

"I fell off the step when Lani bolted," I say. Does he

know what's going on outside? I can still hear the screaming, distant now—or is it only in my head? "I caught up when you stopped."

"And then?" Maman stands too, her voice low, urgent. "I felt the axle crack like a bone."

It sounds like a statement, but I know it is an accusation. I glance down at my bloody palms, clenching them into fists, trying to hold on to my temper, but it slips through my grasp. "What would you rather I had done?"

"I'd rather you kept your promise," she says through her teeth. "Never show, never tell."

"I saved our lives!" I whisper fiercely—in frustration or pride? But she slams her own palms down on the table.

"At what cost?" All around us, the sudden silence seems to echo, and I can feel it then—the eyes of an audience. Cheeky is watching us from near the bar, joined by another girl, this one blond and vaguely familiar.

Maman notices them too—she presses her lips together and sits back down in her chair. But I can't help myself. "I don't know, Maman," I say under my breath, only loud enough for my parents to hear. "Is it worse than death?"

I lift my chin, triumphant—our savior in the fray—ready for the praise I deserve. It doesn't come. Instead, her face goes sallow, sickly. "It could be," she whispers. "Depending on who finds out."

Her expression shakes my conviction. Was I right to risk it—or was I only arrogant? My malheur makes it hard to know for sure. But even if Legarde had somehow noticed something odd about the wagon, was arrest worse than being shot in a fallow field?

I cannot ask, not here, not where others can hear me: never show, never tell. Not that Maman would answer, anyway. The blond girl is approaching now, carrying a wide wooden bowl of water. A fresh green smell drifts up with the steam, and the vana of a minnow makes the water glimmer. "Sit." The blond nods to an empty chair, and her voice is low and soothing. "Before you fall."

I sink down, my knees suddenly weak, and reach across the table to take Papa's hand. It's bandaged with a strip of pale silk. "Are you hurt?"

"Some splinters and scrapes. But we've had good care. This is Tia." Papa bows his head in respect as she sets the bowl at my feet. I frown—though the girl is familiar, the name is not. Then Papa gestures as another girl approaches in a long silk wrap, carrying a handful of clean rags. "And this is Eve. They're performers here."

Eve smiles sweetly from behind a thick curtain of dark hair, but I can't stop staring at the live snake draped around her neck. "That's just Garter," she says, swirling a rag in the water and dabbing at my muddy, bloody feet. "Get it? Don't worry, she doesn't bite. Not unless you're a rat. Where are your shoes?" She bites her lip then, suddenly uncertain. "Do you have shoes?"

"They're in our wagon outside." I do not mention that my only pair is one I wear on the stage. Embroidered silk is too fine to risk in the street—and too expensive to waste. But I'm too ashamed to say so in front of these lovely girls, lush and well-fed, draped in glitter and rhinestones. Then I wince—she's gentle, but everything hurts. "I was getting ready for the show when the stage exploded."

"We heard the bombs." Cheeky plops down into a chair on my other side, sliding a glass of cloudy liquid across the table. I reach for it, but Maman gives me a sharp look.

"What is that?" she asks, and Cheeky gives her a look right back.

"Same thing you gulped down two minutes ago."

I can't help the laugh that bursts past my lips—she is so bold. But Maman's eyes narrow, and I turn it into a cough as the girl grabs a frilly scrap of lacy silk from Eve's lap and dips it into the glass.

"Don't worry," she adds with a wink. "They're clean."

I have half a second to digest this claim before she puts the silk to my shoulder and I yelp. "That burns!"

"Drink, then!"

Ignoring Maman's disapproval, I take a sip of the liquid. Then I cough again, for real this time. "That burns too," I choke, my voice suddenly hoarse.

Unconcerned, Cheeky keeps dabbing at my skin. "Next time, arrange to be rescued by a docteur. What happened here?" she adds then, tracing the edge of the scar with one cool finger. I turn away, embarrassed, and she pulls her hand back. "Sorry. It just seems that as far as burning goes, you've dealt with worse."

"Haven't we all?" Tia says to Cheeky, and the two of them laugh like bells, chiming.

"It was the first time I'd had to rig the scrim alone," I say, avoiding my parents' eyes and trying not to blush. The first touring season after my brother joined the armée, though it doesn't feel right to mention him, not in this irreverent place. "The knots were loose and the wind took the silk into the fire bowl. I must have been . . . distracted."

"So you're shadow players?" Eve says hopefully. "I love shadow plays. I try to go to La Fête every year. Not this year, obviously. We were working tonight." Her smile falters for a moment—so quick I almost missed it. "But almost every year."

"I saw a shadow play in Nokhor Khat once," Tia says, tossing back her blond curls. "Just a few months ago, on my world-famous tour."

"World-famous?" Cheeky drops the rag to the floor and takes another. "In what world?"

"Don't be jealous, darling, green's not your color." Tia speaks without malice, reaching over to chuck Cheeky under the chin. Cheeky blows her a kiss. But now I'm drawn in.

"You've been to the capital?" I say, a bit breathless. "What's it like?"

"Oh, darling." Tia smiles at me like a benediction. "It shines twice as bright as the stars in your eyes. Fine people and finer dress. Champagne and sugar and electric lights around the Ruby Palace."

"I used to dream of performing at the royal opera," I admit, but Maman frowns.

"Better to perform for an emperor than a king." On the surface, it's true, but she doesn't fool me. Even though troupes in the capital make far more money than those in the villages, Maman has always hated the idea of performing there. She's never told me why, but I'm certain it has nothing to do with the king's status. More likely it's her fear of Le Trépas; so many Chakrans who lived through his reign are certain that the stone walls of his prison are not half as thick as they should be.

I am not so fainthearted. But on the way to Aquitan, I doubt Maman will give me the chance to stop for a show.

"Nice work if you can get it," Tia is saying. "But the Boy King does love his entertainment."

Cheeky winks. "The Playboy King, you mean?"

They laugh, but Papa shifts at the disrespect. For a moment, I tense; I can still hear the echoes of his voice—a whisper from the past. "He's the rightful heir," he used to say, "why don't they let him rule?" But only to his brother, and never loud enough the words might pass beyond the walls of our shack. Papa was too cautious for that—not like Uncle was. Maybe that's why Papa is still around.

It's not that Papa doesn't appreciate the Aquitans, and what they did at La Victoire. We all do. But we also remember the Hungry Year, when the rains never came and the stores were depleted and we realized just how many fields had gone over from rice to sugar. We have performed in the parlors of plantations owned by foreigners—seen their fine things, smelled their rich foods—and gone back outside afterward to eat rice from our cookpot and sleep in the roulotte. And we remember—Papa and Maman and I, we cannot forget—how Akra put on the uniform d'armée and that was the last time we saw him.

But Papa is still cautious, even here. Especially here. "I've never heard that term," is all he says.

Cheeky only flutters the scrap of lace in his direction. "It's been nearly sixteen years since La Victoire. He's not a child anymore, and it's not like they let him govern. What would you do with your time if you were young and rich?"

"Shadow plays," Papa says with a wry smile, and Cheeky grins at him.

"Lucky you."

"All that will change after the coronation," Eve says, but Cheeky tosses her pin curls.

"It'll change right back after the wedding," she says. "Men are weak for beautiful women. Trust me on this."

"I could always take her place," Tia says, framing her face with an open palm while the other girls giggle. "No one would ever know the difference."

"The king might figure it out on the wedding night," Cheeky snickers, and Tia winks.

"I don't think he'd complain."

Watching Tia, I realize why she looks familiar. "You're an impersonator," I say, but she flaps a hand at me.

"I prefer the term 'long-lost twin.' Tragically separated at birth from my sister, Theodora Legarde."

I cock my head. In the last few months, the posters of General Legarde had been joined by posters of his daughter— La Fleur d'Aquitan, they call her. The only woman beautiful enough to tame Raik Alendra, the Boy King, the last of his line and heir to the Chakran throne. An historic marriage— between a Chakran and an Aquitaine, and a symbolic one too. But on the posters, Theodora is pale as porcelain, with eyes like sapphires, and luxuriously fat. Tia's eyes are black, and under the powder, her cheeks are golden brown and faintly stubbled; this close, I can see the shape of extra padding under her dress. But Tia is beautiful too, with all the hauteur of royalty; she makes her rickety chair a throne just by sitting in it. Besides, at the heart of theater is the suspension of disbelief.

"I thought it was her, when I first saw you," I say, though even as the words come, they sound too eager, too obsequious. "The spit and image."

Inside, I cringe—why do I want their approval so badly? But Tia puts her hand over her heart, as though touched by the compliment. Then Cheeky leans close to whisper loudly. "Mostly spit."

Pulling the blond wig off her own head, Tia pretends to swat the other girl with it. Their laughter puts me at ease— even Papa is smiling. Once the giggling subsides, Tia fits the wig over one hand, gently rearranging the curls.

"I saw her in real life once, you know. While I was in the capital." She gestures to her hair—short and black under the wig—and grimaces. "I went incognito, of course. You know their *laws*. But one night I went to a shadow play and there she was, sitting in the front row with her father and every other foreigner in the city. They're all wild for fantouches d'ombre."

Eve nods. "Last year at La Fête, someone told me that Le Roi Fou converted his ballroom to a shadow theater."

I tense at the word *fou*—mad—but they aren't looking at me. And a slow grin is spreading across Cheeky's face. "So then," she says deliberately, "how does he hold his balls?"

The girls burst out laughing again, but the numb feeling is returning. "We were on our way to La Fête," I say softly. "We were trying to get to Aquitan."

Across the table, Maman's face cracks like a bowl, and the bleak despair in her eyes is somehow the worst thing I've seen tonight. It eats at me too: we've come all this way, and our destination has never been further out of reach. Seeking comfort, giving comfort, I take her hand in mine. "Don't worry, Maman," I say, though the words are hollow. "There's bound to be another way."

"Another way?" Maman grips my fingers—her whole body tenses, as though she's trying to hold herself together. "And what will that be?"

My fingers hurt, but I only squeeze her back until our knuckles both turn white. A hundred answers flit through my head—to build a boat with a turtle's soul, and ride it across the Hundred Days Sea. To step from behind the scrim—no longer a wonder but a marvel, and wait for the world to shower us with coin. To march to Nokhor Khat and demand an audience with the Boy King himself. He would be amazed by what I can do. Or would he be afraid? Either way, I'm sure I could convince him to help.

Papa puts his hand over our twisted fists, his voice low— trying to soothe, or to silence? "We'll find a way," he says. "In the morning, we'll ask around. They may rebuild the stages. Le Fête may still go on. The Boy King is still getting married, after all. The royal couple is still going to Aquitan. And Le Roi Fou will still want his shadow plays."

Ever the optimist—ever the storyteller. But under Maman's strict eye, what other option do we have?

The girls are shifting uncomfortably, pretending not to listen. The snake slithers across Eve's bare shoulders. "I was trying to save enough to leave," she says finally, into the prickly silence. "But the river gods raise the prices after each attack."

Papa cocks his head. "River gods?"

"The men who sell passage on the boats." Carefully, Eve wraps a bandage around my heel. "They stand between this life and the next, judging your worth. Somehow they find me wanting," she adds with a winsome smile, but I can see the fear underneath.

I glance around the room then: Cheeky with her jokes, Tia with her pride, Eve with her sweet smile. But ultimately, just some girls in a dirty dive along the northern jungle, with smudged makeup and holes in their stockings. I understand their laughter now—it is just another act. How many people want to flee but have no route to safety? We were lucky we had a chance—*have* a chance, if the money in our roulotte is still there by morning.

"How much is passage?" I ask. Across the table, Maman's eyes snap to mine, and hope creeps back across her face.

Eve only shrugs. "You'll have to go ask at the dock. I stopped checking a while back. Or Leo might know."

Tia frowns, looking up from her wig. "Where is Leo, anyway?"

"Never ask where a man goes," Cheeky says loftily. "He might get the impression you want him to come back." Then she puts a gentle hand on my shoulder as I start to rise. "The dock will still be there in the morning. Even I wouldn't go out there alone tonight."

"Will the armée keep us safe in here?" I ask, and she grins.

"Sure," she says. "As long as they stay out there."

Sent at 2106h
General Legarde at Luda
To: King Alendra at Nokhor Khat

    GUERRILLA ATTACKS ACROSS VERDU STOP TWO
    REBELS CAPTURED IN LUDA STOP SITUATION
    UNDER CONTROL STOP QUESTIONEUR
    EXTRACTING INFORMATION

Sent at 0136h
Theodora Legarde at Nokhor Khat
To: General Legarde at Luda

    ON THE CUSP OF IMPORTANT DISCOVERY STOP
    URGE YOU TO RECONSIDER SENDING ME TO
    AQUITAN

Sent at 0343h
General Legarde at Luda
To: Capitaine Chantray at Nokhor Khat

    TIGHTEN SECURITY AT PALACE STOP
    RETURNING TO NOKHOR KHAT

Sent at 0346h
General Legarde at Luda
To: Theodora Legarde at Nokhor Khat

    LE RÊVE WILL SAIL AS PLANNED AND YOU
    WILL BE ABOARD STOP URGE YOU TO WORK
    FASTER

ACT 1,

SCENE 5

At the encampment, predawn; inside the general's tent. Through the canvas comes the sound of men and horses waking. Though the tent is roomier than the others, the sparse decoration gives it an empty feel; there is a single kerosene lamp, a standard armée cot, a lone travel trunk holding spare uniforms. Indeed, the only nod to the general's status is the field desk, and the fine fountain pen in his hands.

GENERAL JULIAN LEGARDE is marking a map with the locations of last night's attacks when his son, CAPITAINE XAVIER LEGARDE, steps into his tent. He waits for a moment—patient, even tentative, but the general does not look up.

XAVIER: Sir?

LEGARDE: Reportez.

XAVIER: I sent the telegrams and alerted the cavalry. They're readying the horses. Your men should be ready to move before dawn. And I updated the recherche for the Tiger, adding these newest crimes.

LEGARDE: You distributed it via telegraph?

XAVIER: And in Chakran, sir. Before dawn, the country will know there were shadow players among the dead.

LEGARDE (*nodding, satisfied*): That should do some good. The locals love their storytellers.

XAVIER: Not only the locals. Speaking of which, a letter came.

XAVIER hands it over. LEGARDE looks at the envelope— weather-stained from long travel, but finely milled and sealed with gold-flecked wax stamped with a sunburst: the symbol of Le Roi Fou, LEGARDE's half brother. He tosses it on his desk.

LEGARDE: Any response from Nokhor Khat?

XAVIER: Not yet, but it's still very early.

LEGARDE: If anything comes after I leave, send it on downriver. Unless it's from your sister.

XAVIER: Is there trouble?

LEGARDE (*making a wry face*): She keeps trying to get out of going to Aquitan.

XAVIER: If I may, sir . . .

LEGARDE: You too?

XAVIER: Her work here has been vital to the effort.

LEGARDE: Her marriage will be as well. And she won't be gone as long as she thinks. What about the prisoners?

A flicker of distaste crosses XAVIER's face.

XAVIER: The two dead will be put on display, as per your standing orders. What do you want done with the last one?

Now LEGARDE looks up, surprised, impressed.

LEGARDE: He's still alive?

XAVIER: Barely.

LEGARDE: Hmm. *(Idly, he taps the desk with his pen.)* See if the docteur can patch up what's left of him. He'll set a different example.

XAVIER: Which example is that?

LEGARDE: We show strength in mercy, Xavier.

XAVIER: The questioneur is many things, but merciful is not one of them.

LEGARDE gives his son a look, his eyes dropping to the gold pendant XAVIER wears—a golden circle on a chain.

LEGARDE: I know at times our tactics are at odds with your beliefs, but this information will save lives on both sides.

Finally XAVIER's frustration breaks through his calm facade.

XAVIER: What information? Every claim the rebels made contradicted the last! After the first hour they would have said anything. Besides, there's no way a green farm boy knows what the Tiger himself is planning.

LEGARDE: Not *his* information. The information we send when his comrades see exactly what they're risking.

XAVIER: I don't think the threat of torture will sway the rebels.

LEGARDE: It isn't just the rebels that concern me.

He leans back in his chair, regarding his son.

LEGARDE: These guerrilla attacks are cowards' tactics. The Tiger's men creep in the dark, strike as fast as they can, then throw down their weapons and melt back into the population. Unfortunately, they get the job done. The locals are intimidated. Maybe even impressed. Especially when the perpetrators escape with no consequences. This country is full of green farm boys, Xavier. Most who leave the fields join the armée. But the stronger the Tiger looks, the more likely they are to take his side. The rebellion is still relatively small. I'd like to keep it that way.

XAVIER: But one of the crimes on the Tiger's recherche is torture, and you know how the locals feel about that. If we denounce him for that, then publicly stoop to his level—

LEGARDE: The difference is, he does it to his own people. We only do it to our enemies. Besides, it might boost morale in our own ranks. I'm not unaware of the . . . ugliness brewing.

XAVIER: It might help if you let the men pursue the rebels when they strike.

LEGARDE: We don't have the numbers to chase them through their own territory. Or the ability to tell the Tiger's men from innocent villagers, out in the jungle.

XAVIER nods reluctantly. Then he frowns.

XAVIER: If you know the rebels' information isn't any good, why are you going back to Nokhor Khat?

LEGARDE smiles a little, gesturing to the map laid out before him.

LEGARDE: Tell me what you see here, capitaine.

XAVIER approaches his father's desk to glance over his shoulder. His jaw clenches, unclenches, as he considers.

XAVIER: Points of attack, all along Le Verdu.
LEGARDE: What kinds of attacks?
XAVIER: . . . Sabotage.
LEGARDE: And close to their own territory. Why? We know they hide all over the country. Farm the fields until they get their orders. Attacks like these only need half a dozen men. Why limit strikes to Le Verdu?
XAVIER (*slowly*): You think they're trying to draw your attention away from the capital?
LEGARDE: Away from the wedding. The last thing they want is an Aquitan queen.

XAVIER considers this for a moment.

XAVIER: What if it's only a ruse to get you to leave the area?
LEGARDE: They'll have you to contend with in my absence. I'm leaving you in command.

XAVIER raises an eyebrow.

XAVIER: Not Pique?

LEGARDE: Certainly not. We want the locals managed, not terrorized.

XAVIER: He has seniority. Experience.

LEGARDE: Are you a coward now too?

XAVIER: No, sir.

XAVIER straightens his back, but LEGARDE sighs.

LEGARDE: Pique has been here too long. In war, there are some experiences that do more harm than good.

XAVIER hesitates, then, shifting on his feet . . .

XAVIER: Are the rumors true, sir? The rebels going south to . . . to—

LEGARDE: To free Le Trépas?

Now XAVIER shudders, fishing the gold pendant from his uniform and raising it to his lips in a motion that borders on ritual. LEGARDE only shakes his head.

LEGARDE: The Tiger is ruthless, but he isn't mad. He wants the throne for himself.

XAVIER: Perhaps he hopes they can set their differences aside to fight a common enemy.

LEGARDE: Le Trépas can't be bargained with. You were too young to remember—

XAVIER: I've heard the stories.

LEGARDE: Then you know the man was a zealot and his followers just as bad. Live burials. Dark magic. Abominations.

XAVIER: Why have you kept him alive all these years? Why not an execution? Or an unfortunate accident in prison?

LEGARDE does not answer right away. Instead, he steeples his fingers, watching his son over his hands.

LEGARDE: There is a story in this country. I saw it first in shadow plays, but as Le Trépas gained power, it kept cropping up in rumors. That through pain, certain spirits could gain powers after death.

XAVIER: I've heard those too. The n'akela. How they haunt their tormentors.

LEGARDE: Some of his disciples believed they could do more than haunt. I saw men cut their own throats because they were sure their souls could simply steal new bodies, dead or living.

XAVIER: And you believe that?

LEGARDE: The Chakrans do. You must have noticed that they won't look you in the eye. The blue color scares them. They think it means we're possessed.

XAVIER: I know. They're superstitious. But what does that have to do with Le Trépas?

LEGARDE: If the old monk were dead, someone could claim to be him—or his soul. The King of Death reborn. Do you understand? And I won't let anyone drag this country back into a dark age of mysticism. The king's marriage to your sister sends a symbol—that Chakrana is wedded to civilization, not savagery.

XAVIER: Wedded to Aquitan, you mean.

LEGARDE: We *are* civilization, in this place. We will bring them into the modern age, whether they like it or not.

Then he frowns, glancing at the guns.

That reminds me. What did the last rebel say about the missing weapons?

XAVIER: Nothing believable. *(He hesitates.)* But the questioneur is Eduard Dumond—one of the men who lost a rifle. He says the story doesn't make sense—that the guns must have been taken by a separate group of rebels.

LEGARDE: Have him keep asking.

XAVIER: I don't know that the boy will live through more questioning.

LEGARDE shrugs, rolling up the map—clearing his desk, except for the letter XAVIER brought.

LEGARDE: C'est dommage. But isn't that what you preferred? And it will save our docteur a visit.

XAVIER's face is carefully bland, but he salutes and leaves the tent. At his desk, LEGARDE sighs. Then he breaks the elaborate wax seal and bends his head over the letter.

Pour Général Julian Legarde, Shepherd of Chakrana, leader at La Victoire, et mon demi-frère;

Cher Julian,

I read your letter from last month with great consternation concerning your report of the local rebellion gathering strength.

I have long put my trust in you, giving you free rein to run our affairs in Chakrana as you see fit. Unfortunately, your most recent request for additional funding is still too opaque. A ragtag band of insurgents can't possibly warrant such an expense. What armée are you trying to build with so much money?

Chakrana has always been a profitable venture—especially since your famed victory, for which you were rightly commended. But I must weigh the costs of goods against the costs of protecting them. Can you elaborate on your need?

As this letter will take another month to reach

you there across land and sea, it is quite possible that you have already pacified the uprising. If not, I trust that the upcoming coronation will quell the resistance by giving the general population exactly what they want—a Chakran in a position of power. It is a lucky thing that by all reports, this particular Chakran wants nothing to do with governance. And while I've only met Theodora once, knowing you, I'm certain her influence on her fiancé will allow you to exert your own on the future king's decisions.

Cordialement,
Votre demi-frère,

Antoine Le Fou

Roi des Aquitains

AVIS DE RECHERCHE

❈ ❈ ❈

The Tiger

The leader of the rebellion, a Chakran man approximately seventeen years of age, true name unknown. Physical descriptions vary.

❈ ❈ ❈

WANTED FOR:

Treason against the empire

Arson and destruction of property

Murder

The most heinous and unspeakable acts of torture against Chakran and Aquitaine alike.

REWARD 10,000 sols

CHAPTER FOUR

Later, after our wounds are dressed and we've picked apart a meal of cold rice and hot tea, I lie awake on a pallet in Cheeky's ramshackle room, listening to her soft snoring. She's sharing a blanket on the floor with Tia; the girls insisted on giving my parents their own room, and me, a bed. Their generosity is overwhelming—I haven't laid in a proper bed since the start of this year's touring season, when we left Lak Na for the last time. Too bad I can't enjoy it.

How can anyone sleep after a day like this? I toss and turn, my mind racing in circles, spiraling gently down, like the flyers, fluttering in the golden light, snatched away by the blast. The gunshots, the fire. The soldiers giving chase, the rebels clinging to the side of the roulotte. *Help me*, the boy says again and again, but he has my brother's face.

I bury my head in the thin pillow. Behind my eyelids, Akra's easy smile dissolves into a skull's rictus. My brother went off to fight the rebels—he was likely killed by one. So why do this boy's screams still echo in my head? Guilt for watching him die? Or is it a hallucination brought on by my malheur?

They crop up from time to time, when times are bad, but I haven't had one of Akra in a while. The old ones were better—the ones just after he joined up. I would hear his voice in the fields, singing one of the story songs, the one about the three brothers and the King of Death. It was always the same part too: the middle brother asking death to spare him. But the sound was so real—so rich—that the first few times it happened, I would walk through the dusty paddies to look for him. Of course he was never there. And by the time his first letter arrived, along with a fistful of sols, the sound of his singing had faded away. It never came back—not even while we waited for his seventh letter, and the weeks stretched to months before, one by one, Maman, Papa, and I admitted in the silence of our hearts that he wasn't coming back.

I'd give all the money he sent and more to hear his voice again, even if it is only in my head.

I'd give almost as much to stop the screaming.

But perhaps this is to be expected. What is a normal reaction to an explosion—to a boy shot like a dog? *Help me.*

Tossing aside the pillow, I slip out of bed on bandaged feet. I shouldn't have finished that drink. Or maybe I should have asked for another. My mind flits to the bar down the hall—the rhum in the old kerosene jars—but though my mouth is watering, I will not stoop to theft. I need something else to do, something to settle my nerves, to take my mind off the dead, off dying. Usually, when I can't sleep, I work on my fantouches. I could do so now, if the soldiers are gone.

The room is lit dimly by a few hopeful souls, but I bat them out of my way as I creep to the door. Spirits are such strange things, or perhaps I'm still unused to their presence. It was only after the fire I started seeing them—I thought they were hallucinations too, at first. Shifting patterns of red, orange, gold—the memory of flame. But they persisted long after I could breathe again, after my blisters healed, after I could leave my bed. And over time, I noticed their movements—similar in death as in life—and I began to recognize them for what they were. The tiny vana of moths, drawn to candlelight; the arvana of songbirds, flitting through trees. And the akela of dead men, like tongues of flame, wandering the fields where they worked, or standing in empty doorways, remembering.

No, the spirit sight is not the same as my malheur. The ups and downs, the sudden passions or the deep melancholy—those are things that grew as I did, like my limbs, my hips, my hair. But the spirits only appeared after my brush with death. It's like the old comedies about the Fool Who Could Not Die, though I only faced fire, and not the other two calamities that befell the hapless monk in the stories. And the spirits don't share gossip or try to trick me like they do him—they don't say anything at all. They only follow, eager for another chance at life, as though they know I have come close enough to death that I could lead the way there and back. And I'm happy enough to give them what they want.

Maman, less so.

I didn't tell my parents about the souls until after I was almost certain they weren't symptoms. But Maman's reaction made me wish they were. Never show, never tell. The fear in her face was shocking. Of course I'd known the old ways were forbidden, but the capital and its laws are very far away from where we lived in Lak Na. Even though the old temple at the back of our valley was reduced to rubble and jungle like all the rest, everyone I knew left a bit of rice in their bowls for the ancestors, or burned incense for the King and the Maiden and the Keeper of Knowledge.

But Maman's fear left no room for argument—at least, not from me. Papa has always been the only person who could ever change her mind. It was his idea to try to harness the souls—to use them to bring the fantouches to life—but it was hers to parlay our growing fame into a ticket out of Chakrana.

How did she learn what she taught me? Whenever I ask, her lips thin and her eyes go flat. Still, she was the first one to prick my finger, to guide my hand to draw the symbol. Even though Maman hates to talk about the old ways now, she lived half her life before La Victoire—before the new laws. And she has never failed to leave a bit of rice out for the spirits.

But hadn't I meant to stop thinking about the dead?

Carefully I ease open the door, stepping lightly; my feet are swathed in linen, but the floor still creaks. The air in the hall is cool, raising chicken skin along my arms. The little bedrooms line the hall from the entry; the distance seems shorter now. Before long, the crooked red door looms in front of me, and suddenly my heart is pounding again. I wait for the sound of gunshots, but they do not come, so I gather my courage to peer outside.

The pale moon silvers the stones and blackens the pool of blood. The soldiers and the rebels are gone, but our roulotte is still there. Dust and night dull the bright paint, making the white scar of a bullet hole that much brighter, but at least in the shadows, the broken axle is invisible. And Lani looks unhurt, even though she's been in the harness all night and hasn't eaten. Guilt pushes me through the door, but I hesitate just past the threshold. There is someone sitting on the back step of the wagon, long legs crossed on the stair.

A soldier? No—it's Leo, tucked into the cove of the rear step. His collar is loose and his eyes are closed; the moonlight pales his skin but darkens his hair as it curls loosely over his brow. Asleep, he looks much younger—perhaps my age. How does he run a theater by himself? Is that why he's so tense, so defensive? Or is it only that he's had to be, to survive?

I've never met a . . . a person with his heritage before—though I've seen them on the fringes with the beggars, the thieves, the fallen monks. Marriage between Aquitans and Chakrans isn't quite forbidden, but it isn't quite proper, either—just one more reason the king's engagement made waves. Then again, considering the sort of entertainment La Perl offers, perhaps Leo's parents were never married. Who were they? Where are his ancestors? Can they see him from across the sea?

And will mine be able to see me once we're gone?

"What are you doing here?" Leo says then, and I jump. His eyes are barely open—has he seen me staring?

"This is my roulotte," I say quickly. "What's your excuse?"

He sits up straighter, uncrossing his arms, and just like that, the softness about him is gone. His mouth slides into a grin, and I can't help but notice he's holding a dark glass bottle by the neck. "I'm keeping watch, as promised. Wouldn't want anyone making off with all this good meat." Leo gestures at Lani with the bottle; then he notices me staring. "Want a drink?"

"No, thank you," I lie. I know it's not wise to drink with a strange man in a dark alley—or even to drink much at all. But want wrestles with wisdom in my heart—the danger is what makes it so tempting. "Wait . . . yes."

Leo offers me the bottle. It's heavier than I expected, nearly full; I realize why when I take a sip and splutter. It's the same thing I had earlier. Tears spring to my eyes. I take another pull.

"Easy," he says. "Didn't you already have a glass?"

"Hours ago." I lift my chin—a challenge. "And you have a whole bottle."

"Fair enough," he says with a small smile. "I hoped it would help me sleep."

"Me too," I say, taking one more pull. His smile fades. He takes the bottle back then, and pushes the cork into the top.

My cheeks grow hot—is that the alcohol already, or is it shame at his look? But why do I care about this boy's opinion? I pretend to study the damage to the roulotte. "That's only Cheeky's costume box," Leo says quickly.

"What is?" I follow his gesture to the rear wheel. A battered wooden traveler's trunk is tucked right beside it, propping up the corner of the roulotte. I hadn't even noticed it in the dark. "Oh."

"The wheel was at an angle and Eduard was worried the wagon would topple over with him inside," he says. "She lent it to him on the promise he wouldn't paw through her underthings."

I bite my lip; inside, my heart races. Did Leo notice anything odd about the roulotte when he tucked the trunk underneath? Did Eduard wonder how the wagon had run so smoothly with a broken wheel? But the shadows are deep, and the questioneur was drunk—or so I tell myself. "Wait . . . he searched the wagon?"

"He took a quick look." He cocks his head. "Why do you ask? Were you carrying contraband?"

Fear opens a pit in my stomach. "Move," I tell him, and his expression turns serious as he slides off the steps. I open the door and scramble inside. But the fantouches are still bound in their burlap sacks—everything looks untouched. Still, I don't breathe until I slide my hand beneath Maman's pillow and feel the hard edge of the red money box.

It's not that I don't trust the armée, but this is our entire savings—over two hundred sols. Thankfully, it's still safely hidden. Relief floods me as I sit back on my heels.

Outside, Lani lows plaintively, as if to remind me of my guilt. In the far corner of the wagon there are some old rice bags stuffed with grass that I gathered this morning—or is it yesterday by now? She must be starving. I toss a bag through the open door. It bounces on the cobbles by Leo's feet, but he doesn't seem to notice. He's holding a piece of paper—one of our flyers. Realization sweeps like light across his face. "The Ros Nai?"

Pleasure creeps in at the awe in his voice, the shine our growing fame brings, even here—even now. "You've heard of us."

"Hasn't everyone?" he murmurs, but my laugh is short and bitter.

"They were supposed to," I say, stooping to grab the bag. "Tonight."

"At La Fête?" Leo puts the flyer down on the pile and follows me to the front of the wagon, where Lani is stamping her feet. "I'm sorry."

I rub Lani's neck and dump the contents of the bag out under her nose. She dips her head to eat. "It's not your fault," I say to Leo, but he flashes a grin.

"I mean I'm sorry I didn't get to see the show. When's the next one?"

"I'm not sure," I say. "How long does it take to get to Aquitan?"

"Aquitan?" Leo frowns. "Are you traveling by hope or by dream?"

"By boat. I had hoped the general would sponsor us, but if that doesn't work, Eve says they sell passage at the docks."

Now it's Leo's turn to laugh. "Not unless you're a crate of sugar loaves! The river gods sell passage down the Riv Syr to the capital. From there, you'll have to find a bigger ship."

"So will you, then," I say. "If you want to see us perform."

The humor fades. "You shouldn't take a boat downriver."

"Why not?"

"You have a wagon." He pats Lani's neck. "Take the roads."

"With the Tiger prowling around? The roads will be dangerous."

"You haven't seen the boats, I'm guessing?" My silence is his answer. Leo shakes his head.

"Why?" I ask. "What's wrong with them?"

"Nothing, if you're rich." Leo curls his lip, and my own heart sinks—rich means different things in the city than it does in the village. "This wasn't the only attack, you know. The rebels struck at sunset last night, all along Le Verdu."

I frown. "Who told you that?"

"Tia. The girl at the telegraph office has a crush on her. Came by to check and see if she was safe." He only shrugs, but my mouth is suddenly dry, and the tips of my fingers are tingling.

For years, there have been rumors that the Tiger would come south to drive the Aquitans from the country, from the capital, from the Boy King's circle of advisers. Some even said he would free Le Trépas to steal the foreigners' souls. I don't believe that—not truly. But where the Tiger goes, blood runs. And if the Aquitans decide to flee, how much room would be left on the boats?

"The point is," Leo adds, "every new attack means a higher price. And even if you are rich, you'll need every étoile once you get to Nokhor Khat. Passage across the sea doesn't come cheap. Besides, if you *are* carrying contraband, the river gods turn into river rats at the checkpoints, unless you give them a generous cut. What's wrong with your wagon?"

"You said it yourself," I tell him. "The wheel is loose. We cracked the axle running from the explosions. I was going to ask the general for help with a new one."

"The general?" He makes a face. "Why do you think he'd help you?"

Because we're the Ros Nai, I want to say, but I swallow the retort. What had Papa said? "Because the Boy King is still getting married, and Le Roi Fou still needs his shadow plays."

But Leo raises a mocking eyebrow. "Can't you fix a wagon, cher?"

"Iron is rationed, cher," I tell him tartly.

"So is rhum," he says with a wink, sloshing the liquid in the bottle. "But that's never stopped me."

"I'm not so well connected."

"You could be." Leo gives me a cocky smile. "Perhaps we can make a deal."

"A deal?" His look is offensively certain. The flush in my cheeks spreads and prickles the skin of my throat. Not just the alcohol now. But what did I expect from a man like him? "How dare you?" Spinning on my heel, I storm away, but he catches up with me beneath the painted sign: GIRLS GIRLS GIRLS.

"How dare I what?" he says, his eyes as hard as onyx. "Open my doors to your family when there is blood in the street? Or consider fixing your wagon in exchange for a ride to Nokhor Khat? How dare *you*, mamselle?" he adds. Then he presses his lips together in a grimace, as though trying to stop himself from saying more.

"That's what you want? A ride to the capital?" I stare at him, flustered, shame creeping in, but I'm not going to admit to it. "We'll be traveling with the general," I say at last, trying to sound more confident than I feel. "But thank you anyway."

"As you say." Leo waves a hand, dismissive, and starts back toward the theater. "But you better hurry if you want to catch up with him."

"Catch up?" I frown. "He's gone?"

"If not yet, soon." He tosses the answer over his shoulder. "He'd rather go to his daughter's wedding than grapple with the Tiger."

His words carry to me, but distantly; I'm already racing down the alleyway into the broad street. Sure enough, past the dock, where the road meets the fields, the armée is already on the move by torchlight, striking tents, saddling horses. Legarde is leaving . . . but he can't. Not without seeing us first.

What could make him stop and pay attention?

Whirling, I return to the roulotte, yanking open the back door and then grabbing the first fantouche I lay my hands on. Quickly I unwind the rope from the burlap, unwrapping a hulking heap of knotted black leather. The King of Death—a good omen. His stories have always been my favorites.

Leo has turned, watching me with a quizzical expression. "What are you doing?"

"Do you want to see a show?" I heave the puppet over my shoulder and march up to him, grabbing the bottle for one last pull—for luck. Then I hand it back and turn to run down the road. "Follow me!"

The King of Death and the Three Brothers

(Or, The First Shadow Puppet)

Part 1

In the days when our ancestors were young, there lived three brothers, though not for very long. A plague came to their village, and the King of Death came with it, carrying his lamp.

The first night, he knocked upon the eldest brother's door. It was a fine door, in a fine home, filled with fine things, for the eldest brother was rich, and he offered his wealth to the King of Death if only he could live.

But the King of Death was patient: "Everything comes to me in the end."

And he drew the flame of the eldest brother's soul into his lamp, and the eldest brother fell down dead.

The next night, the King of Death came to the house of the second brother. The second brother was humble, and begged Death to spare him. "Who will care for my parents if I am gone?" he asked.

But the King of Death was merciless: "I will take care of them."

And he took the fire of the second brother's soul into his lamp and went away.

But the third brother was cunning. So he fashioned a man out of leather, with clever joints and glassy eyes and a body that moved like his own. And the next night, when the King of Death came calling, the man lit a lamp behind the puppet and called out. "Here I am," he said. "I will give you no trouble."

And the King of Death was fooled. He pulled the light of the lantern flame into his own lamp, and the youngest brother let the puppet fall, and the King of Death went away.

CHAPTER FIVE

I run down the road in the creeping light of dawn. Is Leo following? I don't know, I don't care. The fantouche bounces on my shoulder, the wind takes my hair, and in my chest, hope blooms. Sefondre. When everything comes together.

La Fête was cut short; Legarde is leaving too soon. If he cannot stay for the show, I will bring the show to him. And I have a chance now that I did not have on the main stage: to perform without competition.

But it is strange to have the fantouche out in the open—without the scrim, without any cover but the predawn darkness. In my arms, he moves, restless as I am, eager to be seen. Under my breath, I whisper commands I do not follow myself: "Be calm, stay still." And unbidden, unwanted, Maman's voice creeps in over the sound of my pounding heart, my racing feet: never show, never tell.

I have to be cautious—I know that. I do. Nothing too showy, nothing too impossible. Just a taste of our skill, nothing more, nothing less. Doesn't theater always look like magic? Desperate times call for desperate measures— besides, don't I want to catch Legarde's eye? And there is something thrilling in it, isn't there? In the idea of such a dangerous show.

Along the road, little souls glimmer under scrub and on the breeze. Some of the living drift toward the horsemen, too: farmers pushing wheelbarrows or pulling carts, carrying children or driving animals. People following the armée toward the capital. People afraid of the Tiger.

People who can't get the general to stop and take notice.

I dodge around them, breathing hard. I see him now— Legarde, astride his golden horse, as the cavalry forms in rows at his side. He is only one soldier among many, and all wearing the same colors, the dark knee boots and drab green uniform of the armée, but even the firelight seems pulled to him, glittering on the bright buttons of his uniform, the medals on his chest, the silver in his hair. "General!" I shout, but he doesn't even turn to look. "General Legarde!"

Others stare as I pass. A foot soldier puts a hand on his gun and my heart stutters, but he doesn't take aim. What do they think of me, with my bandaged feet and my torn silk dress and the black bulk of the puppet in my arms? They must know I'm a performer, at least. But this show is not for them.

Speeding past startled livestock and surprised civilians, I skid to a halt at the side of the road and spin the King of Death to the side, like a partner in a foreign Aquitan dance. "Follow my lead," I whisper, and the arvana in the fantouche obeys as I stretch out one arm.

The King ripples through the air, unfolding, and hovers a few inches above the dusty road. A strange beast—I crafted him of stranded leather after a dream I had, where death crawled toward me on a hundred scuttling legs, and gave him the soul of a vulture. I keep hold of one bent wing, the other spread wide, and he slouches at my side—all without stick or string.

Now people are watching. There are gasps and murmurs. This is my first time facing an audience—behind the scrim, they are only a murmur of voices, a round of applause. I can't hide my grin. I bow with a flourish, and the King of Death does the same. But when we straighten up, instead of the wonder I expected to see, there is only fear in their eyes.

The crowd falters, stepping back in a widening ring around me, the older Chakrans pulling the younger away. At first I think they are afraid of the fantouche. I know he's intimidating—I made him that way. But no . . . the crowd is staring at me. For a moment, my heart quavers. Then it hardens. This show is not for them, either. "General!" I call again, and he has heard the commotion. At last he looks at me.

The full force of his gaze is almost physical; all the charisma of an actor, but the country is his stage. I draw myself up straighter as Legarde narrows his eyes—bright blue. Ghost eyes.

"My name is Jetta of the Ros Nai," I begin—and why didn't I bring the flyers? But before I can go on, a familiar voice calls my name. This time, it isn't only in my head.

"Jetta!" Maman is racing down the road. Just my name, but in it, a warning: never show, never tell. My mouth goes dry.

"You may have heard of us," I croak, trying to ignore her, but I've lost the audience. They've all turned at the sound of her voice.

"Jetta!" She pushes through the thick ring of the crowd and stumbles into the clearing. How did she find me? Part of me wants to run; the other part has no idea where. But I came here to get Legarde's attention, didn't I? And here he is, still watching. Fear mixes with something else in my gut—is it anticipation? Surely she must see the opportunity I've made for us—our best chance to get to Aquitan.

But as she nears, she draws her hand back. I am too stunned to cower, but she only snatches the fantouche out of the air, clutching it to her chest. For a moment, she glares at me—then past, to the audience as they wait for the next act in this drama. Even Legarde is rapt. She points her other hand at me. "You charlatan!"

My eyes go wide. "What?"

"How dare you try to impress the Shepherd with a parlor trick? Forgive us, general," she says, bowing low, nearly groveling. The leather tendrils of the fantouche drag in the dirt. "My daughter didn't mean any disrespect. She merely wanted to perform for you, but she has no sense of timing."

"Maman!" I try to protest, but she has stolen my show.

"A new marionette with silk strings!" The lie slips smoothly from her tongue; she's spoken this line a dozen times: Aquitanians always ask how it's done, and they never take "trade secrets" for an answer. "The thinness of a spider's web," she says, pretending to grasp a strand between her thumb and forefinger, pulling it taut to show him something that doesn't exist. "See? Almost completely invisible, especially in the dark!"

Legarde waves her into silence, still watching me. But shadows can hide many things, and Maman has been an actor longer than I. The general dips a hand into his saddlebag, tossing something to the road at our feet.

A five-étoile coin.

Without a word, Legarde puts his heels to his horse. The armée follows him in a cloud of dust and hooves, and they are off. Leaving the coin in the dirt, Maman grabs my wrist and shoulders through the crowd, back toward the theater. "Come with me."

"We should be going with them!" I say, pulling back toward the armée. "He would have taken us to the capital—"

"He would have taken you to prison!" she says. "Or worse. Legarde is the one who banned the old ways. What were you thinking, to shove them in his face?"

"And how would he know what they were?" My voice bursts out, too loud; strangers glance my way. I lower to a whisper. "How would he know about the souls?"

"How do you think they did?" Maman jerks her chin to the crowd. She pulls me close, hissing in my ear. "You're too young to have seen anyone else toy with the dead, but not all of us are so lucky."

I stop in my tracks. The crowd is thinner here . . . or people are giving us a wide berth. Still, I feel eyes crawling like insects over my skin. Souls are drifting closer, as though they've seen what I did. As though they hope I could give them new life too. "Who else?" I say, and by her silence I know the answer. "Le Trépas?"

She flinches at the name. "Don't ever say that name again."

Frustration bites at me. "What else am I supposed to call him? Kuzhujan?"

The name, his real name, trips up my tongue as it falls from my mouth. I've never said it aloud before—only heard it whispered or, once, shouted by one of Akra's friends. A taunt, a dare—answered only when his father came running from their house to give him a cuff across the mouth. Maman's eyes go wide. She shoves the black fantouche into my arms; it squirms against my chest. "Don't call him. Don't speak of him. Don't think of him."

I scoff. "You think he can hear me?"

"No. But the dead can."

"And what can they do about it?"

"Pray you never find out."

Her words take my breath away—so much anger in them. But I'm angry too, now. I open my mouth to make a retort, but in the corner of my vision, something flickers.

Bright blue, like the heart of a flame, like the waters of Les Chanceux—yet the sight leaves me cold. I turn my head, but it's gone.

No. It's on the other side now, just behind me. I whirl, but it's vanished again. Part of me wishes I could convince myself it was never there in the first place, but something about it shakes me, and I know it wasn't only my malheur. I have never seen a n'akela before, but there are tales about them. Rare souls—and dangerous. The ones who died in pain . . . the ones who want revenge . . . the sort Le Trépas created to send against his enemies. They do not want a new life—only more death. And they use their fading days to seek it out.

Did I draw it near, simply by speaking the old monk's name? A chill seizes me; I shiver, and Maman frowns. "What's wrong, Jetta?"

Everything. "Nothing."

I hate how Maman looks at me, like I might break. But she takes my arm again, gentler this time. "Tell me."

I grit my teeth, wavering—is she only going to blame me if she knows? "N'akela," I say at last, and she goes still.

I am so close to her that I can hear her breath falter in her throat, and her fingers tighten around my wrist. "Where?"

"Gone now," I say, but she searches the dark, like she could see it if she looks hard enough.

"Back by the road?"

"I . . . yes. But—"

Suddenly Maman clutches my hand. "Look there."

My eyes go wide—Maman has always denied being able to see souls—but then she points and I peer into the dark, not toward a flicker of blue, but something . . . stranger.

At first I think it is a man in the fields, dressed all in black, his face floating like a moon above a shadowy landscape. But as I stare, I realize that it is only a man's head, spiked through the chin on a spear of green bamboo. Farther down the roadside, a torso, striped and spotted with red wounds. Past that, another piece—a leg or an arm? I hadn't noticed them before, in the dark, in the crowd, or maybe I'd only had eyes for Legarde. Now flies crawl across the swollen tongue of the man's open mouth, and though it's been beaten bloody, the face is familiar. I can still hear his plea: *Help me.* A scream builds in my throat. I bite down, trying to breathe, to gather my scattered thoughts. They ruined his body, twisted his soul. But it's only a rebel . . . only a rebel . . . and it's no worse than the Tiger would do—is it?

"Come," Maman says, pulling me down the road. "Let's go."

I follow her with faltering steps, but the skin on the back of my neck is crawling, as though someone is watching me run. The eyes of the dead man? His vengeful soul? Then a voice drifts behind us on the road. "Madame?"

It's a commanding voice, smooth, accented. It reminds me of the general—but Legarde has gone, hasn't he? And Maman keeps walking, as if she didn't hear, though her arm tenses and she picks up her pace, ever so slightly. Behind us, the heavy tread of a soldier's boots comes at a jog.

"Madame!"

In my arms, the fantouche writhes. I clutch him tighter as the soldier steps in front of us, forcing us to stop. He's younger than Legarde, younger than Maman too—but old enough to be decorated, with medals on his chest. Maman looks at those, instead of into his pale blue eyes. But I can't look away—the color is too unnerving. "Yes, sir?"

"You forgot this." The soldier extends his hand—in it, a five-étoile coin. The one the general threw. A simple gesture, but his urgency gives me pause. Why would a soldier d'armée chase us down just to bring us some pocket change? I don't want the money, not from him, but Maman takes it, bowing low.

"Thank you, sir," she says. "Thank you."

He inclines his head; his eyes bore into mine. Then he stands aside. My palm is slick around Maman's arm. Together we leave at a measured pace, fearing another call. Nothing comes, but I don't breathe easier till we reach the docks. I lean down then, pretending to check my bandages while I glance behind us. The soldier has disappeared, thank the ancestors. A false alarm.

Still, my heart is pounding. "I thought the rebels were the only ones who used torture."

"There are no rules in war."

Maman's harsh whisper takes me aback. "The armée is supposed to be civilized!"

"Civilization is only another act. We have to get out of

the area," she says. "I don't want to be here if the general decides he wants an encore."

I blink at her. "What about Le Roi Fou? The Boy King? The boat to Aquitan?"

"We'll have to find another boat," she says grimly. I follow her gaze to the wharf. Already there is a small crowd gathering—news must have spread of the other attacks.

"Leo says the prices are an outrage," I murmur, with the peculiar feeling of taking a side I'd only just argued against. "If we pay to travel downriver, we may not be able to afford a ship to Aquitan."

"It's worth asking," she insists, chewing her lip. So I wait on the road while she goes to inquire with the other hopeful passengers. As I watch her, I feel watched myself. I try to ignore it, to fight the urge to turn around. When I finally give in, there is no one behind me.

It must be my malheur . . . the sight of the dead rebels . . . or the talk of Le Trépas. I grew up free of his reign—he's been imprisoned as long as I've been alive. Still, his shadow lingered after he was shot and jailed by Legarde, like an infection in the world, like poison on the skin. The older Chakrans remembered—they couldn't forget. I cannot get their stares out of my mind.

Did they think I might be just as bad as him? Another thought comes to me then—are we really leaving to find a cure, or are we running from something darker?

Maman is returning now, and even in the predawn light, I can see by the droop of her shoulders that Leo was right about the price. I clench my jaw. If travel downriver is so expensive, how much would it cost to cross an ocean? Perhaps it was a good thing the soldier brought us the general's coin. "So," I say to Maman when she's close enough to hear me. "We're following the armée after all?"

"At a safe distance," she snaps. "So the general doesn't ask to see you perform in broad daylight."

My skin prickles. Does she have to throw it in my face? "Good thing the wagon will run," I say, but she gives me a skeptical look.

"Only so long as no one notices it's running on a broken axle."

I narrow my eyes. "What would you prefer, Maman? The boats we can't afford or the wagon that shouldn't run?"

"I don't know, Jetta!" she shouts, rounding on me; at first I think she's furious, but then I see the despair in her face. "I don't know."

I swallow all the other angry words gathering in my

throat; they turn into guilt in my stomach. Why am I being so cruel? It isn't helping—and perhaps she's right to be angry. After all, if it weren't for my malheur, we wouldn't be here in the first place. I collect my thoughts, trying to breathe—trying to find a solution instead of more angry words.

"I have an idea," I say at last, taking her hand again. "Let's go back to the theater."

The King of Death

Part 2

The Man Who Cheated Death

In the days when our ancestors were young, the youngest brother rejoiced, for he had cheated death. Time stretched out before him, a road with no end, and he journeyed boldly down the length of it. But as the years went by, he began to grow weary.

His back bent and his eyes grew dim; his fingers went crooked and his feet flat. His teeth wore to nubs and all his hair fell out. His parents had passed on to be reborn, and so had his children, and even their children were growing old. Still, the third brother could not die; his soul was tied to his body and could not get free.

Lying on his bed, he called out in as loud a voice as he could—though that was not very loud at all. "King of Death," he said. "King of Death! Many years ago you came to me, and I sent you away with only a candle. Let me come with you now."

The King of Death was furious. "Why should I take you away with me?" he cried. "You had your chance." And he left the man's soul in his body.

The youngest brother despaired. Where could he turn? Who was more powerful than Death?

Why, Life, of course.

So the youngest brother left the house of his children's children and went into the wilds to search for the spirit maiden, the goddess who gave life. Years passed, and his children's children died, and so did their children, and their children, until no one knew his name or his village. Still he wandered, until at last he found her and fell to dust at her feet. But when his soul sprang free at last, it was twisted and angry, having suffered too much to remember anything but pain.

The spirit maiden knew better than to stitch his soul into a new skin, so she left him there, an abomination, longing to be reborn.

CHAPTER SIX

Maman goes back to her room to tell Papa the plan, and I find Leo in the bar, counting a fistful of money. The floor creaks as I approach—I know he can hear it—but he doesn't acknowledge me. Still, I wait quietly, one minute, two, trying to be respectful. He keeps counting. "Leo?"

"How was the show?" His words are polite, but his tone is absent, nonchalant. His eyes stay on his money. There is so much of it.

My jaw clenches, but I won't let him bait me. "It could have gone better."

"Too bad."

"I wanted to apologize for my assumption," I say, a little too loud. Now he looks up, and hope creeps into my voice. "It wasn't fair. But your offer is. An axle for a ride to the capital. We can leave as soon as you have the roulotte repaired."

"Apology accepted," he says, returning my tentative smile with a broad grin of his own. "But the deal is off."

His words are at odds with his expression; it takes me a moment to understand. "Why?"

"With what I would pay for an axle, I could afford a ticket on a boat."

"I thought you didn't trust the river gods."

"I don't have to trust someone to make a deal with them." His tone is pointed. I narrow my eyes, and his smile deepens.

"You're enjoying this."

"You aren't? I'm not forcing you to stay." Leo waves me away with his money, tossing the words at me like copper coins. "I don't force anyone to do anything."

I grit my teeth. "Can you at least introduce me to your source?"

"Give you the name of a friend selling contraband?" Leo shakes his head at the cash. "Why should I trust your discretion when you don't trust my motives?"

"I thought you accepted my apology!"

"Oh, but I do!" He meets my eyes again, and his face is earnest. "Your assumption was unkind, but so is the world—especially to girls, I'm well aware. You have no reason to trust me. Of course I have no reason to trust you either. And an apology won't buy a contact in the Souterrain."

The Souterrain—the underground. Where you can buy what is rationed—or what is forbidden. If we were back in Lak Na, I'd know who to ask. But here in Luda, I'm stuck with Leo. I glare at him, but he seems to enjoy the attention as he finishes his count. "So," I say at last. "What will?"

Leo leans across the bar with a grin. "Put on a show for me."

I clench my fists, holding tight to my anger. "I'm not a dancer."

"That's for the best," he says. "Your audience will be, and they're very discerning."

I frown. "The girls?"

"They love shadow plays."

"Shadow plays?" I glance around the dirty room. "Here?"

Leo turns back to his money, laying it out across the bar

in four stacks. His response, when he makes it, is a bit too casual. "Something wrong with La Perl?"

"No." I take a breath, calculating; we could rig the scrim from the flies between the curtains—though we'd have to be extra careful with the flame. At least it would be easy to protect our privacy backstage—everyone usually in the wings would be seated in the audience. "No. But . . . why?"

Leo takes a deep breath before he answers. When he speaks, his voice is low and steady, balanced on the edge of a long dark drop. "Because I asked the girls to work the night of La Fête. Because I have to leave tomorrow and I will miss them. Because not everyone can afford a more permanent escape from this place. Or maybe because of the look on your face when you ask me why."

I smother the next question: what look? Instead, I catalog my own expression: the curve of my eyebrow, the curl at the corner of my lip—perilously close to disdain. How long had that sneer been on my face? Carefully I smooth my features. "It will be an honor to perform here."

"You're a very good actor, cher." His smile is grim as he slips the smallest stack of bills into his own pocket. He picks up the other three and gestures with them. "I'll go tell the girls. They'll be thrilled. When's the show?"

"After sunset," I say automatically. "Shadow plays always start at nightfall."

"Bien." Leo slaps the pile of cash against the bar with a grin, and hope stirs in my chest. Still, I'm cautious.

"So we have a deal, then?"

"Yes. No. One more thing," he says then, narrowing his eyes. "Why on earth do you want to go to Aquitan?"

I open my mouth as all of the answers come to mind—I select the one that makes me least vulnerable. "We'll be rich. Shadow plays are famous there, and we're the best troupe in Chakrana."

"Is that really all it is? Fame and fortune?"

I bite my lip. "There are no Tigers overseas."

"There are wolves."

"How do you know?" I say then, my frustration building. "Have you been there?"

Leo leans in with a laugh. "Look at me," he says, gesturing to his face. "Do I look like I belong in Aquitan?"

It's a question . . . but not one that I can answer. So I look at him, like he wants me to. His features—handsome, yes, but strange. Mixed. It was one of the first things I had noticed about him, I remember now—and is that why I don't trust him? "It's hard," I say at last. "Not belonging."

"You say that like you know what you're talking about." The words are cocky, but his voice is gentle, sad. He holds out his free hand, as if to shake, Aquitan style, on our deal, but when I put mine in his, he kisses it. Startled, I pull my hand back, but Leo has already turned away. "I'll go get the mechanic started. Maybe even drum up a bigger audience. Who knows? At the right price, tickets could cover the cost of the iron."

Leo leaves to make his arrangements, and after a deep breath, I find Maman and Papa to make our own. "A show?" Maman asks, looking askance at me. "I thought he only wanted a ride."

I make a face. "The price has apparently gone up."

"It was already quite high," Maman says. "I don't like having strangers so close."

"You liked the cost of boat tickets less," I remind her. Still, she hesitates, and I brace myself for the questions— *Can you control yourself, Jetta? Can you keep your secrets?* But we haven't always traveled alone—or been this lonely.

Before the Hungry Year, before the spirits, before Akra left and my uncle vanished, we used to travel with other troupes on the circuit during the dry season, when the roads were clear and the fields were fallow. Jugglers or ribbon dancers, contortionists or other shadow players. We would come together for meals on the road or roll in caravans between stops. Sometimes Akra would walk up and down the lines, trading stories or advice with the others—he was so good at making friends. So was I, during the bright times, when my malheur masqueraded as an expansive bonhomie. These days, we have too much to hide.

But Papa puts his arm around my shoulders. "Traveling together seems like our best option. But tell me. Why does he need to go to Nokhor Khat?"

"I didn't ask," I say blithely, but Papa's brows draw down. "Should I?"

He takes a breath, but then he hesitates. After a moment, he shakes his head. "No. No. He's certainly not the only one in Luda who wants to leave." He drops his arm with a sigh. But then the ghost of his showman's smile crosses his face. "It's not quite La Fête, but we've done more with less. Come. Let's get ready for the show."

At his words, the thrill stirs in me again—a performance, an audience, an ovation. A collective breath held on my smallest gesture, a crowd in the palm of my hand. My heart drums in my chest—but first things first. It isn't easy to convert the burlesque hall into a shadow theater.

The stage is fairly shallow for our needs, but an audience always wants to be closer to a scantily clad girl than to a scrim on which shadows are dancing. At least I will be alone behind the curtain. If we were a traditional troupe, we would need a dozen players to control such large fantouches, but there is no room for half so many here. Of course, before the fire, we used to perform in even smaller spaces, Akra and I kneeling side by side below the apron of the scrim, trying not to elbow each other or jostle each other's fantouches. Our puppets were smaller, then, too. Less work for fewer hands—but so much less impressive. At least, to an audience.

When I first started casting souls as puppeteers, I worried that what I did was no longer art—a break from what Papa had taught me, and his parents had taught him. Some of our most prized fantouches were crafted by their hands. What would my ancestors say, watching me now? But Papa was the one who corrected me. "I taught you the traditions so you would know them," he said. "Not so you would be bound by them."

And lucky I am not, for this is not our traditional venue. But we find a rickety ladder in the wings and use it to stretch the thin silk scrim. It goes from the very front of the stage, just behind the footlights, all the way up the top of the proscenium. This is the screen on which the shadows will be cast by the flames.

Usually, we pile up wood to build a fire, making sure it's dry and stripped of bark to keep the smoke down, but even that won't work indoors. Cheeky comes to our rescue when she wakes, clearing old props from a short set of shelves backstage. She puts it against the back wall while Eve gathers candles; tucked inside glasses from the bar and lined up on the shelf, they will shed plenty of light.

Maman brings in the instruments—the drums, the flutes—while Papa goes through his warmups, his rich voice reverberating through the room. Tia harmonizes from the little kitchen as she makes congee, enough to share. I'm grateful again for their generosity, and not least because we're low on rice ourselves. The camaraderie eases something in me: a tightness in my chest, a tension in my heart, and soon enough, a smile tugs at the corner of my lips. When Cheeky makes a joke about throwing Garter into the porridge, I have to bite back a laughing retort about borrowing the snake to clear the rat's nest of my hair. It isn't my place, in more ways than one, and Maman's words hang over my head: never show, never tell. So I go back to the roulotte to prepare.

My once-best dress goes in a heap in the corner—a terrible waste, all that expensive fabric. Perhaps later I can clean off the dust and the blood and make repairs—or more likely, use parts of it for scrap to make a new fantouche. But for now, I rifle through my other costumes—silk and velvet, brocade and damask—choosing my second-best outfit: a soft sarong of rose silk with a red corset laced over it, and a bright brass pin holding back my hair.

Back before we were so well known, I used to wear plain and faded black. Maman and Papa still do, but as our fame grew, more than one rich member of the audience simply had to meet the puppeteer after the show. I am not pale enough to be judged classically beautiful by the Aquitans, but an expensive dress goes a long way. Fancy clothes have become part of the show—it feels like a wanton indulgence, but I can't say I don't enjoy it. Besides, I have a feeling Leo would know if I cut corners tonight.

But more important than my outfit is the show itself. What story should we tell? *The Shepherd and the Tiger* seems irreverent now; Legarde is not some wily country boy, but a hunter in his own right, like the wolf on his banner.

Should we sing the story of the seven swans instead? Or tell the tale of the arrogant man? Or maybe one of the King of Death's stories? I run my hand over the black leather of the fantouche; Maman had tossed it on the floor of the wagon, as if she didn't want to touch it any longer than she had to. And now something about him makes me shudder too. Not tonight.

Under my hands, the puppet trembles—sympathetic. Gently, I take him up, wrapping him back in burlap, winding him in silk rope. Then I place the bundle back on the shelf, beside the spirit maiden. My hands still. Why not a comedy?

It seems incongruous, but after the horrors of last night, there might be nothing left to do but laugh. Nodding to myself, I take the puppets from their shelves—the spirit maiden and the hapless fool, the river, the rocks, the flame—unwrapping them gently and laying them next to the door. They rustle, moving ever so slightly, and not with the natural settling of gravity. "Quiet," I whisper, and they fall still.

A giggle bubbles up in me—pure delight for these creatures of my own making. Or is it a touch of hysteria? I press my lips together and keep working.

As I'm gathering the fantouches, I hear voices in the alley. Two men—Leo and someone else. Peering through the curl of a dragon's eye, I see the stranger carrying a thick bamboo pole over his shoulders. Two buckets hang from it, one on each end, both clanking gently. As he puts them down, I see they're filled with tools. The mechanic.

They are deep in conversation pitched too low for me to hear, but Leo gestures to the wagon, the rattling wheel, Cheeky's battered trunk. A burst of gratitude floods through me that Leo put the box beneath the roulotte to hold up the wagon, or at least to appear to. A prop . . . and a prop. Smothering another laugh, I put a hand on the scrollwork of the roulotte and whisper to the soul inside, "Stay down."

The wagon creaks a bit as it settles; at the sound, the men fall silent. I take the opportunity to open the door, the maiden and the fool in my arms. "Hello," I say, because no one else is speaking.

The mechanic only stares, but after a wide-eyed moment, Leo holds out his hands. Is it my imagination, or do the puppets move a little? "Can I help you carry anything?"

"No," I say. Too quickly? "They're delicate. I'll come back for the others."

"Then let me get the door." He walks by my side, leaving the mechanic to start his work. The silence stretches half a beat too long. "You look lovely," he says.

"You look nervous," I reply, and he laughs.

"You might be too, if you had walked across town with seven feet of iron axle hidden in a bamboo pole," he says smoothly. "There are soldiers in the street."

At his words, I feel eyes on me; I can't stop myself from glancing around, but there are no soldiers lurking—not that I can see. Still. "Is there a place to hide the wagon while the mechanic works? A stable, or . . . ?"

Leo shakes his head as he pushes open the door. "I'll be keeping watch at the head of the alley. And it shouldn't take more than a few hours. Besides, any soldiers hanging around La Perl will know the usual rules don't apply here. Most of them are still hung over from their last run-in with my contraband."

I press my lips together, taking in his posture—leaning against the door, so casual as he flouts the law. For a moment, jealousy stabs at me—what must it be like, to make your own rules? "You were right, you know."

"About what, cher?"

"I have no reason to trust you."

"Didn't I tell you earlier? You don't have to trust someone to make a deal with them." He grins again, his teeth bright. "You only have to have something you know they want."

"No," I snap back. "You have to be out of other options."

I regret my words as they cross my teeth. The mechanic has barely started his work, and already I'm risking Leo's anger. But to my surprise—and my annoyance—he only laughs.

"C'est vrai," he says as he lets the door swing shut between us. "It's true."

ACT 1,

SCENE 9

Another opening, another show at La Perl.

LEO is still slinging drinks at the crowd gathers. But this time, the girls are in the front row of the audience, and it is not the tinny piano, out of tune, nor the smoky murmur of TIA's voice that silences the crowd.

Instead, the sound of a bird flute floats out over the audience, followed by the steady beat of a thom, like the thrum of a giant's heart. An old sound, ancient, the sort one can remember despite never hearing it before.

The melody's familiar too, at least to all the locals: the old tale of the Fool Who Could Not Die. Every shadow puppet troupe has its own version—anyone born in Chakrana would know it by heart.

But of course the trick's not in the tale, but in the telling. And as the Ros Nai tell the story, even LEO puts down his bottles and glasses and turns to the stage to watch the show.

PAPA (*offstage*): In the days when our ancestors were young . . .

The Fool Who Could Not Die

In the days when our ancestors were young, there lived a foolish monk. He walked from town to town to talk about the gods, but neither gods nor villagers paid him any mind. So he went into the jungle to preach to the birds in the trees. Not watching his step, he fell into a hole and the earth swallowed him up. But even Death ignored the fool, and after some time, he climbed out and went on his way.

Soon enough the fool came to a river, so at last he left the birds alone to sing to the fish. But the fish did not gather to listen, so he stepped into the river to follow them, and walked until he drowned. But still Death ignored him and so did the fish, and eventually the fool came to the other side of the river and walked out again.

Night was falling and his robes were wet, so the fool built a fire and preached to the flames. But he built the fire too high, and the embers leaped into the trees. Still Death ignored him, and the monk took the inferno as high praise for his preaching.

At last the spirit maiden took pity on this man who had been rejected thrice by Death, and as the flames fell and the smoke cleared, she revealed to him the souls of those who Death had not ignored. So he spoke to them as they waited for their next lives to begin, and the spirits listened.

ACT 1,
SCENE 9 (CONTINUED)

At the door of La Perl. Distantly, we can hear the sound of the shadow play—the drumming, the song. Then a bell jangles at the bar; Leo sets down his glass and goes to the door. He pulls it open to find CAPITAINE XAVIER LEGARDE, his pressed uniform and perfect posture at odds with the dirty alley.

XAVIER: Sava, Leo?

XAVIER's tone is polite. Leo's is not.

LEO: What are you doing here?

XAVIER: I wanted to see a shadow play, and this is the only place to find one. You must have heard what happened last night at La Fête.

LEO: You must have heard what happened last year at La Perl.

XAVIER: What does that have to do with me?

LEO: It has to do with the general. Your father.

LEO spits the word; XAVIER pauses a moment to consider.

XAVIER: Of course. And it was a tragedy. You have my sympathies.

LEO: Sympathy and a ticket will get you admission to the show. Too bad we're sold out.

XAVIER: Good thing I already have my ticket.

XAVIER puts his hand on the pistol on his hip. LEO tenses.

LEO: What do you really want, Xavier?

XAVIER: I just want to talk to the shadow troupe.

LEO (*pointedly*): Talk?

XAVIER sighs, lifting his hand from his weapon and letting it fall back to his side.

XAVIER: I spoke to the girl earlier today. I only have a few additional questions for her.

LEO: Questions? What about?

XAVIER: Maybe I'll answer yours after she answers mine.

Still LEO hesitates; the two men stand, face-to-face, neither backing down. But when applause erupts from the audience, XAVIER raises an eyebrow.

Is now a good time?

Without waiting for an answer, he pushes through the door; LEO walks backward rapidly, keeping himself between XAVIER and the theater.

LEO: This is only intermission. You'll have to wait till after the second half of the show.
XAVIER: Another shadow play?
LEO: The girls are taking the stage. Don't make that face— you should see why your best men come here on payday. No charge for you, of course. Sit anywhere you like.

When they reach the bar, LEO puts his hand on XAVIER's chest, stopping him.

But you have to leave your gun at the bar.
XAVIER: My gun?
LEO: House rule. If you know what happened last year, you know why.

XAVIER hesitates, but after a moment, he takes the bullets out of his gun and pockets them. Then he hands the gun to LEO, who tosses it behind the bar. The applause is still going strong; cries of "Encore!" mix with whistles and stomping feet.

Quickly, LEO grabs a violin case and pushes through the crowd. As he passes the table where the girls are sitting, he murmurs something to CHEEKY. She stiffens, nodding, then whispers to TIA and EVE before heading for the dressing room. The other girls follow as LEO steps toward the stage.

CHAPTER SEVEN

The applause washes over me like the rush of the season's first rain—a few drops at first, building quickly to a storm. A comedy was the right choice after the drama of the explosions last night. The crowd is effusive, excited, loud. For a moment, I imagine they can hear the cheering in Aquitan. They will . . . they will.

Papa has blown out the candles, but I can still feel the heat of the flame, warm on my back, in my hair, under my skin. Everything is more intense, more real. Joy purrs in the pit of my stomach, and my blood fizzes like ginger beer. The air rings like a struck bell; I drink it in like honey. The dark itself is like velvet on the bare flesh of my arm.

Eventually the applause begins to fade—a natural ebb, like a waning moon; I steel myself against the emptiness it will leave when it is gone. But then, into the hollow, Leo's voice comes from just beyond the scrim. "Mesdames, messieurs, et mes autres!" It's a stage voice—it cuts easily through the ovation. "Thank you, thank you! Un plaisir, to have the Ros Nai here tonight! But settle down in your seats, the show is only beginning."

I frown, glancing at Maman, but she looks as puzzled as I am. No one mentioned more performances. Into our confused silence, a note falls—exquisite! The sound of a violin.

Then I see him: Leo, or rather his silhouette. The footlights are fading up on the other side of the screen; he's standing on the stage, leaning into his instrument, bending like a palm in the storm of his song.

It's beautiful, and familiar: a Chakran folk reel that reminds me of Lak Na. I've never heard it performed on a foreign instrument before.

The notes fall like water, they soar like swallows, they shimmer more vibrant than the stars. Leo is playing the audience back into silence. Chairs scrape, feet shuffle, people murmur—how dare they? But the music rises over it all, and his shadow dances with it. I take a step toward the scrim, and another, reaching out with tentative fingers to the outline of his form—the dark space he's cut from the light. Are any of my shadows half so graceful?

"Jetta?" I whirl, snatching my hand back at Cheeky's soft voice. But where is she? The call comes again from a crack—a trapdoor in the center of the stage: she's peeking through, her eyes rising just above the floor. "Jetta!"

I approach on quiet feet, hunkering down to whisper. "What is it?"

"Capitaine Legarde is looking for you," she says. My brow furrows, then my heart stutters. The soldier in the road—the one who gave us back the coin. He must be the general's son. What could he want now? "You have to go."

My eyebrows go up. "Now?"

"Easier now than later!" she hisses. "Leo will meet you at the roulotte when Tia takes the stage. We'll keep the capitaine distracted as long as we can. But you have to hurry."

I chew my lip. Is it wise to run from the armée? What if he only wants something innocuous—something small, an innocent question?

How did you do it?

Hidden strings . . .

But when I straighten up, Maman and Papa are standing close—by their faces, I can tell they've heard what Cheeky said, and they know there is nothing innocent about the capitaine's request. Without a word, Maman nods to the trapdoor. My fantouches are scattered across the stage, near the scrim. I move to gather them, but she puts her hand on my arm and shakes her head.

Inside me, something shrivels. Leave my fantouches?

Each one represents hours, days, weeks of work—not only mine. Our version of the spirit maiden was the last fantouche Akra made.

And what of the souls sewn into these skins? Will they behave without me near, or will they grow bored and start to wander without my permission? Would they be trapped forever in their bodies as they slowly waste away, longing for reprieve, unable to be reborn?

There's little time for the dead when the living are in danger. So when the next round of applause comes, I slip down through the stage and walk empty-handed into the dark. With a bitter twist of my lips, I see Papa holding his bird flute, and Maman with the little painted thom she loves so well—but they are small things, easy to carry, and close to hand. The delicate lute that belonged to my grandmother is still in the dark backstage—not to mention our silk scrim, hiding us from the audience. Still, these are not the first things we've had to leave behind. They will not be the last.

The creak of the stairs underfoot is covered by the cheers of the audience. Cheeky lowers the trapdoor behind us; the thick wood muffles the first few notes of the piano. Tia's voice comes in from above: "J'errais avec les fous, je me retrouve chez les âmes perdues. Nul ne sait où il est parti, mais je me suis languis de toi, de toi . . ."

The song fades as we pick our way through the warren of the basement. The ceiling is so low we have to duck, and the air here is cool and damp and smells of mildew and river water. Old munitions crates hold dusty props; touring trunks are stacked with empty barrels marked RHUM, all of them gently moldering. Little souls glimmer in the dim. We pass a peeling vanity, finely carved in Aquitan style—expensive once. I sound out the red writing on the cracked mirror: AU REVOIR.

Cheeky leads us to another stair, this one leading up to a pair of slanted cellar doors at street level. "I have to go back and get dressed," she says. Then she grins brightly in the dark. "Then undressed again. Break a leg. Preferably someone else's."

"Do me a favor," I say quickly, and she rolls her eyes.

"Another one? Usually I charge."

"Burn the fantouches."

Her eyes go wide in the dark. "Why?"

I bite my lip—there's no time to explain, but even if there was, I couldn't say. Never show, never tell. "Just do it. Please."

She looks at me, uncertain, but then she nods, and I trust her to do what I've asked. Fear hits me as she disappears into the dark—when the capitaine discovers we've fled, will he take it out on the girls? But she must know how to take care of herself. Or am I only telling myself that? Either way, I can't make myself call her back.

Instead we slip up the stairs. Reaching the top, I press my shoulder against the heavy door and heave. Grit trickles down the back of my neck as the panel lifts. Then someone outside takes the weight of the door, lifting it all the way open.

It's Leo. His jacket is unbuttoned and a violin case is slung over his back; he beckons us up into the moonlight. We have exited the theater just a few steps from the alley door. Everything is so quiet—odd, for a city the size of Luda. A deep, layered silence, the kind that comes from fear. Even the spirits seem furtive, gleaming from deep corners and shining between cracks in buildings. The feeling of being watched is back; I turn my head quickly. Was that a flicker of blue, beneath the roulotte? No matter—not now. Soon enough we will be far away from here.

On quiet feet, we steal to the wagon. To my surprise, Leo ushers us toward the door. "Get in the back."

Maman shakes her head. "I'll drive."

"He's looking for you, not me," Leo murmurs. "Besides, you don't know the route."

Maman eyes him skeptically. "Out of the city?"

"Out of the city without driving past the entire encampment."

But Papa is wasting no time; he swings open the door and starts in. Maman follows, and I have my foot on the stair when I hear a little metal click. A chill, cold as cruelty, drips down my spine. I lift my chin. There is a man lying atop the roulotte. A soldier. Moonlight shines on the steel barrel of his gun.

"Sava, Leo?" the man says, and beside me, Leo sighs through his teeth.

"Sava, Eduard. I see you've still got my pistol."

"You really ought to stop misplacing guns. But right now all I need is the girl. Your brother has a few questions for her. You likely know that already."

At first I don't understand, but the look on Leo's face says it all. "The capitaine is your brother?"

"Quiet, girl." The soldier gestures with the gun, and I swallow the lump in my throat. "And close the door of the wagon."

In the deep shadows in the roulotte, the whites of Maman's wide eyes gleam. "What's going on, Jetta?"

The soldier raps on the roof with his fist. "Ferme ta gueule and close the door! Is there a way to lock it?"

My hands are shaking, but better that my parents are safe inside—that they cannot chase after me, that they cannot be shot for fighting back. Maman scrambles toward the doorway as I swing it closed; I lower the latch as she pounds on the door, cursing the armée. The soldier pays her no mind. He only jerks his chin at the theater. "Now step back against the wall."

My heart is a wild bird in the cage of my ribs; I am watching the gun, waiting for the bullet. What will happen when the capitaine comes out? Can Leo intercede? Or will they drag Maman and Papa from the wagon? Will they line us up, three in a row, kneeling in the dirty alley? Was the death of the rebel boy only a premonition of my own?

Just behind me, out of my field of vision, it burns—the blue flame. What color will my soul be when it springs from my body?

"Did you hear me? Step back!"

At the soldier's shout, I jump, but I do not obey. Instead, I whisper to the soul I put in the wagon—the old dog, eager to please. "Throw him down," I murmur. "Throw him down."

The spirit obeys. The roulotte tilts, two wheels lifting with a groan, then slamming back to the earth. The soldier tumbles to the ground with a shout. The gun skitters across the stones and Leo leaps after it. But as his hands close around the pistol, the soldier is on him. They struggle, but Eduard is bigger; he smashes Leo's knuckles bloody against the cobbles and the gun tumbles free again. I race toward it, but the soldier wraps his hand around my ankle and pulls me off my feet; I fall, hard, on my stomach, and the jolt knocks the wind out of me. Leo is scrambling after the gun on his hands and knees, but Eduard hauls me up, pressing my back to his chest, one thick arm cinched around my waist, another across my shoulders. And up under my chin, a painful point—the tip of a knife. I cannot see it, but oh, I can feel it as I breathe, as I swallow, as my pulse pounds against the coldness of the steel.

My free hand flies to my throat. Eduard tightens his grip and I hiss. Blood is already slipping down, slick on my fingers. Spirits are gathering in the still air, and the blue fire is just over my shoulder, as though to whisper in my ear.

Leo is on his feet again, holding the gun, but he lowers it when he sees me in Eduard's arms. Against my shoulders, the soldier's heart is pounding. "Put it on the ground," he growls.

"The capitaine can't question a dead girl," Leo says, but the point of the knife digs deeper; I stop breathing.

"There's a long road between life and death," Eduard says. "And I can get answers out of almost anyone along the way. Put the gun on the ground."

Visions of the bodies displayed on the roadside float behind my eyes like shadows on a screen. Am I in the hands of the torturer? Is the knife he used to flay their skin pressed against my throat? Is the soul of the rebel here now, waiting for revenge on the man who put his head on a pike?

Would his vengeance doom the soldier—and save us?

Carefully, slowly, Leo obeys; ever so slightly, the soldier relaxes his grip. And gently, softly, I lower my arm to my side, to where the questioneur's fingers dig into my ribs. With my bloody hand, I trace the sign of life on the back of his hand.

There is a flash of blue. Eduard screams as he stumbles back, convulsing. The sound splits the night—it pierces my skull—it rings in my ears. It goes on and on, an alarm, an accusation. His eyes roll, his body writhes, his head lolls like a mad thing. Then it ends, and the soldier drops in a heap.

Is he still breathing? I am cold all over. What have I done? The sudden silence is a void, filling now with other sounds—Maman's muffled cries, a dog barking . . . and the wet hiss of air through the soldier's clenched teeth.

Leo turns to me, his eyes wide in the dark; he's still holding the gun, and it's not exactly pointed at the ground. "What happened to him?"

I open my mouth but no explanation comes. "Why are you asking me?"

"Because you don't look all that surprised."

I grit my teeth—too late to don a mask of shock. "We should go," I say instead, and he only nods. I follow Leo onto the bench of the roulotte. Lani is snorting, stamping, afraid and impatient; she practically bolts down the alley when Leo snaps the reins. The wagon lurches forward. As we turn onto the main street, the theater door opens and the capitaine's voice calls, "Arret!" Like the general. We don't stop.

ACT 1,
SCENE 11

For the second night in a row, a show at La Perl ends before curtain call, and somehow, tonight's screams are even more disturbing than last night's explosions. When CAPITAINE XAVIER LEGARDE leaps from his seat and runs from the theater, CHEEKY doesn't even bother with a bow before she hops offstage and hurries down the hall. TIA leaves the piano to follow her, and EVE joins them both, watching through the crack in the door.

Outside, EDUARD still twitches on the ground. EVE looks at TIA, but CHEEKY shakes her head, mouthing an exaggerated "no" to the question she did not ask.

EVE: What happened to him?
CHEEKY: You couldn't pay me enough to check.

XAVIER is coming back down the street, cursing the roulotte for disappearing around the corner. Reaching the prone questioneur, the capitaine kneels beside him, checking his

airway, his pulse, slapping his slack cheek. At last EDUARD's
eyelids flutter open. XAVIER draws back in alarm.

XAVIER: Putain.

The stricken soldier's eyes slide closed again, but it takes
XAVIER a moment to reach out, to peel back the eyelid on
the vacant face.

A trick of the dark, of the crescent moon, or perhaps a
symptom of a strange jungle poison . . . but the iris is a cold,
ethereal blue.

XAVIER stands, wiping his hands on his uniform. Then he
grits his teeth and strides toward the corner, where the rattled
audience is spilling into the street. The capitaine conscripts
two strong men from the crowd.

XAVIER: You. And you. Help me take this man to the
docteur's tent at the encampment.

Though they are not soldiers, the two Chakrans know better
than to disobey a direct order from the armée. XAVIER leads

them back to the camp as they drag EDUARD between them, directing them to the docteur's tent before dismissing them with a curt thanks.

He has just sat down to prepare a telegram when the screaming starts. XAVIER looks up from his field desk. Then comes the sound of gunfire and panic, the trumpeting of horses—and someone raising the alarm.

Sent at 2236h
Capitaine Legarde at Luda
To: General Legarde at Lysan

   ATTACK ON GARRISON STOP POSSIBLE REBEL
   PLOT STOP SITUATION UNFOLDING

Sent at 0913h
General Legarde at Lysan
To: Capitaine Legarde at Luda

   HOLD THE LINE

ACT 2

La Lumière

music and lyrics by
Mei Rath

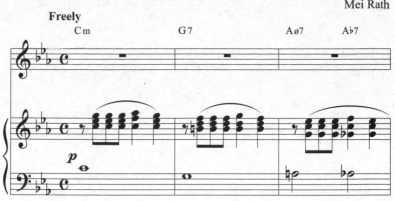

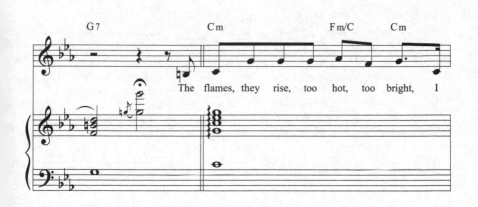

The flames, they rise, too hot, too bright, I

know they can-not last the night, But oh, they give a love-ly light,

Slow Blues Tempo

path is dark, with no re - turn, But I would ra - ther go than yearn, What

pur - pose have I but to burn, LA LU - MI - ÈR - E? Some

seem to walk in sun-shine, in the lo-ving warmth of day. For

those be-neath the new moon, per - haps I'll light the

way. So let us love and let us hate, The

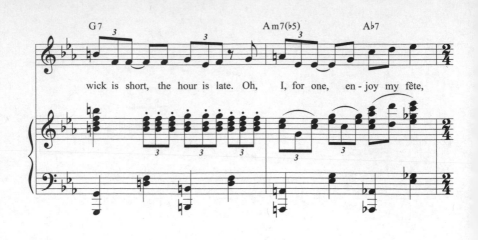

wick is short, the hour is late. Oh, I, for one, en - joy my fête,

LA LU - MI - ÈR - E.

poco rit.

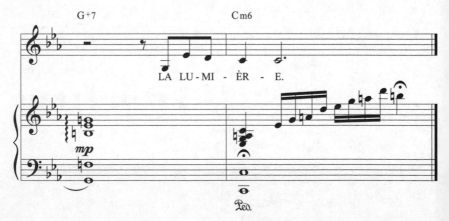

LA LU - MI - ÈR - E.

mp

Ped.

142 ✻

CHAPTER EIGHT

As Lani stretches her legs into a gallop, my own heart pounds. The soldier's scream still echoes in my skull. My back is pressed to the scrollwork; my whole body is so tense I'm shaking. I keep expecting more shouting or shooting, for the capitaine to chase us down on a great gray horse, for Legarde himself to return and drag us back to the killing spot.

How could I have missed that Leo was the general's son? They have the same jaw, the same nose—the same voice, the kind that can cut across a crowd. But where Legarde commands, Leo charms. Why hadn't he mentioned it before? I shouldn't have trusted him.

Then again, he hadn't handed us over to his brother. We are still rolling on through the city, away from the wharf and the warehouses and the armée, and no one is chasing us—not yet, anyway.

Maman will be harder to escape. I swallow my heart and turn around on the bench, bracing myself for her reprimands. Leo's question echoes in my skull: "What happened to him?"

I had acted on instinct—a hope and a prayer . . . and something else. Some dark draw—vengeance or just curiosity? Never before had I put a spirit into a body that already had a soul. Some people say that's what madness is. Two souls in one skin. And a n'akela isn't just any spirit.

Would it drive him mad? Or kill him—or something worse? Now I can begin to imagine fates worth than death. Nevertheless, that fate wasn't ours tonight. I had saved us yet again. So I square my shoulders and open the panel, ready to reject Maman's condemnation. But when my eyes adjust to the dimness inside the roulotte, instead of the anger I expect, Maman is curled against Papa's side like a frightened animal. My tension slips into uncertainty. "Are you both all right?"

"I saw," she says. Nothing more—but her eyes gleam in

the slices of moonlight that slip through the scrollwork. I balk at the expression on her face. Fear. Is she afraid for me, or of me? For a moment, I wonder if she hates me.

But Papa shushes her, stroking damp hair from her forehead. "He was armée," he says darkly. "He had a gun."

I draw myself up. "If it was me or the soldier, Maman—who would you try to save?"

At my question, she lifts her head as though surprised. "You, Jetta. I'm always trying to save you."

Her words leave me breathless. "From what?"

Maman only glances at Leo, sitting beside me on the bench, and I know she will not answer. I look to Papa for help, but he only sighs, nodding to his other side—an invitation. "Come, Jetta. Come rest awhile."

Rest. At the word, my shoulders sink, losing some of the tension I hadn't known I was carrying. I long for the comfort of my parents' warm embrace. More than that—for the closeness of feeling like family. When was the last time I felt it? Years ago, before the fire and the souls. . . . It was during the Hungry Year—the day Akra left, and Papa, who had been so angry he hadn't looked at my brother for a week, finally pulled him close and sobbed into his uniform. We had all wrapped our arms around one another—I can still remember feeling Papa's ribs through his shirt. We were all so hungry, but we'd had one another.

Looking at Maman now, I think she needs comfort more than she can give it. I shake my head. "We can't stop yet."

"When?" Papa's tone is pointed. "You need to sleep."

I hesitate—I am tired. But my mind is still racing, and something about the thought of sleep makes my skin crawl. "Soon," I lie, sliding the panel shut.

Turning, I face forward on the seat. Leo glances my way, but only briefly—maintaining the decorous silence of any gentleman who has overheard an argument. Together, we watch the town blur by, but only I see the vana swirl in the breeze of our passing. We're moving fast. The roulotte is light with the arvana inside, and Lani has been resting all day. We've left the slapdash shacks of the dockworkers and the sugar millers far behind. Just beyond the telegraph office is the center of town. Here are old Chakran houses with upturned roofs, new Aquitan buildings of terra-cotta tile and white stone—fine homes for fine people. A perfect place to scatter flyers, if there was to be yet another show tonight. A laugh tries to scramble up my throat; I press my lips together to suffocate it.

But this road leads north, winding into the old mountains—in the opposite direction of the capital. If we go far enough this way, we'll pass into the Tiger's territory—beyond that, to the source of all the rivers, where old dragons live in icy pools in the caldera of dead volcanoes. "Where are we going?" I murmur to Leo.

"A secret route out of the city," Leo says. "The capitaine will certainly have the roads watched."

I hesitate, almost afraid to ask. "Did he tell you what he wanted?"

"I was hoping you would know." Leo glances at me, then winces. Holding the reins in one hand, he tugs a handkerchief out of his breast pocket. "There's blood on your throat."

"Thank you." Gingerly, I press the cloth against the cut, eyeing his battered knuckles, the swelling skin on his cheekbone just below his eye, the faint bruise mottling the bridge of his nose. "Are you all right?"

He waves my concern away as if he doesn't deserve it. "I should have checked the roof of the wagon. I should have known he'd have a sentry."

I wet my lips. "Your brother?"

Leo stiffens. "I have no brother."

I shift on my seat—but that is anger in his voice, not confusion. I didn't misunderstand what the soldier had said. We roll along in more decorous silence. Vana buzz around my head, my neck. The cool night air kisses my cheek, and Leo's shoulder is warm against mine. "I have a brother," I say softly. "Or . . . I had one, once."

All around us, the jungle is closing in, the fine homes turning back to modest cottages interspersed with stands of bananas along the hill. Luda has no walls, so the city is simply fading away. The road is rougher here too, rutted from long rains and little repair. I can smell the greenery, the scent of the flowers, the sweet hint of water in the air. Birds call to one another in the blackness, and insects bow their limbs over their legs, making music. Leo keeps his gaze on the road ahead, though his jaw is clenched. When he finally speaks, his voice is almost too quiet. "What happened?"

I take a breath. My memory feels strangely disjointed tonight. It's all a jumble: the click of my brother's lighter as he toys with the lid, his earnest smile, his hollow cheeks. The shame on Papa's face when Akra first donned his newest costume. The way the uniform hung loose on his body. The way everything changed that day. "He joined the armée, three years back. During the famine, do you remember?"

"No room for rice," he says, and I nod, remembering the whispers that swelled to shouts as the months dragged on. Rice is life—if there is no room for rice, there was no room for Chakrans. And while plantation owners moaned about their lack of income and how they couldn't afford their dresses or their entertainment, the rest of us starved, unable to afford the rising price of food. That was the year the rebels coalesced around the Tiger—the year they first burned a plantation, the year they began to make war instead of trouble. "It wasn't so bad at Luda," Leo adds. "But we had a lot of country people move to town. That's when Eve came to La Perl."

I bite my lip, trying to imagine it. What would I have had to do to eat, if my brother hadn't left? "That was before we . . . before the troupe was so well known. We didn't have much, so he gave us his sign-up money, and sent us his pay at first—long enough for us to get by, till the rains came back. Especially since he ate so much," I say, trying on a smile. It falls away quickly. "I kept all seven of his letters."

"And the last one came . . . ?"

"Over a year ago."

Leo bows his head under the weight of my words. "Did you ever hear anything from the armée?"

"No," I say. "But sometimes silence says it all."

"That's true." Leo sighs. "I suppose I could be grateful I was only disowned."

My hands twist the handkerchief in my lap. "That's terrible."

"To be fair, the general's original ownership was . . . tenuous." Leo's tone is deceptively light. "He would visit once or twice a year at best. When the rebellion started heating up, he was worried someone would use us against him."

"You and the girls?"

"Me and my mother," Leo says, and his laugh belies the pain on his face. "He told us we were on our own. Though he left us his gun. Self-protection, he said. Of course, that's not how she used it." Leo shrugs, his voice wistful. "She was a chanteuse, among other things. Very popular, before she died. Those were the glory days of La Perl. She always burned so brightly. It's no wonder she burned out."

My breath hitches; his words strike a chord in me. La Perl. His inheritance. And the red writing on the cracked mirror of the vanity in the basement: AU REVOIR.

The silence is delicate—the quiet of moonlight, of

escape, of heartbreak and whispers. "I'm so sorry," I say at last.

A smile twists the corner of his mouth. "Xavier never said anything, though I'm sure he prayed over it. But I had a letter from my . . . from Theodora. Just afterward."

Theodora—La Fleur. His sister, I realize. "What did it say?"

"It doesn't matter," he says, but he's a violinist, not an actor. "I never wrote back because I couldn't find the words to . . . contain what had happened. To put it all down on a slip of paper. But I wonder what my silence meant to her."

I stare unseeing at the winding road, trying to imagine posters of Akra, news of his wedding. Knowing he was alive and well—famous, even—but no longer mine. Hearing people refer to him by a ruler's honorific, while never being able to call him brother. "You could still write back, when you think of something."

"Maybe someday," he says, in the way that means never. "And I still have the girls. They're like sisters to me. Well, not Cheeky," he adds. "She's a human cannonball of filth and glitter, but I love her just the same."

My ear tweaks at the word, spoken so openly. Is this a city mannerism, or is there something more between them?

"Are you two together?" I ask carefully. But he only laughs.

"I'm not her type. You can tell by the level of sass. If she's ever tongue-tied, you'll know she's found the one."

"Ah," I say with a theatrical sigh and a tiny pang. But we were never staying in Luda. "So I never had a chance."

Leo laughs. "Very few do. But that doesn't stop most from trying. The girls adored the show, by the way. I saw them cheering. Too bad we didn't have time for an encore."

Usually I enjoy praise, but his makes me shy. "You too." I nod at his violin case, nestled at his feet. "You play beautifully."

"We could turn this into a tour," he muses with faux seriousness. "Stop in a few towns on the way to the capital."

"Dodging the armée wherever we go?"

"No, no, we have to charge them extra. We could make a mint that way."

"Divided equally between performers?" I say with mock hope; he gives me a stern look.

"Between acts."

"But I'm top billing," I say. "After all, they're looking for me."

"Fine," he says, trying to hide a smile. He holds out his hand. "We make a good company."

We shake, Aquitan style—and this time, he does not kiss my hand. But his fingers are warm and calloused where he holds his bow . . . does he hold my hand a little longer than he must? In my stomach, a spark of light, like the soul of a butterfly. I tighten my fingers as though to crush it. With my malheur, is his company a wise place to be?

"How did you do it?" he says then.

I blink at him. "Do what?"

"The puppetry, of course! Cheeky was convinced it's done with wires from the flies, but I don't think you could have rigged pulleys. Is it hot air? Like balloons?"

I pull my hand away. "Trade secrets." The words fall from my lips—a line learned by rote—but my heart isn't in them. What would he say if he knew?

"She and I made a bet, you know," he says with a wink. He leans close and lowers his voice, as if Cheeky might somehow hear. "I'll split the winnings with you if you swear I'm right."

"Or I could tell her you tried to rig the game," I counter. "My silence might be worth the whole pot."

"Vicious!" he says, pretending to be shocked, but his eyes are intent. "And what you did to Eduard? Is that another trade secret?"

My mouth goes dry. I pull back. "I—I don't know what you mean."

"All right." For a moment, I wonder if he will ask again, but he is quiet, and the night flies by. Above the tree line, the glow of the rising moon smears the stars. Leo passes me the reins. "Hold these, will you?"

I take them, and he turns around to stand on the bench, looking back over the top of the wagon. "What's wrong?"

"Just making sure we're still alone," he says. He slides back to his seat and I look at him sideways.

"Why?"

"Because." He takes the reins back and turns Lani off the main road. The wagon bounces out of the ruts and onto a little path. "This is a trade secret too, remember?"

The jungle closes in overhead on the track; through the greenery, I can see lights glimmering. Souls? No—a little hut roofed in palm leaves, tucked into a clearing. Moonlight shines on a kitchen garden and a nearby shack, almost as large as the cottage. A goat house, perhaps, or a shelter for pigs. "Not a very well-kept one," I say, but Leo only smiles as he pulls Lani to a stop.

Immediately, the water buffalo lowers her head, pulling up a wad of fresh grass as the cottage door creaks open. An ancient woman steps out—at least a grandmother, perhaps twice over. She's holding a lamp in one gnarled hand, and a gun in the other.

"Daiyu!" Leo waves from the seat of the wagon; she squints at him in the dark. "It's Leo," he says; only then does she nod.

Tucking the gun into the rolled waist of her sarong, she totters over to the shed. Leo twitches the reins, urging Lani to follow. The water buffalo obliges, always ready to rest. I am too. I stand, preparing to hop down from the wagon, to unharness Lani, but Leo shakes his head a little. "Not yet."

Frowning, I sit back as Daiyu hands Leo the lantern to fumble with the door. "You're always hanging around with the prettiest girls," she murmurs, shaking her head.

I try to hide my smile, but Leo winks as he hangs the lamp on the wagon's eaves. "None to rival you, Daiyu."

"I was talking about me, Leo." She cackles as she swings the doors open. But instead of a pen and the smell of goats, a cold gust swirls out of the blackness inside, where a wide tunnel leads down into the dark. Spirits glimmer among the roots that writhe through the earthen walls.

"What is this?" I whisper, awed.

"I told you. A secret route." Leo winks and flicks the reins;

tentatively, Lani steps into the tunnel. "The Souterrain."

I sit back on the bench. "You're a smuggler too?"

"Music doesn't pay all the bills," he says with a winsome smile. "But what about you, Jetta? What are you?"

"Just a shadow player," I say, but my voice breaks on the words. The fading light turns his smile wicked as we ride into the dark.

ACT 2,
SCENE 13

Back at the encampment, all is blood and chaos. In the dark, in the confusion, in the rapid fire of the guns, XAVIER LEGARDE takes cover behind a tent as men fall around him in the night. As he loads his weapon, another soldier scrambles through the smoke to huddle beside him. Young. Chakran. Green. Another farm boy. His eyes are wide in the dark, and he is breathing fast and loud—a panicky sound. XAVIER glances at his nameplate.

XAVIER: Vang.

Beside him, the boy startles at the sound, looking up as though dazed.

VANG: Sir?

XAVIER ducks his head, putting his face before the young soldier's, trying to catch his eye—to make him focus.

XAVIER: What did you see out there?

VANG blinks, as though he hadn't expected the question.

VANG: Rebels, capitaine.

XAVIER: How many?

VANG: I don't know. Dozens, maybe hundreds!

XAVIER frowns.

XAVIER: Did you actually see them?

VANG: No, sir. But who else would it be? Probably came back with the guns they stole. Trying to kill us all!

XAVIER listens. Sure enough, the sound of repeating rifles tatters the night air. But he shakes his head.

XAVIER: They've never had the numbers to risk a direct attack on a battalion. And how could they get all the way to the center of camp without a patrol noticing? Cover my back.

VANG only stares as XAVIER creeps out from behind the tent. Come on, soldier!

Startled, the boy follows. Rifles crack, soldiers cry out. Horses have broken their tethers; they careen through the dark, trampling limbs and tents alike. Turning his face so VANG can't see, XAVIER mouths a prayer to his god as they slip behind another row of tents for cover.

But as the men catch their breath behind the tents, a bullet rips through the canvas. Without a word, VANG topples over face down in the dusty field. XAVIER's heart thunders into a gallop, and his own breath starts to come fast. The tents are no protection. His hand goes to the pendant hanging around his neck, but now his prayer changes—whispered to a different god.

XAVIER: Are you a coward now, too?

Gripping his gun and gritting his teeth, XAVIER springs from cover and runs toward the fray. Dodging around wounded men and blazing tents, he rounds a corner and sees an armed figure taking aim. The capitaine lifts his gun, but he doesn't shoot. The man is silhouetted against the flames, and it takes a moment to recognize him.

XAVIER: Eduard!

The questioneur is bleeding from a dozen gunshots, but he stands firmly on his own two feet. The capitaine hesitates, just a moment. EDUARD does not. There is a flash—a bang. A bullet hits XAVIER's thigh.

XAVIER staggers left, barely escaping a second shot. But despite his wound, his own aim is true—a single bullet, right between EDUARD's ice-blue eyes. The soldier stumbles back in silence, falling against the fiery canvas of a burning tent. As XAVIER slumps to the muddy earth, he looks up at the night sky.

His fingers creep toward the golden pendant he wears around his neck, but his hand stops halfway across his chest. His next whisper is not a prayer, but a curse.

XAVIER: Nécromancien.

CHAPTER NINE

Moonlight follows us into the tunnel, but stops a few feet past the entry. Then Daiyu shuts the doors behind us, and all the light in the world seems to shrink toward the lamp swinging from our eaves. My eyes adjust slowly. There aren't many spirits here, so we move through the long dark like a falling star drifting through an endless void.

The silence between Leo and me is deeper still. I knew he had contacts on the black market—but so do we, back in our little valley. Everyone always needed something, a little iron to fix a plow, a bit of dye for wedding silks. And so many plantation mansions are lit at all hours by kerosene lamps . . . and the owners' extravagant parties fueled with rationed liquor. Buying contraband was one thing—smuggling it was quite another.

Rumor is, the smugglers fund the rebellion, routing sapphires stolen from the mines in Le Coffret to buyers in Nokhor Khat. The offense was technically punishable by imprisonment, but the more likely penalty was an armée bullet. I wet my lips and look once more to the violin case at Leo's feet, half intrigued, half afraid. Is there anything in there aside from the violin—anything else that could get us in trouble? "You never told me why you need to go to Nokhor Khat."

"Didn't I?" He follows my gaze down to the violin. "Maybe I'm going to seek my fame and fortune."

"You're smuggling something in the case."

He laughs then—sudden, surprising in the dark. "Are you going to turn me in?"

I blink. "You're not even going to deny it?"

"Why should I? You've made up your mind."

"But . . ." I falter. "Am I right?"

"No."

"Are you lying?"

"Yes."

"You're impossible!" I say, throwing my hands in the air.

"For someone who won't answer many questions, you expect a lot of answers."

"Shall we trade?" I say then. "One of mine for one of yours."

"A fair deal," he says, appearing to mull it over. "Though I suppose you want to go first."

"What's in your violin case?" I ask, triumphant.

He grins. "A violin."

"That's cheating."

"It's true," he says, nudging the case closer with his foot. "Go on. Open it."

Suddenly less sure, I take the case, placing it across my knees. It is carved of mahogany, and the hardware is faded brass. I flip the clasp and lift the lid. The violin gleams back at me in the low light, nestled in a bed of red velvet. "There must be a secret compartment."

"There's a slot for the bow in the lid. Some rosin, wrapped in the handkerchief there. And sheet music underneath. Careful with it, please—it's precious to me."

Reaching beneath the instrument, I find the folded sheaf of paper. I flip through it gingerly, looking for a secret letter tucked into the packet, or a set of plans—something worth smuggling, but it's only music, written in a delicate, graceful hand. I don't recognize the song titles—they're all in Aquitan—but beneath them, a woman's name. "Mei Rath," I say, sounding it out.

"My mother."

"She wrote these?"

"It's my turn for a question."

"Right." Gently I tuck the music back into the case, feeling a bit ashamed of myself for not believing him. And worse, I am certain he will ask about the puppets again, and now I will have to answer with a lie. I run the line in my head—the one Maman always gives: strings, the thinness of a spider's web. But Leo surprises me.

"Why do you really want to go to Aquitan?"

I take a breath, taken aback; to cover, I close the violin case, tucking it carefully at his feet. No one has ever asked that before—fame and fortune are too believable a tale. My mind races, trying to formulate a new story, but nothing comes. The silence pulls at me—an empty stage, a waiting audience. How many secrets am I keeping? What was the last true thing I said? There is so much danger in being myself, and danger always draws me. Who better to tell than a boy I'll never see again? "I'm told there's a spring in

Aquitan," I say at last, speaking slowly—testing these new lines. "Just outside of Lephare. Le Roi Fou makes a monthly trip there to take the water."

"Les Chanceux?" Leo nods, his expression a mystery. "I've heard of it."

"You have?" The revelation is a surprise; I only learned about Les Chanceux last year, from a painting at Madame Audrinne's plantation. Then again, General Legarde was Le Roi Fou's bastard brother . . . perhaps it's not so strange that Leo would know the family stories. "I'm told it's magic," I say, eager for confirmation. "That anyone who bathes there is cured."

"Not just anyone," he says. "Le Roi Fou is insane. Les Chanceux is supposed to cure *madness*."

The word is sibilant—a hiss in the dark. I swallow. "That's what they say."

There is a long silence. He cocks his head and glances at me. "Are you sick, Jetta?"

I open my mouth to give an answer—a single word. It should be simple, easy, but it sticks in my throat. "It's my turn for a question."

"So it is."

We ride for a while in silence as the packed earth walls

turn to rounded stone. Chakrana is riven with old lava tubes, formed by hot rock flowing beneath the crusted, cooled surface centuries and centuries ago. Years ago, back in our valley, the rainy season exposed a shallow section of an old lava tunnel; we would dare each other to stand ever closer to the crumbling edge, to spit into the water rushing by, as though into the face of the King of Death himself. "Are you a rebel, Leo?"

"No." He says it simply, and for once I believe him. "But I don't side with the armée, either. Which is good for you, all things considered. As for my question: how are we on food?"

I laugh a little, startled. "Food?"

He gives me a knowing smile. "Well, with everything I'm smuggling in the violin case, I just didn't have enough room for rice."

It is a reprieve. I relax against the seat as I consider our inventory. "We have maybe a quarter bag left. Some yams. A little dried mango."

"Not a lot, then."

"How much do you eat?"

"It's hungry work, fleeing for your life. No matter, we can get some supplies."

I cock my head. "Are there markets in the Souterrain?"

"Two questions in a row?"

"I thought we were done playing."

"No matter, I'm feeling generous. There are no markets, but there is forage just up ahead."

I wrinkle my nose. Forage? In the earth? My mind calls up white grubs, red worms, black beetles; staples of the Hungry Year. But my speculation fades into curiosity as I notice a light far down the tunnel, distant but growing brighter. I almost ask about it—almost. But wouldn't Leo say something if he could see it too? Besides, I've already had two questions. Three might push my luck. And as I watch the patterns eddy and swirl, I'm glad I kept my mouth shut.

The tunnel opens up into a wide stone cavern lit with souls. Most of them are vana, but there are arvana too. They crouch in the corners . . . they scamper across the floor . . . they perch like bats along the vaulted ceiling. The spirit of something hungry lands on my shoulder, sidling close to the blood drying on my throat. I shrug it off as surreptitiously as I can, but another soul starts climbing the hem of my sarong. There are so many of them, an incandescence, illuminating the cracked carvings along the wall. Dancing demons, laughing gods. . . . "This is a temple."

I can't keep the awe out of my voice. I have never been so close to one. I have only seen them from a distance, smoldering with soullight; hundreds of spirits, drawn in as though the buildings were the King of Death's lamps. They say the temples were built three days apart as a person walks—so no matter where you die, your soul can find its way to the gods.

"It was." Leo speaks so casually as he pulls Lani to a halt. He slips down from the bench, barely glancing around. "Come on."

"The temples are forbidden by the armée." And by Maman, I do not add. What dangers wait in these walls? What wonders?

Leo only grins. "So is our entire trip, so far. But you can stay with the wagon if you like. I'm taking the lantern, though."

He lifts the lamp from the eaves and starts toward a stair leading up. A smattering of moonlight spills down from above, almost eclipsed by the light of the dead. I can see perfectly well without the lamp, and part of me wants to stay and wait in what Leo thinks is near blackness. I could even search his violin case again to pass the time, to see if there is anything I missed. But the draw of the temple is stronger. This is my best chance to see one—maybe even my last. Gnawing the inside of my cheek, I peek through the scrollwork; both my parents are fast asleep. I send my thanks to whatever god this temple used to honor. "Leo?"

"What?"

"Wait."

I slide off the bench, and my bare feet sink into the loamy floor. But beneath the layer of dirt, carved stone shows in patches: a bold, graphic pattern that shifts in the soullight. It takes me a moment to recognize it as writing—old Chakran—though I don't know how to read it. Few people can. It is a language for prayers, for spells. For monks. But here and there, the symbol of life stands out. Though I suppose that is a spell too.

My footsteps quicken; I fall in with Leo on the stairs. They are patterned as well, though the center of each step is worn thin by the tread of hundreds, thousands of feet. All gone now. After La Victoire, the monks who did not flee were killed or imprisoned—not just Le Trépas, but all across the country, from every temple. Those who predicted the floods and harnessed the rains, who tended the ill and brought new life into the world—all were tainted by association . . . at least according to the royal edicts, signed by the Boy King, written by Legarde. The general did not want anyone left to step into Le Trépas's role.

In our village, there were people I was sure had been monks, once—midwives now, or teachers, or healers, or the ones who washed the dead. No one ever admitted it, but you could tell by what they wore: shirts with high collars and long sleeves, even on the hottest days, for monks tattooed their sins on their backs, to bear the weight of them.

A few months after I started seeing souls, I had gathered my courage along with a bunch of bananas and gone to ask Auntie Rael—not my real aunt, but the quiet, nervous woman who taught reading and writing, the edges of her long sleeves always stained with mulberry ink.

"Were you a monk once?" I'd whispered as I'd put the fruit in her hands. "Do you know about spirits?" I was close enough to hear the breath catch in her throat, but she acted like she hadn't heard me. She only put the bananas on her table and shooed me back out the door, tugging on the ragged pink edges of her cuffs. Never show, never tell.

Past the stairs, Leo and I emerge into the shattered ruins; the moonlight falls around in a silver curtain. The shrine has been broken like old bones scraped for marrow: a heap of rubble, grown over with vines and saplings, the carvings defaced with chisels, the statues facedown on the ground. The gold was rubbed from their faces and hands, the gems pulled from their hollow eyes. Now the gods are only celebrated in shadow plays. And isn't it strange how the Aquitans devour our stories but silence our prayers?

Still, official edicts could never banish the souls. There are so many here! Vana, swirling with the breeze; arvana, flying in circles between broken pillars and piles of black rubble. And akela, drifting through fallen archways in the silvery light of the moon. "Beautiful, aren't they?" Leo says.

I stare at him askance. "What?"

"The carvings."

"Oh! Yes," I say, looking anew at the tumbled stone as we pick our way across the floor. A pang hits me; despite the desecration, I can tell the work was art, once. "I've never been inside a temple."

"Yes, yes," Leo says. "You're a very upstanding citizen."

"Hard for a smuggler to understand?"

"Especially the part where in spite of it all, you're on the run from the law." Smiling, he offers me his hand to help me over a fallen pillar, but I remember the spark I felt before. Though the temptation is there, I keep my hand to myself.

We have reached the heart of the shrine; like the eye of a

storm, it is oddly unaffected by destruction. No . . . looking closer, I see the black block of the altar is cracked into three pieces; they've only been pushed back together. The statue of the deity is harder to repair—it was too large and heavy for the armée to topple, but the faces were smashed into blank stone.

Still, I recognize them: the Keeper of Knowledge. The deity of many faces and all genders, the unraveler of mysteries. Between death and birth, a soul whispers its past life into the Keeper's ears. Before the armée came, the brightest jewels in Chakrana were set in their eyes.

Laid at the Keeper's lap are the offerings—long orchid stems and strands of red chrysanthemums draped over piles of knobby tamarind and spiked jackfruit, glossy mangos and bumpy lychee. Souls swirl around the fruit, as if remembering what it was to taste, to smell, to enjoy, to consume. Such a bounty—and all of it fresh. A chill breeze stirs in my hair, prickles the skin on the back of my neck. Who has left the offerings? Are they still nearby?

I glance around the ruins, but we are the only living souls I see. Beside me, Leo sighs, shaking his head at the pile of fruit. "Sometimes I wonder why people believe in gods when the gods do not seem to believe in us."

Spirits flit between us, cold and silent fire. I smother my

smile. "There must be something you believe in."

"I believe in family," he says softly. "But it doesn't always believe in me either."

I shift on my feet. "I'm sorry if I've made things worse between you and your . . . capitaine."

Leo's sudden laugh echoes in the empty temple. "No. No. It would be hard to make it worse than I already have."

Then, in a motion so quick it startles me, Leo shrugs off his jacket and pulls his shirt over his head. I gape at him until he tosses the shirt at my face. The smell makes my heart beat faster—molasses and vanilla and the tang of iron. Still, I sputter as I struggle free. "What are you doing?"

"Knot the arms over the neck, will you?" He's putting his jacket back on over his bare chest. His muscles flex and ripple in the soullight, and a thought boils up, unbidden, unwelcome: what would his skin would feel like against mine? "So it makes a bag."

"What?"

"Forget it, I'll do it." He takes the shirt back from me and ties the sleeves together. Then he plucks a ripe orange right off the pedestal and puts it in his makeshift pouch.

My mouth drops open—am I appalled, or impressed? "Leo!"

"People bring more every day." He gathers more fruit—mangos, bananas, even some rambutan, tucking them all into the shirt. "They'll rot otherwise."

"But . . . they're for the spirits!"

"Strange, isn't it?" Leo plucks a red rambutan from the pile and holds it out to me with a smile. "When hunger is for the living?"

I bite my lip—in truth, the ripe smell of the fruit is making my mouth water, and rambutan are my favorite. So after a moment, I take it, and when I do, my fingers brush his. An accident—but the spark I'd felt before kindles into flame, hot in my belly, warm in my cheeks. I draw back as though burned, clutching the fruit, but Leo only raises an eyebrow. Does he know what I'm thinking? Can he see it on my face?

Is he thinking the same things?

Our game of questions is over, but asking is not the only way to get an answer. Tossing aside the fruit, I take his hand in mine. But as I pull him toward me, tilting my face to his, the cocky look in his eyes fades to uncertainty. "Jetta—"

"What?" The word is just a breath through my parted lips, but he's close enough to hear it—almost close enough to taste it. Almost. But he only stands there, back stiff.

"I was thinking. . . ." He glances down, avoiding my eyes. "What you said earlier. About Les Chanceux . . ."

Now I am the one to draw back, and the flush on my cheeks is not excitement, but shame. Of course. Who would want to kiss a mad girl? I should have known not to tell. "It isn't contagious," I say bitterly, but now I sound like a beggar. I push away from him, but he takes my hand again.

"It isn't that," he says, but I don't want excuses. I pull free and start back toward the stairs. Then I jump, muffling a scream.

There is a woman standing there in the shadows.

She wears a red sarong, tied to leave her back bare. The soullight gleams on the writing tattooed across her shoulders. A monk, and unashamed of it. How did she get so close so quietly? My heart is in my throat, but she only inclines her head. "Welcome, lailee," she says—little sister. Akra used to call me that. "Have you come to join us?"

"Just leaving," Leo says, coming up behind me. His voice is more calm than I feel. But he holds the bag of fruit in his left hand; his right hovers so casually near his gun.

Though she is unarmed, the monk only smiles, her expression unconcerned. "I wasn't asking you." She turns to me; her black eyes are depthless. "The dead are coming, lailee. You've sent us so many. Won't you help us bless them?"

I wet my lips; my mouth is dry. "What dead?"

"Soldiers. From the camp outside the city."

Leo frowns. "What are you talking about?"

She doesn't answer—she doesn't even look at him. I open my mouth to ask her, but before I can, her voice comes close and soft, like a whisper in my ear, though her lips don't move: *He doesn't know what you are, but I do.*

I reel backward; Leo steadies me. I can almost feel the heat of her breath stirring my hair. But the woman hasn't moved a muscle. And though Leo couldn't have heard, he's looking at me now, his face troubled. Was it only in my head? Hands shaking, I draw myself up. Then the night shatters in a scream.

Maman's voice—and she's calling my name. Is she in trouble, or am I? Whirling, I race through the rubble, and Leo is right behind me. We leap over the stones and down the steps as her cries echo from the heart of the temple. I glance back once—I can't help it—but the monk has disappeared.

Are her fellows downstairs? Or the rebels? Or a band of smugglers—thieves or bandits?

But there is nothing in the belly of the temple but the roulotte and the souls, and Maman can't see those. The back door judders as she pounds on it. My heart sinks, but I lift the latch and she spills through the doorway, furious.

"Where were the two of you?" she shouts. "What were you doing alone together?"

The implication is jarring after the run-in with the monk—though it isn't as ludicrous as I wish. The shame of Leo's rejection covers me like a mantle; I want to throw it off along with her accusation. But she knows me better—or at least, she knows my malheur, and the rush and temptations it brings. And what can I tell her? That we were robbing the altar? That we met a monk? That the monk claimed to know my secrets?

In the silence, Leo straightens up, buttoning the jacket over his bare chest. "I assure you," he says. "Nothing happened."

The reminder makes it even worse, but Maman doesn't respond. Already her anger is faltering as her eyes sweep across the room; her face falls—she stares wide-eyed at the carvings in the light of the lantern. Then Papa emerges just behind her; he realizes a moment after she does. The look he gives me is practically a snarl. "You've brought us to a temple?"

"I have," Leo says quickly, but Papa's expression does not change. He grabs the lantern.

"Get inside the wagon, Jetta. Meliss, you too."

"Samrin . . ." She grabs his arm, but he herds her gently inside. She scrambles through the door and I follow, knowing better than to argue.

Papa shuts the door behind us and heads toward the driver's seat, Leo hurrying after him. His voice drifts in through the scrollwork. "I swear to you—" he starts again, but Papa cuts him off.

"Spare me your promises. Just steer us out of this place."

Leo doesn't respond, and they climb in prickly silence to the bench. In a moment, we're off once more through the tunnels.

The soullight dims and fades as we leave the temple behind. Maman huddles in the dappled pool of lamplight that shines through the scrollwork. The air in the tunnel is not cool, but she is trembling. And in the silence, the monk's whisper echoes. *He doesn't know what you are, but I do.*

But he knows enough, doesn't he? A mad girl, out of control. And what else? What could the monk see just by looking? Or was her voice just another hallucination?

"Maman," I say at last. "What am I?"

She looks up at me as though startled. "You're my daughter, Jetta. Mine." And then, to my surprise, she takes my hand and pulls me close. I can still feel her shaking, but she holds me like she's unafraid. Her arms are so warm. After a while, the monk's voice fades, and I let the rocking of the roulotte carry me off to sleep.

Rapport Postérior Aux Mesures

Lieutenant Armand Pique
The Incident at Luda
Attn: General Julian Legarde

Last night in Luda, Questioneur Eduard Dumond was involved in a skirmish during the attempted capture of suspects wanted in regards to the rebel sabotage at the celebration known as La Fête des Ombres. Unfortunately, they escaped—or were released—while Dumond was left seemingly unconscious in the street. Identified as a girl and her mother, both Chakran, they were last seen driving a carved and painted mummers' wagon.

The suspects lost, Capitaine Xavier Legarde ordered Dumond brought to the medic's tent. There, in the dead of night, Dumond awoke— or more likely dropped his subterfuge. Possibly in league with the rebels, he attacked and killed Docteur Benoit Cariveau and the patients recovering from the previous night's insurrection.

Dumond then left the tent to continue his assault on the rest of his battalion, killing quite a few before the alarm was raised. In the dark and confusion, several soldiers returned fire, resulting in unfortunate casualties. At last, Dumond was shot and killed by the capitaine, who was himself grievously—possibly mortally—wounded in the fight.

Frightened by the shooting, the Chakrans in the surrounding areas swarmed the docks in an attempt to flee the town. Due in part to the avarice and cowardice native to their race, a riot broke out between the boat owners and the refugees unwilling or unable to pay the fee for passage. The ships were set ablaze, and the fire spread through the dock and the shantytowns of the sugar cutters. As the 314th Battalion does not have a fire suppression team and local housing is not a priority, it is still burning as of my writing. Unfortunately, the telegraph building was damaged as well, which is why this report is following you by rider. Please send all responses by horse or pigeon until the lines can be repaired.

Naturally Dumond could not be questioned, but rebel collusion is clearly indicated in his mutiny. A swift and decisive response is required. As Capitaine Legarde is still unconscious, I am left in charge of some three hundred men. I have made the determination to lead them into the surrounding villages to purge the area of insurrectionists and find the wanted rebels.

CHAPTER
TEN

I don't know what time it is when I wake. It could have been hours or days. The roulotte still clatters through the tunnels, the dark still presses in through the scrollwork. Maman and Papa have traded places, but everything else is still the same.

I lift my head—it seems to take all my energy. But as I move, Papa opens his eyes. "Are you all right, Jetta?"

"Yes." The word comes out on a sigh—even nodding seems like too much work. Is it exhaustion? It makes sense after the show, the running, the monk in the temple. But I don't feel tired. I don't feel much of anything. Still, Papa is watching me, and the look on his face—it's so different than

Maman's fear. It's a look of love. So I force my lips into a little smile. "I'm fine. Just tired."

He smiles back, but he shakes his head. "I'm not an audience, Jetta. You don't have to pretend."

The words are a balm. I want to go to him, to lay my head in his lap, but I don't have the will. "You're not angry with me," I say instead.

"No." He sighs. "But what were you doing up there?"

Now a spark of emotion stirs in me. A faint blush works its way to my cheeks: the memory of shame. "Not what Maman thought."

"The boy told me you stopped for supplies." Papa makes a face—the same face I must have made when Leo proposed stealing from the feet of the god. "But you know the temples are forbidden."

"Then why were there so many offerings?" I hadn't meant to say it—the words just slipped out. But I want to know. "Leo said that people come every day."

I do not mention the monk, but her voice drifts through my head. *I know what you are.* But Papa only smiles a little. "What else did Leo say?"

"Papa."

"I remember how it was, you know. I'm not so old."

"Papa!" Now the blush is full-fledged, as is his grin. Disbelief propels me upright. It takes me another beat to realize what he's doing. "Right," I say, settling back against the wall of the roulotte. But now the smile on my own face—however small—is real.

And Papa knows it; his look softens as he drops the act. "It's not so strange, you know." Idly, he picks up Maman's painted thom, running his fingers across the top before tucking it back in its spot on the shelf. "Romance isn't always two lovers under a golden moon. Sometimes it's stolen moments on the run."

"There was no moment, stolen or otherwise," I say— not for lack of my trying, I do not add. But even the embarrassment seems distant now—like something I overheard, not something I felt myself. Then I frown. "You never answered my question, Papa. If the temples are forbidden, why do so many people still go?"

Papa sighs, and I realize then . . . he wasn't only trying to make me laugh. He was also trying to make me drop the question. I expect him to brush me off—to tell me that anyone who goes to the temple is a fool, or evil. But when he speaks, his voice is thoughtful. "They're losing control—the armée. It's not a good sign, for them."

"For them?" Something about the way he says it tweaks my ear. "And for us?"

"It's good that we're leaving," Papa says firmly, though there is regret in his voice—there always is, when he talks about going away. He passes a hand over the scrim on the side of the roulotte, where the bullet hole has torn through the silk. "It's not safe here."

"I know," I say. "I meant for us Chakrans. For the country."

"Ah. For that, who can say?" He drops his hand and gives me a little shrug. "It wasn't all bad, before."

I blink at him, taken aback. My uncle used to talk that way, but I'd never heard Papa say as much. "Maman hates the old ways."

"It isn't the old ways she hates, Jetta."

"It's Le Trépas." I whisper the name, and though Papa purses his lips, he doesn't try to hush me.

"Before he took power . . ." Papa's voice trails off. Silence creeps back into the roulotte, and at first I think he won't finish the story. I lean against the wall, letting my head rock gently as we rattle on through the tunnel. I have just closed my eyes again when he speaks. "When I was a boy, I spent rainy seasons at the temple. A lot of us did. The ones who didn't have our own fields to work. We planted if we were able, but if we weren't, we still had dry beds and full bowls. At night they taught us all to read, and at the end of the season, they sent us home with bags of rice. That's how it used to be."

I have not opened my eyes—instead, I see his story, as though on a scrim. The children tucking blades of young rice into the shimmering water, the monks with their turmeric robes pulled up through their belts to keep them dry. "What happened, then? What made Le Trépas different?"

"Don't get me wrong," Papa says. "Even when I was a boy, there were problems. Land going over to sugar. People who craved riches more than rice. Boys started wanting to learn to smuggle and shoot more than to read and write. Do you want to know what I think?" Papa lowers his voice then, like he used to when he would speak to his brother, so his words wouldn't go beyond the thin walls. But this time, it's not the armée or the neighbors he is afraid will hear. It's Maman. "I think the gods went a little mad when the Aquitans came."

The word should chill me, but instead it saps the last of my energy. The silence returns as we roll on.

Capitaine Xavier Legarde
to Lieutenant Armand Pique

9 Août 1874

Lieutenant,

I recently learned of your sortie from Luda not
from your own hand, but from a copy of the letter
you sent to my father. My adjutant rightly guessed
I would want to see the report when I awoke;
though I am, as you say, "grievously wounded," I
am not mortally so. Nor am I incapable of reading
correspondence, and I expect to be kept apprised
of developments. I saw nothing in your report to
indicate rebel collusion, nor, in the case of such
an alliance, any hint of how the rebels involved
might be found.

I am told you rode southeast toward Dar
Som. What drew you there? I have instructed the
rider to wait for your response.

Capitaine Xavier Legarde

Lieutenant Armand Pique
to Capitaine Xavier Legarde

10 Août 1874

Capitaine,

I am very pleased to hear you are recovering. Prognosis was poor when I left, and I did not know if you would wake. Forgive me for not addressing the report to you. Still, I have in no way disregarded the chain of command.

Have no fear; the men are restless and eager for the fray. I have the honor to report that at four o'clock this morning, I attacked and routed a rebel camp consisting of roughly a hundred people. The enemy made a small show of fight but quickly yielded. I suffered no losses. Weapons were discovered among their belongings.

Pique

CHAPTER ELEVEN

The tunnels roll on forever, a dark and winding path. I lose hours watching through the scrollwork. Here, the tunnel branches; there, cavernous openings yawn in the rippled rock walls, leading off into shadows or, sometimes, toward a faraway light. We pass rivulets glimmering like streams of stars, where tiny fish and their vana nibble black algae; other times, I hear the crash of distant waterfalls in the deep gloom of wide caverns. Twice we come across other people— other smugglers—going the opposite way. They pass by with murmured greetings and furtive looks, as do we.

Maman and Papa trade places again. I want to ask her

about her own childhood. She never talks about it. Had she ever worked the temple fields, planting rice beside the monks? Had she sat at a long wooden table, sharing rice with tattooed women, learning to read their sins? Is that where she heard about the blood offering, and the symbol of life?

But I am too tired to bring it up—no. Too tired to risk the anger the question might provoke. She'd always told me never show, never tell. But there was a third lesson, I realize now. Never ask.

But the monk's voice won't stop. What am I?

Capitaine Xavier Legarde
to Lieutenant Armand Pique

12 Août 1874

Lieutenant,

You did not answer my question: how did you
identify the people in the encampment as rebels?
The weapons you recovered—do they match the
missing rifles stolen during the attack at La Fête?
Did you question the prisoners?

Capitaine Xavier Legarde

CHAPTER

TWELVE

Time passes differently underground; I cannot count the days. We have stopped to eat several times, though I can't remember exactly how many, nor what we ate. Nor if I ate. But it doesn't matter much. I am not hungry.

The crawling feeling persists on my skin, like the brush of hair or a spider's legs, skittering across the back of my neck. At least the monk's voice is gone. Was it ever truly there?

Lieutenant Armand Pique
to Capitaine Xavier Legarde

14 Août 1874

Capitaine,

The weapons found were machetes, of the type usually used by rebels when they cannot steal guns. But rest assured, we will continue to search for the missing rifles.

Unfortunately we were unable to accommodate prisoners; the rules of war are by necessity circumvented when the enemy follows no such compunctions. But tomorrow we expect victory over a rebel hideout in the valley nearby. I'll ensure any survivors are thoroughly questioned.

Pique

Capitaine Xavier Legarde
to Lieutenant Armand Pique

16 Août 1874

Lieutenant,

Machetes are common weapons among the rebels because they are also common tools for foragers in the jungle, as you well know.

Report back to Luda at once.

Capitaine Xavier Legarde

Lieutenant Armand Pique
to Capitaine Xavier Legarde

17 Août 1874

Capitaine,

I will not leave my men to fight without me, nor abandon the field at the edge of Dar Som, where just last week a rebel force executed a routine patrol.

I have watched your betters bleed to death in these savage jungles for sixteen years at the whim of diplomacy and half measures. For the glory of Aquitan, I will break this stalemate here and now. The rebels will be taught a lesson. I look forward to sending you word of our victory.

Pique

CHAPTER THIRTEEN

I wake from a dream, but it is still dark. If it was a dream. If I am awake.

Capitaine Xavier Legarde
to Lieutenant Pique

19 Août 1874

Lieutenant Armand Pique, you are hereby relieved of command. You are to surrender to Lieutenant Hyo and B Company at once.

Capitaine Xavier Legarde

This letter was never delivered, but found later on Lieutenant Hyo's body in a shallow grave outside Dar Som. B Company never reported back to Luda.

ACT 2,

SCENE 19

The tunnels. Outside the roulotte. Idly, LEO tunes his violin while PAPA pokes the fire, though both men watch the door of the wagon out of the corners of their eyes. When it finally opens, they look up expectantly, settling back when they see it's only MAMAN.

PAPA: Well?
MAMAN: Still not hungry.

PAPA's shoulders fall. MAMAN offers him the bowl she carries—it's still full of rice and greens—but he shakes his head.

She hesitates for a long moment before offering it to LEO.

LEO: No, thank you.

MAMAN sits down on the steps of the wagon and picks at the food. LEO is still watching her. After a few bites, she puts down the spoon with a look of exasperation and holds out the bowl again. Embarrassed to be staring, he turns back to his violin.

LEO: Sorry. It's only . . .

He hesitates. When he speaks, the words come out all in a rush.

She told me. About why you're going to Aquitan. About Les Chanceux. I think it's wise. And brave. I wish I'd been able to take my mother there.

A long silence. MAMAN's look softens.

MAMAN: You lost her.
LEO: Last year.

Another long pause. MAMAN holds out the bowl again.

MAMAN: No wonder you're so thin.
LEO: I'm not hungry.
MAMAN: Eat anyway.

With a small smile, LEO takes the bowl.

LEO: Does this mean I'm forgiven?

MAMAN: Don't test your luck.

CHAPTER

FOURTEEN

The next time I open my eyes, something is different, though at first I am not sure what.

The light? The location? No, we are still traveling in the Souterrain, and maybe we'll never leave. I am alone in the roulotte, but that isn't it either.

I push myself out of the nest of pillows that surrounds me and take a deep breath. The air is cool and clear. The crawling feeling is gone, replaced by a new energy under my skin.

The difference is in me.

I stretch my legs—I clench my fists. Suddenly I need

something to do. Looking around the roulotte, I find it easily. The place is a mess, and so am I.

The first thing I do is strip off my old sarong and don a fresh one; the clean fabric is like heaven on my skin. I wipe my face with a damp scrap of cloth, then scrub it across my teeth till the mossy feeling is gone. Then I brush my hair and pull it into a low bun.

It seems like such a small thing—to comb hair, to clean teeth, to change clothes. Why is it so hard sometimes? And why does it make such a difference?

Refreshed, I toss the dirty things into the corner. They land atop my other ruined dresses—one tattered, one bloody. Kneeling beside the basket, I run the fabric through my hands, holding up the skirts to look at them from various angles, trying to consider what I might do with the remains, how I might give them new life. This panel might become the silk wing of a bird; this line of ruffles might be salvaged to decorate another skirt. My fingers itch for the shears, the steady challenge of the needle and thread. Of course I'll have to wash the dresses first. With a sigh, I tuck them back into the basket for later.

Then I stand, brushing the dust off my knees. Though I am put back together, the roulotte is . . . not. There is bedding scattered everywhere, and a musty smell: dust and sorrow. So I collect my makeshift nest, shaking out the pillows and stacking them on my parents' little bed. There is a soft straw broom in the corner; I run it across the floor, pushing the dust toward the back door of the wagon. But there—on the boards, a flattened ball of crumpled paper trembles.

The kitten. I had forgotten about her, poor thing. I set down the broom and pick up the page. It rustles on my palm. It's long past time I freed her from this middling incarnation.

Tucked onto a shelf, beside my folded sarongs, there is a little bag I made from a scrap of silk and a drawstring ribbon. I tip the contents out onto the floor—some incense, a few grains of black rice, my brother's letters, and his battered lighter.

He'd given it to me the day he'd left. I still use it to light the lanterns before any performance—a way to keep him with us. I rub the dented steel with my thumb as vana drift in through the scrollwork, drawn by the rice. Then I flip the cap and hit the strike. A little flame springs to the wick; I touch it to the paper. In a curl of flame and ash, the kitten's soul tumbles free.

She sits at my feet for a moment, as though stunned.

Then she flicks her tail and bounds after the spirit of a fly.

As she cavorts around the roulotte, I pluck up the grains of rice and pour them back into the bag, followed by the incense and the lighter. Then I finish sweeping as the soul of the kitten bats at the broom. Now I remember why I put her in the flyer in the first place. But she has to get bored soon. And if she doesn't, it's only three days.

What next? The floor is clean, the shelves are straight— rows and rows of fantouches wrapped in burlap bundles. All but one, still in pieces. My eye is drawn to it like an old friend's face in a crowd: my dragon.

I flex my fingers, and a smile touches my lips at the thought of real work—of creation. I've been crafting this fantouche on and off for nearly two years—ever since our old one burned up in the fire. When it's done, it will be a masterpiece. Is now the time to finish? Better now than later. After all, if Aquitan has different gods, the souls there may be different too. And the dragon is much too large to control without their help: twice as long as I am tall, cut and crafted from water buffalo hide. Each scale is scraped translucent and rubbed in gold and carmine; the teeth are carved of cow bone. The skin is painted with two pots of red kermes and one of saffron, along with half an ounce of ground gold for shine. But a soul is not the only thing the fantouche needs. We are still missing the rivets to hold it all together. I had hoped to find some along the way, but copper is much scarcer than spirits these days. In the battle between war and art, war has better weapons, and the armée needs its bullets.

Kneeling on the floor of the wagon, I lay out the pieces around me in a long arc, the way the dragon will look when it's done. Should I string the joints with knotted leather, or will cords only fall apart mid-show? Absently, I shoo the kitten away from the tasseled tail. Then I frown as the roulotte slows and stops, rocking gently as someone hops down from the bench. A voice drifts in from outside—Leo's.

"—another three days to the capital. We should make it well in time for the coronation. Might pick up a bit of extra cash there, if you want to do a play."

He sounds in high spirits, and his voice is richer than I remember. There is a creaking sound, and suddenly—light. Even filtered through the scrollwork, the sun is blinding after so long in the dark. I lift my palm against the glare, then marvel at the scarlet glow limning the thin skin of my hand.

The roulotte rolls forward and a cool breeze pushes in, carrying a hint of greenery and the smell of rain. My ears feel like petals as they catch the light patter of droplets on the roof. We are back above the ground in the realm of the living. "Nuriya?" Leo shouts. "Das?"

I listen, but the only response is the wind in the leaves and the winnowing of a snipe. Leaving off my work, I crawl across the floor of the roulotte. The handle of the door feels strange in my fingers. But when it swings open, I'm looking out on a familiar clearing: a cottage, a kitchen garden, a grove of dragon-eye trees, the glossy green leaves shining with rain and the last flare of the setting sun through the clouds.

La Fête des Ombres always marked the end of the dry season, when rains like these—light and sun-dappled— would chase us back home to Lak Na. Is it raining in the village too? As I let the droplets kiss my cheeks, the soul of the kitten leaps down from the roulotte to stalk the grass outside the hut. I half expect Daiyu to open the door, tottering toward us with her faded sarong and her wicked humor. But we are alone. No one answers Leo's call; when he ducks into the cottage, he comes back out shortly after, shaking his head.

"They're gone," he says. Then he sees me and stops in his tracks. "You're outside."

I shift a little on my feet. "So are you."

It's a glib answer, and he opens his mouth to retort—but Papa interrupts. "What do you mean, gone?"

Leo shrugs, affecting nonchalance, but I can see the little worry line, just between his brows. "They've packed and left. I don't know why. There's no sign of trouble. Just . . . no sign of them, either. This is still the best place to stop for the night," he adds. "There's good grazing for Lani and a spring behind the cottage. And we can all sleep indoors for once."

Papa nods a little, but he studies the trees, the cottage, the dewy clearing. "They must have left for a reason."

"Not all reasons are nefarious." Leo glances at me again, hesitating, but by then Maman has seen me. She rushes over and smooths back my hair; under her hand, it feels lank and tangled.

"Are you hungry?" she says, standing a bit too close. "Will you finally eat?"

It takes me a moment to recognize the gnawing feeling in my stomach as emptiness—as hunger. Thinking back, I can't remember my last meal. "D'accord, Maman."

"I'll make coconut rice. Your favorite." She gives me that look I hate—the careful one, as though she is not sure if too strong a glance will push me over the edge.

But my mouth is watering at the thought, and I only nod.

She takes the black pot behind the house to the spring while Papa unharnesses Lani and leads her to a stand of thick grass. I linger at the back of the wagon, a bit at odds with the world. My legs feel shaky and my skin, too delicate—like the outside air has a texture that isn't entirely pleasant. Rain sticks to my shoulders; the air is too humid. And Leo is still standing there on the grass, watching me. A flush creeps up my neck as I remember our last conversation—his rejection, his mention of my malheur. "What?" I say at last, and he blinks.

"I just . . ." He shakes his head. "How are you feeling?"

"Why do you ask?"

"Because I haven't seen you in over a week!" His tone is incredulous, as though the answer were obvious—but it takes me aback. A week? The memories are dim and distant: sleeping, waking, the long journey underground.

"I was working on a new fantouche," I say, which is not technically a lie. Trepidation turns to interest on his face.

"Oh?"

"Look," I say, gesturing inside the roulotte; he peers over my shoulder, frowning at the pieces scattered across the floor.

"Look at what, exactly?"

I scowl, crawling into the roulotte to gather the scraps—

the horned head, the fearsome jaw. "Here, see? Like this."

I lay them out under the eave, along on the back step. He traces a finger along the curve of a scale, then picks up a section, holding it to the light, so the fading flame of the setting sun rushes red through the thin leather. "It's beautiful."

Pride floods in; I try to summon some modesty. "It's hard with the rationing. Copper rivets are impossible to find."

He puts the piece back down, out of the rain, and gives me a crooked smile. "I'll keep that in mind the next time I want something from you."

I widen my eyes, taken aback. Is he toying with me, or have I misunderstood him? A week ago, his look might have made my heart beat faster, but after the temple, I'm not sure what to think. And more than that . . . I seem to have lost my rhythm during the long days in the dark; the spark has flared out, along with the manic energy of my malheur. Is that why he pushed me away in the first place? Not because I am mad, but because he knows my madness clouds my judgment? "I . . . I was only talking," I say at last, leaning back, just a little. But he takes the cue, shifting on his feet, giving me space.

"And I'm just listening." His smile softens; I return it. Around us, vana shine, bright spots in the gathering dark. "We should go in," he adds then. "I don't want to miss out on that coconut rice."

Carefully, so as not to brush my skin, he reaches past me into the roulotte, gathering an armful of bedding and starting toward the cottage. Bemused, I watch his back as he goes, and after a moment, I follow.

The hut is a typical Chakran home, lifted a little off the ground on poles of thick bamboo and thatched with palm leaves. More bamboo makes up the springy floor, covered with an old woven mat. There are two rooms, separated by a curtain, but aside from the grass screen hanging from the ceiling, there is not much left behind.

A flat stone fire pit, some broken bowls, and a few chipped pots full of brine. Pickled vegetables float in the pungent liquid, too old to risk eating. Papa has a fire going to chase away the damp, and Maman is boiling rice fragrant with sweet oil. But despite the scent of food and the cheery flames, the cottage is anything but welcoming. The fire casts long shadows against the bare walls, and the rain rustles in the wet thatch. It's not a cool night, but I sit close to the fire.

While the rice is cooking, Leo ducks outside once more,

returning with a bottle of rice wine crusted with earth—stored in the dusty dark beneath the hut. He breaks the twine seal and lifts the jar by the neck. "To those who aren't here." He takes a deep draft and whistles before passing the bottle to Papa. "And everything they leave behind."

"To those we miss," Papa agrees. He drinks and passes the bottle. Maman wipes the rim with her sleeve before she takes a mouthful. Then she adds a splash to the pot and passes the wine to me. The glass is cool and heavy in my hands; I watch the three of them across the fire, feeling a bit at loose ends. Something has happened over the last few days—some sort of harmony between them, a melody coalescing while I wasn't listening. "To Akra," I whisper under my breath. The wine is bittersweet.

We pass the bottle around again. My cheeks get warm and my head begins to float. I haven't eaten enough to drink deeply. The next time Papa takes the bottle, he holds it awhile, turning it over in his hands. "The people who lived here. They were your friends?"

"Oh," Leo says, leaning back against the wall. "Nuriya worked at La Perl years ago. Das was a cane cutter who came in to see her. My mother got them a post here when she heard Nuriya was pregnant." He gives Papa a little smile—sad, or mocking—and gestures to himself. "La Perl was clearly no place to raise a child."

When dinner is ready, Maman gives me a heaping bowlful—the silky rice salty sweet and rich with coconut meat. My mouth waters as the fragrant steam purls across the back of my throat. Still, I send another quick prayer to my brother before shoveling the rice into my mouth, and I leave a bit of food in the bottom of my bowl. Maman does too, though she can't see the souls collecting in the air, or the kitten that has wandered in to circle the offerings.

I watch the little arvana as she plays at eating, then curls up beside the fire. Around us, tiny spirits dance and dip. What do they do with the things we give? Can they smell but not taste? See but not touch? Or is it not the substance but the sacrifice that they cherish? The value we assign when we deny ourselves something they can never consume? Or is it something else entirely? Something I will never understand in this life? Maudlin thoughts swirl around me like the souls, broken then by the sound of a violin.

Leo has set his empty bowl aside and settled his instrument in the crook of his arm, and as the last of the daylight fades, he plays a song that brings the dark to life. He is even more beautiful to watch than his shadow was, that night at La Perl. In concentration, his mouth is soft and his eyes are distant. He moves as though the music inhabits his body—or perhaps it is the other way around. Embers drift up with the notes of his song, another tune I know. The one about the lovers—the one we perform each time we visit a new town. Papa joins in at the chorus as Maman drums gently on her knees.

A smile creeps across my face. This is the rhythm I had missed, and I am more hungry for the kinship than the coconut rice.

The fire is still high enough to cast a good shadow. I rush outside to the roulotte to rummage through the fantouches. The rain has stopped, and the tattered clouds drape a lacy shawl over the half-moon. I search by the silvery light—I know I have something here, at the bottom of the pile. An older puppet, soulless silk—a swallow on a stick. It will paint a graceful picture on the walls as I twirl it in swooping circles overhead. Grinning, I shut the door of the roulotte just as a filthy hand clamps down over my mouth and an arm snakes around my waist. Struggling, screaming into a stranger's palm, I am dragged backward into the jungle.

CHAPTER
FIFTEEN

I am thrashing, biting, my fingers like claws, my mouth a maw. I am an animal, vicious, tasting blood. The man curses and rips his hand from between my teeth. For a moment, I can breathe again—I turn a shallow breath into a short scream. But the man behind me muffles his own curses and clamps his hand back over my mouth. The lights of the cottage disappear quickly as he pulls me deeper into the wet green.

"Arret," he growls. "Stop fighting!"

But I don't—not until another man comes into view, his gun glinting in the dim and dappled moonlight. At the sight of it, I go still. My first thought is that the soldiers have found me. My second thought is that these men aren't soldiers.

Both are wearing the green uniforms, but they are dirty, disheveled—stained and wrinkled and open at the throat. There is stubble on their chins, which the armée never suffers, and the man before me is wearing leather sandals instead of the armée boots. Deserters—or grave robbers? Defilers of the dead? I don't know which is worse, or if it matters.

"Qu'est ce que c'est, Jian?" the bootless man whispers— armée words in a Chakran accent. The smell of unwashed flesh scrapes the roof of my mouth. Even more stomach turning is the look on the man's face: recognition. "What do we have here?"

With a grin, the second man tosses me to the muddy ground. I start to scramble up, but Bootless cocks his gun—a warning. I sink back as Jian gives me a gap-toothed smile. "I know you saw the wagon," he says to his friend. "A carved roulotte, just like the lieutenant said. And a Chakran girl inside it who might just be wanted for questioning."

"Sound familiar?" The bootless man squints at me. "Ever had a run-in with Capitaine Legarde?"

I blink at him, wide-eyed in the low light, acting. "Who?"

Bootless hesitates, but Jian lashes out, driving his foot into my stomach. "There's a recherche for you, girl. It describes your wagon perfectly! And I think the lieutenant will forgive our little leave of absence if we come back bearing gifts."

Wheezing, I clutch my belly, but my mind is racing. I try to remember the terrain south of Luda. What had Leo said? Three days from the capital? What was nearby? "I don't know what you mean," I croak, my weak protest stirring in the damp leaves. "We've only just come from Dar Som—"

He kicks me again, this time in my ribs. "Now I know you're lying," he says through his teeth. "No one escaped Dar Som."

"Wh-what?" Blinking away the tears in my eyes, I stare up at him through a haze of pain. Little souls float between us on a night breeze. "What happened at Dar Som?"

Bootless drops to a knee on my chest, pushing me into the sodden earth. I gasp for breath as he takes my wrists and binds them. "Lieutenant Pique."

Then his hand clamps down over my lips and both men go still. I hear it in the distant dark. Leo's voice, calling my name. Renewing my struggles, I try to respond, but Jian's fist collides with my temple in a spray of stars that fades to fuzzy black.

The first thing to break the blackness is not light, but sound. A distant wail—high and familiar and chilling—but it draws me back to the world. When I wake, I almost regret it. My head is throbbing in time with a bruise on my ribs that makes it hard to breathe. My wrists are tied painfully tight, and my fingers are cold and numb. But I am alone—or at least, the soldiers have gone. In the corner, an akela sits, bright gold, playing with a scrap of cloth twisted into a makeshift doll. The arvana of mice scramble in the thatch overhead.

Painfully, I use my knuckles to push myself to my knees—slowly, slowly. A wave of nausea ripples through me and I clamp my lips together, trying to keep from retching, taking deep breaths through my nose. Cold sweat beads on my forehead, but at last the feeling passes enough for me to look around the room.

I am on the packed-earth floor of an empty hut—no, not empty. Abandoned. Unlike the smugglers' cottage, people left this place in a hurry, unwilling or unable to stop and pack their meager possessions. A thin woven mat makes a humble bed. A faded orchid blossom wilts in a shallow stone cup, the water dark with algae. Coconut-shell bowls are still stacked on a rickety bamboo shelf, along with a metal cooking pot—a prize for a poor family. They wouldn't have left it behind if they'd had a choice in the matter. My heart sinks as I look back to the akela. Perhaps they didn't make it far.

Gingerly, I take a deep breath, wincing at the pain in my ribs, at the sour taste of smoke on the air, and something else . . . something sweet: the swampy smell of rot. Then the sound comes again—the one that woke me. High and long, a howling wail. It is answered by another and another; they overlap in a mournful song. It's the sound of the ke'cherk—I know it well. A pack of them used to roam the mountains above Lak Na. When I was a girl, I found their music beautiful. Then came the Hungry Year, when all the death tempted them into the valleys and they flitted through the fields like white ghosts under the moon.

Everyone said they were afraid of humans, but I saw the aftermath of their scavenging—the opened graves, the carcasses rent and torn—and that year, I became afraid of them too. The howls fade away, but the dread remains, coiled under my tongue like a snake beneath a stone. Death draws them near. I glance once more to the akela in the corner, but she pays me no mind. And then I hear laughter outside—the soldiers' voices, and they are much closer than the ke'cherk.

"I'm telling you, it's not desertion if you're in pursuit of the enemy." Bootless's voice.

"We weren't when we deserted," Jian replies.

"We don't have to tell him that."

Slowly, quietly, I creep toward the door on my knees, peeking through the tattered flap of woven reeds hanging over the doorway. Beneath it, I can make out the merry dance of a cookfire, and one of the men . . . Bootless, maybe, though I can only see his back.

I cast about the hut for another way out. The windows are small and high up, near the roof, to let out heat—but this was not a rich family. The walls are not bamboo, but thatch.

First things first. Lifting my hands to my mouth, I pick at the knot with my teeth, but it's tied tightly, and soon blood fills my mouth from the split on my lip. So I spit on the rope and curl my numb finger to draw the symbol of life on the fiber. The akela wavers briefly, but returns to her doll, uninterested in such humble flesh. Something slips in, though—something small. A vana, maybe a worm. At first it grips me tighter, coiling up in its new skin. The pain makes me gasp, but I stay as still as I can, trying to soothe the little soul. Finally it begins to relax, to twist itself free of its knots. Gently I try to help, to pluck at the rope, and the blood starts returning to my hands.

Outside, the soldiers laugh again at some shared joke. For a moment I go still, but the man I can see doesn't move, so I redouble my efforts, hoping they both stay there, by the fire. Their voices rise again into the ebb of their laughter.

"The real question is," Jian says, "do we want to go back?"

"I'm hungry," Bootless replies. "Not much left to eat around here."

"We could move on."

"Where? The jungle? You know what the rebels would do to us?"

"The ones here didn't have much fight in them."

"These weren't rebels, connard. Not all of them." Bootless spits into the fire, and something cold twists in my stomach. But then the rope falls free from my wrists, twitching and coiling on the ground. I pick it up, winding it around my wrist like a bracelet. "Stay," I murmur, and it cinches up close. I'll burn it later, when I'm back safe with my parents around my own cook fire.

Taking one last glance through the door to make sure the soldiers are still there, I crawl across to the opposite wall and push my hands through the palm fronds. They rustle and I freeze again, heart fluttering, but the soldiers don't stir. Moving more slowly, I slip my arms through the dry leaves in a wedge, letting the crinkle of the grass blend into the crackle of the fire. The edges of the leaves are sharp as razors, drawing little lines of blood where they brush along my bare skin, but I press forward—ducking my head, twisting my shoulders, slow and steady as the arvana scramble closer through the leaves.

But I stop halfway through.

My hands are on the rutted ground behind the hut, where rain drips down from the eaves and scores the earth, looking out on the gutted remains of a village. The smoke I had smelled came not from the cook fire, but from the smoldering ash of burned-out hovels. I am in one of the only ones left standing. Coals still glow dimly in the ashen husks: still-beating hearts in broken rib cages. Wisps of smoke hang in the air like memories, and everywhere I look, there are columns of cold fire: n'akela. The deaths here were not easy.

I know without being told that I am in Dar Som.

But why? Anger roils in my gut along with the bile. These weren't all rebels—even Bootless had known that. The spirit with her rag doll, the orchid in the bowl—the people who lived here were families like mine. And Jian's face comes back to me, twisted into a leering grin: *No one escaped.* As I clench my fists against the rocky earth, the n'akela drift closer, as though they can hear my thoughts. As though they know I am tempted to help them with their vengeance.

Then a gunshot cracks like a whip—once, twice, thrice. I stifle a scream . . . but it came from the jungle on the far side of the hut. Nowhere near me. One of the soldiers is screaming too—Bootless, I think. "They're in the trees!" Jian shouts, returning fire. "Get inside!"

I hesitate. Who is out there? Rebels? The armée? Am I in more danger out in the open or back in the hut with the soldiers? In the dark, in a firefight, I don't want to be caught between them. I struggle through the thatch, but I waited too long. As I slip through, a hand shoots out from the hut and wraps around my ankle. I hear Bootless cursing just inside. He pulls me back, but his grip is weak and slick with sweat or blood. "She's getting away!"

Frantic, I kick back through the thatch. The fronds slice my skin as my heel connects with his shoulder, his head, his jaw. A muffled grunt, and I am free. Scrambling to my feet, I careen toward the jungle—running headfirst into Jian coming around the side of the hovel.

He lunges for me. I spin away. His fingers barely brush my back, but he grabs a fistful of my sarong and nearly jerks me off my feet. I stumble back, close enough to hear him snarl in my ear—no words, just a sound like a beast. He wraps his arm around my neck, so tight I can't breathe. "Let go of me," I whisper, clawing at his arm. The n'akela creep closer, hopeful. "I'll kill you if you don't."

He only laughs. "With what?"

My blood and bare hands, I do not say. The souls of the dead and the damned. But the memory of fleeing La Perl, of Eduard's screams—they still rattle in my head like dust in a dry skull. So instead, I tug the rope from my wrist and whip it back over my shoulder. The vana twists inside the fiber, wrapping tight around his neck.

Jian's hands fly to his throat, and I am free. He reels sideways, falling against the wall of the hut, eyes bulging, struggling to breathe. His fingers gouge at the soft skin of his neck as he sinks to his knees. In my chest there is a feeling, distantly familiar, like the applause after a show, like the thrill of having all eyes on me. It is power.

All around me, n'akela gather, a rapt audience. But this is not a shadow play—death is not a puppet, here. Still, something dark tempts me . . . could I play this role? Doesn't he deserve it?

I am caught between shadow and flame, hesitating, but the rope only wraps itself tighter. Jian's lips turn blue, and the n'akela drift closer still, waiting for the vengeance that is their final purpose. If Jian dies now, what color will his soul be? Will I be watching over my own shoulder for a flash of blue light?

"Stop," I whisper to the spirit in the rope, and just like that, it falls away. I snatch it back as Jian drags a single breath—ragged, desperate, eager. Then another shot rings out from the jungle, and a spray of red explodes across the wall of the hut.

With a strangled scream, I turn away—but not before the image is pressed into my mind in shards of bone and teeth all red with blood. Jian's body slides sideways to lie against the rutted earth. Nausea hits me again like a punch to the gut, too fast to fight. This time I retch, tottering away from the body, spitting, gasping, gagging. A man crashes out of the tangled greenery behind the hut, a gun in his fist. "Jetta?"

"Leo!" I wipe my mouth on the back of my hand, stifling a sob—relief, and dread. I want to run to him, I want to run away. Instead I try to breathe. His hair and eyes are a little wild and his shirt is in tatters under his jacket, but otherwise he seems unhurt. "What are you doing here?"

"I came to save you," he says—an echo of Maman's words. *I'm always trying to save you.* Where is she now?

I look behind him, toward the trees, but all I see are the n'akela, drifting away; the show is over. "Are my parents with you?"

"I made them stay with the roulotte, in case . . ." He doesn't finish his sentence—and I don't want him to. His lip curls as he glances over my shoulder, at the soldier slumped on the ground. I do not turn; I do not follow his gaze. I do not want to see Jian's body or his soul. "Did they hurt you?"

"A bad headache," I say. "But nothing worse. They were going to bring me to their lieutenant. They said I'm wanted for questioning on a . . . a recherche."

Leo frowns, pushing past me; out of the corner of my

eye, I see him crouch beside Jian's prone body. He rifles through the dead man's pockets, drawing out a few étoiles, some cigarettes, a crumpled piece of paper. Then another howl cuts through the night—much closer.

"We should go," I murmur, winding the rope back around my wrist for safekeeping, but Leo's still staring at the page, swearing softly. "What is that?"

"The recherche, like you said." He looks up at me, almost hesitant. "They have a description of you, and of the roulotte."

I suck air through my teeth—a description printed on paper? I've only ever seen those for the Tiger. How much of the armée is looking for us? Has word reached Nokhor Khat? But before I can ask, the palm thatch rustles, and the tip of a bayonet slides through the wall of the hut. Leo twists away—too late. The bright blade lays open his jacket and cuts a scarlet line across his chest. With a grimace, he raises his gun and fires back through the thatch; inside, Bootless's scream cuts off in a gurgling sigh.

Wincing, I turn away. All I can smell is blood and smoke and bile. But another howl floats through the air along with the smoke. I see her then—the ke'cherk, standing in the village square, pale as bone. Her sleek muzzle is raised toward the night sky, the white fur stained red. The silvery scales on her slender legs gleam in the moonlight. Can she smell Leo's blood above the rest?

My heart pounding, I pull him toward the trees, plunging into the jungle along a muddy track. Leo's face is pale; he presses his fist against the jacket, over the wound, trying to stanch the bleeding. Another howl floats through the air—but surrounded by thick greenery on both sides, I cannot tell if it comes from behind us or up ahead. I stop to get my bearings, but Leo keeps going. He is only maybe a wagon's length away from me when I hear him yelp.

"Leo!" I whirl, but he has vanished . . . though ahead, there is splashing and cursing in Chakran and Aquitan. I take a step toward the sound, and the smell of blood grows stronger, mixed with the sweet taint of rot. There, where he disappeared—the track ends suddenly in a deep shadow before a wall of jungle. "Are you all right?"

"Don't come any closer!"

"What's wrong?" I say, my heart pounding in response to the panic in his voice. I take another step. Where is he?

"Stay back!" he calls, but I ignore him. As I approach, the shadow on the track resolves itself into a hole dug in the earth—as wide as the roulotte, and several times as long. He must have slid down the side.

"Leo!" My heart drops as I teeter on the edge of the pit. I think I see him then, lying in the mud, half submerged by the rainwater that fills the bottom of the ditch, but I'm wrong, so wrong. It isn't him at all.

Leo is scrambling up the side of the gully, clawing at the white roots that worm through the fresh-cut earth, eyes wide and shoulder bloody, but alive. And at the bottom of the ditch, a body. And another, and another, stacked like cane—men and women and children and even babies, the whole village, sinking in the muck, a mire of the dead.

AVIS DE RECHERCHE

"Jetta of the Ros Nai"

A Chakran girl in her teenage years with dark hair just past her shoulders, medium height and build, burn scars on her left shoulder. Traveling in the company of her mother and a moitié man aged eighteen. Fled Luda in a covered roulotte, carved and painted, and pulled by a white water buffalo.

CHAPTER SIXTEEN

So much death. I knew it was happening—I'd heard the stories. The rebels attack, the armée retaliates, back and forth, blood in the jungle. But this is not a story, and these are not rebels. I can't get the images out of my head—the bobbing backs and bloody limbs and the hair of a girl, drifting round the cracked porcelain of her shattered skull.

I should have killed Jian myself. Bootless too.

The anger is like a flame inside me, but there's nothing I can do about it now. Instead Leo and I stumble through the trees, away from the murdered village of Dar Som, though the smell follows me. It may never leave. I forget to scan the shadows for the flash of white fur, the ripple of silvery scales, the eyes that shine green in the dark. But the next time I hear the ke'cherk howling, they are farther away—back where death tempts them like souls to the god's lamp.

I shiver as I walk, but I tell myself it's only the cold night air. As we press through the jungle, moonlight barely penetrates the thick greenery, but the spirits are bright. Where Leo hesitates, I lead the way; in following the soldiers, he had tied strips of white cloth to branches at eye level, torn from the tail of his shirt.

His jacket is ruined now too, stained with blood that seeps from the wound on his chest. His own pants are soaked with the filth from the ditch, plastered to his legs—he must be cold. His face is pale, but he keeps pace with me until we've gone far enough that I can no longer hear the howling. Still, the scent of smoke clings to my hair like a dark crown. But we stop—just for a moment—to catch our breath. I am nauseated, and my head is pounding; Leo must see it on my face. "Are you all right?" he asks.

"Yes," I say, not trusting myself to nod, and he sags back against a tree, as though relieved—or exhausted. "You?"

His lip curls, dismissive. "I'll be fine. I'm just . . . tired."

"Let me see."

"I don't know how you can see anything in these shadows."
He turns toward me, letting his head fall back against the tree
and his eyes slide shut. Peeling back the blood-soaked linen
of his jacket, I inspect the cut by soullight—a deep slash, just
below his collarbone: pale skin, red flesh.

"You're going to need stitches," I say, but he only nods.
Still, his jacket is filthy—it hasn't been washed for days.
"Infection is the real risk."

"Can't do much about that out here," he says grimly, but
I frown, scanning the trees. Under the leaves, the souls swirl
and dance, a cloud of vana buzzing in the bromeliads, the
spirit of a moonrat lingering over a fallen piece of jungle
fruit. They illuminate a winding fall of heart-shaped betel
vine, crawling across the earth.

"That's where you're wrong." I reach out, stripping a
handful of leaves from the vine. "Here."

He takes them between his bloody fingers. "What are
these for?"

I cock my head. "You need to make a paste from the
leaves," I say slowly, but his look is blank. "Chew on them
a bit."

"Oh. Oh!" Leo grimaces, but he tucks the leaves into his
cheek. "You know, I like our way better."

I raise an eyebrow. "What way is that?"

"Alcohol."

"Next time, arrange to be rescued by a dancer," I say loftily, and he tries to laugh as he chews. The leaves are a good antiseptic, and a natural painkiller. But what to use for a bandage? I reach into his breast pocket, where I'd seen him tuck a handkerchief before—was it only days ago? When I pull it out, it's already soaked through. But behind it, the gleam of silver . . .

"What are you doing?"

"Looking for something to cover the wound," I say, but he shrugs his jacket shut, putting his hand over the cigarette case still tucked in his pocket.

"It can wait."

I want to ask him what's the matter—why he's glaring at me like he's afraid I'll steal his silver. But there is pain in his eyes, deeper even than the cut on his chest. So I don't press the issue. Instead, I toss the bloody handkerchief aside and unwind the cloth belt from my sarong—only a little dirty. "Here. Use this."

As I offer him the folded cloth, he spits the paste almost delicately onto the fabric. Then he hisses through his teeth as I press the cloth against the wound. "This isn't some kind of joke, is it?"

"Like how the Aquitans think we eat bugs as a delicacy? No. Take off your jacket," I add. "I need to tie this over your shoulder."

He narrows his eyes, but he obeys, slipping his left arm free, and I wrap the cloth around his chest, up over his shoulder, down under his arm, making a bandage of my belt.

"No one ever taught you these things?" I say as I move behind him to tie off the fabric.

"My mother wasn't very traditional," he says softly. Then he sighs, shifting his shoulders under the silk. "But I learned other lessons."

My hands still . . . not only at his tone. I might not have noticed it, if not for the light of the souls, but there is a mark on his back, just over his left shoulder blade. Nothing fancy, just a line and a dot—the symbol of life—in blue ink under his skin. But it takes my breath away. "I thought you didn't follow the old ways," I say softly.

"What do you mean?"

"Tattoos are for monks." I step back, confused, but he turns, quickly, as though to hide the mark from me.

"Tattoos are for sins," he corrects softly.

"Is life your sin, Leo?" I ask the question without

thinking, and see the answer on his face. But he pulls the jacket shut again.

"It's every bastard's sin," he murmurs, staring through the trees. Then he shakes his head, laughing a little. "A moitié man."

"What?"

"The recherche. 'A moitié man,' it said. But Xavier saw me, driving the roulotte. My brother," he explains at my look. "The capitaine. He didn't list my name."

"Do you think he was trying to protect you, somehow?"

For a moment, a wistful look crosses his face; quickly, he mars it with a grimace. "There are few things he cares about more than doing the right thing. The family name is one of them. That's all he was protecting."

"Ah." What else can I say? I search his eyes, his pale face, the bandaged wound, still bleeding. His rambling worries me. "We should get back," I say, and he doesn't argue.

It is only another hour till we see the smugglers' hut under the pearl-pink light of dawn. When I see the clearing through the trees, tears come to my eyes; all I want to do is go inside and sleep. But I take a deep breath, hesitating in the shadows beneath a stand of elephant ears. "Don't tell my parents."

"Don't tell them what, exactly?"

At first, the answers come not in words, but feelings—the red rush of power as I watched Jian struggle to breathe, the sickening spray of blood as it spattered the wall of the hut. The girl's hair in the muddy water, drifting like ribbons in the wind. "About how bad it was. In the village."

"D'accord," he says softly, rolling his wounded shoulder with a grimace. "But when we get to the main road I'm sure they'll put it together."

"What do you mean?"

He nods at the little hut. "Nuriya and Das fled. They won't be the only ones."

I pause with one hand on the door to the roulotte, remembering the families following the armée, pushing wheelbarrows full of bedding and valuables. And the crowd on the docks in Luda after the last attack. How many people will be traveling south to try to avoid the fighting? "We better hurry to the capital, then."

I am rummaging through the back of the roulotte for a needle when my parents come boiling out of the house. Papa rushes toward me, but there is a grim look on his face, and Maman has tears in her eyes. "Are you all right?" she murmurs into my hair. "Did they hurt you?"

"I'm fine," I murmur back, letting her hold me close even though my skin is crawling. "It's Leo who needs help."

"What happened?" Papa says.

"They won't bother us anymore." Leo sinks down on the back step of the roulotte. Wincing, he shifts his weight, pulling the recherche out of his pocket. "But they won't be the only ones looking."

Papa takes the paper gingerly—it is wet and stained from Leo's tumble down the ditch—and I take Maman's arm. "Can you get some clean water?" I say, but she hesitates, trying to watch as Papa peels the folded paper apart. I squeeze her wrist gently. "He risked his life to bring me back, Maman."

At last she nods. "There's some morning glory growing on the side of the house," she says. "I'll brew some tea. Come, Samrin. Bring the paper."

Together they go to the house, leaving me to pick through my supplies—silk and steel, needle and thread, and a long strip of clean cloth from my once-best dress. By the time I have what I need, Maman has brought the fire back to life, and the water is starting to steam. She pours a little into a bowl and adds a handful of morning-glory seeds to steep. I toss some rags into the pot to boil as Leo balls his jacket into a pillow and lies down to rest his head.

Papa is still holding the poster, but his eyes are far away. At last he puts the paper down with a sigh. "What do we do?"

"Just keep going." Maman uses a long pair of chopsticks to lift a piece of steaming cloth from the pot. "Stay on the back roads. Out of sight."

"What about when we get to Nokhor Khat?" Papa says. "There will be soldiers at the gates."

Gingerly, I take the hot fabric, letting it cool for a moment. Then I peel away Leo's bloodstained bandage and squeeze the clean cloth out over the wound. Red water drips across the skin and through the bamboo flooring; Leo grits his teeth but makes no sound. "We could split up," I muse. "The poster doesn't mention you, Papa. They're less likely to recognize us if you and I go together, and Leo goes with Maman."

"It could work," he says slowly. "But what about the roulotte?"

My hand stills as I consider it. The description is unmistakable—and I have never seen another roulotte like ours. Papa built it himself, along with his brother, when they were both young and had just begun to tour. They carved and painted each frieze with their own hands.

There is a silence in the room. Maman lifts another strip

of cloth from the bubbling pot, letting steam rise toward the ceiling. The water drips and drops from the fabric. I take the cloth in my hand—hot enough to redden the skin of my palm.

Finally Papa answers his own question. "We have to leave it behind."

Leo's eyes spring open, and I lift my head quickly. "Papa—"

"We would have had to leave it at the dock, anyway. We can pack the best fantouches on Lani's back," he says gruffly. "That's all we'll really need. The fantouches and the instruments and each other."

Across the fire, Maman nods slowly, and though the thought hurts, I know Papa is right. Gently I dab at Leo's wound, but in my mind, I am making an inventory. What we have to bring, and many more things that we'll have to leave. But then Leo pushes himself up on one elbow, shaking his head. "No. No, we'll find a way to bring it with us."

Papa smiles gently. "I'm open to suggestions."

"A secret entrance?" I say, hopeful, but Leo makes a face. "A lava tunnel under the city?"

"If there is, I don't know about it," he says, but Maman looks to Papa, and there is a soft silence between them—

like the pause before a nervous actor says her line.

"Maman," I start, but she shakes her head.

"It's not wide enough for the wagon!"

"A hidden route?" Leo's face is eager. "You have to show me."

"I'm not going back there," she says, her face ashen. "I'm never going back."

"Then tell me and I'll go," he says, trying to sit up. I push him back down as fresh blood flows from the cut on his chest. "The location could be worth hundreds. Thousands—"

With a clatter, Maman throws down the chopsticks, pushing back from the fire and starting toward the other room. Leo looks to Papa, but Papa shakes his head; in his eyes, a warning. "Money doesn't solve as many problems as you think."

"Maybe not," Leo says. "But Jetta will be safest if she can avoid the soldiers at the gate. They don't take money, either."

Though Maman doesn't stop, she falters as she passes through the curtain. Papa gives him a long look. "We all need some rest," Papa says. "Let's talk about it when we wake."

Before Leo can say anything else, Papa follows Maman, leaving us by the fire in a strange and fragile silence. I can hear Maman whispering behind the curtain, her voice strangled, as though her words are trying to escape, as though she cannot catch her breath. But Leo turns to me. "How does your mother know a hidden route out of Nokhor Khat?"

"I'm not sure," I tell him, though my own imagination is aflame. I know so little about her past, and she had no family for me to ask—no sisters, no mother. Strange in our village, though not unheard of—not after the fighting that lead to La Victoire. But what if she wasn't from the village? What if she'd left her own family behind in Nokhor Khat? Leo is still watching me. To cover for my racing thoughts, I pass him the morning-glory tea, dark and bitter. "Drink up," I say, dabbing at the wound with the last warm cloth.

He takes a quick swallow and wrinkles his nose. "Ugh."

"The worse it tastes, the better you'll feel." I chew my lip, watching as he drinks, waiting for the tension to ease from his brow, for his breathing to slow. It only takes a few more sips. The tea is strong.

I pick up Maman's chopsticks as he takes the last draft; delicately, I close them around the needle and dunk it into the boiling water. "Could we disguise the roulotte?" I murmur, half to myself. "Paint it, maybe?"

"That won't fool anyone," Leo mutters into his empty cup. "They'll be searching every wagon—especially one with so many carvings."

"What if the rest of us went through the gate separately?" I say, lifting out the needle. "We could send Papa on ahead with the roulotte. Even if they search it, they won't find us."

"That won't work," Leo says, chewing his lip, but I frown. "Why not?"

His eyes slide away from mine. "We could do so much with a secret route into the city."

I let the needle drip into the pot. "You didn't answer my question."

Leo sets down the cup. In the silence, steam rises to the ceiling. A soul glimmers in the thatch overhead. I thread the needle with a length of undyed thread. No explanation comes. What is he hiding? Or is it only the blood loss, the long night, the village, the tea? "How's the pain?"

"Less."

"Do you want to wait a while?"

Leo shakes his head and leans back, adjusting the pillow of his jacket. As he does, the gleam of metal catches my eye—the silver cigarette box, peeking out of the pocket. "Best get it over with," he says, closing his eyes.

Putting the case out of my mind, I lean over his chest and start to sew. He tenses when I put my hand on his skin, to hold the wound closed, and again when the needle touches his flesh, but he suffers in silence, breathing deeply. At first I too struggle for calm—for focus. But as I sew, taking care to keep the stitching neat and straight and the edges even, my heart slows and I relax. It is no different than other fine work—except that I can feel his blood on my hands, his pulse under my fingers. As I tie the last knot, I glance up and see that his eyes are no longer closed. Carefully I cut the thread close to the skin. "Are you all right?"

He takes a slow breath, and when he speaks, his voice is thoughtful—dreamy. "You're the expert. You tell me."

"I think you'll live," I say with a smile. But he shifts his head, looking down at the wound with a grimace.

"I feel like I could use a little more paint and polish," he says, and I laugh.

"It's a bit more serious than paint can fix."

"Sequins, then? Glitter?"

"Rhinestones, maybe."

"That bad?"

"Might be best to scrap you. Start over."

"If you do, build me better next time." He gives me

a wan smile—there is such sadness in his face. I reach out to put my hand on his arm; his other hand comes up to cover mine. It is tacky with blood and grime, but I do not pull away, not for a long while, not until his breathing is slow and easy. And as he sleeps, the fire burns low, but the light still gleams on the corner of the silver cigarette box.

What's inside your violin case?

A violin.

But I have never seen Leo smoking.

So I slip the case out of his jacket pocket with my free hand, and slowly, gently, snap it open. Inside—no cigarettes. But there is a piece of paper, folded in thirds, then in half. This must be what he is smuggling.

My mind races through the possibilities. Secret plans for the next rebel attack? A map of the locations of armée camps or ammunition? A schematic for a new weapon? Gingerly, I unfold the page, making sure it doesn't crinkle, but the paper is worn and soft, as though it's been read many times, and when I tip it toward the dying light, I see it is a letter.

Dearest Leonin, it begins, in the precise, delicate hand of a lady. *I was so saddened to hear of your mother's death, and so is our father, though he'll never admit it. And yes, I say "our father," for you are my brother always, no matter what he says. . . .*

My stomach flips; shame chases my eyes from the page. Hurriedly, I fold the letter and tuck it back into the case, sliding the whole thing under his jacket. After all he's done—the risks he's taken, the knowledge he's shared, from the first day outside the theater when he opened his door to us. What is wrong with me?

With a sigh, I pull my hand free of his, but when I move, he stirs. "Where are you going?" he murmurs, eyelids fluttering open. I can't meet his gaze.

"I need to get more betel," I say, hoping the dark hides the flush on my cheeks. "Make a fresh bandage."

To my surprise, he struggles up to his feet, searching his jacket for the gun. The cigarette case clatters to the floor; he grabs for it, but he is still wobbly from the tea, and it takes him two tries before he picks it up and tucks it back into the pocket. "You can't go alone."

I want to protest—then again, I did not know who might be lingering outside. And though I'd used the leaves as an excuse, it wasn't a lie. He did need a new bandage. So I peek through the curtain at my parents; they are lying together on the makeshift bed. At first I think they are sleeping, but then I see Maman's eyes, glinting in the glow of the firelight. "I'm just going to the garden," I say, and she nods a little. By the time I turn back, Leo is waiting by the door.

I glance outside, but the clearing is empty save for Lani. Aside from the call of the birds, the jungle is quiet. Over the tree line, the rising sun is chasing away the shadows. So I step outside into the morning light, Leo right behind me. His hand is on his gun, but his steps are slow, tentative, and his focus is not on the trees, but on the roulotte. I do not know how well he could defend us, if he had to, but no one rushes from the jungle or bursts from behind the house as I make my way through the kitchen garden.

Past waving stalks of chive and the feathery fronds of carrots, there is a bamboo trellis sewn with a bright green betel vine. I pluck a handful of leaves and turn back to Leo, but he's still staring at the roulotte, his eyes like glass.

"We have to find the secret route," he murmurs, almost to himself. His words are slurred . . . his guard is down.

"Why is it so important to you, Leo?"

Emotions cross his face—shame, fear, frustration. "Can I tell you something?"

A knot forms in my stomach. "You'd better."

Leo hesitates a moment longer. Then he beckons. I follow him to the side of the roulotte, where he kneels in the grass. I lean down, following his finger as he points between the wheels. Then I gasp. Beside the new axle, a dozen rifles are strapped to the bottom of the roulotte.

Dearest Leonin,

I was so saddened to hear of your mother's death, and so is our father, though he'll never admit it. And yes, I say "our father," for you are my brother always, no matter what he says.

But perhaps you will say I'm only making his excuses. I found your letter on his desk. I know you blame him. You may blame me too, for not insisting he send Mei to Aquitan to take the cure there. You aren't wrong. I regret it too, with the perfect certainty of hindsight.

Of course my own regrets are unimportant . . . but I cannot sleep at night for trying to find something to do, something to ease your pain or honor her life. She was a beautiful person, a bright star—she shone on stage with a light of her own. At the very least, I will not forget her.

And if there is anything you need, any help I can give, any favor you ask, tell me and you shall have it.

Your sister,

Theodora

CHAPTER
SEVENTEEN

I straighten up so fast I nearly hit my head on Leo's chin. Then I shove him, hard, my hands connecting with his bare stomach. "I trusted you!"

Leo staggers backward, losing his balance, one hand out as though to defend himself—his actions. But when he straightens up, it's there in his bleary eyes: the apology. "I took the rifles the night we met," he says quietly. "The night of the explosion. I was supposed to send them south from Luda with the rebels after the dust settled. But the general had other plans for the Tiger's men."

There is regret on his face—it tugs at my heart, but I

ignore it. My mind races, trying to put it all together. "You had the mechanic put them under the wagon," I mutter. Then my eyes narrow. "You brought them out in Cheeky's linen box! And you had the nerve to ask me what I had done?"

"I had to get the guns out of the theater! I was afraid the soldiers would search the place," Leo says, desperate. "They were supposed to run toward the explosion, not wait at my door while you drove my couriers into their hands!"

"You said you weren't a rebel!"

"I'm not," he says wearily. "I only made a deal—"

"A deal with the rebels!"

"A deal to keep the girls safe!" Leo's cheeks are flushed, his eyes wild. He runs a hand through his hair. In his other hand, the gun gleams as he gestures. Is it a threat? "Look, cher. Everyone knows the Tiger is coming south. Everyone also knows who my father is, and that the girls have made quite a bit of money from the soldiers. But the rebels swore they'd overlook it all if I only did them this favor. And I would do *anything* to protect the girls!"

"Anything?" I can't help it—my eyes cut to the gun. I don't think he'd shoot us to take the wagon . . . but I never imagined he'd strapped guns beneath the axle, either.

But Leo's face falls. "You think so little of me?"

"I don't know what to think."

With a grimace, he opens the chamber and tips the bullets out into his hand. The tightness in my chest eases. "I have money," he says softly, but I shake my head.

"Money won't buy our way out of prison. And you said it yourself, they'll be giving the wagons extra scrutiny. They'll find the guns in a search."

"Then the secret route."

"Maman said the wagon won't fit through the passage, and you can't carry a dozen rifles by yourself."

"You could help me carry them."

"And risk my life?"

Leo grits his teeth, rolling the bullets across his palm—six of them. Most of them are only casings, I can see now. "I could get you a place on the boat to Aquitan."

There is silence in the clearing, so long that a bird nearby starts to call. I watch Leo; he sounds so earnest—but he has fooled me before. "You're lying."

"I never lied," he says, but at my look, he drops his eyes. "I . . . may have kept things from you. But I've never gone back on a deal."

I bite my lip, thinking it over—but this, at least, was

true. And it isn't so unbelievable that Leo Legarde would have a way aboard the ship where his sister will spend her honeymoon. "What about the recherche? There are bound to be soldiers on the boat."

"The wagon is the real problem. Cover your scar and that description could be of a thousand other girls. You can use a different name. And no one will suspect a wanted criminal to be La Fleur's special guest. Is it a deal?" He tucks his gun into his belt and holds out his hand, Aquitan style. "You help me bring the rifles through the passage, and I'll get you a place aboard *Le Rêve*."

I look into his eyes, hoping for a sense of clarity. All I see is his own apprehension; he needs my help at least as much as I need his. "It's a deal," I say, and the relief on his face is like the dawn breaking.

We shake, once. The copper casings jingle like bells in his other fist. "How are you going to convince Meliss?" he says, and I sigh.

"Because it's the only way."

"I know that feeling." He turns my hand over and pours the empty shells into my palm. "These should work for rivets, by the way."

"Rivets?" It takes me a moment to understand what he's

talking about. Was it only yesterday he held my work in his hands and called it beautiful? I close my fingers over the metal, still warm. What else he could want in exchange?

Before I can ask, the door opens, and Maman peeks out at me, worry written all over her face. "What's taking you so long?"

"Just checking on Lani," I call back. Under my breath, I murmur to Leo. "I'll talk to her. You take the guns off the roulotte. Hide them in the jungle till we can figure out a better place. And then get some more betel leaves," I add—I had dropped the others in my surprise. "You can make your own bandage this time."

To his credit, he barely makes a face; he only nods and turns back to the roulotte as I follow Maman inside. It is warmer in the hut, almost cozy, and for a moment, my heart aches for our little cottage back in the valley. But this is not home, nor is Lak Na. Not anymore. I take a breath, trying to figure out what to say to Maman about the passage—how to phrase the request. But as she shuts the door behind me, I see a scrap of paper in her hand. It's the wanted poster, dry now, and stiff from being near the fire. But the back is covered with markings—dark lines made with a charred stick. "I spoke with your father," she says softly. "Leo was right."

"About what?"

"The soldiers are looking for you. And if they find you . . ." She sighs, leaving the rest unsaid; my imagination is worse than her words. "Papa and I will travel through the gates, but you and Leo . . ." She shakes her head. "I can't go back there, but you have to."

Gingerly, I take the paper from her hand; it is a map, crudely drawn—a winding tunnel, a cavern, a stairway. "Back where, Maman?"

She takes a breath. She wets her lips. She lowers her voice. "To Hell."

"Maman—"

"There is a path," she says, her voice no louder than a whisper. "From the temple grounds to the middens. Outside the city. Where the dung carts haul the trash."

I chew my lip. Her words are innocuous, but her voice . . . her face. "The path comes up inside?"

"To the gardens between the temple and the Ruby Palace," she says, her voice shaking. "At least, it did sixteen years ago. You'll have to be careful. The temple is a prison now, remember? There will be guards nearby, and maybe worse, depending."

"Worse?"

"Fallen monks. Restless souls. His disciples."

"Disciples?" The question is on the tip of my tongue—about the woman we met in the temple. Had Maman known that monks still brought offerings to the gods? "I thought Le . . . I thought all the monks in Nokhor Khat were killed."

"They were," she says, but the fact doesn't seem to soothe her fear. I look down at the map, then up into her eyes.

"How do you know about this passage, Maman?"

She opens her mouth, but it takes her a long time to let the words past her teeth. "I lived there, Jetta. When I was only a little older than you."

"You lived in Hell's Court?" I blink at her. "You were there before Le Trépas was imprisoned?"

"Don't!" She raises her hand to my lips; I press them together, but my eyes are wide. She must have seen him, known him. A monster, out of legend, when he was still roaming free with death at the tips of his fingers. No wonder she hated his name.

Then my brow furrows—Maman has no tattoos. "You weren't a monk. What were you doing there?"

"I told you, Jetta. I'm not going back. Not even in my memory." She turns away, slipping back into her room, but

I am already putting things together. The only people who lived in the temple were the monks and the brides.

For Le Trépas kept a court, like any man who styled himself a king. Another break with what was holy: he had wives in his temple—though he never kept his children. People say he killed them for their souls.

My hands are shaking. Sixteen years ago, she'd said. She left the temple just around the time I was born. But Akra is three years older than I am. He has Papa's eyes, his chin, his nose. And Papa was never a monk.

Alone in the room, I sink down by the remains of the fire. The soul of the kitten climbs into my lap, and we both watch the embers for a while. My mind is its own shifting hellscape. So many questions, but so much more makes sense. The souls . . . the magic . . . the malheur. But what of the shadow plays? The work and the art? The joy of the stage, the things Papa taught me—were they ever mine to share in?

Behind me, the floor creaks. Papa comes to sit beside me, as though I have summoned him. A thousand questions flit through my head, but at heart they are all the same—the one I asked Maman. What am I? But Papa has never been at a loss for words. "Blood may matter to the spirits. But what we share is even better."

My words come slowly. "And what is that?"

"We share history," he says. "We share tradition. We share years and memories and everything that makes a family."

"But not blood."

"What is blood?" he says with a gentle smile. "We share a heart."

I can hear it—my heartbeat, and the blood rushing in my ears. The blood that draws the spirits near. The blood that brings them back to life, the blood that sang in my veins when I considered killing a man. Who else shares it?

What am I?

I do not ask—Papa doesn't know, not truly. The fire crackles before us, the charred wood collapses inward on itself, the coals glow and fade. Finally he pushes himself to his feet with a groan. "Come," he says. "Let's go unpack the roulotte."

I follow him outside, and we spend the rest of the day sorting through our possessions. I throw myself into the hard choices—what to leave, what to take—and ignore the part of me that says that none of it is truly mine. It is easier to run my hands over silk and leather, paint and paper, than it is to wrap my mind around this new truth. So I pore over each item, savoring each memory as a past I never knew casts shadows in my head.

My third-best costume is a given—or my best, now that the first is torn and ashen and the second stained with blood. Maman had bought the fabric for it toward the end of our first season using souls in fantouches, just as our fame had begun to spread. We'd spent hours sewing together—unused to working with so much fine silk. And here—the little lighter my brother left me, to light the fires for our shadow plays. The letters he sent us, all seven of them. My makeup: bone black and lucky red. Our money, so hard earned.

Papa makes Leo a gift of a shirt and a pair of trousers. Maman packs the instruments and the old linen scrim; our silk one is still back at La Perl. The fantouches are more difficult—we have nearly fifty, and though they are light, many are bulky. We can't bring them all. But which ones?

I dither for a long time—packing is delicious distraction—but the wisest choice is to start with the ones that would cost the most to replace, the biggest puppets, the most colorful. The Tiger, the Peacock, the King of Death, the Flame. And of course my dragon. It may be untested, unfinished, but it is beautiful, and too expensive to burn.

So I take up my hammer and the copper casings and set to work piecing it together. When I am through, I wrap it along with half a dozen other fantouches, making lumpy parcels topped with canvas to keep out the rain. At first, they writhe, protesting being packed so tightly, but I whisper as I load them onto Lani's back. *Be still, be still.*

I could bring more with me if I wasn't going to carry the rifles. But I keep my parents talking in the hut while Leo makes up our packs, with clothes and bedding wrapped around the weapons.

Everything else, we leave in the back of the roulotte, which is where we build the pyre.

Papa sings as he works, dragging old branches from the jungle, pulling bark into kindling, but though his voice is strong and brash, his smile wouldn't fool a discerning audience. Still, Maman and I pretend along with him, and since the instruments are packed, we sing too. My voice is rough, untrained. Between the two of us, Akra was always the better singer. Still, I know the harmonies, and for a moment . . . sefondre. We have come together.

But Leo is standing a bit apart, and he does not pretend. After all, he has the least to lose. "Why?" he says. "Why not just leave it all here for someone else to find?"

"It's tradition," I say, and it's not truly a lie: in our village, we burn the dead. "These fantouches belong to my family—to my ancestors. If we can't use them, no one else should."

He grits his teeth, but he doesn't argue. I am grateful. It pains me far more than it does him—but I know the story of the third brother. It would be so much worse to condemn these souls to rot in their skins. Then, as I toy with the lighter, I remember how I'd tucked the soul of the kitten into the page for safekeeping. Do I truly have to leave them all behind?

There, under the branches and the dry leaves: the rest of the flyers—the ones we were going to use in Luda. I pull out the stack and set it beside me as Papa lights the kindling. The fire starts slow, tentative, but soon enough the paint of the roulotte starts to bubble, and the carvings to char. All the work—months, years—all that's left of our touring, all that's left of my uncle. Papa has stopped singing, but his lips still move in a silent prayer before he turns to go back into the cottage.

Maman and Leo follow, but I can't go—not yet. Through the open door, I watch for the fantouches to burn.

As the souls drift free with the bright embers, I draw each of them into a slip of paper. A pangolin freed from the leather puppet of the Swine, my hummingbirds from the two lovers, the old dog from the roulotte itself. The sweet scent of sandalwood weaves through the char of burning leather as it all falls to coal and ash. And as the pages fill with souls, I bind them with a ribbon—a collection to carry with me across the sea. The pages stir gently; anyone watching might think it was only the hot wind of the blaze. It wraps around me, smoky warmth, and dries the tears as they fall.

By dawn, I am exhausted, and the fire is too. The lingering wisps of smoke will not stand out, not now. As sunlight shines over the trees and raises the steam from the greenery, the little kitten approaches. My surprise is a distant emotion beneath the bone-deep weariness, but I smile when she makes a half-hearted attempt to bat at the pages.

She is as pale and wan as I feel—is it already three days since I freed her from the flyer? "Why haven't you gone to a temple?" I say to her, but she only paces around the book.

I look for more pages, but I've burned the ones I haven't used. Suddenly, fresh tears spring to my eyes. I dash them away. Ridiculous, isn't it? After all I've let go? But when she puts a paw on my knee, I know I can't just let her fade away.

Where to put her? A leaf? A scrap of cloth? Somehow I

can't bring myself to offer her such a crude skin. But I have one fantouche left unsouled, don't I?

It is the matter of a moment to find my dragon in the packs—it is so large, it is hard to miss. A drop of blood, and the kitten has her claws in the leather. In a flash of light, the whole pack rustles with new life, but I rest my hand on the leather, and whisper to her. *Be still.*

She does—but now I am uneasy. The largest, most expensive fantouche I have ever made now houses the soul of a kitten. What is wrong with me?

But I already know that, don't I?

And then Maman's voice drifts to me from the cottage, along with the smell of breakfast cooking. I go inside and throw myself down beside the fire to sleep. But too soon, the food is ready, and after we eat, we grab our packs and leave the rest behind, taking the winding jungle track to the main road.

We move slowly south toward Nokhor Khat, past twisted falls of strangler figs where parrotlets scream at lemurs over ripe fruit, and stands of wild taro where raindrops pool like diamonds on the bright blue leaves. The road is never empty. There are always people traveling—farmers to market, performers to shows, armée soldiers on the march, or horsemen carrying messages. But passing from the jungle into the valley, where fields of cane whisper in the wind, we fall in with a different sort of traveler. Wagons loaded not with eggs or fruit, but with possessions, furniture, family. Grandmothers and grandfathers, riding in vegetable carts, children in their laps, nestled among their effects.

My family has traveled every year for as long as I remember; when we left home for good, we knew what we'd need to take, and what we'd have to leave behind. But these people—they have brought everything they could carry. Not just the everyday necessities like cooking pots and changes of clothes, but the fine things they couldn't bear to let go. Fancy porcelain tea sets tucked into bamboo boxes, a copper washtub large enough to sit in, an Aquitan sewing machine on a wrought-iron base. Beautiful things, heavy things—like all reminders of home.

The first few groups we see, Papa stops to ask them why they're on the move, but none of them agree. Many mention Dar Som, but some of them speak of rebels too. They give reports of blue-eyed demons—but do they mean n'akela, or foreign soldiers? They say they know of people who disappeared into the jungle and never came back—certainly the Tiger. Or perhaps the armée. No one knows anything, but everyone is sure of something, and they're getting out before it's too late. And though fear is invisible, there is a weight and size to it; it wraps round our necks, it drags at our feet, it sits on our backs like a sin, making every step a journey.

But all we can do is carry on. Toward the walls of the capital, the fort at Nokhor Khat, the docks at the edge of our country. Toward the certainty that what lies ahead cannot be worse than what we've left behind.

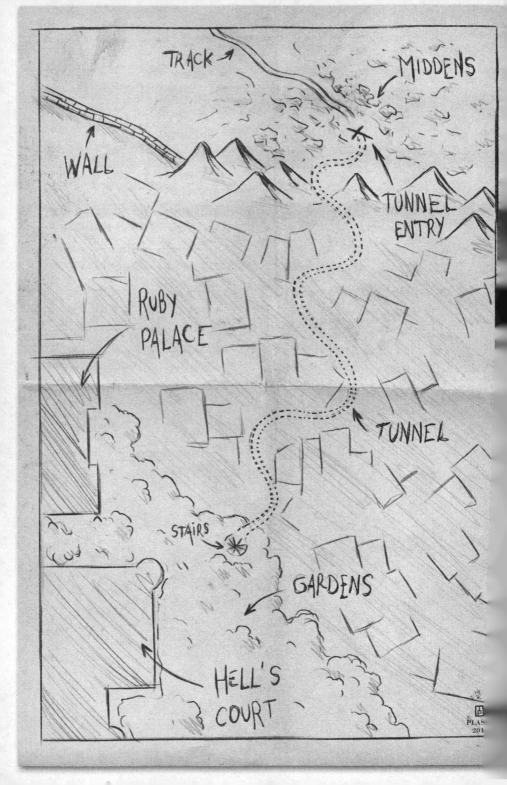

CHAPTER

EIGHTEEN

I can smell the midden long before I see it. At first it is just a hint of rot, the touch of decay—though still far too familiar after Dar Som. But as we trudge on and the afternoon lengthens, the scent swells like a poisonous mushroom, like a tumor. By the time we reach the fork in the road, where refuse wagons from the capital turn off the main route and trundle into the jungle, the taste of putrescence is sticking to the back of my throat.

We left my parents at the crossroad; they continued toward the long lines and the shantytowns outside the city gates while Leo and I waited for a dung cart to pass us on the track. Now we're trudging after it. My feet ache, and my shoulders are red under the weight of the guns. Another early rain has left the road muddy and the air thick with steam. I hope for a cool breath as the green tunnel closes in above us, but it only traps the putrid humidity.

The cart moves slowly, pulled by a Chakran man under a wide-brimmed hat. His shovel and broom are thrown over the detritus piled high on the wagon—horse dung and rotting vegetables and the fly-specked carcass of a dead dog. It was a fine animal once, with a wide jaw and muscular shoulders, the sort the Aquitan aristocracy use for hunting. Now just another bit of trash.

"Walk slower," Leo says. "The smell of that dog is about to knock me off my feet."

"But the slower we walk, the longer we're here," I say, and he makes a face.

"Good point."

So we plod after the cart, but when we pass a rumdal tree, I pluck a handful of blossoms, tucking one beside my ear and holding another up to my nose. Leo takes one and does the same, but it does little good. The smell only intensifies as we walk, until at last, we emerge again into the hot sun and a swarm of flies, both living and dead.

The midden is in a massive clearing at the base of the caldera—a swampy, stony field where instead of rice or sugar, the refuse of the city has been sown. Broken things, dead animals, waste, and detritus. And more souls than I expected. Things die here. Rats by the dozens; I might have guessed about those. But other things too—a handful of kittens, playing with the ties of the bag they were discarded in. Gulls and vultures, picking over the heaps just like their living comrades. Even a n'akela— cold fire—walking round the edge of the clearing. I try and fail to suppress a shudder. What must its death have been, here in the middens?

The street sweeper doesn't stop to watch them, of course. He only trundles along a path that skirts the trees—the heaps near the main road are piled too high to climb. But when he peels off toward a collapsing mass midway along the glade, Leo and I continue on the little road.

We are not the only others here. People roam through the hazy air, through the clouds of insects, picking over the piles. Scavengers dressed in rags, some with long sleeves that make me wonder what's beneath. I reach up to adjust my own shawl over the scar on my shoulder. These people are thin, desperate, but not dangerous. They keep their heads down as we pass, never meeting my eyes.

As we walk, the piles get smaller and older—bones instead of bodies, dirt more than decay. At last the clearing ends in a scattering of gray trunks and green vines climbing steeply up the side of the caldera that borders the city. As we step through the scraggly jungle, I see the rocky outcrop Maman told me to look for: a black pile of stone streaked with guano and sewn with thick roots.

The passage is there somewhere—a slender crack in the slab, leading beneath the city. I scan the stone, looking for the entrance, then stumble over a rounded rock. Unbalanced by the heavy pack, I fall to my knees with a grunt.

"Are you all right?" Leo takes my arm, helping me up. My stubbed toe stings, but I nod, glaring at the earth. Then my frown softens. There, in the grass, the stone that tripped me. Not a worn chunk of lava rock, but something smooth, the size of a cat. Carefully I lean down to look closer. Brushing back the leaves, I reveal a familiar sign carved into the rock—the stroke and the dot, like the sun rising: life.

A chill takes me; I step back. Leo furrows his brow. "What is this?" he asks.

"It looks like a grave." Now that I'm looking for them, I can see stones dotting the earth—tucked between roots, peeking from under fallen leaves.

He follows my gaze. "So many."

"And so small." I turn back to look at the middens—the trash heaps, the refuse of the city. Beside it, the tiny graves, just outside the tunnel that leads to the temple. With a sick feeling in my stomach, I realize why Maman knew about the path. Swallowing bile, I try to keep my voice steady. "Leo . . . what do you know about Le Trépas?"

His face twists. "Enough."

"Did you ever hear the stories about his brides?"

"That's a nice word for it," he mutters. "I heard they were girls from the street. He'd give them food and shelter and money. In return all he wanted was the souls of their children." Leo's voice falters; he glances around the clearing again. "Though maybe they weren't just stories."

His words settle like ashes around my head. "Do you think they knew?"

"The girls? No." His voice is firm. "How could they?"

"How could they miss it?" I cry, suddenly shouting. In the trees above, a pair of pigeons startles, taking flight. "How could they not know, with a man like him?"

"Men like him never tell the truth about what they're really offering." Leo's jaw clenches; he speaks through his teeth. "And even if some of them suspected . . . Jetta. You know what it is to be hungry. And desperate. And to gamble on paying a price later for survival now."

There is truth in his words, but I don't want to admit it. So I turn and start toward the cleft in the rock, but Leo reaches out and grabs my arm. "Jetta, wait."

"What?"

"You're angry and I don't know why. I . . ." He takes a deep breath and lets go of my arm, but I don't try to leave again. "I don't know if it's a mood, or something I can fix."

I stiffen—how casually he mentions my malheur. "It's not your responsibility to fix me, Leo."

"I know, but I . . ." He smiles a little, awkwardly, and taps his chest, still bandaged under the shirt Papa gave him. "I'm just trying to pay a debt."

I hesitate, remembering what else is there under the bandage—his tattoo, his sin. Life. What debt is he truly trying to repay? And all of these stones in the clearing, marked with the same symbol—graves for those whose only sin was being born. My sin too, but I survived. Maybe that's why I'm cursed. Is there any freedom in bearing your marks? In telling the world?

Or if not the world, then the ones who will listen?

"I know how Maman knew about the passage," I say at last, nodding to the cleft in the rock. "She lived in Hell's Court before she met Papa. She escaped during La Victoire. I was newly born at the time."

Leo takes a deep breath, digesting the words. Overhead, the leaves rustle in a rare breeze. At last he takes the white flower from his pocket and drops it on the grave at his feet. "I'm glad you both got out. So many others didn't."

I gape at him. "That's not the point."

"Then what is?"

"Le Trépas is my . . ." I trail off—I don't want to finish the sentence. But Leo only smiles a little.

"You forget who you're talking to."

"Legarde isn't evil," I say, and his smile falls away.

"You weren't the one who found my mother." Leo sighs. "These men—they are nothing. Your real father—he's a kind man. A good one. He loves you. You love him."

"But this . . . thing I've inherited." I clench my fists in the fabric of my sarong, as though I could reach inside my own flesh and pull out the offending parts of me. "It's his. It must be."

"Your madness?" Leo quirks an eyebrow—and though that is not what I meant, I cannot correct him. "Madness doesn't make you good or evil. Actions do. And those are all your own."

"I know," I say, but it is small comfort. I cannot stop thinking of my actions—of watching Jian writhe on the ground, of giving Eduard over to the vengeful dead. The way power felt—like sugar on my tongue. But Leo only frowns, and glances through the trees.

"We should go," he says softly, and something about his tone raises the hair on the back of my neck.

"What's wrong?"

"I don't know," he says, no louder than a whisper. "But it just got very quiet."

I blink—but he's right. No longer do the birds call, or the rats rustle. I glance around the clearing, but all I see are little souls drifting. Then I frown. The n'akela is here too, standing at the edge of the trees. Had it followed us across the middens? And if so, what does it want? I wet my lips, recalling Maman's words. Fallen monks, restless souls. "Let's go."

His only reply is a curt nod. Adjusting the pack on my shoulders, I stride toward the rocks. Leo follows close behind, his hand on his gun. Here, the tunnel, where a cold wind sighs between stone lips like Death's whisper. I slip through, into the dark. Maman had walked out this way at least once.

Had she ever walked back in empty-handed?

"Wait. Jetta." Behind me, I hear Leo fumbling with the lantern—I had forgotten the pretext of needing light. When he catches up to me, the lamp makes my shadow dance on the rocky wall: a girl and her burden in the shadows. But before I can start off again, he takes my arm. "Stay still."

"Why?"

"Shh."

Gritting my teeth, I wait as he listens, but there is only the sound of the wind in the tunnel. As last he shakes his head.

"Nothing."

He sounds relieved, but it doesn't ease my fears. Souls make no sound. And is that a light, coming down the tunnel, or just the movement of our shadows? "Come on," I say, starting off again.

Ducking through the narrow passage, we wind our way into the cool earth. The map trembles in my hand; I read its lines by the light of the dead. The volcanic rock of the tunnel is rounded and rippled, like the great throat of some stone beast. Here and there, patches of obsidian line the walls, black and glassy as water in a midnight pond, catching the dim shades of our reflections. Ahead comes the soft rush of wings: bats, mostly likely. Their souls hang from the top of the tunnel like lamps.

And behind us? Still no sound, and the light from Leo's lamp makes it hard to tell if anything is coming. "Did you hear something?" he says then, and I tense.

"No, did you?"

"No, but you keep looking back."

"It's nothing," I say, praying it's the truth. Why would a n'akela follow us? And even if it caught up, what could it do? I brush my fear away—it is only paranoia, the sight of the graves, the dark oppression of the tunnel. I take a deep breath to try to clear my head, but is that a whiff of rot on my tongue? It must be the clinging smell of the middens, nothing more.

Crouching under bulky crags, plashing through milky puddles, we make our way through the earth, but the smell of decay only gets stronger. When we reach the end of the tunnel, I see why. The map has led us to the bottom of a damp well, gouged from the earth by human hands. Stairs circle the side, climbing upward into the gloom. But at their base, lying on the muddy ground, is the graying body of a dead man.

Startled, I whirl, but there is no one else here—no lurking murderer, ready to strike. And by the smell, the body has been here a while. There is no soul attending, no spark in this dank hole aside from the lantern, and the souls of the bats spiraling above.

"What happened to him?" Leo says, his voice muffled. He has brought his sleeve up over his mouth, breathing through the cloth of his jacket. With his other hand, he holds the lantern out, though he stays near the wall, away from the body.

"You check, if you're so curious." Still, I can't help but stare. There is no clear sign of death—no bullet wound, no cut throat—though there is a mark on the man's forehead. A familiar symbol. The dot and the line. Life.

A chill takes me, deeper than the cold of the tunnel:

fallen monks, restless souls—or disciples. How had this man died? Had someone marked him like I had marked Eduard? Were there others like me, who could tuck a wandering soul into a skin?

It is a mystery I have no desire to solve. Gingerly, I step around the body to the coiling stairway ringing the well. Then I curse. It ends in a metal grille, far above. The souls of bats fly through, spiraling into the sky.

Leo follows me, squinting. In the low light of the lamp, can he see the grate? "I don't think Maman knew about the bars," I tell him.

He shifts the pack on his shoulders. "Maybe we can find a way to get them open. If all else fails, I can go back and make my way here, aboveground. Try to open it from the outside."

"If you think I'm staying here overnight, alone with a corpse, you're the crazy one." I glance back at him, to give him a look, but then, out of the corner of my eye, I see a flicker of blue.

The n'akela. It's followed us all this way. At my gasp, Leo whirls—but how can I explain what I'm seeing? Then, like a shadow, a massive dog appears just behind the soul, and this, we both can see. The smell hits me a moment before the realization does: I recognize it from the dung cart, fly specked and thick shouldered.

"Mon dieu." Leo's whisper echoes in the well as the mastiff pulls black lips from yellow teeth. "I thought that thing was dead!"

It was—I'm sure of it—but I cannot tell him so. I can barely comprehend it myself. New life in a dead body? Then again, isn't that what I do? The difference is I paint the skins first.

A wave of revulsion overtakes me as the dog steps closer. But as Leo fumbles for his gun, I cover his hand with mine. "There might be guards above," I say, nodding to the grate. Then a low growl rattles like gravel in the dog's throat. Leo shrugs me off.

"I'm more concerned about what's down here," he murmurs through his teeth. But how can you kill what's already dead? The answer comes after another moment: fire. So before he can shoot, I snatch the lantern from Leo's other hand and hurl it at the animal.

The glass breaks at the dog's feet in a shower of burning oil; the creature yelps, wreathed in flame, and flees down the tunnel, the firelight fading as it goes. Only I can see the blue blaze of the n'akela as it crosses to the corpse lying at the stairs and crawls inside as though it is a suit of skin.

A flash of soullight, and the dead man opens his milky

eyes. I gasp, the scent of death sour in my throat.

"What is it?" Leo says, his own eyes wide as he casts about in the sudden blackness. What can I say? Never show, never tell. But I am still reeling. I have never seen a soul take a body without my help—my blood. Now I know why Maman was not assuaged by the thought that all Le Trépas's monks had been killed in La Victoire.

Had they leaped from body to body for the last sixteen years? There is no shortage of bodies in Chakrana. I clear my throat, trying to steady my voice. "Up the stairs, Leo. Check the grate."

But in the dark, the dead man laughs. "Light or no, I can smell your blood, my sister."

At the word, I go cold. Sister? But Leo jerks his gun toward the sound—the muzzle weaves in the air like a snake's head. *Who is that?*

"I guard the path." The body pushes itself to its feet, and turns to me. "Welcome home."

"What do you want?" I whisper.

The corpse grins—bruised lips, white teeth . . . and bright blue eyes. "You should be dead."

"Get behind me, Jetta!" Leo cocks his weapon. His hand is trembling, but the dead man does not flinch.

"Just go, Leo!" I say, pushing him up the stairs.

"Not without you!" Blindly, he reaches for my arm. The dead man does too.

Wrenching away from the both of them, I make a fist, smashing my knuckles against the rough stone wall. Then I drop to my knees at the corpse's feet. All around me, crawling souls creep closer—grubs and bugs and creatures that burrow in the earth. As the dead man's gray fingers twine in my hair, I draw a worm into his shoe. "Down," I whisper, and the vana pulls his foot into the muddy earth.

Thrown off-balance, the corpse lurches sideways. I wrench free of his grasp and scramble back toward the stairs.

"Jetta?" Leo's eyes are wide in the dark. When I take his hand, he hauls me up. But as we race up the slippery stone steps, a rasping rattle of laughter follows. It flies like the souls of the bats, up to the grate—where Leo and I stop. He puts his shoulder against the iron and heaves, but though the bars shake, they don't open.

"It's locked," Leo says, but I push him aside.

"Move." Slipping my hand through the bars, I feel along the rusted rim of the grate. My hands close around the lock: solid, heavy. Crooking my finger, I trace the symbol with my bloody knuckle. I do not see what soul slips inside, just the small flash, and I whisper, "Open."

The metal groans; the tumblers turn. I pull the lock away and toss it to the ground. Air hisses through Leo's teeth as I heave the grate wide on rusty hinges, but he says nothing as we climb up into the light. Looking back into the well, I see the dead man gazing back at me.

Before it can follow, I shut the gate behind us, and though I do not know if it will help, I lock it up tight.

We Meet by the Light of the Moon

wan-ders all a-lone at night un-der star-ry skies. Her

smile's a bro-ken pro-mise, there are se-crets in her eyes. She

slips from shade to sha-dow, and she is gone too

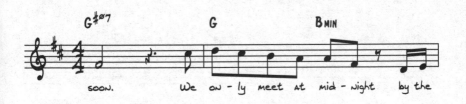

soon. We on-ly meet at mid-night by the

light of the sil-ver-y moon. She

BMIN   /A   GMAJ7   F#MIN7

will not stay past sun-rise, though my heart is hers to keep. I am

EMIN7   F#MIN7   GMAJ7   F#7

on-ly tru-ly liv-ing   while the whole world is a-sleep. We'll

BMIN   /A   GMAJ7

nev-er wake to-ge-ther, or while a - way an af-ter-

G#ø7   G   BMIN

noon.   We on-ly meet at mid-night   by the

EMIN7   F#7   BMIN

light of the sil-ver-y   moon.   By

B7   EMIN   /D

day I won-der All__ a-lone__ un-der

CMAJ7   G/B   AMIN   EMIN/G

sun-ny skies— was it the bro-ken pro-mise or the

se - crets or the lies? But ev-'ry

night I dream her back, though she is gone too

soon. We on - ly meet at mid - night by the

light of the sil - ver - y moon. We

on - ly meet at mid - night by the light of the sil - ver - y

moon. _____

CHAPTER NINETEEN

Leo and I have emerged from the earth into an overgrown garden. Ragged palms litter the scrubby grass with dried leaves; huge patches of elephant ears ripple in the breeze. Limes rot at the base of a tangled old tree, and green ponds lined with stones dot the grounds.

It must have been beautiful once, this meditation garden nestled behind the hulking stone temple: Hell's Court, they called it. Death's Palace. Now it is a prison: a dark heap of stone squatting behind the line of palms, the walls carved with demons, the openings laced with iron bars. I shudder looking at it—but it is not the legend that scares me. It is the darkness. Every other temple I've seen has glowed with the light of spirits. Hell's Court is lit only by torches.

Then again, after meeting the dead man at the bottom of the well, I can see why the other souls have abandoned this place.

Crouched behind an overgrown fall of morning glory, Leo stands so close to me I can feel him shaking. "They were dead, weren't they?" he says, his face pale. But it's not a question. I swallow.

"You saw him."

"I *smelled* him! Mon dieu, Jetta!" Leo runs his hands through his hair. "But he stood. He spoke! It was one of the old monks, wasn't it? Le Trépas's followers."

"Shh!" His voice is too loud and the name is a curse—I see it now. The stone walls of the prison would never be thick enough to hold a soul. Neither would the grate that covers the well, if it came to that. Uneasy, I reach for Leo's hand, to pull him away through the gardens, but though he wraps his fingers around mine, he won't budge. "What is it?"

"Jetta . . ." Leo swallows, the muscles in his throat working. The leaves rustle in a sultry breeze; a mosquito whines past my ear. He takes another breath. "He called you sister."

Despite the humid air in the garden, a chill settles over me. I want to explain the words away: a mockery, twisting a term of endearment. But I know it was more than that.

All my life, I'd thought Akra was my only brother. Who else should I have been praying for?

Welcome home, the corpse had said. Such an ugly thing—an evil spirit in corrupt flesh. But the n'akela had taken the dead body as easily as any of the souls I've ever commanded. No wonder Maman hated what I could do.

Leo turns to me, his face pale in the moonlight. "Are you . . ." Then he stops—shakes his head. But I can't let it go.

"Am I what? Dead? Alive? One of them?" Before he can answer, I take his fingers and press them to my throat, where my pulse pounds. Even faster now, at the warmth of his hand. He is close enough for me to hear his breath hitch.

"Are you all right, I was going to say."

"Liar."

He only shrugs. But his eyes are boring deep into mine, and he brings his thumb up to brush my chin with a touch like a feather. I barely suppress a shiver. "You saw something following us through the middens," he says.

I blink at him, releasing his hand, but he doesn't let it fall. "A premonition."

"And how did you open the lock on the grate?" he murmurs. "You had no key."

"It must have been rusted out."

Only now does he pull his hand back, but he doesn't drop his eyes. "I can't make you answer me, I know that. But we've come an awful long way since that night in Luda, when you marked Eduard's hand with your blood."

At his words, I stiffen. I want to shove my bloody hands in the folds of my sarong. Instead, I clench them into fists. "And we still have farther to go. Which way to the inn?"

For a moment, I think he will argue—but he only shakes his head. "Come on, then."

Ducking through a tangle of bougainvillea, we skirt one of the ponds. Carved stone statues seem to watch us from the tangled greenery. At the edge of the garden, a crumbled wall. Leo makes a stirrup of his hands to help me climb over, following a moment later. As we emerge from the shadows, we go from a sneak to a stroll, leaving the temple grounds behind.

There on the main road, Leo pauses to orient himself. Though we can't linger on the street, I can't help but stare.

When we used to do the circuit—was that only last year?—one of our regular stops was Monsieur Audrinne's plantation. His wife was young and beautiful and hailed from Lephare, the capital of Aquitan, the land of gold and glamour. Monsieur, on the other hand, was old and rich and lived in a back valley in Chakrana—paradise for some, but not to Madame. Naturally, she expected very fine things in return for joining him so far from what she deemed "civilization," so much of her husband's wealth went to bring civilization to her.

Players and poets, musicians and singers, all came to perform in Madame's parlor. She hosted a circus troupe from the Lion Lands on her great lawn, including a live elephant with tusks trimmed in silver leaf. Her mansion held a vast collection of paintings from artists all over the world, each canvas framed in gold.

Even before I learned about the spring's healing properties, my favorite had always been one that depicted Les Chanceux: a group of pale, languid women bathing in a hazy pool. But the biggest painting, given pride of place over the enormous mantle, was of Lephare itself, the Light of the West: steepled stone roofs and copper spires, gables and windows going on and on into the far distance, and all washed in a lovely golden dawn.

Nokhor Khat must be almost as big.

At first, all is wonder—glitter and glow. Past the rundown sector near the temple, we move through an empty market. The colorful stalls are shuttered for the day, but the square is lit with slender glass lamps and lined with grand buildings twice as tall as the tallest I've seen in Luda. The windows, also glassed, gleam with light: a clear, clean glow that must be electricity. I've heard of that strange fire without fuel, but I've never seen it before tonight.

It lights the fine buildings: upturned roofs lapped with curved tiles of blue copper in old Chakran style, entrances lined with carved scrollwork, massive doors gilded and decorated with bronze knockers in the shape of dragons—the king's symbol, here in his capital. The streets are straight and wide and so clean, patrolled by sweepers and their carts.

But despite the glamour of the city, something winds tighter in my gut as we walk. What is it? The lingering scent of decay? The threats of the dead man—or his words of welcome? Or is it the soldiers, the electric light gleaming on their black boots?

They patrol the streets more zealously than the sweepers. Each time we pass them, I'm sure my shawl will slip from my scarred shoulder. If they look too close, will they catch the shape of the rifles in our packs? My spine prickles, as though a chitinous thing with many legs is crawling down the back of my neck. Despite the weight of the guns, I walk faster and faster; by the time we reach the inn, I am practically running.

Le Livre is a long, low building glowing with light, shaped like a plantation house and oriented along the water so it catches the breeze through the shutters of the many windows. Leo leads me right to the ornate door, peeking out from under a fall of jasmine. The scent mingles with the smell of sweat and the reek of the middens still trapped in my hair. I feel too filthy to even touch the handle, but Leo barges right in with a smile.

I follow a few steps, then freeze on the threshold. The main room is huge, nearly the height of the entire building, and beautifully appointed. Enormous open doorways face the back gardens; the ceiling is studded with lazy fans ushering the fragrant breeze. Woven chairs cluster in small groups around low teak tea tables, where a handful of well-dressed men read the paper. The room is brightly lit with gas lamps, illuminating the richest sight of all: a shelf in pride of place, directly across from the front door, and all lined with books.

I've never seen so many all at once. I didn't know there were so many in the world. Some of the plantation owners kept a few—or at least, they bragged that they did, though usually the books were locked away in a study. Madame Audrinne had a prized collection of seventeen, most of which she kept in the parlor and never read, though her servants dusted them daily. But here were dozens—hundreds, maybe.

Standing in the doorway, blinking in the light, I find I can't take another step—I am not meant to be here. I do not belong. But Leo pulls me into the room, toward the bookshelf and the wide desk before it. A man sits there, slender and dignified, with black skin and a warm smile.

"Siris!" Leo calls, grinning. "Sava?"

"Sava." His voice is rich, with a soft accent—but that makes sense, and the books do too, of course. He must be from the Lion Lands, to the south and west of Chakrana. They say the countries there are rich in knowledge—that the crowns of their cities are universities. He stands to shake Leo's hand across the desk. "And you?"

"Sava," Leo replies, less enthusiastically. Then he grimaces, teetering his hand in an equivocating gesture. "Though it was comme ci, comme ça for a while."

"I heard about that." Siris's face is grave, but he gives me a small smile. "You must be Jetta. Your parents are here already.

My daughters are preparing your rooms. The baths should still be warm if you want to shed the dust of the road."

"Baths?" I'm out of breath—from the idea of such a luxury, or perhaps from the pace I'd kept through the streets. But he only waves to a girl, tall and dark as he is.

She smiles and beckons me toward a hall. "Just this way."

"I'll be happy to shed more than dust," Leo says, relieved. He shrugs off his pack, setting it on the floor carefully—I only hear the clink of metal because I'm listening for it. I follow suit as Leo flicks his eyes down, then back up to Siris. "Is there anyone around who can take our bags?"

"Certainly," Siris says smoothly, motioning to a table in the corner where two well-dressed Chakran men are sipping drinks. When Siris nods, one man murmurs to the other; they both drain their cups as Siris turns his attention back to us. "Now it's time for you to rest. I can see it's been a long journey. I'm just glad you got out of Luda before the fighting started."

"You mean at La Fête?" Leo shakes his head. "We were there for that."

"The night after."

Leo stiffens. Emotions flicker across his face like shadows: shock to pain, fear to uncertainty. My own heart drops like a stone through muck. "What happened?"

Before he answers, Siris raises a hand. Smoothly, the tall girl steps back, pretending to straighten the curtains, and the men at the table settle back into their seats. "I've only heard rumors, of course," the innkeeper murmurs. "And rumors are always worse—"

"Tell me."

"Reports vary, but . . . there was some sort of rebellion among the soldiers. A quarter of the battalion was slaughtered," he says, almost apologetically. As though it were his fault.

As his words sink in, Leo leans heavily against the desk. My own gut clenches at the news. "How?"

Siris shrugs, uncomfortable. "Some people are sure it was the rebels. But some say it was Legarde's own men turning against him. The questioneur, they say."

"Eduard?" Leo looks at me and my heart sinks.

I open my mouth—but what to say? A quarter of the battalion. The monk at the temple—what had she said? *The dead are coming—you've sent us so many.*

"Unfortunately, Capitaine Legarde was gravely injured," Siris adds delicately; he must know Leo and the capitaine's history. "But he'll likely make a full recovery."

"So who's in charge?" Leo says. Then his mouth twists. "Not Pique." Siris only makes a face, and Leo swears under his breath. "That explains Dar Som."

"Rumor is that Capitaine Legarde left his sickbed to rein him in, but not soon enough. Word is, morale was quite low. There were more than a few officers ready to take their frustrations out on somebody. Anybody."

"I need a pen and paper," Leo says. "Can you have someone run to the telegraph office for me? If not, I'll go myself."

"The telegraph at Luda was damaged in the fire, I'm afraid."

"The *fire*?"

"A riot at the docks. People were already jumpy after the explosions. When they heard the gunfire . . ."

With sudden rage, Leo kicks the bundle of guns at our feet. "The telegraph office is nearly in the center of town! How far did the fire spread?"

Siris takes a careful breath. "Like I said, it's only rumor—"

"How far?"

"Almost certainly the theater was affected."

The theater. The girls. And all because of Eduard.

Because of me. My hands start to shake, but Leo takes a deep breath. His face is pale, and the pain in his eyes is deeper than a wound. I reach out to him, but he shrugs me off. "Leo—"

"Go rest, Jetta. Your part of the deal is done. I won't forget mine." Leo pulls a fistful of coins from his pocket and turns to Siris. "I'll need you to get a letter to the palace. And I need a fast horse too. I have to get back to Luda."

My eyes go wide, but Siris waves the money away. "Just tell me when you're leaving. I'll have everything prepared."

"As soon as possible," Leo says. "Tonight." Then he turns to me, and for a moment, I catch a glimpse of the softness about him that I had first seen while he had slept on the back stair of our roulotte. He reaches out to tug on the shawl I'm wearing, drawing it tighter over the scar on my shoulder. Then his mouth twists into that old smile, but the charm has been hollowed out of his eyes. "Good-bye, Jetta."

Before I can protest, Siris gestures again. The men at the tables approach, and each of them shoulders a bag—mine and Leo's. They follow Leo and Siris around the desk into a little office and shut the door firmly behind them. The tall girl leaves the curtains and takes my arm. "Come, cher," she says. "I'll have your things brought to your room. Let me show you to the baths."

I follow her down the hall in a daze, and in my mind, memories play like shadows on a scrim. The cold fire of the n'akela, the sting of the knife, the moment I marked Eduard's hand. And the sound of his screaming. But then— even worse—the smell of the theater, stale sweat and old perfume. Cheeky's wicked grin, her soft hands. The sweet, aching song of the violin.

If La Perl is lost, it's because I couldn't control myself. Eduard was after me because of what Capitaine Legarde had seen me do—because of my performance on the road. The weight of guilt presses down like a yoke on my shoulders, like sins on my back. I try to tell myself that I couldn't have known; I call up Leo's words about the gamble of survival. But the lines are hollow in my head—I cannot fool myself.

The baths are as luxurious and inviting as the rest of the inn, with deep tubs carved of basalt and hammered copper showerheads that sluice warm water from catchments on the roof. There is even soap in powdery flakes, sprinkled with dried lavender blossoms, and soft robes thicker than quilts hanging on the walls. The hour is so late that I have the space all to myself.

So no one can hear me crying.

Dear Theodora,

I am sorry I did not write back sooner. It's hard to believe it's already been more than a year. I hope you didn't spend these months thinking my silence was born of anger or blame. To tell the truth, until today, I had no answer to your question.

In your letter, you asked me if there was anything you could do. There was not, at the time. Some acts are final. But I hope it is not an imposition to answer you now.

I've met a girl, and I owe her a favor. She needs to get to Aquitan to take the cure Mei deserved.

I know what you're thinking. I know what *he* would say. But this is not some secret mistress or a hurried elopement. She is a shadow player traveling with her family, and we've never so much as kissed. But there is something about her,

something I want to save. Or to stop. And I can—
but only with your help.

So if your offer is still open, here is something
you can do. The troupe is staying at Le Livre. They
need a place on your boat.

Ever hopeful,

Leonin

CHAPTER
TWENTY

It takes me some time to fall asleep. First there is the reunion with my parents, and I realize that somewhere in the back of my mind, I wasn't sure if I would look at Maman differently after I had walked in her footsteps through the tunnels. But when she holds out her arms, I rush into her warm embrace. I do see her differently, but not how I worried I might.

"I'm so glad you're safe," she murmurs, but I only nod and paint on a smile. She doesn't need to know what I saw in the tunnels. Or maybe she already does.

Even though we are all together again, and the bed is warm and soft, I lie restless and awake. It isn't as bad as the night at La Perl . . . but I can't get the theater out of my head. For a while, I smell smoke, and I wonder if it's my imagination, or something burning at the inn. When I finally slip from my bed and throw open the shutters, the night is quiet—there is nothing ablaze. I take a deep breath of the cool night air, sweetened with the scent of flowers blooming. Overhead, the sky is turning pink.

Does dawn break the same in Aquitan? Are there rumdal trees across the sea? Turning from the garden window, I see a white envelope on the floor. Someone must have slipped it under the door in the night.

Lifting it from the floor with shaking hands, I slide my finger beneath the flap. Carefully, I pull out the thick card, staring at the invitation with disbelieving eyes. The letters— black on white, like shadows on a scrim. I don't have to read the words to know the story they are telling.

I must have made a sound, because Maman stirs and sits up in her bed, and though I never want to let go of the paper, hasn't she earned this, just as much as I? So I pass it to her, and she wakes Papa, and both of them exclaim at the soft, heavy paper, tracing the gold scrollwork, breathing in the fresh ink, like perfume. Such a small thing, but we have traded so much for it.

Then I frown. Inside the envelope that held the invitation is something else: a thin sheet of paper, folded shut, the outside marked with only an *L*. Even through the page, I recognize the precise, delicate hand of La Fleur. This note is meant for Leo.

As Maman and Papa marvel over the invitation, I consider the letter. The temptation is there—there is no seal. But instead I tuck the paper, still folded, back into the now-empty envelope.

Murmuring an excuse to Maman about finding breakfast, I slip from the room and make my way into the front of the inn. It is too early to be crowded, but Siris is there, reading one of the many books from his shelf. For a moment, I am just another girl from Le Verdu, with muddy feet and a sun-faded wrap—well aware that we haven't paid for his hospitality, and probably can't afford it. But he looks up as I approach, tucking a faded ribbon between the pages and closing the book, as though to assure me I have his full attention. I lift my chin a little. "I'd like to send a letter to Luda."

"Luda! There aren't many people traveling that way—at least, not since Leo left." He looks down at the envelope in my hand. "Isn't that the letter you just received?"

"No . . . well. Yes. But there was a note inside for Leo as

well." I take a breath, trying to quash the sudden swell of strange emotion.

Siris only holds out his hand. "Would you like me to hold it? I can ask around. Find a rider. Though it may take a while."

I open my mouth—I almost agree, but something stops me. I do not want this letter lost, for Leo to never know his sister sent it, for her not to know whether it reached him or if he's just ignoring her again. Or maybe I just don't want to let go of this last connection between Leo and me. We traveled so long together—and our good-bye was too rushed. And at the very least, I will see Theodora on the ship; I could return the letter to her instead. That's what I tell myself as I stand in front of Siris, clutching the envelope. "No, merci," I manage at last. Then I hesitate again; I can smell, very distantly, the scent of coffee—that rich dark brew the Audrinnes adored. "What's the cost of breakfast here?"

Siris waves a hand. "Gratis, gratis. I'll have it brought to your rooms."

"Thank you," I say, but he shakes his head.

"Thank Leo," he says. "If you see him again."

The words twist inside me like a knife, but I only nod and try to smile. Returning to my room, I tuck the letter into my bags next to my little booklet—the one full of souls. And when breakfast arrives, it looks so tempting that it almost brings my appetite back.

Cut ripe fruit like a pile of gems. An omelet so thin it's nearly translucent, folded around thinly sliced pork and ribbons of green onion. Little fingers of fried dough dusted with real white sugar like tiny stars. And a whole pot of coffee, boiled with cardamom and lightened with cream, so sweet it makes my stomach ache.

Maman is eating heartily, but Papa too is only picking at the food. He holds a porcelain coffee cup, still full, as though it might explode. "I've been wondering what to do about Lani," he says at last. "We'll have to leave her behind."

Tears spring to my eyes—but hadn't I known that all along? And I know my father; I know what he's thinking. "You want to give her to Siris."

"If you both agree," Papa says, looking at me and Maman. "His youngest daughter cares for the stable. She put her in a stall. Alongside all the fine horses. Lani might like it here."

I nod, trying to smile, trying to ignore the fact that no one here has any reason to keep a water buffalo—that she'll likely be sold, and we can only hope it will be for muscle and not for meat. "Wouldn't anyone?" I say, picking up a piece of fried dough. Papa smiles, relieved; at last he starts to eat. But despite the sugar, there is a sour taste in my mouth.

After breakfast, we bathe again, dressing in the best of what remains. Then I spend some time repacking our bags; now that the rifles are gone, I can carry my fantouches again. I gather them up, running my hands over them as they shift and rustle: my old friends. They are all I have left. I want to be the one to carry them from here to there—the one to bear the weight of them on my back as we leave home behind for good.

Outside the haven of Le Livre, the whole city is out in force—the celebration has been going since noon at least. The streets are full, boisterous. Tumblers and ribbon dancers perform in pockets carved out from the surging masses. Vendors careen through the crowds, selling delicacies out of wheelbarrows: candied fruit and coconut, sizzling scallion pancakes, pillowy pork buns. Firecrackers pop in the muggy air, scaring away the drifting vana.

But there are more soldiers in the streets, their hands on their rifles, and no one is allowed to stand in one place too long, not that we want to. I keep my head down, my hair falling over my face. Despite the heat, I keep the silk scrap tight around my shoulders. I am just one Chakran girl among hundreds, thousands, but I don't want to give the soldiers an excuse to look too long at my face.

Thankfully, it's just a short walk from the inn to the docks, but the closer we get, the more the celebration edges toward a riot. There is a frantic energy in the air, a frisson of hysteria, something more like fear than festivity.

The north side of the dock is bordered with a wishing wall. It might have once enclosed a livestock pen, but the yard beyond it is empty now. Instead, the bamboo fence holds messages for those left behind—the missing, the dead. Amulets and ribbons, scraps of paper and cloth, some with writing, some with pictures, and some too faded to tell. *Miss you, love you, waiting down the road* . . . And lining the base of the wall are oranges and other offerings. Tiny spirits cluster around the tributes. The decorations almost cover the peeling posters beneath: VICTOIRE over a dashing profile of General Legarde.

I've seen walls like this, in other towns we've passed, but never one so large. There's even a bit of industry grown up around it: women with lap desks and ink-stained fingers selling transcriptions for those who cannot write, five étoiles for mulberry paper, ten for a strip of silk. I wish I could leave one for Akra, but the crowd sweeps us past too quickly, and over their heads, I finally catch a glimpse of the ship.

It's the largest I've ever seen—far bigger than the little riverboats with their small gods, far bigger even than the sugar ships that carry cargo to the capital—and she is not built for transport, but pleasure. *Le Rêve* is painted gold and lucky red; her sails are silk and embroidered with scales, and in the center of the ship, steam curls from a stack shaped like the fearsome head of a dragon. Just like my own dragon puppet, strapped in my pack. The rail is decorated with pennants and strings of flowers—chrysanthemum and jasmine, orchid and rumdal. And there are porters trotting up and down the gangplank, loading crates of champagne— nothing is rationed for the king.

We approach the wharf, slipping in behind a group of men dressed in servants' livery, carrying one of the crates. They push through the crowd until we reach a cordon of soldiers protecting the pier—a line of pressed green uniforms against the motley local dress of revelers and refugees. An officer waves the servants past, but when we try to follow, he shoves us back with a look. Is it recognition? No . . . it is a glare he gives to all the riffraff who come too near to the king's ship. But once he sees our invitation, his fierce expression softens. An invitation from La Fleur sets us apart from the rest.

Just past the cordon, the dock is clear, and I can breathe again. I do, deeply, until my lungs ache with the sweet scent of the vast sapphire ocean. The river mouth opens up right into it—the Hundred Days Sea, a boundless blue. The same color as the waters of Les Chanceux. But here the rolling waves stretch to the horizon and beyond.

If someone had told me it went on forever, I would not have doubted them. How far is the distant shore? I know it's not a hundred days' journey—not truly. Troupes saving up for tours say it takes a week, maybe two. But the miles and miles between my future and my past have never looked so long.

My hands are shaking; suddenly, I cannot move my feet. But behind us, a man shouts at the officer who just let us through. "Why them?" he says, pointing. "Why them and not me?"

At his question, rage flares. Does he know what we've lost? Does he know what I've done? I turn to ask, the question like a shard of glass on my tongue, but when I see his face, I recognize him—not the man, but the look.

Haggard and hollow. I swallow my question; of course he knows. The lines may be different, but our stories are the same. The officer only curses the man, dropping his hand to the butt of his gun. "Move back," he roars. "Or I'll send you floating downriver, but not in a boat!"

Shames twists in my heart like a worm into fruit as I duck my head and force my feet to move. I can't stop now. It's the culmination of all our travel—the end of the road. The journey has been so hard. Why are these last few steps harder still? I try to gather my courage around me, the way an Aquitan woman might gather her wide ruffled skirts. We wait at the gangway until the servants and their crate are clear. Then we hand the gold-edged letter to a crewman. "Bien," he says, gesturing toward the ship. "Welcome aboard."

Papa nods, and Maman sighs. I take the handrail and climb the wooden stairs with my eyes shut tight. And instead of thinking of what lies across the sea, I am remembering the long roads we traveled in the roulotte. The whisper of wind through the scrollwork. The smell of smoke and rouge. Even Lani, as eager to work as she was to eat. And my brother, his brow furrowed as he polished the sandalwood face of the spirit maiden we'd left in the theater in Luda. My heart clenches tight around the memories, like a fist around any precious thing.

But I step from the dock to the deck, and just like that, I've walked off the edge of my world. Nothing is the same. Nothing will ever be the same again.

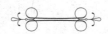

To the shadow players at Le Livre

Join us

aboard Le Rêve

For the moonrise coronation

of

King Raik Alendra

And his wedding to

Theodora Legarde, La Fleur

Theodora

ACT 3

To celebrate the eighteenth birthday of our beloved King Raik Alendra at the eighth Turn of the Tide in the 745th year (30 Août in the calendrier), we have marked this historic occasion by providing for our subjects a day of entertainment throughout the city. A parade of lions, music, and dancing in the streets shall be followed by shadow plays on the plaza once night falls. In between, at the exact moment of sunset and moonrise, at 7:14 heures, the fireworks will announce the coronation of our king, long may he reign.

6:00

Cocktail reception aboard Le Rêve

7:00

Coronation ceremony begins

7:14

Fireworks. After which, dancing

CHAPTER TWENTY-ONE

Looking back at the dock is a strange feeling. From here, the movement of the crowd looks like a scandalous dance; the press of bodies, writhing back to belly, faces contorted, slick with sweat. Individuals elbow through, their violence rippling outward in jabs and shoves, before they are turned away by the cordon and pulled back into the crush. Near the ship, a thin woman clings to a piling to keep from being swept back into the crowd. She meets my eyes as she reaches out, as though I can save her, but I turn my head hurriedly, cheeks flaming. I have barely saved myself.

Eyes down, I walk from the gangplank toward the front

of the ship, running my hand along the rail. The contrast between the ship and the shore is overwhelming. In the afternoon sunlight, bright pennants snap in the breeze from the ocean. The rails are wrapped in silk ribbon and studded with bouquets of flowers—white rumdal and orchids, and twining falls of jasmine, their scent rich and heady. Even the decking beneath my feet is changed. No longer the rough gray wood of the pier, but polished mahogany that seems to glow with a golden shine. It spotlights the dust and the scuffed silk on my shoes, the mud and dangling thread on the hem of my sarong. My finest clothes are reduced to rags by this strange new set. It is too beautiful for the likes of me.

From the ship's rail, I can see up the river, past the dock and the slapdash bamboo houses that sit on stilts above the dirty reeds, all the way to the high moon bridge: a rounded stone arch that links the fort on the far bank to the palace grounds. It is an ancient structure, built long before the Aquitans came to Chakrana—too low for their tall sails and their sugar ships. Now I see why the riverboats cannot make it to the open waters.

Every month, at full moon, the Boy King stands upon its rounded crest to call the river up from the sea. Or rather, every month but this one. Today he will call the waters from the prow of his dragon boat. The crown will be placed on his head as the tide surges upriver; after the coronation party and the wedding, the functionaries will depart in little shallow-bottomed river craft. Then those of us staying aboard will be on the way to Aquitan. Will the waters still rise a month from now, when they boy king is drinking fine champagne and watching operas in Lephare?

Two strangers approach—one pale, one dark, but both in servants' livery—and their presence shakes me out of my thoughts. I step back against the rail to let them pass, but the Aquitan man stops before us.

"The last-minute guests? Friends of La Fleur," he adds, not bothering to hide the puzzlement in his voice. He looks us up and down, his eyes lingering on my stained silk shoes, but I meet his gaze head-on, and he is the first to look away. "I am the majordome. If there are any problems on our journey, you will bring them to me. May I show you to your rooms? Cha, take the bags."

My face twists at the slur, but the majordome has already spun on his well-heeled dress boots. He steps crisply across the mahogany deck as the Chakran man bends to carry our packs. I keep hold of mine. I am tired, but I am strong, and something feels odd about slapping my last few fantouches into the hands of a stranger. Especially one who looks like he's only barely made it aboard the ship himself. While his uniform is crisp and new, it hangs off his skinny body, and his eyes are hard and haunted.

The majordome shows us to our little room—a berth below the top deck, with a tiny round window overlooking the water. The Chakran servant puts our bags down in the middle of the floor. They look like a pile of rags abandoned by a transient. "There's only one bed," the majordome says matter-of-factly. "The arrangements were very last minute."

"This will be fine," Maman says. Is she smiling? I can feel it too—the sense of relief, bordering on wonder.

I nod. "I can sleep on the floor."

"Bien." The man's face is carefully smooth. "I'll have cha find you some extra bedding. The reception will start within the hour. As soon as you've freshened up, you're invited back abovedecks." He glances significantly at the washbasin in the corner, but I keep my face smooth too.

Maman watches the door a long while after the men let it close behind them. "I never really thought it would happen," she says softly. "There are so many people out there on the dock."

Papa puts his arms around her and kisses the top of her

head. "It's been a long road," he says. Is that regret in his voice? It strikes a chord in me, and all of a sudden, I am back at the start of it all, in our grass shack at the base of the mountain, looking out the door at the mango tree.

Deliberately, I drop my own bag to the floor and sit beside it, running my hand over the bundled fantouches. "I don't know how I'm supposed to freshen up. This is my best dress now."

"Do what you can," Papa says. "It's our chance to catch the eye of La Fleur."

"Is there a stage on the ship?" Maman says. "A place for performances? The trip is a week or more. Surely the Playboy King will need entertainment."

"We can ask the majordome," Papa says with a wry smile. "Any questions, he said."

"Any problems," I correct. But Maman only laughs.

"Once he sees what we can do, he'll show more respect. Jetta." She turns to me, her eyes shining. When had I last seen her so happy? "Do you want to come find the man?"

I hesitate, thinking of the look on the majordome's face. "Let me wash up a bit. Maybe clean my shoes."

"All right." She takes Papa's hand, almost floating as she leaves. Alone in the little room, I try to breath, to relax, but the air is too warm, tainted with the bitterness of fresh varnish. Somehow, without my parents there, the space seems smaller. It's just as big as our roulotte, but there are no signs of life here—no fantouches hanging from the ceiling, no scraps of fabric scattered on the floor, no scratches in the paint on the clean white wall. The starkness is a fresh reminder of what we've left behind.

I try to open the window, but the glass is fastened shut, so instead I turn to the basin. A porcelain bowl, painted with pink roses and set into a low wooden dresser. A metal ewer of water stands beside it. I pour some over my hands and scrub my face, my arms, even my neck, where sweat has beaded under my thick hair, but the water is lukewarm and only adds to the sticky feeling on my skin. Sweeping my hair up into a knot, I pull a few tendrils down to frame my face. Then I brush the dust from my shoes and smooth the wrinkles from my third-best skirt, but it is red raw silk. There is no way to hide the wear and the stains.

I go to my pack for my makeup, something to make me feel less dirty. Less mundane. But opening the bag, I am met with a sea of vibrant scarlet: the scales of my dragon fantouche.

"Shh," I tell her as she wriggles. I try to dig around her,

but she is too bulky, so I pull her out, emptying the whole bag onto the bed. The fantouches tumble out in a pile of silk and leather, paint and rivets; the dragon's body unscrolls, a river of red and gold. But there too is my makeup—along with my combs, some ribbons, a necklace, my book of souls . . . and the envelope. I turn the letter over in my hand, wondering what Theodora has written. Will Leo ever read it?

The sound of a violin drifts down like a memory, and I look up in wonder. But then another instrument joins in, deeper. A cello, perhaps, then a viola. The dragon flicks her tail. It is only a quartet, playing songs from Aquitan. The reception must be starting.

With a sigh, I toss the letter back on the bed and turn to the vanity. I sharpen my cheekbones with the rouge, then paint on a winged line to deepen my eyes. I want to look dramatic—dangerous. But underneath the paint, my skin is bloodless and sallow. What I wouldn't give for Tia's skill with makeup. The thought floats through my head, as careless as an ember, and my hand falters. Where are the girls now? Did they make it through the fire?

I turn from the mirror, no longer able to look myself in the eye. But as I pick up my bag to repack, there is a knock at the door. For a moment, I hesitate—but it must be the man with the bedding. "Come in," I say, but the door is already opening.

The man who slips into the room is wearing servants' livery, though he is not a servant. My breath hitches in my chest. "Leo?"

"Jetta." He shuts the door behind his back, his eyes casting about the little room. When he turns to me, he pauses for just a moment. "You're all dressed up."

"So are you." Hope rises in me—unexpected, but warm. "Are you . . . are you working on the ship?"

He grimaces, looking down at his livery. "I'm here for a job, but not this one. Where's your family?"

"Looking for the majordome. I never thought I'd see you again." The words are bold, but he doesn't seem to notice.

"No such luck." His tone brings me up short, and though it's only been a day, he looks different. Something about him, gone cold, or scared; there is no hint of the easy smile I've grown used to. He takes my hands and looks into my eyes. "You have to get off the ship."

"What?" My voice has gone up an octave. Leo puts his finger to my lips; I breathe the next word into his palm. "Explain."

Leo clenches his jaw. "The king won't be going to

Aquitan. The rifles we brought through the tunnels—they were bound for *Le Rêve.*"

My eyes go wide. "How do you know?"

"Because," he says carefully. "I just helped bring them aboard in a case marked champagne."

It takes a moment to make sense of the words. When I do, my mouth falls open. Had I seen him on the dock? Among the group of servants carrying the last crate, loaded just before we came aboard? He'd walked right past me—past all of us who were dreaming of escape—and he'd sunk those dreams as if he'd blown a hole in the ship itself. Anger blazes red and hot. "How could you?"

I shove him back, as hard as I can, and he reels, catching himself against the wall. The dragon lifts her head, her interest piqued, and I growl. "Go." She needs no more urging; in an instant, she has bowled him to the floor.

"Connard!" Leo struggles, but she is strong and fast— tail lashing, claws against his shoulders. She pins him to the decking. "What the hell is this, Jetta?"

I kneel beside him, to look him in the eye. "Did you know about this when you made our deal?"

"No, I swear! What is this thing?" He struggles with the dragon, and she clamps her jaws around his arm. He cries out, and I put my hand on her ridged back.

"Gentle," I say, and she loosens her grip—but only a little. "Why did you help them? You knew we were aboard this ship!"

"It was the only way I could get word to you! I only just learned myself! Jetta, please!"

"Tell me how to stop them!"

"If I knew how, I would have tried!" Leo's eyes are wide; he glances between me and the dragon. "My god, Jetta, what are you?"

The question shakes me—the same question the monk had made me ask Maman. I sit back on my heels, breathing hard. As if she can sense my hesitation, the dragon eases back as well, though her tail is twitching across the floor. I open my mouth—but do I owe him an explanation? Then Leo answers his own question.

"You're one of them, aren't you? A nécromancien. Like Le Trépas."

The name is a punch to the gut; suddenly, I can't catch my breath. "I'm a shadow player," I say softly—as much to him as to myself, but if it's not a lie, then it's not the whole truth either. I clear my throat. "I'm just trying to get out of this place."

It's so quiet in the room that I can hear him swallow. Distantly, the revelers clap for the quartet; a new melody floats down like a mist. Leo wets his lips. "Let me help you find a different way."

A laugh slips out—bitter and too loud. "Because our last deal went so well?" Then I take a breath, trying to slow my heart, to gather my thoughts. Leo is hard to pin down when it comes to his deals . . . but he's good with his gun. "Help me stop the plot instead."

It seems so obvious, but he gives me that look—the one Maman gives me, the one I despise. "Jetta. That's madness."

"No!" I say again, clenching my fists, struggling for control. "No. What's madness is you thinking I would come so far and give so much just to turn away now."

I run my hand down his sides, around the back of his belt. There—the pistol. I pull it free. Leo laughs, half startled, half afraid. "You think you can take down a dozen men carrying the latest rifles?"

"You could double my chances if you helped me."

"I am not going to watch you get shot."

"Stay here then." I pause, considering. "But give me your uniform."

"Jetta—"

I hold up the gun, and he falls silent. But when he raises a hand toward the buttons, the dragon tightens her grip, her carved claws pricking the fabric. "Let him," I tell her, and she relaxes.

"Trade secrets," Leo mutters, shrugging off the red jacket. "I should have asked what trade. I should have known from the night we left La Perl. From Eduard. From the show!"

"How can I find the other rebels?" I say brusquely, but he shakes his head.

"I don't know their names. They're all Chakran, in livery like mine." His hand moves to his belt, and he avoids my eyes as he slips off the dark pants. Is that a faint blush on his cheek? I look away too, but a laugh lodges in my throat at the absurdity. To steal a rebel's uniform but try to preserve his modesty. "Is it too much to ask for a pair of your father's trousers?"

"Don't worry," I say, reaching for the pile on the bed— the makeup, the book of souls, the letter . . . the ribbons. "No one will see you in here."

"Jetta, please." He searches my face as I bind his hands and feet—more gently than I need to. "There's still time to get out of here. To find your parents. We can go back to Le Livre. Figure out something else. There's bound to be another boat—"

"One that I could afford? One that would take me to the Roi Fou? You saw the crowds on the docks, same as I did. There's a reason they're so desperate." I scoot back then, and so does the dragon. She sits on her haunches, immensely pleased, and starts to groom her tail. "I'll come back to let you go once the rebels are taken care of. I know you have to get back to Luda."

Only then does Leo turn away. "There's nothing left for me in Luda."

Something cracks in my chest—but I have no time for sentiment. Still, I take a pillow from the bed and shove it under his head. I take the letter too, and put it on the pillow. "This came for you, along with the invitation. From your sister. Theodora. I'm going to go and save her fiancé." I stand, hesitating. "Watch him," I say to the dragon, before slipping out the door.

Dearest Leonin,

Your letter brought me more joy than I've had all year. Thank you for writing. I hope you'll make it a habit.

Your friend is welcome on our ship and we will take care of her family. I will ask no questions of her, but you must know I'm intensely curious. Even I can see that it all looks terribly romantic. Will you by any chance be joining her aboard the ship? I hope so, and not just to satisfy my need for gossip. Though can you blame me? I haven't heard from you in too long.

Something else is troubling me. Our father says it's only the wedding, but I think it's something more. The rebellion is gaining strength, and I'm leaving the country for half a year with so much unfinished business. I've told him that this trip to Aquitan is a bad idea—how better to quell a rebellion than to return the crown to the rightful king, and put that king before his people? But Father thinks the king must be kept out of harm's way so the armée can rout the insurgents. He's sure it will all be over in a few months—or so he says, anyway, though I get the feeling there's something he isn't telling me.

I do hope you are joining us. I won't lie to you—our father will be here too, at least for the coronation. Please don't let that keep you away. One thing is sure, you will be safer with us than back at La Perl with the Tiger breathing down your neck. Please let me know—in person, preferably, and with your bags and your violin in hand.

Theodora

PS I nearly forgot to mention, but Les Chanceux is not the only cure. Have I piqued your interest? Come see me and I'll tell you all about it—after we push off from the dock.

CHAPTER TWENTY-TWO

Flinging open the door, I look both ways, but the narrow hall is empty. Where would the rebels be?

Upstairs, most likely, on the top deck. That's where the king is. I can hear the party now—music, murmuring, mingling. They should be easy to find, shouldn't they? All the other servants will have trays of champagne and hors d'oeuvres. The rebels will be the ones with the rifles.

How are they hiding them? Surely they won't just carry them over their shoulders. Far easier if they'd had Leo steal some pistols—the one I'd taken from him is tucked into my pocket, where it bangs against my thigh. Maybe they've stashed them around the ship, to pick up at some secret signal. Or maybe they're carrying them covered in flowers, or shoved down the backs of their jackets as they walk stiffly across the deck.

No matter—I'll find them. And when I do? Shooting an assassin would hardly be the worst thing I'd done. And this is one sure way to catch the king's eye.

My palms are sweating; I wipe them on the livery trousers I stole from Leo. Then I hike the belt back up. I'm shaking, but not afraid—it is a different feeling. The pressure before a show with too few rehearsals. A tension like I'm made of facets and edges and string strung too tight.

The belt keeps slipping lower as I jog down the hall. I haven't gone far when I meet a man going the opposite way. A servant—a Chakran. But no rifle. Still, he's carrying a load of bedding—is he heading to our room? Will he find Leo there, sound an alarm? Will something so small be what stops the ship—or what gets me thrown back to the dock?

Then I realize it is not the same man who'd helped us earlier. What if he isn't a servant at all? I glance at the soft quilts in his arms—a pile large enough to hide rifles inside.

The man peers at me too, stopping in the hall. "What's that on your face?" he says, and my hand goes to my cheek before I realize he's talking about my makeup. "Are you trying to be noticed?"

The question is an odd one. "Noticed by who?"

"By anyone looking," he says, but as my suspicion builds, so does his. His eyes go to my jacket . . . too big. My trousers . . . too loose. "You're not one of us."

"No, I'm not." I pull the gun from my pocket, and the man's eyes go wide as he backs against the wall. "What's in the quilt?" I ask, but he only gapes at me—at the gun. So I reach out and snatch the blankets out of his hand. They fall to the floor—pillows, sheets, quilts. Nothing more.

And as my heart sinks, a soldier rounds the corner, his own rifle gleaming on his back. He stops dead in the hall when he sees us, and in an instant, I see what Leo meant. This is madness.

But rather than arrest me, the soldier turns and runs.

I stare after him, dumbfounded, but as he glances back over his shoulder, I recognize his face. The man the major-dome had called cha. The man dressed as a servant only an hour ago.

The man now running toward the party with a rifle strapped to his back.

Swearing, I start after him, tripping in the tangle of

blankets, but the servant grabs me by the wrist. Without thinking, I lash out with the butt of the gun and strike him across the face. He reels, bright blood bursting from his nose. The sight of it shakes me almost as much as the fear in his eyes. "I'm sorry," I say, backing away. "I'm sorry."

Before he can try again to stop me, I race down the hallway, past the noisy kitchens, where the real servants pass in and out with trays for the guests. They draw back as I careen up the stairs. But on deck, I falter; the sight takes my breath away.

The scene: a party in full swing under a sky painted gold and pink. The lavish light of sunset glitters on gowns and glasses, on jewels and medals—so many people, and all in their very best attire. Aquitan soldiers in pressed uniforms stand at attention along the rails. Functionaries and courtiers, sugar barons and officers, women in lovely gowns and men in fine tuxedos with tall hats. All of them pale, all of them Aquitan.

No sign of the rebels.

Hurriedly, I shove the gun back in my pocket, but all eyes are turned toward the prow, where a man makes a speech no one can hear. The acoustics on the ship are terrible, but I know who he is without hearing what he's saying. His is the one dark face in a pale sea, and the ivory crown is already resting on his head.

Beside him is his fiancée, Theodora Legarde, the Flower of Aquitan, and the legends of her beauty have not been exaggerated. Her dress is pale rose and picks up the blush of her cheeks, the high waist gathers under ample breasts, the diaphanous skirt skims her rounded waist. She wears a flower behind one ear in Chakran style, but her blond hair is done in pin curls, like Tia's wig, though she doesn't have Tia's hauteur. Instead she seems nervous, ill at ease— glancing around the ship.

Does she know something? Does she suspect? But there is a ring of soldiers to protect the royal couple—all officers with gleaming epaulets, all Aquitan. General Legarde too—I drop my eyes when I see him, and duck behind a woman in a deep green gown. There's no way a rebel could get close to the king—not with Legarde by his side. He must know the faces of his officers. Then again, with a rifle, an assassin needn't come anywhere near him.

Desperately, I scan the crowd—the businessmen clustered around the champagne, the ladies posed prettily near the flowers at the rail—but though I see Chakran soldiers here and there, how can I tell which are rebels at a glance? If I were to pull out the gun and start asking, I wouldn't get far.

And what if they are hiding somewhere? Beneath the skirted tables . . . behind the dais for the band? The prospects are overwhelming; they might be anywhere. A popping sound makes me jump, but it is only a string of red fireworks dangling from the mast. It dances and writhes as it burns, and a cheer goes up from the revelers on the ship as the lines are cast off.

The moment of sunset and moonrise: the ship is leaving the dock. And with a broad smile, the king raises his arms to call to the river.

From the sea, where the last flare of sunset strikes gold on the water, the waves start to rise, lapping against the banks, curling around the piles of the dock and rustling in the reeds. The Aquitans have always scoffed at the magic of the moment—they say it's the tides changing with the full moon. But as the king stands tall and the boat slips free, the water lifts us like the hands of a benevolent god.

The band starts a lively march, and excited chatter drifts up like incense from an offering. But as the ship chugs into the river, shouting erupts on the shore. On the wharf, a refugee grapples with a soldier, breaking free of the cordon.

He races toward the gangplank as though he could leap to the deck—as though, if he could only find himself aboard, he would be safe and sound. But before he reaches the ship, a soldier behind him raises his gun. The shot splits the air, and the man drops like a pile of rags. Blood flows in a scarlet puddle around his head. My cry is lost in the screams of the crowd, and suddenly the rabble on the dock becomes a riot.

Those in the front fall back, trying to retreat as those behind them surge forward, and all along the wharf, people are pushed into the water by the violence of the mob. Others crumple underfoot; the crowd crashes over them like a wave. Soldiers in the cordon draw their weapons, but I can't take my eyes off the one who shot the refugee.

"Akra." The word is barely a whisper, but all the wind has been knocked out of me. I take a deep breath and scream. "Akra!" His head jerks up just as the rioters sweep past him, hiding him from view—but it wasn't him. It couldn't be. My brother is dead. And if he were alive, he would never shoot a frightened man in the back.

Beneath my feet, the ship's engines growl as the captain pushes her faster; the band falters, and the majordome screams to play on. But before we're out of range, a flaming bottle arcs out of the crowd on the dock and bursts against the rail. Fire splashes across the boards, licking up the fresh varnish, and cries go up from the revelers. Soldiers race to the flames, beating them with their jackets.

Instinctively, I seek out the king—the fire is the sort of show that I would stage to mask an assassination. He is still at the prow, though his face has gone grim, and he is watching neither the riot on the docks nor the crowd on the ship. Instead, his eyes are tilted toward the sky. Suddenly he points. "Up there!" he shouts. "On the funnel!"

I follow his finger to the steam stack. A lone Chakran soldier sits on the edge—a rebel, he must be. He's aiming a rifle at the king, who's still standing frozen at the rail.

"Get down!" I shout, but if he hears me over the screams of the crowd, he does not move. Yanking my own gun from my pocket, I try to take aim at the assassin, but my hands are shaking—I pull the trigger, but nothing happens. The latch . . . the safety. I thumb it back, but as I aim again, the rebel fires. The crowd screams again, as one creature, and the king falls over the rail.

My heart follows—down down down—along with our plans. Forget Aquitan, forget the cure, forget escape from Chakrana. We'll be lucky to escape the ship. What about Leo? Is he safe in the room? And where are my parents?

"Maman! Papa!" My voice is lost in the sharp sound of a second shot. This one comes from the deck. Legarde is there, pistol up, the crowd parting around him. The assassin topples backward into the funnel. Black smoke swirls and billows. Then the sound of gunfire echoes up from the stack as his rifle cartridges explode in the heat.

But it isn't only in the stack. The rest of the rebels are firing on the crowd. Skinny Chakrans with new haircuts and stolen uniforms—they aim at the officers d'armée with the guns I helped put in their hands.

All around me, well-dressed men and women shove past, trying to clear the deck as the real soldiers fire back. The majordome is hit, red blood staining his white shirtfront. Revelers leap from the rails, splashing into the river; others flee down the stairs into the belly of the ship. Souls flare as soldiers and rebels fall; the crowd explodes outward around each body like ripples in a pond.

"Maman!" I shove through the crowds, searching for familiar faces, desperately avoiding anyone dressed in the uniform d'armée. Soon enough, my silk shoes are stained with champagne and blood. "Papa!"

At my voice, I see him, peeking up from behind an overturned table. Then his eyes go wide. "Jetta!"

I see the look in his eyes, the panic, and I turn as he vaults over the table. Behind me, an Aquitan soldier taking aim.

The pistol—it's still in my hands. I throw it aside, but too late. The soldier fires just as my father slams into me, knocking me aside with a grunt.

"Papa!" He tumbles to the ground as another shot comes, this one from a rebel gun. The soldier reels, his rifle clattering to the deck.

My hands shaking, I reach for Papa—the bullet went clean through the meat of his arm. He cries out when I touch it. But all around us, the gunshots are dying down. Akela dot the deck, illuminating the bodies. The rebels are done—but so is the damage.

Maman is scrambling over the table now, her face streaked with tears. She rushes to Papa's side, and for a moment, her hands flutter like leaves in a breeze. Then she tears the sash from her sarong to wind it around his arm.

Air hisses through his teeth as she handles the wound. I reach out to brush the sweat from his brow, but his blood is all over my hands. Instead, I daub his forehead with my sleeve. "You're going to be all right, Papa."

"The armée," Maman says softly, her expression one of

disbelief. "They just started shooting."

"It was the rebels," I say. "A plot against the king."

"How do you know that?" Maman looks up at me then, her brow furrowed. "And what are you wearing?"

I open my mouth—but where to begin? With Leo's warning? With the guns we smuggled into the city? With the fact that if I'd listened to him, we could have left before the shooting started? And where is he now? Still trapped below? There is a feeling in the pit of my stomach, familiar but askew, like sefondre, but instead of coming together, everything has fallen apart.

But before I can say anything, footsteps approach—heavy boots on the deck. Glancing up, I see we are surrounded by soldiers. One of them reaches for me; I take his hand automatically. Then I cry out as he twists my arm up behind me. Pain shoots through my shoulders as he grabs the other wrist.

"What are you doing?" I say, struggling.

"You're being detained," the guard replies, tying my hands behind me.

"Why?"

Another guard steps in front of me; in his hands, the pistol I had only just discarded. "Treason."

ACT 3,

SCENE 29

Jetta's room aboard Le Rêve. From above, the sound of music—no gunfire yet. LEO is still sitting, on the ground. The dragon puppet watches him, her tail lashing.

LEO chews his lip. Then, slowly, deliberately, he starts to work on his bonds. The dragon's tail lashes faster.

LEO: I'm not doing anything.

The dragon only cocks her head. Gently, LEO picks at the knot. JETTA had tied him with a hair ribbon—the silk slides through his fingers, easy to loosen. But the fantouche hunkers down into a crouch.

She said to watch me. Not to eat me.

The dragon doesn't move, and LEO keeps plucking at the ribbon. At last it slips free. But he hesitates, watching the fantouche.

What were you, before this?

The dragon does not answer, but her hindquarters wriggle. LEO narrows his eyes. Then he flicks the ribbon at the dragon and she leaps up to bat at it. For a moment, LEO grins. Then, from above, the sound of fireworks.

Merde.

LEO scrambles to his feet; the dragon lifts her head to look at him. He raises an eyebrow.

We haven't got much time if we want to get out of here.

The dragon only returns to her play. LEO turns—slowly, this time—and starts digging through the packs, searching for a pair of trousers. Finding one, he sits on the edge of the bed to pull them on, keeping one eye on the fantouche. But as he shifts his weight, the booklet on the quilt rustles slightly. LEO stops for a moment, watching the pages. Then he shakes his head, eyeing the door, then the dragon. She is still toying with the tie.

Are you coming, or should I leave you alone with the ribbon?

He starts toward the door, but stops with his hand on the knob, glancing at the rest of the fantouches still scattered around the floor. Uncertainty flickers across his face. Softer now:

Or drop you in the furnace, like she did with the others?

The dragon turns her head, and then rolls over in one sinuous motion. LEO frowns, glancing at the empty pack. Pressing his lips together, LEO scoops the fantouches inside and throws the bundle over his shoulder. Then he grabs Jetta's book and Theodora's letter from the pillow. Hesitating, he starts to open the envelope, but stops at the sound of a gun from above.

Merde!

LEO jams the note in the booklet and stuffs them both in his pocket. Then he grabs the ribbon and jogs out the door. The dragon bounds after him. From above, the sound of screaming, but LEO runs the other way—toward the dining hall, where porcelain plates and crystal glasses wait for a meal that will grow cold in the kitchens. The dragon follows at his heels.

At the end of the dining hall, they burst through the double doors that open onto a balcony overlooking the water.

Frowning, LEO gauges the distance to shore—too far to swim with the pack. Reluctantly, he heaves it over the side, into the dark river—better that no one have it than to leave it behind for the armée to discover. Then he climbs over the rail, about to follow, but he hesitates when he catches sight of a fishing boat—one of the many little river craft that scull the water. This one is quite close to Le Rêve—especially taking into account the sound of the gunfight above.

Whistling through his teeth, LEO waves to the men in the boat, both in faded fishing gear, though looking closely, he can see that one of the men is dripping wet—and very familiar. The other man ignores him, continuing to row toward the shore. With a grimace, LEO whistles again. Then he whips the ribbon across the rail, and the dragon bounds after it, her long leather body graceful as a snake, the gold paint glimmering in the last light of the setting sun.

Both men are staring now, and after a hurried discussion, the boat turns back. LEO waits impatiently, bouncing on the balls of his feet as the fighting continues above. At last the prow bumps against the back of the ship. The man with the pole steadies the boat as LEO drops down among the netting. The other man holds out a hand to help him. His eyes are sharp, calculating, though his hair is still dripping river water. The dragon slips down between them, coiling at their feet. LEO drops the ribbon across her nose and bows to the man.

LEO: Your Majesty.
RAIK: Not so loud.

RAIK settles back into the boat, among the fishing nets, tossing them over the dragon, who squirms gleefully as she kicks at this new toy. LEO sits down beside him, nodding back toward the ship, the shouting, the confusion.

LEO: From the sound of it, that was quite a show you staged.
RAIK: It had to be a spectacle, to throw Legarde off my trail.
LEO: And to make your people angry enough to join the rebellion? Once word gets out that a soldier shot the Boy King, there will be riots.
RAIK: There were already riots, thanks to the armée. But I had word the general was planning my death soon enough. It was to be a drunken accident at sea. After the wedding, of course. You must be Leo Rath. Your sister has told me about you. *(He glances briefly at the dragon writhing under the nets.)* Though not everything.

LEO: What's a marriage without a little mystery?

RAIK: Unfortunately the wedding is off. Mystery is one thing—secrets are another.

LEO raises his eyebrows and gestures to the dragon.

LEO: This? I assure you, Theodora has no idea. I didn't either, until an hour ago.

RAIK: And how did you learn so quickly?

LEO: Me? No. This belongs to . . . to someone I fell in with for a while.

RAIK leans forward, his face intent.

RAIK: Who?

LEO wets his lips.

LEO: You know, I can't recall her name.

RAIK: What will help you remember?

Together, the men settle down in the boat as it sweeps toward the shore.

The Dream

D MIN⁷   G SUS   C ADD2/E   F MIN⁽ADD9⁾   C ADD2/E   F MIN⁽ADD9⁾

what you lose But I'm the same, where-'er I go.

A MIN   D⁷   F MAJ⁷   G SUS   G

Old-er, yes, but wis-er? No. So

A MIN   F ADD2   C/E   F ADD2

let___ us rest here, you___ and I   And

E⁺/G♯   A MIN⁷   F MAJ⁷   G SUS   G

dream a-bout the days gone by.___

A MIN   F ADD2   C/E   F ADD2

Let___ us rest here, you___ and I   And

E⁺/G♯   A MIN⁷   F MAJ⁷   G SUS   G

dream a-bout the days gone by.___

A MIN   F   C   G   D MIN⁷   A MIN⁷

Long the hours through till dawn We can-not wait, we

CHAPTER TWENTY-THREE

As *Le Rêve* turns back to shore, the city lights blur and shimmer like a mirage. I have never abandoned hope, but at times, hope abandons me.

I can feel it now, trying to escape, like the spark of my soul, all the light in me. I clench my fists as though I can hold it close, but it slips out in my protests, my pleas, and finally, my bitter laughter. One of the soldiers sneers down at me as though he knows I'm mad—but I have never felt more sane. It is the rest of the world that doesn't make sense.

Was reaching Aquitan ever possible, or is it only an illusion? Perhaps the search for a cure was the real lunacy.

To travel to the edge of the world I knew, only to be turned back on the water. To give everything for a better life and still come up short. To try to stop the rebels and be accused of being one.

I should have listened to Leo.

My laughter only fades when the soldiers haul Papa to his feet. He moans when they touch his wounded arm; he cries out when they tie his hands. I try to stay close to him—just to give him a warm look, a bit of comfort—but when the boat returns to the dock, the soldiers pull us apart to march us down the gangplank. The riot has dispersed, leaving nothing but a line of soldiers and a black smear of blood on the wharf. Desperately, I search the face of each man in uniform, looking for my brother among them—or the man I'd thought was my brother. But if I found him, would he help us?

Either way, he does not appear. The soldiers drag us through the streets. The city is dim, subdued; the revelers gone. But when Maman sees our destination loom out of the dark, her cries split the air.

"You can't take me in there! You can't!" Maman struggles, but the soldiers march us inexorably along the carved stone path toward the black temple—Hell's Court—where Le Trépas lurks in the dark. As they haul us over the threshold, Maman's protests turn to screams. They echo in the long hall, over and over and over, wordless shrieks like a hammer to glass. Somewhere, off in the dark, a man starts screaming back.

Shadows flee before us. The only light comes from the smoking torches tacked to the walls, their feeble light swallowed by the blackness of the cavernous vault. At the far end, a stone statue looms, stripped of its gold. Its face is lost in the darkness near the distant ceiling, but his lamp is there, empty at his feet. The King of Death. There are no offerings here, and no souls either, though I can smell death in the air.

At the foot of the statue, a jailer rests his feet on the black stone altar. As we approach, he stands, taking a set of keys and a lamp from his makeshift desk.

"What did they do?" he asks, barely curious, as he leads us down the long hall.

"Traitors," the soldier grunts. "Like the rest of them in here."

The jailer shakes his head as I whisper prayers to our ancestors—but can they hear me here? And if so, which ones are listening?

We trail down the hall, past rows of cells, small square hollows with tiny windows and scarred wooden doors:

the rooms where monks once slept. Now they are full of prisoners. The smell is almost a physical assault—joined soon enough by voices. Curses, threats . . . prayers. I shudder. Is it his voice I hear? Which cell houses Le Trépas?

Finally we stop before a cell just like the others, only empty. The guards thrust us through the door. When the jailer shuts it behind us, the dark comes down like a curtain: stop the show. There is no light—there never has been, and will never be again. But Maman's screams go on and on, reverberating in the room, making the blackness come alive. Then comes a thudding sound, over and over and over, as she flings herself at the door.

A thought—fleeting: at least we are together. I reach out with trembling hands and find Papa first. To my surprise, he is standing—though he's still hunched, his wounded arm hanging at his side. With the other, he pulls Maman close, folding her against his chest, muffling her cries till they turn back from sounds to words.

"He's here," she says, over and over. "He's here."

His arms around us, Papa leans against the wall; we slide down together to huddle on the floor. But then, over her sobs, Papa starts to sing.

He sings songs from our shows, old airs from the valley,

lullabies and reels about home. Songs for remembering, for resting, for laying down to sleep; even songs for children's clapping games, for threshing rice, for herding water buffalo—he sings them all, over and over, all through the night, as hopelessness circles like a vulture and eternity falls into the chasms between hours. I hold on to his voice—no, it holds on to me, wrapping me like a blanket, warming the cold stone. Maman goes quiet too, finally calm or exhausted. And it isn't only her. When Papa sings, the other prisoners are silent in the dark, even the screaming man.

What about Le Trépas? Can he hear Papa's voice? Does he smile at the music?

Finally dawn arrives, a sickly, crepuscular light seeping into the prison through cracks and around corners. Papa brings his performance to a close, looking somehow smaller, as though he's poured something of his substance into his song. As the light grows, it heightens the pallor of his skin. He slumps back against the wall, his shirt stiff with dried blood. I have never seen him look so diminished, and it is somehow worse than the whispers in the walls.

But there is nothing I can do to help him. The cell is bare—there is no water to wash his wounds, no clean cloth to bind them, no betel or alcohol, only stone floors and filth in the corners and the bones of vermin who have died here in the dark. If only their souls had stayed, I could break the lock, twist open the door. But nothing dares come near, not even when I pick at my wounds and blood beads on the skin. Even the dead fear Le Trépas—except the ones who serve him. A brief spark of gratitude for the dark; I'd rather have no light at all than a flicker of blue fire.

Hours pass like years. No one opens our door—why? Had they searched our rooms? Found our bags? Found Leo? Has he told them what I am? What I can do?

Maybe they will never open the door again.

We haven't eaten since yesterday, but I am not hungry. The thirst, though . . . it's like a file in my throat. Worse for Papa—it must be—but he doesn't complain. And what about his arm? It is swollen, limp, hot to the touch. Pain flickers like a flame across his face, and even in the cold of the cell, sweat glistens on his brow.

Now that he is quiet, the sounds of the other prisoners creep in: men whispering, weeping. Someone coughs and coughs with a sound like tearing flesh. The hours pass, and eventually I hear sobbing, soft and close—and I think it's Maman until I touch my face and find the tears, hot as blood.

At least Maman is no longer screaming. She only lies with her head in Papa's lap as the hours pass. Gently he strokes her hair, and her breathing is shallow and even. I think she's sleeping until she speaks. "Do you see them?"

Her voice is so quiet; her lips barely move. But Papa heard her too. "Shhh, Meliss," he says, but I crawl closer.

"Who, Maman?"

"Your brothers and sisters." Her whisper is softer than a dying breath; it chills me more than the stone. "Can you see their souls?"

"No," I say, still cautious—but why? If we cannot talk about it now, when? I may never have another chance. "Not here."

"In the middens," she guesses, with such clarity that I wonder if she'd seen them too, so many years ago.

"In the tunnel," I tell her. "Something like n'akela. But he put himself into a body like I put souls into fantouche."

"Jetta . . ." Though Papa's voice is quiet, there is a warning in it. But I take Maman's hand, unwilling to be silent now.

"What are they, Maman?"

"A perversion," she says with a shudder. "They use the power to give life to take new bodies for their own twisted souls."

My lip curls at her words—but these are my brothers, she said. My sisters. If they are perversions, what am I? "How? Is it Le Trépas's blood that makes us this way?"

"It's the deaths," she murmurs. "Three of them. Drowning. The hole in the earth, to swallow you up. I stole you away before the fire. You survived."

I swallow. When I had walked through the graveyard, had I passed a stone carved for me? "If I hadn't . . . ?"

"You'd be one of them."

I sit back against the wall, the stone cold against my clammy skin. Under the damp rags of my uniform, my scar itches. The fire two years ago—my third brush with death. What will happen to my soul when the King of Death finally comes for me? Will I seek out the bodies of the dead and wear their rotting flesh till it falls away?

The image curdles in my head, but then Papa clears his throat and starts another song. Though his voice is raspy and softer than it was, it is more compelling now than the shadows whispering in my ear—more familiar. What we share is more than blood.

He sings the hours away. It is grueling, to sing without stopping, without food or water, without care for his injuries—and even a performer like Papa can't keep it up forever. But he doesn't stop to complain, and I am carried away by the melody as my heart beats in time to the song.

Time passes—how much? I don't want to guess. What if this all the time I have left? But then, over the song, another sound: footsteps in the hall, and the jingle of keys.

I hold my breath. Is the jailer coming for us? Hope returns, though I hesitate to welcome it. Then again, it is oh, so sweet while it lasts. It grows as the footsteps stop outside our cell, then blooms when the tumblers turn in the lock. As the door swings wide, I stagger to my feet, weak and dizzy but propelled by need—for what? Food, freedom? And water. A sip of something. But the man does not carry a plate or a cup, nor does he say a word. He only steps aside to make way for two grim-faced Aquitan soldiers.

One raises a lantern and peers at our faces—Maman, Papa, and me. The light is painfully bright. I cringe, like a worm pulled from under a stone, but dirtier. My hair is lank and tangled, my skin streaked with muck, and the servants' livery hangs off me, stained with water and worse. I must look like the worst sort of person—a criminal, a convict . . . crazy. But the soldier jerks his chin at me. "Come with us, girl."

My heart judders; my gut twists into knots. "What's going on?"

"Just a few questions."

"Why? What about?"

They do not answer. They only take my arms and march me down the hall, and while a moment ago, I longed for freedom, all I want now is to race back to Maman's arms. But the jailer slams the door behind me, the heavy wood muffling her cries. I struggle as the soldiers lead me down the hall, fighting with a strength I didn't know I still had. I've seen how the armée questions prisoners. In my mind's eye, the rebel's face appears, spitted on a bamboo pike. *Help me.*

But at the end of the hall, the soldiers stop. Instead of a questioneur, General Legarde is waiting beside the altar, under the impassive gaze of the old stone god.

I stiffen, going still. What does he want with me? I can't imagine the general himself is questioning everyone from the ship. Does he remember me from the road in Luda? Has he recognized my description from the recherche? Does he know about the guns I helped smuggle?

Has he found my fantouches?

But whatever he knows, whatever he says, this is my chance to try to convince him we are innocent. Perhaps my only chance. So I shrug off my captors and take a deep breath, lifting my chin, just so, and set my jaw, like this, as

I stride toward my impromptu performance. But a laugh bubbles up in my throat. If only I'd known in Luda that I'd see Legarde again. That this would truly be the most important show of my life. And as I approach the altar, I stumble at a new distraction.

The surface is bare—cleared of the lamp, the inkwell, the jailer's papers, his keys. Instead there is only a glass of water, placed directly in the center. It sparkles in the torchlight like a flute of champagne; in my ears, a ringing sound, as though someone were running an invisible finger around the crystal rim. I can hardly take my eyes from the glass.

"Is that for me?" My voice is a croak. The silence stretches. Legarde gives me a thin smile. He doesn't answer my question.

"How do you know Leo Rath?"

Of course. His son. Legarde must know Leo is involved with the rebels. That is why he would question me personally—here, in the privacy of the prison. Did the soldiers find Leo in my room? And if I admitted to leaving him tied there, would that help or hurt my cause? The general has disowned him. . . . "Leo Rath," he said, not Leo Legarde. But what about Theodora's letter? *You are my brother always, no matter what he says.* I blink, trying to gather my thoughts—but the general takes my hesitation as equivocation.

"I can see by your face you know who I mean. Don't try to be clever, and don't bother protecting him. He's a traitor. A pimp. Familiar with *loose women*." He gives me a significant look, just short of mocking, and I use all the power of the muses not to change my expression. The man gives no indication that he's speaking of his own son, but the words gall me—this, from a man who kept a mistress in a dance hall along Le Verdu.

Or is he only saying as much to draw me in? To get me to insult his son to his face? "We traveled together," I say at last. "For safety on the road."

"When did you last see him?"

"Aboard *Le Rêve*," I say—truthfully. Should I tell him what Leo had said to me there? That he was involved with the rebels? Would Legarde show mercy if he knew I had tried to fight back? I take a breath, but I can't get the words past my teeth. What's stopping me? I want to believe it is caution. "May I have some water, please?"

"Leo was seen leaving the ship aboard a fishing boat with another person of interest." Legarde puts his hand on the glass. My tongue curls. "Where is he going next?"

"I wish I knew," I say, also the truth, though it sounds like a lie. "Maybe Luda? If I knew exactly what you wanted to know, I might be able to help better."

Legarde watches me awhile. I watch the glass, and grit my teeth as he moves his hand to gesture at my filthy costume. "That is the uniform the rebels used to steal aboard the ship. A servant reports you threatened him with a gun. But when we questioned the surviving rebels, none of them knew anything about you. What's more, you were invited aboard at Leo's request. You must know each other well."

I open my mouth to refute the claim—there was so much I didn't know. So much I hadn't suspected. But why, then, can't I lay the blame at Leo's feet? "He wanted to help me," I say at last, and at the thought, the words finally come. "We met in Luda. I was there for La Fête. I'm just a shadow player. We're . . . I was trying to get to Aquitan. To bathe in Les Chanceux. To find a cure for my malheur. Leo said he would help me get there. He said I reminded him of someone he knew."

His mother, I do not say. The woman you left alone with your gun. Was Theodora right? Was Legarde as bereft as Leo at her death?

But if he thinks about her, he does not show it. "A

shadow player from Luda," he murmurs. My heart drops—the recherche. "A girl and her mother, if I recall correctly. We've met before."

"Yes, sir." Inside I am cursing, but I paint gratitude on my face thick as stage makeup. "You remember my little performance. Strings the thinness of a spider's web. You gave me five étoile. Thank you, sir. Thank you."

I bow low, but his expression does not change. "That same night, did you happen to meet Capitaine Legarde?"

"Not that I recall," I lie, and a smile touches his lips, then fades.

"I will telegram him to ask," he says then—a warning. But hadn't Siris said the telegraph building was damaged in the fire? How long would it take to repair? I widen my eyes, just a little, as though I'm confused.

"Yes, sir?"

Legarde watches me for a long time. But I do not break—never show, never tell. Finally, he nods a little, and relief nearly makes my knees buckle. But then he motions to the guards. "Show her back to the cell."

"To the cell?" Panic rises in my chest, sharp and strangling. "But I'm not a rebel!"

"I know," Legarde says. He sips from the glass of water

as the soldiers clamp their hands like vises on my arms. Gone is my stiff back, my brave face. I make them drag me down the hall, fighting the whole way. My own screams are answered in a chorus from the cells as we pass.

I should have given Leo to the general, told Legarde everything I knew. But would it have mattered? He believed me, he said so—I saw it on his face. But he hadn't brought me out to hear that I was innocent . . . only to learn who else was guilty.

Who was the person of interest who left with Leo? Another rebel? If I'd made a different choice aboard *Le Rêve*, it could have been us.

Maman and Papa are both waiting, breathless and afraid, as the guards throw me back through the door. We cling to one another, and I don't know which of us is comforting the other.

"What did he say?" Papa murmurs into my hair, his voice like a rasp over bark. "What's going to happen?"

"They're letting us out in the morning," I lie, and if they don't believe me, no one says it. "Only one more night."

At the door, the jailer clears his throat, but I'm grateful he doesn't disagree aloud. He lingers in the doorway though the soldiers have gone. "I like the singing," he says at last, pulling a metal flask from his jacket and setting it on the floor.

I snatch it up as he shuts the door. It's cool and slick in my shaking hands and nearly half full. At first I wonder if it's liquor, but when I unscrew the cap, I can smell the sweet, pure scent of water. It's the hardest thing I've ever done to pass the flask to my father. But Papa only gives it to Maman with a gentle smile. She hands it back to me, and I shake my head. "You first. The general gave me some," I lie.

She takes a drink so deep I can almost hear it—the sound of water rushing by, like the rising tide as the king called the sea, or the floodwater through the lava tunnel as I stood at the broken stone lip. But then Maman hands the bottle to Papa. He only takes a sip. We pass the flask between us, alone again with the dark. At least for tonight, we have one another.

Sent at 0207h
General Legarde at Nokhor Khat
To: Capitaine Legarde at Luda

REGARDING THE RECHERCHE FOR JETTA OF
THE ROS NAI STOP ELABORATE ON HER CRIMES
STOP WHAT HAS SHE DONE

Sent at 0312h
General Legarde at Nokhor Khat
To: Capitaine Legarde at Luda

REGARDING THE RECHERCHE FOR JETTA OF
THE ROS NAI STOP ELABORATE ON HER CRIMES
STOP WHAT HAS SHE DONE STOP CONFIRM
RECEIPT

To the very excellent and puissant king Antoine,
by the grace of God Le Roi d'Aquitan;

Cher Antoine,

We are at a crucial juncture with the rebellion. The King of Chakrana has been kidnapped under a false flag. As a result, the locals believe the armée attempted his assassination. To make matters worse, there was an unfortunate clash between the 314th Battalion and the local population just a few days north of the capital. There is growing unrest in the city, and I have reports of the rebel ranks swelling.

Quite a few officers fell during the kidnapping, and my men are spread thin. Our priority is to find the king. If the rebels spirit him into the countryside, it will be a heavy blow to our authority here.

I will prove your faith in me is not misplaced, but I would appreciate monetary demonstration of your confidence.

À Votre Service,

General Julian Legarde

ACT 3,

SCENE 31

Inside the prison. Darkness looms above the jailer's station, just out of reach of the meager light of the lantern. Drifting through the gloom, we hear Samrin's song, sung low. The jailer is asleep in his chair, feet up on the altar that makes up his desk.

Three Aquitan soldiers approach: a capitaine, a soldat, and an adjutant, all in uniform. The two junior men are not yet accustomed to the walk of the soldiers—they are so new, their boots still squeak—but the capitaine strides forward, his lips twisted in a permanent frown from the scar that puckers one cheek. Reaching the desk, he claps his hands loudly, an inch from the sleeping jailer's nose. The man startles awake, tipping backward in his chair with a cry. Then he scrambles to his feet with an awkward salute, which the capitaine barely acknowledges.

JAILER: Bonsoir, capitaine.

CAPITAINE: Good *morning*, you mean. I'm here for the puppeteers.

JAILER: So early?

CAPITAINE: The questioneur is ready. Why delay? The information they give us may lead us to the king.

JAILER: Of course, capitaine.

He picks up the keys, but the capitaine snatches them out of his hand.

CAPITAINE: Just tell me the cell number. I wouldn't want your chair to get cold.

JAILER (*shamefaced*): Twenty-seven, capitaine.

In response, the capitaine takes the man's lantern and turns on one heel, leaving the jailer in the dark. He leads his soldiers past the carved stone pillars and into the long hall. In the cells, the prisoners murmur and moan at the sound of their footsteps. The capitaine responds by riling them up, slamming his fist on each door as he passes.

CAPITAINE: Teh-toa! Shut up in there!

The prisoners call back with curses and screams; soon there is a cacophony in the prison. Reaching cell twenty-seven, the capitaine swings the door open. Inside, Meliss and Samrin huddle in the corner, but Jetta scrambles to her feet.

JETTA: What do you want now?

She sways as she stands, but her face is defiant, her fists balled in fury. Her anger fills the cell. The capitaine hesitates a moment. Then he nods to his companions.

CAPITAINE: Allez. Tie her.

Nervously, the soldiers approach. They take Jetta's arms, but she jerks free to lunge at the capitaine. The adjutant cuffs her on the jaw; she reels and the capitaine swears. But Jetta looks up at him, her hand on her cheek.

JETTA: Are you here to shoot us, or to save us, brother?

Puzzled, the adjutant turns, right into the capitaine's fist.

CHAPTER

TWENTY-FOUR

In my heart, rage and relief mix—a sickening concoction, though I have no time to be ill. As the adjutant stumbles back against the wall, the soldat reaches for his gun—but Akra is quicker. He elbows the man in the face, and I wrest his weapon from his belt. The adjutant lurches back into the fray, but stops when I aim the gun between his eyes. The lantern swings wildly from his fist, throwing shadows across the stone. His eyes are wide and white in the dark. I do not shoot, and he does not move, until Akra strikes him across the back of his head with the butt of his own weapon.

The adjutant slumps to the floor beside the soldat,

lantern oil leaking out across the stone. Around us, the prisoners continue their wild cacophony. The fight can't have lasted more than thirty seconds, but my heart is louder than any drum and the taste of blood still fills my mouth. I wait for the sound of footsteps—the jailer, more soldiers—but nothing comes. Then I turn to Akra, and my heart falters.

In the dim light from the hall, the harsh set of his jaw is smoothed into shadow. He looks more like he did when he left two years ago—nothing like the man with the gun on the dock. Still, I cannot bring myself to reach for him.

Maman does, though, springing at him with a cry, pressing her face into his chest, clinging to the strap of his bandolier. "I thought we'd lost you," she murmurs. "I thought you were gone."

"How did you find us?" Papa says, breathless. He is still leaning against the wall—too weak even to stand. But the lines of pain around his eyes have eased into a wan smile. Akra leans down to touch his face, to inspect his arm.

"I saw you on the ship," my brother murmurs. The words are quiet as a closing door.

"I saw you too." My own hands are slick on the butt of the stolen gun. Could I have shot the soldier with it, as Akra shot the refugee? "I had hoped I was wrong."

"Why were you aboard *Le Rêve*?" My brother's face is unreadable in the dark—but is that an accusation in his tone?

Before I can answer, another sound drifts in above the strange symphony of the men in the cells: the low clanging of a gong. Akra stiffens, standing. "What's that?" I ask.

"The city alarm," he says, his voice brusque. "We have to hurry."

"An alarm?" A chill goes up my spine; I glance at the soldiers, out cold on the stone floor. "For this?"

"I don't know," Akra says. "But we're not staying to find out. Come." He goes to the door, drawing his gun and peeking into the hall. "It's clear. For now."

"What about the jailer?" I ask. "How are we going to get past him?"

"I'd hoped to get you all outside before starting this little fight." Akra nudges the adjutant with his boot. "But we have his lantern, and the guns. The cordon sanitaire will be more of a challenge."

My heart beats faster. "What do you mean, a cordon?"

"Since the attack on the king, there's been trouble in the capital. Rebels and riots. The armée is lined up to protect the palace block, and the temple along with it. We could go up and over the ridge behind the temple," he adds. Then, with a glance at Papa, "Or, three of us could."

It takes me a moment to understand. His words shock me—so cold, so simple. "Akra . . ."

But he turns to me quickly, his eyes gleaming. "If you have a better suggestion, out with it."

My mouth hangs open as I try to come up with a plan—shooting our way past the guards, out across the plaza, carrying Papa between us. Then what, if we made it that far? Through the cordon? To the city streets? Past the manned gate? Or down into the tunnel, where the dead man stands guard? I shudder, but Papa wouldn't make it down those stairs, either.

I do not answer—but Papa does. "It's a good plan, Akra, but don't forget the costumes." He nods toward the fallen soldiers. "Jetta, you and Meliss take the uniforms. Quickly. And pull your hair under the caps."

I swallow—despite the water, my mouth is dry. "What about you, Papa?"

He smiles a little. "I'd like to rest here awhile. It's been a very long road."

Akra takes a deep breath, though he doesn't protest—

none of us do. But my brother holds out his hand to me, his palm open. I stare at it, unsure what he wants, but he only repeats the gesture. "What?"

"Give me the gun," he says, but I hesitate, so he takes it from me and tucks it into Papa's hands, wrapping his fingers around the weapon. Then he stands. "Get dressed, Jetta."

I frown. "Why the gun?"

"Get dressed."

"Akra—"

Quick as a bullet, he grabs my arm and pulls me close to his ear. "You want me to leave him with no way out? They sent me here to bring you to the questioneur."

I yank my arm free of his grasp—my skin is crawling at his touch. How many others has he walked to their deaths? I want to yell at him, to spit in his face. But I don't . . . because I don't have another solution. Still, I remember the voices— *Help me*—and the rebel's bodies cut to ribbons and left on the side of the road. Then Papa's voice chases the echoes away.

"Long the hours through till dawn," he sings. "We cannot wait, we carry on."

"Papa . . ."

"But if we stop, the midnight breeze will bring us rain and memories . . ."

"We'll come back for you." I throw my arms around his neck and make promises I don't know how to keep. "We'll come back."

He pulls me close to his heart for just a moment. I can feel it beating through the thinness of his shirt—the heart we share, if not the blood. Then, so gently, he lifts me from his neck and pushes me toward the door. His smile never falters, nor does his song. It carries us up to the light as we leave him behind in the shadows.

My vision is blurring, but I keep my face impassive, staring over Akra's shoulder as we stride down the hall. To my right, Maman does the same thing, her eyes as hollow as dead shells. We walk like soldiers to the altar, though my feet slide in my stolen boots. None of us acknowledges the jailer as we approach. The man salutes nervously as Akra sets the dark lantern down with the keys on his desk. "You're out of oil," my brother says coldly, as though it is the man's fault. He is still a good actor.

"Sorry, capitaine," the jailer responds, shifting on his feet, but Akra has already turned to leave. Maman and I scramble to follow. "Sir!" the jailer calls as we depart, but

Akra doesn't even slow down. "What about the prisoners?"

"Still in the cell, blaireau!" Akra throws the words over his shoulder like étoiles to a ragman. "You think I have time for them now? Don't you hear the alarm?"

If the jailer is suspicious, he doesn't dare show it; we walk out of the prison unmolested. The guards at the main door even salute as we pass. Beside me, Maman shudders as we leave the temple behind—is she relieved or hurting? She does not say. She does not say anything—but my own heart is breaking. I was so foolish to think we had nothing else to leave behind.

Akra does not falter. The gong is still sounding, and people are running to and fro in the dark streets. Uniformed soldiers and half-dressed citizens, some heading toward the fort, others toward the palace, others every which way. But as a young soldier crosses our path, Akra seizes him by the arm. "What's going on?"

"The rebels, capitaine!" The man gives him a nervous salute. "They've set off bombs all over the city!"

Akra swears. "How many?"

"Half a dozen reported. The soldiers are sweeping the streets, but the locals are angry. We might have another riot on our hands."

With another muffled curse, Akra releases the soldier, who stumbles off toward his post. "The rebels have bought us some time," he mutters as he leads toward the street. I have to jog to keep up. "But the fort will be overrun. I'd hoped to steal some horses there."

"For what?"

Akra looks at me askance. "We have to get out of the city."

"And go where?" Maman says. The words are distant, numb. "Where is there to go?"

"Into the jungle," Akra says. "Away from the armée. We can make our way north," he adds then, his voice wistful—and there he is again, the boy who was my brother. "Back home."

I cannot bring myself to tell him the truth—that the home he remembers is not ours anymore. But Maman speaks instead. "We should try the docks. We could sneak onto a boat."

"The docks are past the cordon," Akra says grimly. "And after the riots, all the ships pulled anchor and retreated to the bay."

He turns on his heel, heading away from the heart of the city, toward the ridge of the caldera that rises behind Hell's

Court. As we scramble to follow, Maman's face twists—her footsteps falter. And I know, suddenly. Leaving Chakrana was never about the cure. At least not entirely. Even all these years later, Maman was still trying to escape Le Trépas.

We pass the dark heap of the temple and make our way through the ruined garden. As we get farther from the plaza, from the court and the confusion, the sounds of the city fade, muffled by the foliage, though the distant ringing of the gong continues like the beat of a metal heart. Stone statues peek out of dense camellias and sprays of ginger; there are souls here too—flitting through the still air. Sweat beads on my brow as I watch for a hint of blue fire, for anything following us, but mercifully nothing comes.

Near the ridge, the ground slopes gently up, until the overgrown garden turns into a tangle of jungle. But rather than plunge inside, Akra leads us along the tree line. Though the shadows are deep and the armée is busy, I still feel exposed. "Where are we going, Akra?"

"There's a path," he says. "Halfway up the side of the ridge."

"A path? For who?"

"The armée," he says. "There's a workshop up there. We

can find supplies. Maybe guns. The jungle will be dangerous, Jetta."

I raise an eyebrow. "Do you think I don't know that?"

But he doesn't respond. He only keeps walking, leaving me glaring at his back. Soon enough, the track appears: an opening in the jungle that leads to a rocky switchback road climbing up the side of the ridge. We make our way upward, keeping close to the side, under the shadows of the trees, and soon I am panting, light-headed. A week ago, the climb would have been easy, but lack of food, of sleep and water— all of it is a weight on my back.

Maman is suffering too, but neither of us wastes the air to complain, and Akra only continues forward—though mercifully he slows his pace. At last the path leads us to a long, low building perched on the face of the ridge: the workshop. The walls are made of bamboo and painted in drab green, and the roof is thatched with palm, but one side is open to overlook the city below, and a scaffold of bamboo juts from the wide opening, like a pier in midair.

"What do they work on here?" I say, frowning, but Akra puts his fingers to his lips and points. It takes me a moment to understand what he's showing me: the light that glimmers in the building is not a stray soul, but a lamp.

Drawing his gun, he creeps closer to the door of the workshop; it sits slightly open on the jamb. Akra peers inside, and I try to see over his shoulder, wrinkling my nose. There is a strange smell in the air here—a chemical scent that tingles on my tongue. But the sight is stranger still: a room full of enormous contraptions, crafted of bamboo and iron and leather, each of them different, all in various stages of completion.

For a moment, the scattered pieces remind me of my own fantouches. But these machines are not built for show. There is one like a bat, fearsome and finely jointed, the pieces of one wing scattered on the floor. Another is a basket with some machinery inside—it looks like an iron furnace. Trailing on the ground beside it is a multicolored bag of silk at least two wagon lengths wide. Another creature has skeletal wings resembling a hawk's, but missing cladding or feathers. Beside it, a black hawk is pinned to a board, wings outstretched, one plucked bare to see the joints. Its soul still circles through the rafters of the workshop.

There are half a dozen other half-built heaps scattered about. "What are they?" I breathe softly into my brother's ear.

Akra wets his lips. "Flying machines."

"Flying?"

Akra turns back sharply, raising a finger, warning me into silence. I swallow my next question—what are they for? I already know the answer: war. This is the armée, after all. My jaw drops as I imagine it—men with guns, raining death from the sky. "The rebels won't stand a chance," I whisper, and my brother twitches. But then the next thought comes, too quick to keep quiet. "Akra. We can fly Papa out of the city!"

He rounds on me, but inside the workshop, I hear the clatter of metal and a muffled exclamation. My stomach sinks, but Akra curses, kicking open the door and raising his gun. "Arret!" he calls. "Hands up!"

There, in the shadows, a large figure hesitates. For a moment, the form looks to me like some strange puppet, but when I blink, I realize it's a person covered head to toe: heavy black boots, a thick leather work smock that reaches to the floor, and black rubber gloves up to the elbow. Something about the form is familiar—and about the golden hair.

"Don't shoot, capitaine," the girl says, nudging the goggles up onto her forehead with one elbow. "It's only me, Theodora."

I gape at the Flower of Aquitan in her oil-stained work boots, but Akra's aim doesn't waver. "Hands up," he repeats, cocking his weapon. "Jetta, tie her."

Theodora's voice goes up an octave. "What?"

"Quiet," Akra says. "Or I'll have her gag you too. Jetta?"

My eyes are wide—I glance at Akra for reassurance, but he doesn't take his eyes from La Fleur. Her red lips are sour as bayberries. I approach with caution, looking for something to use as a rope. Rummaging on her workbench in the corner, I see wire, but I cannot imagine letting it bite into her flesh. Akra pulls a short knife from his belt.

"Cut the straps from her apron," he says, holding out the blade, but I've already found some rubber tubing.

"What do you think you're doing?" Theodora hisses as I pull the gloves from her hands and wind the hose around her wrists. "The general is my father."

"Which makes you a perfect hostage," Akra says. He looks at her goggles, her apron, her boots. "You're the scientist."

"Are you surprised?"

"I'm disgusted," Akra spits. "You build machines to kill innocents."

Theodora glances at his gun. "And you use them."

Akra's eyes narrow, but Maman slips past him, toward one of the flying machines, running her hands over a bamboo wing. "Do these work?"

Theodora's eyes dart left, then right. "Not yet," she says, too quickly, but though many of the devices are clearly half finished, some look complete. And while the machinery is far too complex for us to operate—with buttons and levers, dials and throttles—the soul of the hawk still circles over the structure inspired by its own flesh and bone.

"Akra," I whisper to him. "Give me your knife."

He hands it over without asking why, but Maman gives me a look. "Jetta, no."

"You have a better plan?"

Her pained silence is my answer. I approach the skeletal machine, all long bamboo bones fused with bright bronze cartilage. No feathers nor webbing, not yet—but none are needed, not for me. As she looks on, Theodora's lips twist, trying to hold back a laugh. "That will never fly," she says. "Be reasonable. Leave now, and you might have a sporting start before my father tracks you down."

I don't bother responding, but at her words, Akra looks at me sideways. "What are you doing?"

"Just get in." The blade flashes in the low light as I slice the pad of my thumb. Blood wells up in a thin line. When I lift my hand, the arvana stoops, and with a flare of fiery wings, she settles on my wrist.

"Jetta . . ." Akra's uncertainty is plain on his face, but Maman wastes no time scrambling into the belly of the bird. I follow her, daubing the symbol of life onto the bamboo. There is another flash of light, and the soul clambers into her new skin.

With a metallic clang that makes me jump, the wings unfold, knocking the metal barrel on its side. The drum rolls sideways, spilling kerosene across the floor. Theodora leaps out of its path and my brother swears, tracking her with his gun, but she ducks behind one of the machines, disappearing into the shadows. Akra curses again, starting after her, but I call him back as the bird shudders under our feet. "Akra!" I shout. "Get in!"

He hesitates, still scanning the dark corners of the warehouse as kerosene seeps across the floor. "That machine isn't finished. You heard her."

"It doesn't matter!" I call, but though he turns from his pursuit, he keeps his distance from the bird.

"Why not?"

I grit my teeth. "Just get in!"

He wavers for another moment. Then he curses again, shoving his gun into its holster and leaping with wide steps across the spreading chemical puddle. Maman reaches out to him, and he takes her hand, hauling himself up into the bird just as a shot rings out from the shadows of the warehouse. The hot breath of a bullet raises the hair on the back of my neck.

Maman screams and Akra swears, scrambling into the bird. "There's no cover here!" he snarls at me, drawing his gun once more. But Theodora is well hidden in her workshop—and free of the binding. I should have tied her with the wire. Too late now.

Instead, I lean down to murmur to the soul. "Up," I whisper. "Fly."

With a lurch and a shudder, the creature lifts off the ground as another shot rings out from the dark. Akra ducks, though La Fleur's aim is not as good as her craftsmanship. The shot whizzes past his head.

The soul of the hawk is eager for the open sky; too quickly, the roof descends. Maman tries to cover my head with her arms as we burst through the grass ceiling. There is debris in my hair, my eyes, the air around us, but it falls away back into the warehouse below as the bird hovers in the cool night air. Brushing leaves from my stolen uniform, I search for my bearings. Before us, the city is spread as though on a stage—there, the palace; beside it, the temple.

Akra's eyes are as wide as mine, but he isn't looking at the city. "How is this possible?" he says, watching the skeletal wings as they beat. But before I can answer, a great metallic screech floats up from the warehouse.

"What was that?" Maman says, but Akra pulls a lighter and a kerchief from his pocket.

"It won't matter in a minute," he says, knotting the kerchief and flicking the flame to life. Lighting the fabric, he drops it down through the hole in the roof. A moment later, a warm rush of heat buffets us from below as the pool of kerosene catches fire. With a curse, I urge the hawk toward the temple. We haven't gone far when a deep bass boom shatters the air, and the grass roof of the workshop is flung like confetti in a ball of fire.

Debris rockets upward; we are shaken in the blast. The air turns to heat and light. My heart stops . . . my ears ring . . . my stomach lurches, but the soul of the hawk bears us into freer skies, and soon enough I can breathe again.

Then a buzzing sound rips at the air like a swarm of

bees; I glance behind us and curse. Another creature has burst from the inferno, zipping down the bamboo pier and gliding toward us on great wings—and in the cockpit of the soot-black bird is Theodora Legarde.

14 Août
—Progress on the design based on the Chakran top—a child's toy made of bamboo, capable of vertical flight—is promising, but the trouble comes from powering the spring. The machinery necessary is heavier than the craft can reliably lift.

23 Août
—Fixed wing: the curve is of particular importance to keeping it aloft. But for initial lift the craft needs more height. A natural cliff? A scaffolding?
—Movable wing. THE POWER IS THE PROBLEM. I have one machine nearly ready to test, but range is limited. I cannot yet carry enough fuel to travel very far.

2 Septembre
—Kerosene may be a dead end. Methylated spirits???

CHAPTER TWENTY-FIVE

The Flower of Aquitan glares at us from behind a shield of glass, her hair streaming silver in the moonlight. On the wide wings of her contraption, propellers spin, and gunfire flashes from a barrel mounted to the nose of her machine.

Bullets zip by. Akra aims back, firing madly. But his shots go wide as our hawk pulls away, dodging and weaving through the air, as quick on the wing as she was in life. The world seems to tilt and my stomach twists like a snake, but Theodora falls back. As our hawk slows, I scan the horizon—there, the temple, across the garden. Murmuring to the hawk's soul, I point her toward Hell's Court.

Akra swears and reloads his gun, but his face is pale and his hands are shaking; he keeps glancing at the earth below as bullets slip through his fingers. "Turn us around, Jetta! We need to get over the ridge out of the city!"

"Not yet," I say through my teeth, but Theodora is circling too, coming back to meet us head-on. Akra curses as another round of gunfire tears the air. The soul of the hawk dips and turns, sweeping back and away again. "Shoot her, Akra!" I shout; he's already taking aim, but he cannot steady his hand.

"Our bird is faster," he calls. "Just keep going!"

"No!" Maman grips my arm and points south, toward the Hundred Days Sea. "We should leave now while we can!"

"Leave?"

"To Aquitan!"

"We'll never make it that far," Akra says over the rushing wind. "We have no food, no water—"

"What are saying, the both of you?" Disgust curls my lip. "We can't leave Papa behind!"

Under his breath, Akra swears, but Maman doesn't look away. "He made his choice," she says. "To save you. Don't throw it away."

"Don't make this about me." I spit the words through

clenched teeth. "We're going back to the temple!"

At my command, the bird banks again, beating the air as we turn. But Theodora is still waiting over the plaza, and the next round of bullets clips our wing.

Our hawk lurches as the bamboo splinters; she shudders in the air, struggling for balance, for height. I wrench at the controls like reins, but Akra reaches out to take my shoulder. "Jetta!" Something in his tone turns my head. "We were never going back."

He gives me that look . . . Maman's look. Leo's look. The look that fears my reaction to their reality, and at first anger flares in me. But it burns fast into bitter ash. I'd already known about Papa, hadn't I? I'd known when I'd left him with the gun.

I'd known and I'd left anyway.

I want to shout at Akra, to make it his fault, or Maman's—anyone else's. But it's mine, isn't it? Not because Papa chose to save me, but because of my choices along the way. From Legarde in Luda to Leo aboard *Le Rêve*—it was always about me. And at last I urge our hawk toward the ridge as cold wind wipes the tears from my eyes.

We pass high over the garden as Theodora circles to stay on our tail, but when we reach the face of the mountain, the bird works harder for height. Souls are strong, but the crack in the bamboo leaves her off-balance. Still, she pulls at the air, clambering up the side of the caldera. Finally, when we reach the apex, the country unrolls before me like a stage lit by the faint glow of dawn.

For one bright moment, we hover. The horizon levels out, the open sky before us, the night air fresh and cool. Then the roar of the propellers grows as La Fleur pulls up to keep us in her sights, and the rattle of her guns splits the sky. "Down!" I say to the hawk, and she folds her wings and stoops. We tip, dropping below the lip of the ridge, picking up speed as we skim over the jungle. The wind of our passing pulls the leaves from the trees. The earth rushes closer . . . closer . . . too close—then the hawk snaps her wings open to stop the fall. But instead of the whuff of wind, I hear a sickening crack.

A jolt, a snap. The bamboo breaks. The hawk twists in the air as the bent wing clips a branch and sends us spinning, tumbling, falling from the uncaring sky.

Thrown from the bird—

A blur of leaves. Branches lash my cheeks.

I land briefly in a tangle of vines, scrambling for purchase before I lose my grip, flip head over heels, and flop heavily to the earth. A firework flashes behind my eyes; for one eternal moment, I cannot breathe. Is this the end? Has my neck snapped in the fall?

No . . . it was only the wind knocked out of me. My lungs heave and air fills me again. Blood rushes in my ears and vana appear in my vision, buzzing lazy circles around my face. I lie on my back, blinking at the hole in the greenery above. Leaves drift from the canopy as the last stars wink down.

Where are Maman and Akra?

And where is Theodora? Can she make it over the ridge?

I should move . . . I know I should . . . though my body doesn't seem to agree. For a long while, I lie listening to the wind in the trees and the sound of the birds calling. Then I hear something else—a rustle of leaves—and fear pushes me to my feet. The world spins. I fall back to my hands and knees. Panting, I crawl toward the cover of a nearby patch of ferns. Slipping into the greenery, I peer through the fronds, trying to catch my breath. Another rustle—then my brother's whisper. "Jetta?"

He staggers through the undergrowth, holding his ribs, blood flowing from a gash on his left arm. I scramble from hiding and stumble toward him as he leans against a tree to rest. "Are you all right?"

"Broken rib," he says, taking shallow breaths. "Maybe two. You?"

I flex my arms, my legs. "Only bruises."

"And cuts," he says, nodding at my face. I touch my cheek; my hand comes away bloody. "Where's Maman?"

"I don't know." He scans the canopy and the distant sky. "But we have to find her and get out of here."

He turns, pushing off the tree, and I follow. Together we search, one eye on the ground and one on the sky. It is too risky to call out, so we creep across the turned soil and broken branches. There is no sign of Maman, neither body nor soul, though soon enough I hear another shiver of leaves. I freeze; Akra draws his weapon. But as we move closer, the twisted bamboo body of our hawk comes into view.

She is caught in the branches of a mimosa tree, her skeletal wings still trying to beat. Blossoms fall like rain around us, shaken loose by her feeble movements. Akra turns to me, a strange look on his face. "It almost looks alive."

There is an unspoken question in his voice, but I don't have the words—or the time—to explain. "We have to get her down from there."

"After we find Maman." He hesitates. "Do you think . . . you can make it fly again?"

I take a deep breath. I don't have the supplies to make a good repair—the glue, the rope, the rivets, everything was left behind in the roulotte. But perhaps I could cobble something together. It wouldn't have to be graceful as long as we could go slow. "Probably."

"*How*, Jetta?"

I know what he is asking, but I do not have the energy to collect my thoughts, my words. Not yet. "Let's find Maman first."

We search in widening circles, past tumbles of trumpet vines and patches of wild yam. The vana follow me, their glow fading as the daylight filters down through the jungle. An arvana creeps close, peering out of the leaves—an ocelot, perhaps; some sort of jungle cat. Then the souls of birds, gliding from branch to branch in eerie, expectant silence.

Finally we find her behind a thicket lying on her back, her hair across her pale face. I brush it back, but she does not move.

No . . . no. I cannot lose her too. But if she were dead, wouldn't I see the bright light of her soul? Kneeling beside her, I search for a pulse on her throat; I sag with relief when

I find it, still strong. But her breathing is so shallow I didn't notice it at first. Akra hovers behind me. "Is she alive?"

"Yes," I say, forcefully, angry at the question. Then my voice softens. "But I don't know what's wrong." I remember my own fear. "Could she . . . could her neck be broken?"

"Move aside." Akra shoulders me out of the way. First he touches her hands. "Her fingers are warm," he says. "Good circulation. Can you check her feet?"

I struggle with her boots—they are not tightly tied, but my hands are tender. Akra gently probes her skull, running soft hands behind her ears and through her hair. He hisses.

"What's wrong?"

"A knot like a lychee. She hit her head. How are her toes?"

"Warm. That's good, right?"

"Better than the alternative." Akra sits back on his heels. "We'll know more by tonight."

"What happens tonight?"

"Hopefully she'll wake up."

A pit yawns in my stomach. "What if she doesn't?" Akra looks away, and the only answer is the sound of insects in the jungle. Panic rises in me. "We can't just wait and hope, Akra."

"That's actually all we can do," he replies. "And we have to do it somewhere else. Can you take her feet?"

"What?"

"We have to bring her back to the flying machine," Akra says, slipping his hands under Maman's shoulders. Her head lolls against his arm. "We'll pull it down and load her in, if you can get it back into the air."

"And then what?" I chew my lip. "Maman wanted to go to Aquitan, but there's no way we could make it across the sea like this."

"Aquitan? No," Akra says, shaking his head. "We need to go north. Back home."

I open my mouth—but what to say? How to put the last few years into a few words? Home feels even farther away than Aquitan. "Akra . . ."

But before I can say more, the leaves stir again, and a Chakran woman steps out from the shadows.

"Bonjour, capitaine." She's dressed in a traditional sarong, the tail pulled up between her knees and tucked into her belt. She's also holding a rifle, and she aims it square at Akra. "You aren't going anywhere."

Rebels. My heart starts pounding. All the stories come back to me—the sabotage, the torture, the executions. "The uniforms are stolen," I say quickly. "We're only shadow players. Performers. Trying to escape the capital. We just want to get home to Lak Na."

She narrows her eyes, glancing from my too-large boots to my baggy armée jacket. "You, maybe. Not him."

"I swear," I say, widening my eyes, lying through my teeth. "Ask him for a story, let him craft you a fantouche—"

"I recognize him, girl!" The woman swings the barrel of the gun around, jabbing the butt of the rifle into my stomach. My lungs seize as I double over, wheezing. But Akra lunges for the gun, grappling with the rebel, trying to wrench the weapon from her hands. He almost has it when another rebel dashes through the brush, his own gun raised.

"Hands up!" he shouts, and Akra falls back, breathing hard. The woman kicks him in the stomach and he stumbles back against a tree, sliding to the ground.

"I'm not a capitaine," he gasps, clutching his broken ribs. "Not anymore."

The rebel woman sneers, her teeth bright. "Demoted?"

"Deserted."

"You betrayed your own people when you put on that uniform," she says. "I'm not surprised you would betray theirs."

At her words, rage burns on the back of my tongue—suddenly I want to tell her exactly why he joined. But the second rebel steps between her and me: an older man, tattooed but shirtless, unashamed of all of his sins. He kneels at Akra's side, speaking softly. "If you're a deserter, how did you get hold of the flying machine?"

Akra's expression doesn't change. "I'll trade information for medical care and the safety of my mother and sister," he says, but the rebel girl laughs.

"You're in no position to bargain," she says. "Get up. Both of you."

Using her foot, she nudges Maman. "She's unconscious!" I shout, but the woman raises the butt of her gun again and I cringe back, wrapping my arms around my stomach. Slowly, she lowers her weapon, a warning in her eyes.

"Be grateful I'll let you carry her," she says softly, speaking to me, but watching my brother. "It's more than I got when his men burned my village to the ground."

Is the pain in my chest from a lack of air, or shame? I look to Akra, but he will not meet my eyes. The rebel woman laughs like glass breaking.

"You're surprised? How do you think cha made capitaine?"

I don't answer her. What can I say? I only kneel beside Maman, pulling her arm up over my shoulder as I struggle to my feet. Her body is limp and heavy by my side. Akra takes her other arm, sharing the burden. I want to push him away, but I can't carry her alone. So she hangs between us, feet dragging, head lolling, as we follow the rebel woman through the jungle.

The path is winding, long and tangled. Vines grip our ankles and rocks find our toes; slick patches of red mud have us scrambling. Soon I am panting with the effort; worse for Akra, who can't seem to catch his breath. His arm is bleeding freely again. We travel slower and slower. Every so often, the man behind us prods us with his rifle. Finally, when we pass a thicket of bamboo, he calls a halt to build a sling.

He says it's because we're traveling so slowly, but I wonder if it's pity. Either way, I'm grateful. And when the bamboo poles are cut and lashed together with vines, I quietly draw a little vana into the cot to lighten the load. Maman would hate it, but Maman can't complain.

Though carrying her on the sling is easier, it's still grueling work to keep her balanced. I focus on my feet, trying to make sure I don't slip and spill her onto the jungle floor. One foot after the last, one foot after the last. My shoulders burn, and blisters rise and burst on my hands. My world narrows, and soon enough I forget everything but the path in front of me, the space between Maman's feet and my own.

I am bone weary and famished, and I crave water with a deep ache; it's all I can do to hold on and keep walking. What if I just stopped? What if I simply laid down on the path?

The thought of it is so tempting, I nearly do. But then a sound stops me—a whisper. Maman's voice. "Jetta?"

The glint of her eyes is barely visible under her lashes. I smile to see it, though my lips are so parched it hurts. I haven't lost her yet, and for all the times she carried me to safety, now I have the chance to carry her. One foot after the last, one foot after the last.

The day is fading by the time Akra staggers to a stop. I look up, tossing lank hair out of my eyes, and see it before me all at once: the rebel camp.

It's carved into a clearing in the jungle, set in the curve of a wide stream—but instead of the stronghold I imagined, it looks more like a place for refugees. Tents are interspersed with slapdash lean-tos and one-room shacks, all scattered over the muddy earth. Skinny chickens and barefoot children roam throughout, and various cookfires send smoke toward the sky. Then the smell of food drifts toward me on a breeze, and my stomach cramps so hard I double over, dropping the poles of the sling.

Akra staggers, but he manages to lower his side carefully to the ground. Then he kneels heavily beside it. In the dim light, his face is wan.

"Get up," the woman says, but Akra only shakes his head, his breath fast and shallow.

I can't imagine standing either, now that I've stopped moving, not even when she nudges me with the gun. "You didn't make us walk this far," I say, breathing hard. "Just to shoot us at the end of the road." Her eyes narrow, and suddenly I am not so sure. But then, in me, the deep, dark dare. "Do it, then," I growl, the words slipping out, and the woman's expression falters.

But that spark of bravado has taken all my strength. My head drops; my shoulders sag. Other rebels are drifting toward us now . . . children too. Would she kill us before their eyes? The scene plays out in my head—the gunshots, the blood—as another voice floats in: wicked, wry, familiar. "Did you bring me a gift, pussycat?"

Sauntering toward us, as lovely in a long sarong as she was in a scrap of silk—Cheeky. She grins at our captor, and I stare. The world seems to spin, like we are back up in the air. Am I only dreaming her here? But I never would have imagined her a rebel—nor wearing a machete at her waist, and Eve's snake around her neck.

I want to say her name, but my throat is too dry. The rebel woman winks at her. "I found a bird too, but it was too big to drag home."

"Too bad! I could use a new boa," Cheeky says, petting the scales of the snake. "This one doesn't have any feathers. So what are these, then?"

She peers down at Maman with a frown on her face— is that start of recognition? And when she meets my eyes, her own widen in shock. She whirls, barreling right into our guard, shoving the woman back. "Go! Get the docteur, quick!"

Sent at 1630h
General Legarde at Nokhor Khat
To: Capitaine Legarde at Luda

REGARDING THE RECHERCHE FOR JETTA OF
THE ROS NAI STOP ELABORATE ON HER CRIMES
STOP WHAT HAS SHE DONE CONFIRM RECEIPT

Sent at 1811h
Capitaine Legarde at Luda
To: General Legarde at Nokhor Khat

MESSAGE RECEIVED STOP TELEGRAPH
OFFICE OPERATIONAL STOP SUSPECT WANTED
FOR QUESTIONING REGARDING PRACTICE
OF NECROMANCY

Father—

I've just returned from my first successful flight. That's the good news.

The bad news is that one of my other machines was stolen.

The part I can't understand is, it shouldn't have been able to fly.

I want to replicate the conditions under which it took to the air. There is something strange here, but I'm on the verge of discovery, I know it. I told you I could figure it out. Aren't you glad now that I'm not getting married out in the middle of the sea?

Theodora

CHAPTER
TWENTY-SIX

At Cheeky's insistence, we are carried into a long pavilion—a sick house, I realize. Or what the Aquitans called an hôpital. But in Chakran style, it's built on a platform to keep the floor dry. The grass roof is held up by thick trunks, with the sides left open for circulation. Gauzy mosquito nets hang above soft pallets lined up in a neat row. Some of the beds are already occupied—we pass a man with no feet, a woman bandaged and moaning, a youth who seems uninjured except for the empty look in their eyes.

Are they all the victims of rebel torture? But if so, why would the rebels care for them? More and more, the stories of the Tiger's hordes seem exaggerated—or at least, I had seen worse from the armée. It's still hard to let go of the fear, but it is distant. Or maybe I'm too tired to carry it any longer. The sick house smells clean enough . . . moreover, it is a place to rest, and once I'm lowered into a bed, the night fades into a blur, seen narrowly between my heavy eyelids.

I rouse a little when a man comes into the hôpital— the docteur. Another old monk, though he hides his tattoos with a thin shirt. How many have the rebels collected? He leans over Maman first, his face serious but not severe. He treats Akra next, daubing his wounds with something that smells bright and clean. Then he removes the tattered shirt to check my brother's ribs. Akra swears as the docteur probes the bruised flesh, but I am staring blearily at my brother's scars. He seems sewn together—a patchwork of black and blue stitched with white, and something that looks like an old bullet wound in his shoulder. What had he suffered?

What suffering had he caused?

I close my eyes then, trying to shut out the world. How long had I been awake? Everything has become too much. For once, my mind obeys my wishes; I drift away into a soft and secret darkness. Then someone touches my hands and I jolt up, struggling, but the docteur whispers to me—hush,

hush—and I stop fighting. Blackness pools behind my eyes and in my head, swirling like a dark galaxy as I slide into a dreamless sleep.

After a while, I am aware of light . . . sips of water . . . the docteur's touch. But I don't have the will or the strength to open my eyes for a long time. When I do, there is afternoon sun—gentle, golden—filtered through the gauze of the mosquito net. I am lying flat on a pallet, on the floor. Every muscle hurts with the deep ache of exhaustion and hunger. I feel reedy, thin, like even the light of my soul has dimmed.

But the camp outside is full of life, and with my eyes closed, it reminds me for a moment of Lak Na. Giggles and singing as children playing a clapping game—the slap and splash of laundry in the water. . . . *Water.* My breath hisses through cracked lips and I struggle to sit up. Someone sweeps open the netting, and I'm looking up into Cheeky's face. "You're awake," she says, delighted.

"Water," I reply.

"Right. May I?" At my nod, she slips a soft hand behind my neck, lifting my head off the pallet and bringing a cup to my lips. Greedily I drink—it's juice from a young coconut, so sweet, tears start in my eyes. Too soon, it's gone.

"More?" I croak, but she is already refilling the cup. My

eyes focus on her hands—the nails chipped now, the pink stain fading.

"We brought food too," she says to me. "Can you sit all the way up?"

"I think so," I say, and I do—slowly, gingerly, with her help. Then I down the next cup all in one go. "Who's we?"

"Me and Leo," she says, and at his name, a jolt shoots through me, much like pain.

Cheeky pulls back the mosquito net, and there he is—leaning against one of the posts in the pavilion. He gives me a wan smile and steps closer, almost cautiously, holding out a bowl like an apology. "I'm glad you made it," he says softly. I throw my empty cup at his head.

My aim is terrible, but Leo jumps back, and Cheeky scrambles to her feet. "What is this about?"

"My father's still back there, thanks to you!"

"Me?" Leo raises an eyebrow. "What did I do?"

"You should have helped me!" I say, though the accusation feels hollow the moment I make it. Still, he shrugs.

"I did the best I could," he replies quietly, tucking his hand into his jacket and pulling out a stack of paper. He tosses it beside me on the cot; it rustles there, and not with the breeze. My book of souls. Quickly I cover it with one hand. The pages settle. Then I look back up at Leo, searching his face.

"And my fantouches?"

"I threw your pack in the river," he says. "I couldn't carry everything."

A pang in my chest—even though I'd never expected to see them again, the thought is still painful: the last of my old fantouches, gone. But this was why Legarde hadn't known what I was. After all I'd done, Leo had kept my secrets for me.

Why? Was it kindness . . . generosity? Or did he want something? But I cannot ask him. Not in front of Cheeky. "Thank you," I say instead, the words tasting odd on my tongue. I take a deep breath. "How did you escape?"

Leo shifts on his feet. "It's a long story," he says vaguely, and my eyes narrow. But he holds out the bowl. "You should eat something."

Cheeky nods, handing me a spoon. "You're a shadow of yourself. Pun intended."

Pursing my lips, I look down at the congee, warm and rich with bits of egg. My mouth starts to water. I lift the spoon—gently, so as not to disturb my healing blisters. Then

I take a bite and blink away tears. The food is so comforting. "You've changed too," I murmur between bites. "I preferred your other uniform."

"Me too, to be quite honest," she says, grinning. "But the mosquitoes are murder in the jungle."

In spite of myself, her smile sparks a small one in return. "What is this place?"

"Remember all the people on the road from Dar Som?" Leo glances out over the camp. "Not all of them get past the soldiers at the gates."

I frown. "And now . . . they're all rebels?"

Cheeky hesitates. "It's hard to say. First they were just refugees. But then the Tiger came."

A chill goes through me at the name; my eyes dart left to right, as though he might be lurking in the corner of the hôpital. "What did he do?"

"He helped," Cheeky says quietly. "Has his soldiers dig latrines. Build shacks. Bring rice. They send out patrols to keep us safe."

I stare at her, trying to make sense of it: praise for the Tiger. "So you're a rebel now too?"

She arches an eyebrow. "I'm a performer, Jetta," she says, as though it's obvious, but there is a bitter edge to her smile.

"Just temporarily without a stage."

I falter, glancing from her to Leo. He looks away. I swallow. "La Perl?"

Cheeky presses her lips together. "Gone."

I set down the bowl. "Tia and Eve?"

"Tia's out on patrol with the boys. They like her, and she likes the attention. But Eve . . ." Cheeky's hand goes to the snake on her shoulders. She strokes the smooth scales. "She ran back for this ridiculous thing while the armée was trying to quell the unrest at the dock. She made it out, but by then the bullets were flying, and . . ."

The words fade into silence; she lets them go like birds from a cage. I look to Leo again, but his eyes are distant and angled upward. My spoon slips in the bowl, but it doesn't matter—my appetite is gone.

Cheeky sighs; in her ears, the little diamonds sparkle. "You didn't eat much."

"Small stomach," I say miserably.

"Try to keep going," she says. "Why don't you rest a little? I'll come back again at dinner. Maybe by then the others will be up. Your maman, and a brother, right?"

Absently, I nod. But on the pallet beside me, Akra stirs. "I'm awake," he says, his voice rusty. He pulls back the mosquito net; he is propped up on one elbow and blinking blearily. His hair is mussed in black spikes, and he looks at Cheeky through narrowed eyes. "You mentioned dinner?"

She opens her mouth, closes it—like a carp. Her face turns bright red, and she flees.

Akra watches her go, his brow furrowed. "What was that?"

I shake my head, confused, but to my surprise, Leo is grinning again. "I'll go check," he says, jogging off after her. Then I remember what he told me—was it only weeks ago? If Cheeky's ever tongue-tied, you know she's found true love. I do my best to muffle my smile as I hand over my bowl.

"What's so funny?" my brother asks.

"Nothing. Just . . . eat your congee."

Akra stirs the porridge with his spoon, though he doesn't take a bite. Steam rises from the bowl, and for a moment, he looks so much like Papa. I avert my eyes; they fall on the booklet Leo brought back to me. Picking it up, I page through it—they're all here, the souls of my fantouches, if not their bodies. The thought comforts me in a way that even the food did not. Then I pause, pulling something else out from between the pages: an envelope. Inside it, the letter from Theodora.

I stare at the paper; it seems years ago I'd first seen it. Why had Leo given it back to me? It might be the exhaustion—or the fact that after all this time, the privacy of a letter seemed like such a little secret to share—but I unfold the paper.

As I read, the laughter of children floats across the village, but the food sits like mud in my belly. *Les Chanceux is not the only cure.* I read the line again and again until the words seem burned into my mind. When Akra speaks, I jump.

"Why were you going to leave without me?"

Blinking at him, I stuff the letter into my pocket. My brother sets his congee down between us. The bowl is still full. "What do you mean?" I ask, buying time.

"That boat was going to Aquitan." He takes a deep breath, wincing, as though the question hurts to ask—or maybe it's only his ribs. "Did you even send a note?"

"A note?" I stare at him as fragments from his own missives scroll through my head; the armée food, bland enough for the Aquitan soldiers, the blisters from the new boots—we always went barefoot in Lak Na. And the way we waited for months for a letter that never came. "We thought you were dead."

"What?" His expression is appalled. "Why?"

"We haven't heard from you in nearly a year!" I throw my hands out, flustered, frustrated. "Why did you stop writing?"

"I didn't! Every quarter, I sent letters with my pay!" On his face, confusion gives way to anger. "They never arrived."

My mouth opens . . . shuts. "No."

"Salauds!" He spits the word. "Bastards!"

"The rebels?" I ask him, trying to make sense of it. "People say they waylay the post—"

"The damn armée," he mutters darkly. "The white tort à dieu who hire us to die. I heard my men complaining they were being shorted of their wages. That the armée was skimming their cash to pay for the war machines. I told them they were liars." He curses the armée again, in their own tongue. "I knew I should have left earlier."

"Then why didn't you?" I say then, my voice soft. "Why didn't you come home?"

Akra clenches his jaw, that scar twisting his old smile into something cruel, but there is a haunted look in his eyes. He looks at Maman then, and back to me. "It isn't so easy to leave," he says.

I raise an eyebrow, incredulous. "You think the general

would have tracked you down in Lak Na?"

"Maybe not," he murmurs. "But just because he wouldn't follow doesn't mean I can escape. Everyone there would have known where I'd been. What I'd done. And I can't forget either."

There is a bitter taste on the back of my tongue. I look again at his scars—more painful than tattoos, remembering the words of the rebel who'd found us. How had he made capitaine? "What is it you did, exactly?"

"*Besides*," he says, pointedly ignoring the question. "I thought it was better for you. With the extra money I was sending, and one less mouth to feed. I started hearing stories about the troupe—that you were doing so well. . . ." His voice trails off into silence, and I know then what he's going to ask. "How did you manage that, Jetta? With just the three of you? Some of the stories I've heard, of your shows . . . and back at the workshop. How did you make that bamboo scrap heap fly?"

I look to Maman, as if for permission. Of course she says nothing—though I hear her voice: never show, never tell. But this is Akra; this is my brother. Still, the words do not come. So instead I take the book of souls and untie the ribbon binding it together. Finding one—the hummingbird—I slip it free and fold it into a butterfly. "Up."

For a moment, the paper wings flutter on my palm, then lift into the air, dancing in the space between us. Akra's brows dive together as I send the page spiraling above my open hand, trembling between us. A child runs by the open side of the sick house, and I snatch the paper out of the air.

Akra jumps. The afternoon light is reflected in his wide pupils, but awe creeps over his face. "Is it magic?"

"Magic?" I turn the word over in my head as I tuck the folded paper into my pocket. "I suppose so. But it has to do with spirits, not spells."

"The vana, the arvana? Like Maman talked about?"

"Yes . . . but. . ." I hesitate—how to explain? I watch the little souls around us. They drift and flutter through the sick house. "You remember the story of the Fool Who Could Not Die?"

"Of course," he says. Then he frowns. "You met the spirit maiden?"

"No . . . I . . . no. But . . ." My hand creeps up toward my shoulder, the rippled burn hidden now under the uniform. Then I clench my fist and drop it back to my lap. My scars are not half so bad as my brother's. "I faced the trials he did. The three deaths."

Akra straightens up in bed, concern in his eyes. "What happened?"

"I don't remember the first two. But after you left, there was an accident on stage."

"How bad?"

"No one died. But the scrim caught fire. I hadn't tied it right. I wasn't careful enough, all by myself. Too impatient."

He gives me a rueful look. "That sounds like you."

"Well." I make a face. "Ever since then, I see them. The spirits. Like the fool in the story."

"And . . . you talk to them?"

"I can tell them what to do," I say. "Once I give them new bodies."

"Mon dieu, Jetta!" Akra shakes his head; on his face, awe mixes with fear. Then he jerks his chin at Maman. "What does she think about all this?"

"She hates it," I say, slipping the book under my pillow. Then I frown. "You know why."

He picks up the bowl again with a sigh, dragging the spoon through the porridge. Still he doesn't eat. "It's one of my first memories, you know. Meeting Meliss. Holding you. Papa saying I had a new sister."

I lean close—eager for the story, though it doesn't feel like mine. "Tell me."

"I hardly remember myself. I wasn't even four, and you were . . . new. But I asked Papa about it a few years ago." Akra pauses, his voice going distant. "He told me we were in Nokhor Khat for a show when the coup happened. The capital was in upheaval. We fled, and Maman came with us, though I do remember she was just Meliss back then. He never told me exactly what she was running from. And I didn't know that after all these years she'd still be trying to get away."

"She told me we were going to find a cure for me," I say softly. "Les Chanceux. The healing spring."

But in my mind, the words repeat: *Les Chanceux is not the only cure.* Akra raises an eyebrow. "What do you think is more dangerous?" he asks me. "Le Trépas, or your malheur?"

I open my mouth—the answer should be easy. The killer of children, the stealer of souls, the nécromancien who terrorizes the country even now, behind the walls of his prison.

But what about my actions on the ship—the servant I'd threatened, my certainty that I alone could stop a dozen rebels, Leo's words to me? This is madness. I do not have a response to Akra's question. But it wasn't Le Trépas's fault that Eve was dead or La Perl was lost or that we'd left Papa alone with a gun in the bowels of Hell's Court.

ACT 3,

SCENE 32

Legarde's offices at the fort. Painted maps of the country cover the wall; smaller versions of the city and the surrounding areas are scattered. LEGARDE is seated at the table, staring at the schematic of the city, when THEODORA bursts into the room.

She is dirty, disheveled. Still wearing her work clothes. But her eyes are shining.

THEODORA: You asked for me?
LEGARDE: Sit.

She doesn't.

THEODORA: Vertical lift! Do you know what we could do with that power?
LEGARDE: I have some ideas.

LEGARDE watches her as she paces around the table.

LEGARDE: You say one of the machines was stolen.

THEODORA: One that shouldn't have been able to fly.

LEGARDE: Who were the thieves?

THEODORA: Three people—including one of yours. A capitaine.

LEGARDE frowns.

LEGARDE: Chantray?

THEODORA: Maybe.

LEGARDE: The Chakran?

THEODORA: Yes. Why?

LEGARDE: He broke the others out of Hell's Court. The girl with him was a wanted criminal.

THEODORA: Well, they all are now, aren't they?

LEGARDE: How did you say they flew your machine?

THEODORA: I don't know yet. That's why I need a new workshop. I need to rebuild the one they took—

LEGARDE: Where did they go? The thieves?

THEODORA: Over the ridge, a ways north but not far. I damaged their wing with a lucky shot. I need to figure out a better way to mount the guns—

LEGARDE (*cutting her off*): But they were alive when last you saw them?

THEODORA: Yes, Father. Why?

LEGARDE: I want them back. Send in my adjutant on your way out.

THEODORA: Did you hear me about the workshop?

LEGARDE: Did you hear me about the adjutant?

THEODORA: Yes, Father.

Pursing her lips, THEODORA breezes out the door. LEGARDE takes a pen and scribbles down a note on a piece of paper. A moment later, the ADJUTANT comes in.

ADJUTANT: Sir?

LEGARDE: Take this to the dovecote. Have it copied and sent out on every pigeon that will take a path north.

The ADJUTANT frowns, taking the paper, reading the message.

ADJUTANT: To what town?

LEGARDE: Any of them. Now.

CHAPTER
TWENTY-SEVEN

The hours pass, the sun crawls. I am restless. But when I get up from my pallet and try to leave the pavilion, I run into the docteur, and he ushers me back to bed. I don't know what my status is—prisoner, or patient? So I obey, at least for now.

"How are you feeling?" he asks me. He is an older man, his black hair salted, his eyes lined with wrinkles. Kind eyes, like Papa's.

"Better," I lie.

"Good. You still need to rest. Eat and drink." He moves on to Maman then, kneeling beside her pallet and pulling back the mosquito net. "You're awake."

Surprised, I glance over. Maman's eyes are open, and the relief I feel is like balm on a wound. "Maman?"

"How are you feeling?" the docteur says, but she gives no answer. He looks at me. "Can she speak?"

"Yes, of course," I say, waiting for her to prove it, but Maman says nothing.

"You need to drink water," the docteur tells her, his voice soft. He offers her a cup. I hold my breath—at last she takes it. "Good," he says gently. "Good."

She drinks slowly, in silence. When the cup is empty, she hands it back and lies down on the pallet again. Her movements are mechanical—a fantouche held by an unskilled puppeteer. The docteur refills the cup and sets it down at her bedside. "Keep drinking. Try to eat if you can." He looks at me again. "Let me know if there are any changes."

He moves on to Akra then, fussing over his ribs and warning him not to get out of bed. But I roll over to face Maman. Her eyes are still open, but I can't tell what she sees, or where she is in her mind. Back in the temple? With Le Trépas, or with Papa?

Slipping a hand under the netting between us, I take her

fingers loosely in mine. "Thank you," I whisper. "For saving us. For saving me."

If this were a play, they would be the right words—she would turn to me and smile. But she just lies there, staring upward. I squeeze her hand one more time, and let it go. "Don't give up now," I say softly, turning back on the pillow.

By the time the docteur is finished with Akra, Cheeky has returned, this time without Leo. But instead of staying to chat, she only drops off the bowls—one for Maman, one for me, the last for Akra—before she practically flees the hôpital.

But despite the docteur's orders, I am not hungry; besides, the man is nowhere to be seen. So I put my bowl aside and follow her. "Cheeky. Cheeky!"

She turns, then, her face still red—this girl, so worldly, tongue-tied at the sight of my brother. For a second, part of me wants to laugh . . . but I have more important things to do. "Cheeky, I need to talk to Leo."

She cocks her head, and then her wicked grin returns. "He'll be glad to hear that. I'll send him right over."

"No . . ." I glance back at the pavilion, where Maman is still lying on the pallet, staring up at the rafters. "I need to talk to him in private."

One eyebrow goes up. "Oh, sure. *Talk*. I get it."

"Cheeky . . ."

My voice is strangled, but she only laughs. "Come. Lots of privacy at the river. It's about time you had a bath, anyway."

I follow her through the camp, and at first my legs are still weak. But as we walk, the groggy feeling lifts like mist, burned away by the brightness of the setting sun. Little golden vana drift between the tents; in the thatch of the roofs, the breeze whispers. The mud squishes between my toes, cool and comforting. We pass an open kitchen, where a pair of women are plucking soft feathers from a brace of pigeons. "Aren't those messenger birds?"

"Maybe for the armée." Cheeky shrugs. "Generous, aren't they? Not only do they send us news to intercept, but dinner too."

"News?" I glance over toward the women again. One is staring back at me, her arms covered in blood and down. I nod a greeting, but she only frowns, tearing another handful of feathers from the pale pink skin. I wet my lips. "What sort of news?"

"We can ask, if you like."

"Maybe later," I murmur. Cheeky catches my tone,

glancing over to the woman, returning her glare with a wave and a brazen smile.

"It's only the uniform making her nervous," she murmurs to me as we walk on.

I look down at the clothes I'd stolen from the soldat. "I suppose I can't blame them."

"Me neither. That thing is frighteningly filthy. Don't worry, I have something you can wear instead." She winks at me then, coaxing back my smile. "Let me take you back to my place."

She takes a sharp turn, leading me on a detour to a little canvas tent at the end of a row. "Wait there," she says, ducking inside.

I peek in through the open flap. The tent is as messy as the dressing room at La Perl. Garter is there, coiled atop a nest of lace and silk. The boa writhes as Cheeky starts to paw through piles of clothing. Pieces go flying against the sides of the tent. Finally she emerges with a rough-spun towel around her neck and a scrap of fabric in her hand.

"Here," she says with a grin. She shakes it out—it's a little dress in creamy white, trimmed in lace. Practically a slip. "War rags."

"Is that one of your stage costumes?" I say incredulously.

"I grabbed what I could carry." She looks down at the tiny thing. "If you crumple this up, it practically fits in your fist."

"You say it like that's a good thing."

"I have a shawl too, if you absolutely must." She draws a length of raw pink silk out of the tangled pile. Then she holds up something else, shining like a net of stars. "Oh! Or this one's floor-length, but it's dripping with rhinestones."

"Cheeky." I tilt my head to catch her eye, trying to make sure she's looking at me and not at her wardrobe. Then I gesture at the mud, the drifting smoke, the ramshackle tents. "I can't wear any of that here."

"Well, those need washing," she says, pointing at my sooty, muddy uniform. "Or maybe burning. Besides," she adds then, her voice going wistful as she runs the soft silk between her fingers. "Sometimes it's nice to remember what things were like, before."

I take a deep breath. Now I understand. "Of course. You're right. Thank you," I say, holding out my hand, but she snatches the dress away.

"You're not touching this till you wash."

Breezily, she starts off toward the river, the tiny dress in one hand, the towel in the other, and the pink shawl thrown across her neck like a highwayman's scarf. Laughing, I follow. We walk downstream in the twilight. Little vana glimmer in the mud of the bank, and the arvana of fish glow in the water. Under the bubbling music of the stream, the sounds of camp fade. Finally we reach an area where bathing pools have been dug out of the riverbank—one of the Tiger's projects, no doubt. Huge stones divert water in one side and out the other, and the pools are lined with a bamboo screen for privacy.

Seeing the water makes my scalp itch; the dank filth of the prison still clings to my skin. Suddenly I don't care what I'm wearing, as long as it isn't the uniform. I pluck at the buttons as Cheeky folds the silk dress onto a flat rock along with the shawl and the towel. "I'll go get Leo."

"While I'm bathing?"

"He can scrub your back!"

"Cheeky—"

"Don't worry, I'll tell him to wait on the respectable side of the screen. But if you shout, he'll come," she says with a grin. "Or maybe it's the other way around."

She disappears through the curtain, her laughter lingering. As I pull the shirt over my head, I vow to think of some way to tease her about my brother.

Next, I shimmy out of the pants, feeling self-conscious, but the evening is quiet—there are no other bathers nearby, not this late. I can see why when I dip a toe into the water. Chills race up my spine and gooseflesh skitters across my skin. I draw back, but at this point, the feel of the grime is worse. And I'll have to bathe quickly, anyway. How long will it be before Leo arrives?

So I count to three and plunge into the pool.

Gasping and splashing, I wade to the center. The water only reaches to my waist, but the temperature is shocking, and I can hardly catch my breath. I let myself pause a moment, trying to adjust, using one leg to scrub the other—both to clean my skin and to rub away the shivers. Then, gritting my teeth, I bend my knees, letting the water rise to my ribs . . . my breasts . . . my neck.

Quickly, gently, I rub the dirt from my skin. Then I gather my courage, along with a deep breath, before dunking my head. In a strangled scream of bubbles, I scrub my scalp with my fingertips, letting the water lift the grit and muck from my hair. Resurfacing, I gulp in air before plunging back below for one more good scrub.

Then I hear a splashing sound, and the water rocks in waves around me—someone else is in the pool. Startled,

I stand, and see Leo crashing through the water, a crazed look in his eyes. I scream, scrambling backward, covering myself with my hands, and he freezes, waist-deep in the pond. "What the hell are you doing?" I shout in the sudden silence.

"I thought you were drowning," he says at last, his face pale.

I stare at him, crouching to keep my body below the surface of the pool. "In waist-high water?"

"Right." He takes a deep breath. Then embarrassment darkens his face, and he whirls around, wading toward the bank. "Right. Désolée . . . I'm so sorry."

I watch him scramble out of the water. His shoulders are heaving, his jacket is dripping—his leather shoes squelch as he walks. My own heart is pounding, and I'm shivering, but not from the cold. How could he think I couldn't find my footing? Did he not know how shallow the pool was?

"I don't understand," I say, but then I realize I do. "You thought I was doing it on purpose."

I am still watching his back. He hangs his head, but anger sparks in me.

"I would never . . ." I falter then. "I *have* never done anything like that."

"No one does until they do," he says.

The sorrow in his voice only makes it worse. I splash through the pond toward the bank, no longer worried about my modesty. "I don't need you to save me," I tell him through clenched teeth, grabbing the towel from the rock and scrubbing myself dry. "I don't want to be rescued."

"What do you want then?" he snaps, shrugging off his jacket, his back still toward me. He wrings it out, water dripping onto the bank. "Because if Cheeky sent me here on a prank, I swear to god, I will use her fishnets to go fishing."

The mention of Cheeky brings me up short—he's here because I wanted him to be. "No . . . I . . . No." More gently now, I twist the towel around the wet mass of my hair. "I . . . I did want to talk to you."

"About what?" he says, his voice still cold.

"About a cure," I say softly. He is quiet for a moment, and suddenly I am afraid—sure he will scoff, laugh, shrug me off. Why would he want to help me, after all I've done? But he only tosses his jacket over another stone, kicking off his wet shoes. I reach for the silk dress—it's so soft on my fingertips. Gently I slip it over my head, and the smooth clean coolness is heaven on my skin. I wrap the shawl around my shoulders; it smells faintly of perfume, distantly familiar.

"I'm sorry about La Perl," I say then. "About Eve. About Eduard. And leaving you on the boat. You were right. It was all madness. But I don't want to be that way."

Leo says nothing, but between us, the quality of the silence changes—no longer cold, only sad. I reach out a tentative hand and touch his shoulder. After a moment, he laces his fingers through mine. For a long while we stand there, in the cool fragrant evening, and then his shoulders rise and fall. "Can I turn around now?"

I laugh a little, and let go of his hand. "Yes."

He does, slowly, his eyes flicking down at the dress. Then he looks away, embarrassed, glancing at the vines, the rocks, his shoes. "I'm sorry too," he murmurs. "For putting you and your family in danger. You were desperate, back in Luda. But so was I."

I wave his words away—I know too well what desperation does. "You've more than made up for it. Thank you for keeping my secrets."

"Well." He takes a deep breath, looking up into my eyes. "Like I said . . . I did the best I could."

Something about his tone, the hesitation in it—and the cold rushes back. Colder than the water in the pool, colder than the stones of the temple prison. "What does that mean?"

He shifts on his feet, leaning down to tip water out of his right shoe, then his left. "The king knows," he says at last, but the words don't make sense.

"The king was killed aboard *Le Rêve*."

"The king was *rescued* from *Le Rêve*," he says. "The assassination was staged."

"But . . . I saw him shot!"

"You saw a man shoot, and the king fall over the side. Raik is in league with the rebels, Jetta. He needed to get out from under Legarde's thumb. Apparently the general had planned to have him killed after the marriage to my sister."

His words wash over me; I grasp at them, but it's like holding water. "In league . . . ? How could the king be in league with the *Tiger*?"

"What's so strange about it? They both want the Aquitans out of the country."

"But the Tiger is . . ." I trail off, all the stories rising in me only to die on my tongue. Distantly, the sounds of village life drift from the camp—so different than the silence of Dar Som, the screams in the prison, from all the aftermath of the armée's work. What was real, what was show? I shake my head, trying to gather my thoughts. "How do you know all this?"

"We left the ship together." Leo takes a breath, hesitating. "I had your dragon with me at the time."

"My fantouche?" I blink at him. "You didn't drown them all."

His smile is sad. "Well. It is a very beautiful piece of work."

"Where is she now?"

"The king has her," Leo says. "He's very eager to meet you."

A month ago, the thought would have left me breathless. I suppose it still does now, but not for the same reasons. "And where is he?"

"Out in the jungle," Leo says. "Looking for the bird you brought to life."

I shiver, pulling the silk shawl tighter across my shoulders. "What does he want, exactly?"

"Can't you guess, Jetta?" Leo stands then, sliding his feet back into his shoes. "He wants an army. And he might be able to get you what you want in exchange."

"An army." My mind drifts to the flying machines. Could I have given each one a soul? Could I command a flying horde, blazing fire and vengeance? I imagine it for a moment—all the death . . . all the blood. "No. No." I clench my fists, digging my nails into my palms, using the sting to focus. "What about your sister's letter?"

He gives me a cautious look. "What about it?"

"'Les Chanceux is not the only cure,' she says." I paw through the pockets of the uniform, thrusting the letter into his hands when I find it. "So what else?"

"I didn't exactly get a chance to ask her on the boat," Leo says. "And rumor has it, she might not be so receptive to the question at this point."

"What do you mean?"

"You stole one of her machines." He raises an eyebrow. "Destroyed her workshop. You might have burned a bridge there. The king, on the other hand—"

"No," I say again, more emphatically. "I've seen enough war. Enough blood."

"And they haven't?" Leo's voice is incredulous; he gestures to the camp.

"You expect me to save them when I can't even save myself?" I stare at him. "Every choice I make is wrong. Everything I've done has only made things worse!"

"Then maybe this is the chance to set things right!" His words scorch the air; it's hard to breathe. He must see the pain on my face; his look softens and he takes my hand. "I know what it's like to have regrets, Jetta—things you can't undo. The only way to soothe that pain is to try to do better." He hesitates then, wetting his lips. "But I won't make you do anything you don't want to."

"What does that mean?"

"Just what I said! If you want to leave now, I'll tell the king you've vanished. I'll say you went back to the city or . . . wherever it is you aren't going. But I think this is your best option, if you really want the cure."

"What are you getting out of this?" I say, still suspicious, and he cocks his head. "I know you, Leo. You're a smuggler. A dealer." In my words, I hear an echo of Legarde: a traitor, a pimp. Familiar with loose women. "What do you get in return?"

"What do I get?" He stares at me. "Do you know what it's like? Seeing someone you—" He stops then, suddenly, but the unspoken words shimmer in the air between us. I cock my head.

"Someone you what?"

"Someone you *know*," he says. "Watching them struggle with something you can't help them fight."

His voice is so soft, but the hard part is what he isn't saying. I wet my lips. "Do you think I'm your redemption, Leo?"

"No. It's not that."

"What, then? Pity?"

"No! I . . ." He scrubs a hand through his hair. "I care about you."

"Why?" I say, my voice fierce. "Because I'm mad? Because I'm broken? Because you want to fix me?"

"Because you burn too bright for me to see you burn out," he says, and it brings me up short. He takes my hand then, pressing my palm with his fingers—and there it is again. The spark I'd first felt as we rode away from Luda . . . but this time, not a whim, no passing fancy born of my malheur. It is not danger that draws me now—it is Leo himself. What I know of him, and what he knows of me. The way he looks at me makes me feel *seen*.

"And . . ." I brush my thumb over his knuckles, considering the warmth of his hand in mine. "That's all you want."

"Oh, I want many things," he says, quirking an eyebrow. "But only if you want them too."

He gives me that smile, and my anger banks to a different heat. I can no longer help it. I lean closer, as does he, and press my lips against his, my heart beating fast, my thoughts rolling slow. His hands slide around my waist, smooth on the silk, and inside, I no longer spark, but burn. He crushes me close and I drink him in, drowning as I try to quench this sudden flame. It billows in the pit of me—this want, this need—nearly a rage, fierce and frightening. I need him closer . . . so I push him away, hard.

Leo stumbles back, raising his hands. His breath is coming fast, but he doesn't move, and his eyes are cautious—patient. In them, a question: yes or no?

Do I want this?

No. Yes.

Do I?

I hesitate, but before I can decide, the sound of cheering rings out from the village. Leo turns, both of us staring back toward the camp. There, coming through the trees, is a group of rebels all in a line, like ants. On their shoulders, the bound bamboo form of the flying machine; even here I can see her fighting her bonds. And even worse . . . at the head of the column, with my fantouche draped around his neck—the Boy King, alive and well, just as Leo said.

Gone are the fine scarlet silks, the casual posture, the easy smile he wore at his coronation. How had he orchestrated his escape under the noses of his advisers? Between the guns smuggled to the ship, the rebels brought aboard in servants' dress, and the faked assassination pinning blame on the armée, it seems the rumors of his playboy attitude were much exaggerated. Should I go to him? I still don't know. I take a deep breath, trying to collect my thoughts, but then a voice—too close—makes me whirl.

"What are you doing with my sister?"

Akra materializes out of the dark in a flurry of motion, shoving Leo back into the greenery, though I was the one with my hand on his chest. "Akra!" I take his arm, pulling him back, but his muscles are tense under my hand. "Leave him alone!"

"What are *you* doing with *him*, then?" he says, turning to me. "Maman would be furious!"

I can't help it—I laugh. "Trust me, Akra. Leo is the least of her worries."

"I'll see to that," Akra says, his mouth twisted. Then he turns as Leo pulls himself out of the vines. "Stay down, you moitié bastard."

Suddenly, the air is as still as the dead. My eyes go wide, but Leo only brushes off his wet jacket and gives Akra that easy smile. "Good to meet you, capitaine. I've heard so much."

The words are simple but loaded. Akra bristles. "From who?"

"Here and there," Leo says casually, putting out his hand, Aquitan style. "Leo Rath, at your service. Or if you prefer, Leo Legarde."

"Legarde?" Akra's eyes narrow. He ignores Leo's hand to take a step closer, so they are face-to-face. "So whose side are you on?"

Leo's smile doesn't budge, and he doesn't drop his eyes. He only tilts his head toward me. "For now? Hers."

I pull Akra back again, before he can respond, and step between the two of them. "We were just discussing how to get us out of here."

Now my brother looks at me with hope in his eyes. "Back home?"

"To Aquitan," I say, harsher than I have to. I hesitate then. But what are my options? "With the king's help. Or so Leo says."

Leo raises an eyebrow. "You'll do it, then?"

"I'll talk to him," I say. "See what he wants. See what he'll give me in return."

Leo's careful smile breaks into a real grin. He offers me his arm. "Should we go back? I could use a dry set of clothes."

"You go," Akra says, putting his hand on my shoulder. "I need to talk to my sister."

Leo hesitates—why? It takes me a moment to understand the sudden fear in his eyes—fear for me. I draw myself up. Though Akra is angry, he would never hurt me. But Leo doesn't know that. How many men has he had to run off from La Perl? "Go on," I tell him softly. "I need to talk to him too."

Leo narrows his eyes, as though trying to see past the lie, looking from me, to Akra, and back. I lean closer to my brother, suddenly defensive. And after a moment, Leo nods. "I'll tell the king you're coming along shortly." He gives me one last look—a chance to call him back—then starts back up the river.

After he's gone, Akra turns to me. "Who does he think he is?"

"He helped us get here," I say, but Akra scoffs, gesturing at the dark jungle, the rebel camp.

"That's not exactly something to brag about."

"We would still be in Luda without his help."

"Closer to home."

"Home is gone, Akra." The words are hard—I take his hand to try to soften them. "We lost everything getting this far. There's nothing to go back to. The only way is forward."

He takes a deep breath then. His eyes glitter in the dark.

Are those tears? If so, this man who was my brother never lets them fall. "Forward to Aquitan," he says at last, and I nod. "Because of your malheur."

"Yes."

On his face, emotions flicker—the longing for and parting from a home he'll never see again. It had taken me months to make the same journey—and in a way, I'm still on that road. My brother swallows; I can see the muscles moving in his throat. Suddenly, it comes back to me . . . does he remember? The first time I knew there was something wrong with me. It was years ago—I was eleven, maybe twelve. Teetering there, at the edge of the broken stone, looking over the water rushing through the lava tunnel. Inching closer and closer, standing on the edge of oblivion, imagining what might come after.

Akra had found me there as the sun was setting—long after the other children had tired of losing the game of dares to me. He had taken my hand, led me home. He never said anything about it, but I think he knew too. And now, after a long moment, he nods. "D'accord. If you want to get to Aquitan, we'll get there. And if you think the king will help you, we can ask. But I don't trust him, or your *friend*," Akra says, practically spitting the word.

"Because he's m—" I stutter over the word, changing my mind at the last moment. "Mixed?"

"Because I finally spoke to that girl. The quiet one." It takes me a moment to realize he means Cheeky. "That's how I knew where you went. She and another girl. Tia. They had this."

Akra pulls something out of his pocket: a little slip of paper, about the length and width of my finger. It wants to roll up like a scroll—the sort of paper a messenger bird would carry on its leg. I unroll it, squinting in the dark, but even by the light of the spirits, I can't make out the tiny words.

"They said they were told not to give it to you," he says. "There were dozens, all the same. The rebels burned the others. She hid this one in her . . . she took it for you."

"What is it?" I whisper. The paper trembles in my hand.

"It's from Legarde," he says. "An offer. He has Papa. He wants to trade him back to us."

My heart leaps—my mind races. "What could he possibly want?"

Akra raises an eyebrow. "He says he wants Leo."

Jetta of the Ros Nai. Meet me at the temple. You may have your father back if you will bring my son.

CHAPTER TWENTY-EIGHT

The first thing I do is burn the letter.

Akra loans me his lighter—a new one, armée green; I'd lost his old one on the ship. But as the paper goes up in a puff of flame and smoke, tears start in my eyes. I cannot unmake it. I cannot unsee it. And who else knows?

The rebels, of course. Someone will have told the king. And Cheeky . . . Tia. What about Leo?

Had he known what Legarde wanted before he'd asked me to stay?

Is that why he'd done it in the first place?

No. I know better. I flip the lighter shut and hand it back

to my brother. "The girls you spoke to—they're my friends, and Leo's too. If they weren't trying to help us, they would have burned that note with all the rest."

"Fine," Akra says. "Maybe your boy hadn't seen it yet. Maybe he is negotiating in good faith. But do you really think the rebels will?"

"I don't know," I say truthfully. Then again, no matter what the king might offer, nothing was more valuable than what Legarde had—not to me. We had to take his deal. Then I frown. "What about Maman? If we leave now, we're just exchanging a hostage with Legarde for one with the rebels."

"I can try to sneak her out of the sick house tonight," Akra says. "We could all escape on the bird."

"Not all the way to Aquitan. Not without food and water. And that's assuming we don't crash again." I chew my lip. "Legarde is Le Roi Fou's brother. And he has control of the capital . . . of the docks. Of the ships."

Akra looks at me with a level eye. "You think he'll give us passage and Papa too?"

"I can ask."

"And how will you convince Leo to turn himself over to Legarde?"

My eyes widen. "I won't!"

"Not even for Papa?" Akra folds his arms. "How else will Legarde give him over?"

"Because if he doesn't, I'll kill him." The threat falls out of my mouth and buzzes in the air—unexpected, but when I say it aloud, I know it's true. My heart beats in my ears—the rush of my blood, red and deadly.

Akra raises an eyebrow. Is he impressed, or is it mockery? But he doesn't say, either way. "And how will we find the bird? Can you just . . . call it?"

"I don't think so. She was bound when they brought her to the camp. We have to figure out where they put her. See how she's guarded."

"They took my gun," Akra says. "I doubt I can get another. But maybe I can pick up a knife in the kitchens. That might be better, depending on how many guards there are. Quieter."

I make a face. I don't want to watch my brother kill again, but we may not have many options. "So we locate the bird and cut her free. Then we get Maman from the hôpital and escape?"

Akra shakes his head a little. "It's got a lot of holes."

"The alternative is walking back to Nokhor Khat on foot. And there are a lot of soldiers between here and there."

"And rebels," he says. "They'll be looking for you once they know you're gone."

I chew my lip. Despite my words, I'm worried too—cautious, after how poorly my last plan had gone. But no other options present themselves. Beside me, Akra shifts his weight on the vine.

"Do you think your moitié will be suspicious when we don't come back to camp?"

Annoyed, I turn to my brother. "Why do you call him that?"

"Why do you care?"

"Because it's wrong."

His smile is bitter, dismissive. "I've done worse."

"So have I," I snap. "But the smaller the evil, the easier it is to correct."

He tilts his head back, a strange expression in his eyes. "What have you been up to while I was gone, lailee?"

"I could ask you the same question," I mutter, and for a while, we are quiet. The sounds of the jungle creep in. Souls glitter in the leaves around us, little embers. "Why did you shoot that man on the dock?"

My brother's face goes smooth, impassive. "I had orders."

"And the village you burned? That was just orders too?"

"You don't understand."

"Then explain!"

"You *can't* understand." Akra clenches his jaw, the scar twisting like a snake. "You weren't there, Jetta. You don't know. They hang us out like targets, did you know that? The Aquitans. They toss us in harm's way, they pit us against our own people. And the Chakrans don't trust us either. Not that we can trust them, when any one of them could be part of the rebellion. You have to decide very quickly whether to kill or to die."

"And you decided to kill," I say, softer now.

"Do you wish I'd made the other choice?"

I wet my lips, thinking of my own choices. "No."

"Neither do I."

"Did you ever enjoy it?" I blurt out, the words falling from my mouth unbidden.

Now he turns his head, his eyes sharp. "The killing?"

"The power."

"There's no power in it," he says, his lip curling. At my side, my fists clench as the memories play across the scrim of my mind. Dar Som, the rope around Jian's neck . . . my anger that I hadn't killed him when I'd had the chance.

Is Akra lying, or am I more monstrous than I imagined? Either way, who I am to judge?

Sighing, I pick up the dirty uniform—I had carried it all this way, into the brush. I might as well get some use of it. Running my hands over the fabric, I search for a tear or a loose thread. A place to rip, to unravel. But my hands still at the crinkle of paper in the pocket: the little folded butterfly with the soul of the hummingbird. I pull it out, considering . . . but no. Best to use a soul that remembers Nokhor Khat as home.

So I tuck the butterfly down the front of my dress, inside the band of silk that covers my breasts. It ruins the lines of the fabric, but better ruined lines than lost souls.

Then I turn from the uniform and start searching the ground. Akra is watching me. "What are you doing?"

"I need to let Legarde know we're coming. I want to make sure he keeps Papa well." Finding a sharp stone takes some time, especially in the dark, but when I do, I use it to slice through the edge of the uniform sleeve, working the stone against the weave of the fabric until it starts to fray. Finally, there is a tear wide enough for me to rip the rest of the way down, leaving me with a square of fabric the size of a handkerchief.

Next, I use Akra's lighter to burn a few leaves to ash. Once they've cooled, I press the soot into the fabric in roughly formed letters—just one word: TONIGHT.

Akra frowns at me as I fold the fabric lengthwise and knot it in the center. "How will you get it to him?"

"The same way he got his note to me," I say. Then I grit my teeth and ball my fist and nick my knuckle with the stone. The cut stings, the blood wells—but Akra puts his hand on mine.

"Is this wise?" he says. "To let Legarde know what you can do?"

"I think the time for secrets is over," I say. "Theodora saw us take wing on a bird with no feathers. She will have told her father."

Akra only grunts. But a chill has settled over me that has nothing to do with the cold night air. What if Legarde wasn't really after Leo? What if he only wants to put me back in prison, in a cell beside Le Trépas, forever in the dark?

But if I don't go back, aren't I dooming Papa to that same fate?

There is no clear path, but I have already chosen my route. And all around me, the souls are gathering. First the vana—but there are always some close by. The flies and worms, the mosquitoes and the gnats. Their souls swarm in glittering constellations around my head.

Next the arvana creep in. The spirit of a rat skitters down the liana vine; the soul of a songbird perches on a branch overhead. Still I wait, clenching and unclenching my fist, letting the blood run down my finger. The soul of a civet creeps through the underbrush, watching me with fiery eyes, and the spirit of an owl glides in on silent wings.

It takes some time, but I am patient, and soon enough, I see the one I'm waiting for—no, two of them, drifting from tree to tree from the direction of the camp kitchens: the souls of the messenger pigeons.

I call one close; she comes to rest on my hand. It's the matter of a moment to put her soul into the rough body I have fashioned. "Go to Legarde," I tell her, and with a rustle of her new cloth wings, she lifts into the air and flutters off through the night jungle.

Akra watches the message fly, his expression caught between fear and awe. "What are they like?" he says softly. "The souls?"

Pressing my thumb to the wound on my finger, I gaze at the bright spirits around me—dancing, glowing, lighting the night. All the burning longing of the dead to live again.

"Beautiful," I say. "And terrible too."

Akra only nods; he has no more questions for me. Instead, he settles next to me on the loop of liana. As the souls start to scatter again, living mosquitoes whine past my ears, so I take Cheeky's towel and tuck it around my knees. Nearby, the river burbles over the stones. A nightjar starts her trilling call; in the brush, something small rustles. I listen for an alarm to be raised, for someone to come after us. For footsteps in the dark. But no one seems to notice that we haven't come back.

From the camp, very distantly, I hear the sound of music, the distant strains of the violin. And is that Tia's voice? Smoke and brass. I close my eyes and remember her song, the night at La Perl. *J'errais avec les fous . . .*

As the song rises and falls, I relax against my brother's shoulder. Only when he stirs do I realize I've dozed off. The music has faded, the fires burned low. The silvery moon has leaped into the indigo shell of the sky. I run a hand over my face. "Is it time?"

"It is."

Slowly we make our way upriver, past the baths, through the sweet breath of the honeysuckle, back to the sleeping camp. And as we pass through the quiet village,

I can already see the bird, bound and laid out close to the water, out of reach of the stray embers of the campfires.

A makeshift tent has been erected above her—two smaller tents, lapped over an open framework of bamboo. Enough to keep the rain from her wings. And sitting on a barrel beside the tent, a single guard. I recognize him even at a distance, and it's only another moment before he recognizes me.

Leo stands slowly as we approach. The moonlight catches the gleam of his pistol, still at his waist—and for a moment, I want to run, but where would we go? He doesn't shout or draw his gun. He only waits for us, as though we were expected. So I step close enough to whisper. "Cheeky told you about the note," I guess, and he nods.

"As soon as I got back. It took me half a minute to realize what you'd choose. So I told the king you were tired tonight. And I volunteered to guard the bird."

"Why would you help us?" Akra says, his tone mocking. "Do you think you're in love?"

"It matters less what I think than what I do."

"Give her your gun, then," Akra says. "Jetta, you guard him while I get Maman."

"I already spoke to her," Leo says mildly. "If you're going

to the temple, she's not coming with you. She'd only be a liability. Besides, there won't be room for all of us in the bird."

My brother's eyebrows shoot upward. "You're coming?"

"Didn't I tell you I'd help you? And maybe in return, you can help them." Leo jerks his chin toward the camp and I whirl, suddenly afraid, but there is no one creeping up on us in the night. Nothing but the rows of huts and tents, the rebels sleeping alongside the villagers, and Cheeky and Tia somewhere among them. "Come back to the camp after your meeting. The king will still value your help," he says softly. Then his tone turns grim. "Your father can heal here. He might need a good docteur."

"Why would you turn yourself in to Legarde?" Akra turns to me. "I don't trust him, Jetta. I do not trust a word he says."

"You don't have to," I say quietly. "We only have to have no other options."

"There is always another option, Jetta." Akra's eyes gleam, but I shake my head. Still, I am curious, and I turn to Leo now.

"What do you think Legarde wants with you?"

"I don't know, but I want to find out." Then he gives me a heartbreaking smile. "Do you know, that note is the first time he's ever called me his son?" Turning toward the bird, he pulls a knife from his belt and slices through the bindings on her wings. Together, we lead her out into the bright moonlight.

The rebels have made some repairs—rudimentary, to be sure, little more than a strip of silk holding a bamboo splint to the broken wing. She is still battered, still broken, but it is enough. Souls are so strong. And when we climb aboard, the skeletal wings of the hawk tear at the air. Slowly, awkwardly, we lift into the darkness above the rebel camp—back toward Nokhor Khat, back toward Papa. For a moment I feel weightless. Free. Like the boundless sky goes on forever and so could we. But when we rise above the tree line, I see it—a blot of smoke above the lip of the caldera, billowing gray in the moonlight, lit from beneath with the dim glow of the dying flames.

"Nokhor Khat is burning," I call back over the wind.

"Not surprising," Akra says, his voice grim. His knuckles are white as he grips the frame of the bird. "Tensions were high even before *Le Rêve*."

"Were the rebels behind the riots too?" I ask, turning to Leo—remembering my suspicions over their timing. "The attack on the docks?"

But Leo shakes his head. "That was all Pique's fault."

At this, Akra looks up. Disgust cuts through the fear on his face. "Pique? He's not in Nokhor Khat."

"No. But he's rampaging through the north, exacting revenge. People flee south, leaving everything behind, only to see their king drinking champagne with Aquitans."

I frown. I don't know Pique, not the way Leo and Akra seem to. But I know he's the man behind the death in Dar Som. What could make a man seek that kind of vengeance? "What happened to him?"

Both Akra and I look at Leo, but he raises an eyebrow. "The rebellion."

"They hurt him? Tortured him? What?"

"Nothing like that." Leo sighs. "But he's been trying to pacify Chakrana since before I was born. And the rebels are difficult to quell. For men like him, that's enough."

As we struggle upward over the ridge, the pall of smoke widens—it hangs in a gauzy curtain over most of the city, silvered by the first hint of dawn. From the gates to the docks, coals glow in the ruins of gutted buildings. It looks like the capital has fallen ill, covered in ashy pocks like an infection. Through the haze, souls gleam like scattered embers in the streets. I am grateful for the darkness; at least we do not see the fallen bodies of the dead.

But even through the wisps and wafting clouds of smoke, the temple rises proud and solid, resolute and implacable as death itself—a stepped building of black stone, flanked by two long, low platforms: the rooftops of the cells below.

"Where shall we land?" I say, but Leo points. Before the pavilion, a wash of light covers the wide stone stairs leading up to the arched door. At first I mistake it for a cluster of souls, but even as they fill the streets, the spirits avoid Hell's Court. No . . . as we near the temple, the glow resolves into a row of lanterns, set on the plaza and along the steps, as if to lead us inside. There is a gaunt man waiting at the top of the stair. For a moment, I am sure it is the King of Death, and a cold premonition seizes me, but then I see the light gleaming on the epaulets, and on the gold mane of his hair. Legarde got my note.

The hawk banks toward the temple on a draft of shifting smoke. The air is gritty, sour; I breathe through my teeth as I scan the territory. I expected Legarde to bring soldiers, but he is alone. Of course, Papa is not there either. Where has Legarde hidden him? As we drop nearer to the temple, Akra leans in. "Don't land on the plaza."

"Why not?"

"Because that's where he wants you to land. Set down on the roof, there," he says, pointing to the flat stone platform atop the cells. "We'll have high ground and a little bit of cover. Last chance to shoot him," Akra adds, turning to Leo.

Leo only laughs, his voice bitter. "There was never a chance of that."

"Give me your gun and I'll do it," Akra says, but Leo shakes his head.

"I haven't come all this way to leave without an answer."

"Then give me your knife," I murmur. "To protect myself."

Without a word, Leo hands it over, and I slip it through the shawl I've belted around my waist. Guiding the bird around again, we bank toward the rooftop platform.

It is a long, narrow causeway surrounded by a low parapet carved with leering demons—a little cover, as Akra had said, but not much. Still, it is better than being on the plaza below, surrounded by the overgrown tangle of the garden. Anyone could be hiding in those shadows. A chill skitters across my skin; something tells me to turn around, to pull up into the wide sky, to glide back to the jungle, back to the camp. I push that voice down into the pit of my stomach and bury it in bile. I will not leave without Papa.

There is no turning back now.

As the bird settles awkwardly to the roof, I whisper to her spirit—be still, be still. She folds her broken wings and I slide down to the platform. My bare feet are warm against the cold stone. The boys follow—Akra, stiff and proud, his posture concealing his healing ribs, and Leo, who cocks his head and shifts his weight to one foot, so casual. Acting.

I walk to the parapet, looking down on the plaza below, flanked by the two of them. Legarde has come to the base of the narrow stairs, tilting his head up to look at me.

"Sava, Jetta," the general calls, his voice cutting through the smoky wind. "Quite an entrance. I see you have a flare for the dramatic."

He smiles, but there is no joy in it; nor is there any in my short, mocking bow. But in the back of my mind, I wonder . . . why he would greet me before his own son? "Bring me my father, Legarde, and I'll be just as happy to make an exit."

"He's inside," Legarde says, gesturing back toward the arched doorway of the temple prison, where the altar sits at the feet of the old stone god. Is Papa still in the cell, waiting in the dark? I clench my fists and start down the stair, but

Akra puts his hand on my shoulder.

"Bring him out, general!" he shouts, and Legarde raises an eyebrow.

"My erstwhile capitaine. I suppose a salute is not forthcoming. Very well. I'll bring him out in a moment. But first I'd like to make you another offer."

"You haven't kept the first yet!"

The general spreads his hands with a look that's almost chagrined—I would buy it if he weren't the man who led La Victoire. "If you want to go now, I won't stop you. Maybe you and your parents can swim to Aquitan."

That brings me up short. I swallow, an uneasy feeling in the pit of my stomach. "Does your offer include a ship, general?"

"Something better," he says, reaching into his pocket. I tense, and Akra pulls me back from the edge of the parapet—but rather than a gun, Legarde pulls out a crystal bottle, the size of a fist . . . of a heart. The lamplight filters through the cloudy liquid inside. "With this, you don't need a ship at all."

It takes me a moment to understand, but when I do, I wet my lips. I am not thirsty, but suddenly my mouth is so dry. "A cure."

"A *treatment*," he corrects me. "Something my daughter discovered. As you've seen, she's rather inventive. And a year ago, she began to look into madness."

Air hisses through Leo's teeth. His mother died a year ago. I take a breath, still looking at the glass. Now I understand the line in Theodora's letter. But all I can manage is "Oh?"

"She sent to Aquitan for samples of the water from Les Chanceux. Apparently the healing properties come from the minerals dissolved in it." The general tilts the bottle so the water catches the light; it glows like an opal in his hand. "A mineral she has since extracted from a well near the volcano. There's enough in here for a month. Take it. It's for you."

The gleam of the bottle is like a beacon to me—I take a step down on the stair before Akra pulls me back. "A month?" he calls. "And then?"

"That, of course, is her choice," Legarde says. "But Theodora's workshop is here. In the capital."

My mind is racing—this is not how I thought this meeting would go. To find what I'd been looking for all this time, in the last place I ever wanted to be. "You want me to stay," I say. "Why?"

"You'd prefer to go back to the jungle?" he says, answering my question with a question. "Wouldn't you hate to leave Leo behind?"

Blood rushes to my face. Is that why Legarde wanted Leo here?

"What about me?" Akra says. "Am I to be hanged as a deserter?"

"You're not a deserter if you come back," Legarde says. Then his eyes narrow. "There was a woman in the cell with you. Your mother. She's welcome too, of course. We can house all of you here. In the capital. In safety."

Safety. Isn't that what I wanted? And a cure . . . or at least a treatment. Is this the moment it all comes together—at last, sefondre? But nothing on this road has ever come free. "And in return?"

Legarde nods a little, as though satisfied by my question. "I'm glad to see you're not a fool. Let me tell you, I've spent half my life in your country, but there are still things I don't understand. One thing I do know, though, is that when your kings are weak, your people turn to the gods. You must have heard the stories about Le Trépas. Or do you call him Kuzhujan?"

My scar prickles, my skin crawls; how bold the general

is, to name the monster crouching just beneath our feet. "I don't call him anything," I say, but Legarde gives me a small smile.

"Not even Father?"

The word is like a punch to the gut—spoken aloud, reality crystallizes. "I don't know what you mean," I lie, but Legarde smiles.

"I'm no fool either, Jetta. I know about your bloodline. Your mother. Her escape. But unlike Le Trépas, you bring life." He raises an eyebrow, nodding to the bamboo bird. "Your people could use that in a leader."

Another twist. This one leaves me reeling. This, from the man who had the sapphires pulled from the old god's eyes? The man who drove the monks into hiding, who forbade the old ways so that no one could take up where Le Trépas left off? "A leader?" I scoff. "Me? After everything that happened with *him*?"

Legarde's expression turns contemplative; he hefts the flask, once, twice, as though weighing it. "With your madness under control, I think the outcome could be very different."

My breath catches at his words—they sound so much like the truth. Of course Le Trépas and I must share more than the ability to bind the dead. My malheur has left a long shadow behind me, all death and disaster. Have I seen my future in the stories of his own tyranny? Could I save more than just myself with a treatment? Is it the madness that makes us both monstrous . . . or only our actions?

While I hesitate, Akra calls down. "Are you offering Jetta the crown?"

The general raises an eyebrow. "Why shouldn't she have it? The Boy King has vanished and the city is burning. I need someone to quell the rebellion before the whole country goes up in flames. I know you love the public eye," he adds, turning to me. "What better place for you than a throne?"

I try to imagine it then—a kingdom for a stage—but I cannot suspend my disbelief. This isn't my role; I do not know the lines. Then again, how much power did the Boy King ever have? Legarde would never let me rule.

The thought is a strange comfort. Could I trade my independence for a treatment? For a life of luxury, for my family's safety, for a life here in my country? Maybe even a life that could include Leo . . .

Put that way, it doesn't seem so terrible. I squeeze Leo's hand; it's warm in mine. But what else would I be trading away—and who is the man I am bargaining with? Legarde, the Shepherd, who flies a red wolf on his banner. The leader of the armée. The one who gave the orders. The one who would have sent me to the questioneur.

My stomach twists at the next thought. How did Legarde put together a past I only just discovered? What would make Papa tell? Fear creeps up my spine like a spider. "I want to see my father first."

Legarde hesitates. "You must remember, he was shot on the ship. He's still weak, and I can't carry him alone."

Akra digs his hand into my shoulder, holding me back from the stairs. "You're not going down there," he says, but beside me, Leo laughs a little.

"Is that why you asked for me, Legarde? So I could act as your pack mule?"

Legarde's face is neutral, carefully so. "Send the boy down then," he calls—to me, not to Leo—and my heart breaks a little. "We can make the exchange."

But Akra reaches out with his other hand, grabbing Leo's jacket before he starts down the stairs. "Papa's dead," he whispers. "He doesn't want an exchange. He wants a new hostage."

The words are like a coal in my throat—dropping through me, melting my core away. But I know Akra's right.

How had Legarde known Leo would serve the purpose? Had it been so clear when the general had asked me where Leo had gone? When I had lied to protect him?

"Back to the bird," I whisper, but the general must have seen my look. As we turn from the stairs, he raises a hand toward the heavens.

At his signal, the last few stars arc out of the dawning sky. It takes me a moment to realize they are bottle bombs—glass jars full of oil, stoppered with burning rags—thrown by soldiers clinging to the roof.

"Shoot him!" Akra shouts as the glass smashes against the stone. Oil spills from burst bottles. Glittering shards prick my skin. The flame engulfs the dry bamboo of the bird in a rush of heat. In a panic, the hawk takes wing, writhing in the air, a blazing star as she spirals through the sky. But she cannot outfly the fire. Her body breaks apart in falling embers scattered across the dark expanse of the temple grounds, and like a comet, her soul spirals free into the blackness of the sky.

But the oily blaze has covered the platform too, and more bombs are raining down. The fire forces us to the stairs, toward the plaza, and as we stumble across the stone, at last Leo draws his gun. But Legarde only turns, disappearing inside the arched doorway of the darkened temple.

"Let's get out of here," Akra says, tugging us toward the overgrown garden, but then, from the shadows of the tangled vines and the old stone statues, soldiers appear.

They line the edge of the plaza, a dozen men, their rifles pointed at the three of us. Together they step closer, and closer still. "They won't shoot me," I say, though it's more a prayer than a fact. I shove the boys behind me, trying to stay between them and the soldiers as they scramble up the stairs. "Get inside! Get Legarde!"

The fire has spread all the way down the stone steps, and the line of soldiers keeps me from fleeing across the gardens. They advance slowly, herding me toward the temple. And what is waiting inside? Will the boys be able to find the general—to subdue him? To take him hostage and get us out of here? Or did he have more soldiers stationed in the temple?

Desperately I cast around for something that can help us—an errant soul, or a vengeful one—but nothing comes close to the mouth of Hell's Court. Against my pounding heart, the little paper butterfly rustles, as though the soul inside would flee if she could.

My foot falters on the stairs. Perhaps I should let her.

I pull the paper from my dress and toss it onto the oily flames. As the page blackens and burns, the little soul bursts free, hovering. In an instant, I have Leo's knife in my hand. A drop of blood on the blade, then two on the hilt as I draw the symbol of life on the worn ivory handle. In a flash of bright light, the blade begins to hum in my palm. I open my hand and let her fly.

Quicker than an assassin, she darts through the circle of soldiers, dipping toward each as though they were flowers. Red blossoms bloom from the pale skin of their throats. Blood . . . so much blood—black in the light of the fire, smelling of copper and iron and heat. My own courses through my veins as I watch the stains spread on the pavers. The soldiers fall like fruit left to rot on the vine.

Sickened, I turn from the sight, stumbling up the steps, but the knife buzzes back toward me, circling like a pet waiting for praise. Reluctantly I hold out my hand, and she settles there, sticky with gore. I wrap my cringing fingers around the bloody hilt as I step into the darkness of the temple.

"Leo? Akra?" I falter when the stench hits me—too familiar: the rancid scent of death and despair. I hear it too—the screaming man, the prisoners gibbering. There is the black altar, there the stone god; he looms over me, his empty lamp in his hands. The jailer is gone. Instead, another sight, also one I've seen before.

Three prisoners lined up kneeling—and Legarde, holding the gun. At first the scene is so like that night outside La Perl that my mind turns around, trying to convince me that nothing has happened since, that I can go down a hall behind me and find the girls in the theater, and Leo at the bar. But Leo is here, alongside my brother . . . and Papa.

He is slumped in a heap on the floor, and my heart stops when I see him, but he is alive. Broken, bleeding, but alive. His hands are bound, his face and hands swollen and bruised, his eyes lost and hollow. Blood and saliva run from his mouth; his swollen lips are stretched around a grimy cloth tied between his teeth. But he's alive. He's alive, he's alive.

"I can kill at least one of them before you cut my throat," Legarde says, nodding at the knife in my hand. "Would you like to choose, or let it be a surprise?"

"Let it be Leo," Akra says through his teeth. There is fresh blood on his shoulder, a gunshot wound—and his face is pale, his mouth twisted in pain. "The bastard wouldn't take the shot when he could."

"Let them all go," I say, too loudly. "Please."

"Drop the knife first," Legarde says, and I do. It clatters on the stone, rattling a little. *Be still.*

"Will you let them go now?"

"Kick it over here," he says, and I obey without a word. The blade slides across the stone. The general puts his boot on it, and his tone changes, to one of nearly professional curiosity. "How many of the men outside survived?"

I don't want to answer—I don't want to make him angry. But my silence is enough. He raises his eyebrows.

"I see," he murmurs. "The ones from the roof will be down shortly. They'll take you to the palace."

Now it's my turn to be surprised—I hadn't expected him to keep that part of the deal. Is he more reasonable than I'd hoped? Could I bargain with the wolf who styled himself a shepherd? "And my family?" I say, almost breathless with hope.

Legarde looks down at the men before him, lined up in a row. "Three hostages is too many. I only need one." My heart sinks in my chest as he nudges Papa with his foot. "This one's too far gone, of course. But I only expected you to bring the boy. Your brother was an unexpected bonus. After all, romance can burn hot and flame out."

He turns the gun from Leo, to Akra, then back, aiming

at the center of his forehead, just below the dark curl of his hair. My voice falters. "You wouldn't kill your own son."

"Of course not." Legarde cocks the pistol. The sound . . . so soft. But it rings out like a drum strike. "But my *son* isn't here."

I have no response, but Akra does: a gob of spittle that lands wetly on Legarde's boot. Wrinkling his nose, the general swings the gun back to Akra, but in the split second when his aim is off, my brother explodes upward, driving his injured shoulder into Legarde's stomach.

The general grunts, staggering back, leaving the knife there on the stone as he brings up his gun. Thunder cracks . . . lightning flashes . . . someone screams "No!"

My voice? The shot was so close, so loud; it rings in my ears like a bell tolling. Akra falls to one knee, his hand over his chest. His face is sallow; blood pours through his fingers. As he slumps forward, the knife springs into my hand; when Legarde reaches out for me, I bury the blade up under his ribs.

His eyes go wide. He coughs. Blood flows like a spring down my arm—mists on my face, a hot spray; I am bathed in it but not cleansed. I stagger as he slumps against me, trying to lift the gun again, but I slap it out of his hand.

It clatters to the stone. Legarde slides down beside it. His spirit leaves his body in a rush of golden light—but it is not the only soul standing before the altar of the King of Death.

Akra, my brother. His body is pale on the cold floor, but his spirit is bright as a fire beside it. There is blood on the stone. Blood on the bodies. Blood on my hands. So little of it mine. But enough.

Death is too good for Legarde.

With a snarl, I reach out and take the general's soul by the throat. There. The statue. I slap my other hand on its black surface, marking it in red, and push the general's spirit into the stone. The akela writhes, twisting, but my rage is too great, my blood too strong. My own wild laughter rings in the vault of the temple as his soul slides struggling into the bleak darkness that will last a thousand years, but not half so long as mine.

The second brother said: "Hear me now, O my king, hear my plea, O my king. Who will care for the ones who cared for me? O my king... If you tear my soul away They will suf-fer all a-lone. So for mer-cy I must pray —" But no mer-cy was he shown.

CHAPTER

TWENTY-NINE

The song is back in my head.

I can hear my brother singing it. It even echoes in the cavernous stone temple, differently than it did in the field, when I first imagined his voice those years ago. But he is dead. Now he is truly dead. His body lies on the floor, his soul standing beside it, and as I listen to the sound of his voice, the akela turns to walk out the door.

That is what breaks me—I can't bear to watch him go. And before I can think better of it, I drop to my knees beside his prone form and trace the symbol of life on his skin. His soul hesitates, as though ready to refuse the offering—but the pull is irresistible. A flash of light, a moment of stillness. Then under my hands, Akra's body trembles, and he draws a breath so loud it seems to tear the air in two.

A fresh gout of blood bubbles from the wound as his heart begins to beat again. I rip the shawl from my waist and press it to his chest, trying to stanch the bleeding as his teeth chatter like dice in a cup. Air passes through his blue lips—first in a hiss, then in a groan. When he opens his eyes, there is a pain in them deeper than my own. "I'm sorry," I whisper, suddenly afraid. "I'm sorry."

But his eyes slide shut again, and I don't think he can hear me. And then, with a deep rumble, the temple itself shudders.

At first I am sure it is the god himself, ready to strike me down. It was too much—to steal my brother back from Death right before his blank stone eyes. A betrayal. An abomination. This is madness. But then, with a crack like thunder, a rift shoots across the crook of the stone god's elbow. Another breaks the bend of the knee. It is not the god, but Legarde.

Dust and gravel hit the floor as the spirit moves in his new stone skin. Desperately, I try to lift my brother, but he screams like I'm killing him all over again.

"Leo?" I say, my voice shaking. "Help me."

There is no response, so I turn. Leo is standing over the general's body—his father's body. His own face is just as pale. Are those tears in his eyes?

"Leo?"

"What?"

"We have to get out of here. Please." I slip my shoulder beneath Akra's arm, but I lose my balance as he slumps back against the stone. His blood pulses weakly through the silk of the shawl. "Please!"

Another deep rumble strikes the temple, and a chunk of stone tumbles from the shadows above and smashes to pieces. That finally moves Leo, and he comes to my side, helping me lift Akra halfway to his feet. "Where are we going?" Leo murmurs, and I look at him.

"Le Livre?" It is not a question, but a request—and it is a very long moment till he nods. "Get Papa. Please."

"We can't carry them far."

"Just out of the temple, so we're safe."

He presses his lips together, but he goes to Papa, lifting him cradled in his arms. With Akra draped around my shoulders, we stagger out of the temple. Behind us, the statue creaks and groans.

Blocks of stone bounce down the steps as we stumble to the plaza. I try not to look at the bodies of the soldiers— at their fleeing souls, glowing through the tangled temple gardens. But as we gain some distance from the temple, other spirits appear, drifting close to my blood. We stop near the garden wall, breathing hard, and I pull a vana into each of Akra's shoes, to lighten the load, and another into Papa's shirt. It's been torn nearly to rags, and while his eyes are open, his face is vacant. I cut the ropes around his wrists and ankles, but he will not stand on his own. When I pull the gag from his mouth I have to stifle a scream. Even in the dim light, I can see the ragged stump of his tongue.

Then another deep crack makes the ground itself tremble; with Legarde's soul trapped in the stone, the temple is crumbling, the carvings broken, the walls tumbling away. We have to move. Already I can hear the sounds of the prisoners—they are screaming too, in terror as their prison falls, in joy as they see the dawn. Le Trépas is surely among them. What have I done?

For an instant, I consider turning around, tearing the gun from Leo's belt and tracking down the monster, the madman—my father. But then I hear it over the rumbling of the falling stone: the sound of the gong. Someone has raised the alarm, and Akra will not make it to the inn if I do not carry him there.

We flee through the city, ducking and weaving through the shadows till we reach Le Livre. One of Siris's daughters lets us into the inn and shows us directly to a room. They prop Akra with pillows and call a docteur, though I don't know if it's necessary. I don't know if Akra can die, not even if he wanted to.

But the docteur treats Papa too; when she's finally done, the sun is high and the shadows small. She is cagey about his prognosis—it will be weeks before he can leave the bed, much less the inn. Shamefaced, I ask Siris about the cost of a brace of messenger pigeons—something to send to the rebel camp in the hope a note will reach Maman. So that she'll know we are safe, so I can warn her about Le Trépas. But Siris waves away my question, and he pays the docteur as well. Before she leaves, she promises to come back tomorrow, telling me to rest as well. While I doubt I can, I go to my own room, where at least I can be alone.

The bed is wide and inviting, the pillows thick and soft. And there is a bottle on the center of the silk coverlet: the bottle that Legarde had offered me—the treatment his daughter created. I had forgotten it in the fight. Leo must have brought it.

I pick it up now, cool and heavy and so precious. My hands are shaking so much I nearly drop it: a month's worth of the cure I'd sought for so long. What would life be like without my malheur? I hardly dare imagine—for what would life be like after the cure runs out? I cannot get more. La Fleur would never agree to treat the girl who killed her father and trapped his soul in darkness.

I set the bottle aside, gently, gently. But beneath it on the quilt is a note—a creamy page folded neatly in half. I pick it up—and for a breath, I imagine the blood on my hands seeping into the page like ink, a litany of my sins, a book of all the souls I have sent to the King of Death. Will send, now that Le Trépas is free.

But the blood is dry, and I unfold the page. It only takes a second to read, but in that second, a lifetime passes. What had Leo said about regrets? That the only way to soothe the pain was to do better.

For a long time I hold his letter in my hands. Then I go downstairs to write my own—not to Leo, but to the king. To the rebellion.

Au revoir.

Leo Rath Legarde

AUTHOR'S NOTE

Sometimes, the inside of my head seems like the pile of returned books on a library cart. A well-worn high fantasy beside an account of the lives of party girls in Bohemian New York . . . a Shakespeare play sandwiched between a history of French colonialism and a book about shadow puppetry. These flying leaps from topic to topic are one of my favorite things about my own bipolar disorder, and they inform my world-building in unexpected ways.

When I set out to write *For a Muse of Fire*, I wanted to write about a main character who shares my mental illness, and seeks a real life treatment for it. (Lithium, which occurs naturally in springs around the world, is a historical treatment but is still widely prescribed for bipolar. I took it myself for a while.) But I also wanted to create a magical second world out of my obsessions, which are in turn informed by my own malheur: I spent a long time in theatre in my youth, where my manic highs let me shine in the limelight. I was obsessed with death and spirits for a while, those thoughts meshing with my maudlin lows. There is a hedonism to mania as well, which is so often reviled in young women (unfortunately, I was no exception), so the cast of Le Perl gives me especial joy.

And of course, my heritage and upbringing creeps in. I am half Chinese, but raised in a rainy valley in Hawaii down the road from a taro farm where a water buffalo grazed. I must admit, as a biracial person, I have sometimes felt like a man without a country, as it were. In this book, I leaned into the freedom that feeling can bring: inspiration for food, styles of puppetry, and language are taken from a broad cross-section of places and times.

The technology, too, is a bit out of history. Though the headers on the letters from the Aquitans note that the year is 1874, the year is not quite analogous to our own nineteenth-century history. The repeating rifle came a bit earlier;

copper-jacketed bullets came a bit later. Electric streetlights existed in our own 1874, but were not widespread for years. And of course, the evolution of flight came later, as did vaudeville and burlesque.

Lastly, please note that while Aquitan and Chakrana are inspired in part by France and South East Asia, so many cultural, linguistic, political, historical, and religious liberties were taken that the story is truly a fantasy, and not an allegory or a close second-world version. This might be most noticeable in the inexact but French-like nature of the Aquitan words.

ACKNOWLEDGMENTS

There are no stars of a show—instead, there are galaxies, and all of you burn so brightly.

For all the direction she gave in shaping and polishing this piece, my editor Martha Mihalick deserves a standing ovation. Another round of applause for my agent, Molly Ker Hawn, a star in her own right.

Composer Mike Pettry, longtime collaborator and friend, certainly deserves his name in lights for putting the music in *Muse*. As for the muses themselves? That lineup features Zelma Zelma, Bambi Galore, Cheeky Lane, Iris Explosion, and Lewd Alfred Douglas.

Thank you to the expert dramaturgs: John Beeler for the insider knowledge of the stack on a steamship, as well as Audrey Masi-Spencer for advice on the French in the lyrics. Thanks as well to Katie Kennedy and Lori Lee, respectively, for booking them.

Many thanks to Sylvie Le Floc'h, who has designed the set of this piece, and Tim Smith, whose attention to detail would impress even the most jaded stage manager. Words cannot express my gratitude to Gina Rizzo, publicist extraordinaire, who could get any show on the road.

My thanks also to Michael Krass, who taught me how to survive as an artist, and to Justina Ireland, who told me why I should bother. My appreciation always for the most fabulous ensembles: The Fighters and Kidlit Alliance. These communities of generous and talented writers are an inspiration. Thanks, too, to NYU's Graduate Musical Theatre Writing Program, which taught me the value of working together.

And as always, to my boys—Bret, Felix, and Hansen— thank you for my favorite collaboration yet.